In the biz

rules that had

but there were certain lines one never crossed. Keep data in code, shield clients' privacy, and protect the girls at all costs. I'd always honored these precepts to the best of my abilities. It helped me stay afloat while other madams sank like old tires in the Anacostia River.

Yet there I was after one free lunch, considering a partnership with a man who didn't deserve to buckle my boots. Why? Was it the champagne? Drummond's smooth tongue? The fact that creditors were calling on a regular basis? Whatever the reason, I couldn't dismiss him until I exhausted every option. Unfortunately, I only had one. Even worse, she hated my guts.

Full Girlfriend Experience

by

Dana Ross

Full Girlfriend Experience

Cover Art by *Debbie Taylor*

The Wild Rose Press, Inc.
PO Box 708
Adams Basin, NY 14410-0708
Visit us at www.thewildrosepress.com

Publishing History
First Crimson Rose Edition, 2019
Print ISBN 978-1-5092-2501-9
Digital ISBN 978-1-5092-2502-6

Published in the United States of America

Dedication

For my Zs, who were patient,
and for my father, who taught me to never give up

~~*~*

Acknowledgements

Writing is a solitary task, but it takes a village to birth a novel. Critique groups, outside readers, and expert contacts have all contributed to the story you're about to embark upon. If it were not for the help of my dear friends and family, this novel may never have made it beyond my keypad, so, to them, I offer my heartfelt gratitude.

First and foremost, I want to thank the incredible team at The Wild Rose Press for adopting me into their family. El Felder, my amazing editor, was incredibly patient and supportive while I grappled my way through an editorial learning curve, and I am forever grateful for her support, feedback, and suggestions.

Second, I wish to thank my writing community, my misfit cohort at Wilkes University who were my first listeners, Taylor Polites, my Wilkes mentor, Robert Bacon, my first editorial eye, my critique group chums who giggled when appropriate and who gave tough love when necessary, and my personal tribe—those who read my blogs and chapters over the years and waited patiently for this book to (finally) be birthed.

Third, I'd like to thank my relatives, for constantly urging me on. There were days I wanted to give up, but my father and my children reminded me that wasn't an option. Thank you for keeping me on track, understanding when I barricaded myself in my writing cave, and for providing cups of coffee when I needed a boost, tissues when I needed a good cry.

On a personal note, this book must be credited to those nearest and dearest to my heart: Navid, for giving Faith snark and critical thinking, Brian, for our late-night conversations and insight on Macallan, Janine, for her long, painted nails, Gran who instilled my passion for reading, and last, but not least, Eric, my real-life Finn, the person who made me believe that Prince Charmings still exist.

Chapter One

"You boys can keep your virgins give me hot old women in high heels with asses that forgot to get old."

~Charles Bukowski

The elevator pinged, the door slid open, and as I strode down the hallway that led to my office suite, I smelled the ghost aroma of someone's citrusy cologne. The anxiety instigated from waking on the wrong side of someone else's bed subsided as I paused in front of my glass-doored entrance.

My company was my home. My utopia. A reminder that despite everything, I'd arrived.

I scanned the room like a general observing her troops. The main room was a buzzing nest of activity. Leggy beauties wearing our signature paisley scarves, stiletto heels, and fire-engine-red lipstick, darted hither and thither. Classical music drifted from the speakers, and the rain-scented air freshener pleased my olfactory senses.

Everything was in order—well, almost. I pushed a crooked tassel on the Persian carpet back in place with the tip of my shoe and clucked my tongue. There. That was better.

Tiana, a biracial beauty with whiskey-colored eyes, greeted me in a husky tone. "Morning, Faith."

"Morning." I looked up and waved. Even in

stilettoes, I was a half-foot shorter than my employee.

My girls were unique, each with talents that set them apart from others. Sure, we sold their assets on the side, but what company didn't sell people? Ours was just more blatantly open about it. And like other corporations, ours banked on promises. Promises of companionship, promises to alleviate loneliness. But unlike other companies, we ensured satisfaction.

For the right price.

On paper, my consulting company was legal and legit. One team handled the daily operations of helping Washingtonians put their best foot forward, while a select group handled services not listed on our website, or what I liked to call *the secret menu*.

I passed through the reception area and glanced at the gleaming plaque that bore our company logo— *Perfectly Polished*. The sign cost an arm and an ankle, but it was worth every penny because it was the first thing I saw each day.

And better than the second thing I saw each day.

Sitting behind a large teak desk was Jeanine, my overpaid assistant. Her hair was teased into its usual beehive, and her phone headset was curled around her jawline. Cat-eye glasses were perched at the end of her nose, and two chopsticks and a ballpoint pen peeked out from her high hair dome. In all ten years I'd known Jeanine, I'd never seen her hair down. Not once.

Her makeup was applied with a heavy hand and the tangerine frock she wore was bright and inexcusable, even for someone as fashion-challenged as Jeanine. I stared at her dress, wondering what retailer in their right mind would sell anything that tacky? Or that orange.

"Yes. Right. Of course." Jeanine drummed her

long, electric-blue nails against her desk.

Most days, I excused Jeanine's fashion faux pas—challenging since we were in the image-perfecting business—but an effective leader knew which battles to choose and when to turn her cheek. Besides, what Jeanine lacked in style she made up for in loyalty.

I zeroed in on the enameled dog pin clipped to her shoulder. It was my gift to her on her fifth work anniversary. Jeanine was my pit bull. Everyone needed a guard dog in the biz.

"Super. We'll be in touch soon." Jeanine hung up and lowered her headset. "Morning, boss." She gave me the once-over and aimed a blue nail toward my dress. "What on earth is that?"

I looked down and touched a damp spot. A courier had knocked into my drink in the elevator. "Coffee." I rubbed my thumb and forefinger together. "At least, it was."

Jeanine scrunched her nose. "Pretty sure you're supposed to drink it, not wear it."

"Hilarious." I frowned at her.

"My, my, aren't we in a mood?" She popped a gum bubble. "What's the matter, stock market drop or did your vibrator run out of batteries?"

I shrugged one shoulder. "Neither, actually."

"Well, that's good news." Jeanine opened a drawer and removed a pink notepad.

My assistant was old school in many ways and preferred paper over electronics. Though I repeatedly begged her to get with the times and email or text me updates, she insisted on writing things down—in cursive. The supply closet shelves overflowed with her irritating pink pads.

She pushed the drawer closed with her knee. "You want your messages now or later?"

I massaged my temple. Morning messages were never good. They were usually bill collectors or bleeding heart charity cases seeking donations to some hug the trees, save the planet, blah, blah, blah foundation. Screw that. I've donated plenty in the past. Who was going to save my company? Also, until my caffeine craving was satiated, conversation had to be limited.

"Messages later, change those first." I pointed to Jeanine's electric blue nails. "And when you're done, please bring me a refill." I set my empty travel mug on her desk and headed toward my office.

"Hold on," Jeanine called. "Before you disappear into your cave, I need a minute of your time."

I halted in place. Jeanine's *minutes* were usually half hours but there was no point in delaying the inevitable. I turned and crossed my arms. "What can't wait until after coffee?"

"This." She pointed to an oversized binder. "It's been three weeks, and Javier's getting impatient. You still haven't given him your approval on the renovations."

Renovations? The image of a thousand dollar bill with wings flashed before my eyes. I indicated the ornate lacquered screen in the lobby. "Didn't we decorate last year?"

She tapped the binder. "Minimalist is in now. Gotta stay current. Your words, Faith, not mine."

She was right, I had mentioned that, but that was months ago when business was better. My assistant had no idea we were in the hole, which was surprising considering she knew everything, including my menstrual cycle. I hated keeping secrets from her, but Jeanine had a tendency to overreact, and image was everything in this biz. If word leaked that we were having financial difficulties, the girls could get itchy.

I sniffed and tossed back my hair. "Javier can wait. What I need *toute de suite* is something hot and sweet."

Jeanine arched one brow. "The UPS guy doesn't come in until noon."

I let out an exasperated sigh.

"Okay, okay." She snatched up my cup. "One latte, coming your way."

****

My office held the odor of a cherry-scented ashtray. After hours, Jeanine liked to sneak into my room and light scented candles to camouflage the cigarette stench. In her mind, she's helping. In reality, she makes it worse. The furniture was starting to smell like fruit salad.

By the window, an oscillating air filter made lazy half-circle rotations. The contraption was one of Jeanine's high-tech finds, another attempt to sanitize my world. Despite my threats, she never lets up. One time, she maneuvered me into taking Reiki. Another time, she signed me up for hypnosis. There was yoga. Pilates. The last straw was the colon cleanse. I nearly fired her for that one.

After dumping my gear on the desk, I opened the window to air out the room. The view was gray and dreary and a damp chill hung in the air. Long stretches of inclement weather were common in D.C., but we were already into the first week of May, and the dogwood trees still hadn't bloomed. Like my bills, spring was overdue.

In my closet, I swapped my coffee-splattered shoes for a clean pair and paraded around the office. After sex and money, there was nothing better for a mood lift than the feel of virgin soles.

Once the fruity odor had evaporated, I closed the window and powered up my laptop. The news feeds were carbon copies. Election babble, broadcasters spinning their right vs. left predictions, shoe ads popping up in the margins. I was browsing an article about the buzz on an upcoming candidate when Jeanine came into the room, unannounced.

"Here you go." She set a steaming mug on my desk. "Hot and sweet, as promised."

Honoring privacy was not Jeanine's forte, but I refrained from complaining because good assistants who made killer lattes were practically extinct. Also, she'd saved my ass on multiple occasions.

I lifted my mug and inhaled the cinnamon-topped foam. Ahh, sweet nectar of the gods. Jeanine could make a killing at in tips as a barista.

She dug a pink message pad out of her pocket and leaned against my desk. "Ready?"

I wiggled the fingers of my free hand. "Didn't I ask you to change those?"

"You asked for coffee, which I brought. It didn't make sense to repaint and ruin wet nails."

I set down my drink and warmed my palms on the mug. "Leave the messages. I'll call you if I have questions."

"As you wish." She tore off a few sheets and set them by my mug. On her way out the door, she tucked a ballpoint pen into her hair dome.

I was reviewing my second message when Jeanine burst back into the room.

"Quick, Faith." She motioned to my phone. "Pick up line two."

She knew full well that I never talked to customers before my second cup was finished. I licked cinnamon foam off my lip. "Tell whoever it is I'm not in."

She came to my side and snatched the mug out of my hand. "This you need to take." She lifted the receiver and made a face as though she'd smelled bad fish. "It's Drummond."

"Drummond?"

My right eyelid twitched. Seven years prior, William Drummond, aka Slippery Bill, had won the Senate seat by charming the moderates with his pledges to stimulate the economy. He ended up winning because he spent millions on his campaign and the voters were duped into swallowing his spin. Two years after he won, he made every headline when the news was flooded with allegations of conflicts of interest involving federal stimulus funds. As the stories went, Drummond took advantage of some free-flowing federal funds. An already wealthy bastard, he was suspected of breaking ethics rules by taking a few million stimuli to stimulate his family's bank account.

Authorities had asked for an audit of the funds, but Drummond did everything to bury the story, avoided debate and interview questions, and hired a crisis-management specialist to handle the fallout. That was where I came in.

My company fixes problem children. Rock stars, debutants, drug addicts, soiled politicians—we've helped them all. And if they came with a referral and earned my trust, we shared other benefits. Some call it an escort service, but I prefer the term, cultivated companionship.

Drummond had been a steady client until *the incident* happened. I'd shut off communication with him after that, but it seemed like we had unfinished business.

I stared at the phone's flashing red light. "Give me some privacy."

Jeanine crossed her arms. "Since when do we filter?"

"I'll fill you in later." She didn't budge, so I made a shooing motion with my hand. "I promise."

"Details. Lots." She huffed and headed to the door.

Once the room was clear, I cleared my throat and smiled to make my voice sound friendlier, since even snakes could be charmed. I counted to three then hit line two. "Good morning, Senator."

"Ah, Faith. So nice to hear your voice. Did I catch you at a good time?"

"It's always a good time for you." The lie was so obvious, I almost tasted it. "I trust the campaign is running well?"

"We're all optimistic, but only time will tell." He gave what sounded like a well-rehearsed laugh. The kissing babies, fist bumps, kind of laugh. "I was hoping we could talk. There's something I'd like to discuss, something that pertains to a mutual connection."

I shuddered as the image of Nadege's bandaged face flashed before my eyes. "Love to, but it's a crazy week and my schedule is quite—"

"Now look, I know there was a bit of miscommunication with that gal, but I'm sure all that is water under the bridge."

Water under the bridge? Nadege walked with a cane. The water wasn't under the bridge; the dam was overflowing.

I squeezed my armrest. "Of course. Anyway, I'd love to but—"

"We must talk." He sniffed. "Not over the phone. One never knows who might be listening."

Politicians had a tendency to be paranoid, but knowing Drummond's background, I assumed he had reason to be worried.

I opened my appointment book and ran my finger down the page. "I could meet you Tuesday for dinner, if that works."

"Let's make it sooner. How about lunch at The Grille?"

Damn. He knew my Achilles' heel. Thoughts of The Grille's melt-in-your-mouth, dry aged, hand-cut steaks made my taste buds tingle. I rocked in my chair. "Funniest thing, I just had a cancellation. What time were you thinking?"

"Noon."

"Great, I look forward to—"

"Don't be late."

The line went dead.

Heat rose to my neck. No one hangs up on me, especially not a salty pistachio like Drummond. I stared at the receiver fully intending to call him back and give him a piece of my mind then remembered something Angela, my mentor, once told me. *Never kick a junkyard dog.*

Fine. I set the phone back in the cradle. It was only lunch, and a free, expensive one at that. All I had to do was make nice-nice and find out what he wanted.

My fingers sprang into action. On my laptop, I typed in Drummond's name and filtered through the articles I'd read in the past. A post had leaked from the Democratic Congressional Campaign Committee mentioning how Drummond spent over four hours a day making campaign fundraising calls, but that wasn't earth-shattering news since it was common practice for politicians to do such things.

While scanning other articles, I twisted the pearl necklace that hung at my throat. In addition to her employees, I'd inherited Angela's necklace and her endless pearls of wisdom. The advice she'd imparted usually came late at night while we sat on her tufted velvet couch, slugging shots of Irish whiskey. I couldn't remember a time there wasn't a shot glass in her hand and a clove cigarette dangling from the corner of her mouth.

As I fingered a physical pearl, one of Angela's wisdom pearls played in my head.

"Kid," she'd said, "Keep your friends close and your enemies intimate. Never expect an alligator to act like a kitten. You're not careful, they'll bite you in the rump."

Angela wasn't the most eloquent speaker, but she had her master's in street smarts. Even in death, her advice served me well.

I picked up my fountain pen and tapped it against my cheek. What could Drummond possibly want from me?

****

By the time I looked up, it was well past eleven. Punctuality had never been my forte, but being late would give Drummond something to gloat about. Purse and phone in hand, I bolted out of my office.

Jeanine was painting her nails when I approached her desk.

"Hold my calls. I'm heading out for lunch."

"What?" She set her nail polish wand into the bottle. "I just ordered your salad. And what about the renovations?" She pointed at my waist. "Hello, your dress?"

The gun-shaped coffee splotch by my pelvis was barely noticeable and there was no time to change.

"My dress is fine, I'll be back early, and regarding Javier, tell him…" That my company was about to crumble. That I was about to break the dying wish of my mentor. That if something didn't change there'd be no office to decorate. I glanced at the ornate lacquered screen and imagined winged dollar bills flying out the window.

"Tell Javier to go screw himself." I slung my purse over my shoulder and headed toward the entrance.

"You're a real ray of sunshine," Jeanine called.

I let her win that round.

Chapter Two

There were three things I could not stand—cheap shoes, bad wine, and the man seated across the table from me.

William Drummond was staring at me like a half-starved animal. Maybe his greedy gaze was due to my dress's plunging neckline, but the man obviously had other things on his mind—complications that involved me. And like the pan-fried calamari appetizer slowly digesting in my belly, sharing company with the man who almost killed one of my girls did not sit well. Nonetheless, I had problems. I had to at least hear him out.

I lifted my empty champagne flute and motioned for a refill. Drummond obliged.

The bubbly was good and dry, one that cost a pretty penny, which the sockmuppet would probably write off and charge taxpayers. It was tempting to slug my drink down and ask for a third glass, but I refrained since I was dealing with someone less trustworthy than my drycleaners.

As Drummond refilled his glass, I remembered how easily he polished off drinks without showing a hint of an altered mind. In addition to the champagne, there was a glass of whisky with melting ice cubes by his plate. Bells in my head rang a warning.

He was slick. Just like that suit. Which was decent,

though, probably an Italian label that cost more than my rent. He also sported a rose-gold designer watch—last year's model—and diamond pavé cufflinks that practically blinded me with their shine. His nails were trimmed and glossy, like he'd had a recent manicure, and his jet-black hair shined like an asphalt lake. His eyes were a forgettable brown, but they revealed intellect—correction, cunning intellect.

Drummond lifted his champagne glass and aimed the rim in my direction. "Let's make a toast. To old times."

I leaned forward and clinked his glass. "Old times."

As I swallowed the champagne, effervescence tickled my nostrils, and a warm, pleasant feeling swirled in my belly.

A soft ring chimed. While Drummond responded to an alert on his cell, I looked around. Wall-to-ceiling windows. Gleaming ebony wood. Polished brass. *Potentials* at every table.

The restaurant was a landmark, popular with both the old money richy-riches and the frou-frou *nouveau riche*. Big wigs sealed deals with handshakes at The Grille. It was a place one didn't make a scene.

I glanced at my plate. The filet I'd ordered was seared to perfection and smelled heavenly, but my patience was wearing thin. Forty minutes had passed, and Drummond still hadn't mentioned why he'd invited me to lunch. Time was money and I was losing both. We needed to end the pleasantries and get down to business.

I leaned back and folded my hands. "I was surprised you called. But you hinted it was urgent."

Drummond brushed a crumb off the table and took his time adjusting his sleeve. "My apologies for keeping you in suspense. It's not often I get to enjoy the company of such an engaging young woman." He crossed his arms and squinted. "I like what you've done to your hair. That blonde streak gives it pizazz."

Smooth words, but I wasn't softening. "I appreciate the compliment," I smiled sweetly, "but we both have people waiting for us."

Drummond chuckled and dabbed his lips with a napkin. Then he removed a cigar case from his inner breast pocket. In no apparent hurry, he clipped the end of his stogie with a cutter and stroked the cigar's shaft before lighting it. It was a bold move since D.C. restaurants had a strict ban on smoking. The only people who ignored such rules were either fiendishly brazen or disgustingly wealthy. I was the former. Drummond was both.

A waiter approached our table and whispered something in Drummond's ear. I would've bet my entire collection of designer shoes he'd make Drummond stifle his smoke, but instead, the waiter swept the tablecloth with a small rectangular brush and placed an ashtray beside Drummond's glass. My eyebrows were still raised while he gave the waiter our dessert order.

Drummond leaned back and stroked his jaw. "It's unfortunate we lost communication. I forgot how much I enjoy your presence."

Ignoring the trap of another compliment, I toyed with my pearls. Angela would never have gotten into a predicament like mine. I'd failed her, but I was working on making things right.

A drip of condensation slid down the side of my glass. I circled my champagne flute around the damp spot on the tablecloth. "Now that I'm here, tell me what couldn't be discussed over the phone."

"Patience is lost on the youth." He sucked his teeth and examined his cuticles. "All right, here's the deal. It's come to my attention that you and I might have a situation on our hands. Something that could be uncomfortable, were it to come to light."

My spine stiffened. Was he referring to Nadege?

A young Parisian who'd sought employment with my company since her art career hadn't taken off, Nadege had entertained Drummond on a few occasions. He'd ended up requesting her services on a regular basis.

One night, Drummond's antics went too far, and she ended up in the emergency room. The poor girl underwent weeks of physical therapy, and I doubted she'd ever return to work.

I waved Drummond on. "Go on."

He took a long pull on his cigar and tapped an ash in the tray. After expelling another smoke cloud, he pointed his stogie in my direction. "Some wild bucks have been snooping around. They think they've got some dirt on yours truly and our mutual friend."

My arms blossomed with goose bumps. So it *was* her. I took a generous gulp of champagne. "And?"

A cigar ash dropped onto the table. Drummond ignored the mess and held my gaze. "This changes the game a bit, but I've had an epiphany. I assume you've heard of my competition?"

Of course I had; it was all over the news.

"You mean Finn Billings?"

Drummond nodded.

Finn was former Governor Marshall Billing's son. I'd helped Marshall on two fronts. On the PR side, when he first ran, I'd helped brand him as the man in the seersucker suit. In addition to being a client of my image-consulting firm, Marshall had later enjoyed the benefits of my side business. Despite his extramarital affairs, Marshall was a decent man adored by the general public. People openly wept the day he retired, and I was no exception, but from what I'd heard about Finn, he was no magnate like his father.

I looked down at my steak. The meat was going to waste, cooling in a puddle of bloody juice. I pushed my plate to the side. "I didn't realize Finn had officially announced anything yet."

Drummond sniffed. "Not yet. But that's why I called you. Being so skilled in the art of politics yourself, I naturally turned to you for help in my current political situation. They're planning on making the announcement at a fundraiser in June."

The gala. Everyone knew about it. Half the people in Washington had been invited. It was one of those horrible kissy-face shindigs the elite attended to keep up appearances. Since Marshall was a friend, my presence was expected.

Drummond laid his cigar in the ashtray and folded his hands. "You and I both know that Marshall was an admirable politician but his son has no business on the Hill." He tugged his shirt cuff. "I need you to stop it from happening."

My gaze zeroed in on his cufflinks. How many people had Drummond screwed over to pay for those things? I'd screwed plenty of people in my day, but always with consent.

"I appreciate your confidence," I said. "But what can I do?"

Drummond picked up his cigar and sucked on the end. "Oh, come now. Surely you see where I'm heading."

It took me a moment. I leaned back until the chair's wood met my shoulder blades. "You want me to smear him?"

"See that?" A wide grin overtook his face. "I knew you were smart." He rested his cigar in the ashtray then leaned forward and spoke in a low tone. "If that man-boy gets the seat, it'll be extremely unpleasant for both of us."

Drummond had a point. Finn was the conservative party's messiah, and puritans were bad for my business. The Billingses had squeaky-clean reputations, Drummond's was questionable so Marshall's son would undoubtedly win by a landslide. If reporters dug hard enough, they might be able to trace Drummond back to me. I'd be screwed. And not the way I liked.

Drummond leaned closer, wafting over a hint of his spicy aftershave. "You get me incriminating evidence," he looked to the side and leaned closer, "pictures, video, something that'll sway their attention away from me and back to him, I'll make it worth your while."

My foot shook beneath the table but I kept my expression even while feverishly examining the angles. Everything about this arrangement felt wrong, but the ugly truth was, I desperately needed money. I glanced at my flute. And more champagne.

Drummond reached over and took my hand. His was mapped with liver spots and veins that reminded

17

me he'd worked in Washington since the Watergate Era. I knew better than to underestimate someone due to their age, but I wasn't going to let him intimidate me.

I straightened my spine. "I'm not sure I can get what you're asking. Maybe there's another—"

"I'm disappointed." Drummond released my hand and leaned back. "Perhaps someone else would be interested. Your friend Bes, perhaps?"

Bes? My right eyelid spasmed. That scheming harpy would sell her firstborn child for the right price. Not that I was any better, but everything I did, I did to protect my girls. Bes only did what was best for Bes.

A rock on Drummond's index finger appeared to be over two carats and gave off an offensive shine. No doubt about it, he was a fat cat with big pockets, and always had cash at his disposal. I liked Marshall and didn't feel good about betraying an old friend, but this was business, nothing more. If Marshall were in my shoes, he'd probably do the same.

I drummed my nails on the tablecloth. "How much are you offering?"

Drummond picked up his whiskey, swirled the ice in his glass. "Ninety."

Ninety thousand would help, but it wasn't enough to sell my soul for. The story of the famous entertainers who'd lost their career when one of their trusted tigers had turned on them played in my head. Even after the animal had mauled one of the trainers, he'd pleaded for the tiger's life to be spared. Those who didn't learn from their mistakes were apt to repeat them.

I was about to turn him down when a smartly dressed, bleach-bottle blonde, a dead ringer for Angela, passed our table. The day my mentor died, I promised her I'd take care of her team. For years, I'd honored that promise. Until recently.

If Drummond could pay me what I needed, I wouldn't have to worry about losing my company—correction, companies—but the only thing worse than the thought of working with Slippery Bill was an anesthetic-free root canal.

"Sorry." I rubbed my thumb and forefinger together. "Ninety's not nearly enough."

Drummond set down his glass and regarded me with an even expression. "What if I doubled that?"

My butt cheeks clenched. Now we were getting somewhere.

Outside, the sky darkened and sleet ticked at the windows. Thunder rolled in the distance.

The waiter returned to our table. He whisked away my untouched meat then set down a spoon and a plated ramekin in its place. The heavenly aroma of vanilla hit my nostrils.

As Drummond dipped into his matching crème brûlée, I did some calculations. The fundraiser was a month and a half away. If I didn't take his offer, Drummond would go to Bes. Finn had a spotless reputation, but either way, Marshall's son was going down. It wouldn't be too hard to get what Drummond needed, the question was, could I be the person firing the trigger?

I glanced at the blonde now seated at the table to my right. Even her lipstick was similar to the shade Angela used to wear. My sinuses tingled.

Drummond wiped his lips and tossed his napkin on the table. The animal had already finished his dessert—not that it mattered since I wasn't going to eat mine—

but still.

He snapped his finger and a waiter nodded. As he lowered his hand, his cufflink struck the ashtray, emitting a soft clink. I glanced at his cufflinks, his ring, and then paused on his monogramed tie tack. They didn't call him Slippery Bill for nothing.

The waiter returned and slipped a leather folder on the table.

Drummond stared at the folder for a long moment. "You and me, Faith, we aren't so different." He picked up the bill and slipped a steel-colored credit card into the slot on the inside sleeve. "All we want is to protect what we've built."

Protect what we'd built. I let that sink in.

Once upon a time, I was living large. Year after year, company profits rose and skirt lengths shrank, but a few months after the New Year's postage stamp dropped our numbers started dwindling. At first I didn't panic, because business tends to fluctuate during election years, but once I realized the dip wasn't linked to the economy, my blood pressure skyrocketed. There was nothing worse than losing money.

Drummond pushed the bill to the side and lifted my hand, kissed my knuckles.

As his lips lingered on my fingers, the image of Nadege's face painted with ugly purple-and-blue bruises flashed before my eyes. I kept my spine straight. Everything was a battle of wits with Drummond; appearing weak was not an option. Unfortunately, he'd caught me at a less than favorable time.

Outside, the wind toppled a planter. A tuxedoed employee whizzed past our table, probably hurrying to fix the damage.

Drummond released my hand and turned toward the sound, and I took the opportunity to wipe my palm on my lap.

Drummond swiveled back to face me. "Well?" He sniffed. "Do we have a deal?"

I glanced at his ring, his cufflinks, his—not one, but two—drinks. A wise person never made big decisions in haste. I needed time. I needed to think. Dammit, I needed more champagne. "Tempting," I smiled and blew on my cuticles, "but I need to mull this over."

Drummond puffed on his cigar. "I'm a patient man, but I'll expect an answer soon." He set down his cigar and rotated it in the ashtray. "And should you accept, everything must be resolved before Finn makes the official announcement."

There it was, the catch. It wasn't a lot of time, but I'd worked under tight deadlines before. Was it worth the risk?

There was no way I was going to let a sweet deal like that fizzle out, even one with heavy strings, but I wouldn't agree until I'd exhausted every option.

I pushed back my chair, stood tall and straight, and downed the remains of my champagne. "I'll let you know by the end of the day."

Chapter Three

I'd feigned assurance in front of Drummond, but by the time I exited The Grille, my heart was beating faster than the time I chased an eight ball of *coke* with a six-pack of energy drinks.

My hands shook so badly, it took three tries to light my smoke. After two drags, I chucked my cigarette into the gutter and leaned against one of the restaurant's concrete lion sculptures to shield me from the wind. Cars were passing at sluggish speeds, spraying dingy gray water onto the sidewalk.

The on-demand car service map indicated my driver was five minutes from picking me up, but the car icon seemed to be stuck in place. Every second away from the office was costing me more money. I paced the sidewalk to stay warm while vignettes from the conversation with Drummond replayed like a skipping record in my head. Plain and simple, he offered good money, but I'd be a fool to think he'd changed.

In the biz, your word was golden, and there were rules that had to be upheld. White lies were acceptable, but there were certain lines one never crossed. Keep data in code, shield clients' privacy, and protect the girls at all costs. I'd always honored these precepts to the best of my abilities. It helped me stay afloat while other madams sank like old tires in the Anacostia River.

Yet there I was after one free lunch, considering a

partnership with a man who didn't deserve to buckle my boots. Why? Was it the champagne? Drummond's smooth tongue? The fact that creditors were calling on a regular basis? Whatever the reason, I couldn't dismiss him until I exhausted every option. Unfortunately, I only had one. Even worse, she hated my guts.

A blast of cold wind hit my back. I blew warm breath on my hands then removed my cell from my pocket and scrolled through my contact list. Bailey, Barber, Bernard—there!

I hesitated before dialing. The idea of partnership had as much appeal as flossing my teeth with razorblades, however, if I didn't convince Bes to team up, Drummond would. Together, they'd crush me—or worse, give the feds info.

I stared at her number. Once upon a time she'd said it was me and her against the world. Maybe after hearing me out, she and I could finally mend fences and move on. I pressed the number and held my breath until a nasally voice answered.

"Maryland Matchmakers, how may I direct your call?"

I cleared my throat and smiled. "Hi. May I speak with Bes?"

"Who shall I say is calling?"

"Tell her it's Faith. Faith Crawley."

A pause. "One moment please."

While I waited, I pictured our history together. Bes and I eating over our hot plate. The two of us sleeping beneath our window air conditioning unit during a heat wave. Bes reading the comics aloud on Sunday mornings.

I never subscribed to the belief that fate brought

people together, but the undeniable truth was Bes had saved my life.

We met in a coffee shop where I'd been hanging out, about a week after I landed in D.C. and couldn't find legitimate work. No one wanted to hire a teen without a high school diploma or a legal address. The shelters were crowded and dangerous, and the city layout—safe on one street, sketchy on the next—confused me.

Bes approached the booth I was sitting in and struck up a conversation. She was near my age, but had cash in her pockets, enough to buy us both breakfast. During our conversation, she explained that someone like me, alone on the streets, would be dead within six months. Either a pimp would snatch me up and hook me on smack or I'd succumb to the elements. Bes danced at a gentleman's club, which, she joked, was flush with men who weren't gentlemanly. I wasn't used to trusting people, but what she'd said made sense. Practically every girl I'd met had track marks or bruises and those were the lucky ones.

Since Bes was on good terms with the owner of the club where she worked, she landed me a gig waiting tables, then later, dancing. We moved in together and lived on the bare minimum. Even with tips, we barely broke even, so I did private dances and odd jobs—anything to bring home extra cash. Bes promised we'd get out of the hole someday, but the money was never enough and plans got delayed.

Until the day fate again intervened.

The operator came back and informed me that Bes couldn't talk at that moment but she agreed to see me in person.

I had just hung up when my cell phone chirped, alerting me my driver was in the vicinity.

As I climbed inside the black SUV, another memory played in my head. It was the day Bes told me to never come back.

Hopefully, time had healed old wounds.

****

The driver dropped me off at the corner of Western and Wisconsin Avenue. As I crossed the street and headed toward a tall Chevy Chase high-rise, I caught the aroma of tangy chili coming from the well-known restaurant across the street. My stomach growled, probably in response to me remembering my untouched filet.

Before entering the building, I looked up and counted floors, pausing on the fifth. Bes's office faced the street. Was she inside looking out?

Inside the lobby, I bypassed the directory and headed straight to the elevators. It had been ages since my last visit, but the place hadn't changed. Same couches, same fake plants, same sundries shop around the corner, same predictable crowd by the elevators—women in skirts with running shoes, bike couriers with bulging calves, and men in suits with closely-cropped hair.

The lobby of Maryland Matchmakers was tawdrier than the makeup on a TV evangelist's wife. Splashes of crimson and gold adorned wall sconces, artwork, and suggestive sculptures. I crossed shag carpeting and paused beside a bronze sculpture of two lovers, bodies intertwined. Bes always did have an eye for gaudy.

The receptionist at the front desk wore orangey blush and lipstick in desperate needed of blotting. Her cleavage burst from the confines of her dress, but in our biz this wasn't something that raised eyebrows.

As I gave her my name, recognition set in, and her smile quickly evaporated. She pushed back her chair and hurried through a set of double doors without knocking. I grinned, comforted by the fact that Jeanine wasn't the only assistant who disregarded privacy.

After a minute, the receptionist returned and offered a cool apology.

"Sorry. She's running behind. May I offer you something to drink?" Her smile seemed half-hearted.

I looked around. If the carpet and decorations were indicators of Bes's taste, I doubted the refreshments were good. "Thanks. I'm fine."

She motioned to a couch. "I'll call you when she's ready."

The room was quiet, minus the sounds of Bes's secretary chatting on the phone and canned music playing instrumental versions of pop songs I'd heard played at grocery stores.

The leaves on a fake plastic tree rippled, injected with motion from the air blowing from an overhead vent.

While waiting, I tapped my nails on the armrest, keeping time to an acoustic version of REO Speedwagon's "Keep on Loving You."

I stacked the magazines on the coffee table into a neat pile. My mission wasn't easy. Not only did I have to convince an estranged friend to forgive me, but I also had to convince her to form a partnership. A stain on the rug beneath the coffee table caught my eye. It was tempting to leave but I stayed in place.

To pass the time, I leafed through the outdated

magazines, some older than the towels in my guest closet. One of the magazines had a picture of Marshall Billings on the cover. After flipping past ads for exotic travel spots, realtors, and erectile dysfunction medication, I came to the featured article.

The headline photo was of Marshall on the steps of the Capitol building. According to the date, the picture had been taken years ago, in the winter, and Marshall looked out of place with his Florida tan, seersucker suit, suspenders, and wavy white hair. His supporters held banners and wore looks of devotion. The former king of the Beltway was adored by his disciples, even in his semi-retirement. I stifled a laugh while staring at their self-righteous signs, thinking of a different side of the man.

While in office, Marshall publicly wooed the conservatives with his talks on family values all the while he was privately wooing my employee, Evangeline. Marshall loved Evangeline as much as I loved Italian shoes, but he never left his wife Clara. That would've caused a scandal, and scandals were not permitted in the Billings clan.

Despite his extramarital affair, Marshall had a good heart. His only crime was loving the wrong woman. For years, I kept his secret safe, because he paid me well to do so, and because secrets were what sustained my business.

Everyone had secrets, even the pious, who were sometimes the ones with the most to hide.

I gripped the magazine the way my evangelist father used to grip his podium. He'd been worshiped by his flock, the sheep who came to him Sunday mornings with starved souls that needed nourishment. My father fed on their desperation, and in that aspect, we were almost alike. We both used people's needs to accelerate our careers.

My father shared kindness to those who followed him blindly and donated to the church collection plate. All he reserved for me were looks of disappointment and bible quotes to memorize. I guess I was a sheep, too. Black. Bad. Both.

I pictured his face and the way the ends of his bolo tie grazed his podium. The feverous look in his eye was accompanied by one of his bible quotes playing in my head—a passage from Proverbs 17:23—"The wicked accepts a bribe in secret to pervert the ways of justice."

My gastric juices bubbled. I buried the magazine beneath the others on the table.

A buzzer sounded, and the receptionist waved for my attention. "Bes will see you now."

****

Bes's office was a throwback to the seventies. Listless spider plants hung from ceiling beams, framed by splashes of gold accents, black lacquer furniture, and, yuck, more shag carpeting. The room reeked of cigarette smoke and the taint of heavy perfume. A knockoff of a classic gilded Art Nouveau painting hung on the wall, and an enameled Russian Easter egg knockoff paperweight sat on her desk. Javier would go into cardiac arrest if he saw this place.

Bes's chair was facing the window. Her assistant motioned for me to take a seat and again offered me a beverage. I politely declined.

Seated, I crossed my legs at the ankles and waited. A desk clock ticked the time.

Finally, Bes swiveled her chair. "Well, well. To

what do I owe the honor?"

I leaned forward to offer her my hand. "Good to see you. It's been too long."

My empty hand remained outstretched for an uncomfortable moment. Eventually, she shook it, but her palm, like her stare, felt chilly. I held eye contact and took inventory of my former friend.

Once, she'd been a beauty. Her lustrous red hair and ample bosom drew men to her like crack addicts came to the pipe. Her hazel eyes were similar to mine, but her caked-on eye shadow and false lashes made her features look cartoonish. Even her hair looked wrong, all done up in a pillar of loops and swirls like Medusa's crown of snakes. Her dress looked pricey but it bunched in all the wrong places. Time and the biz had apparently taken its toll.

After the façade of pleasantries, Bes leaned back and lit a cigarette. "Well, get on with it. You said it was important."

I glanced at a framed picture on her desk. "I'm sorry about your father. I meant to call."

"Thanks." Her tone was cooler than her hand.

I pushed the thought of my own father aside. "I came because there's a situation. Someone we're both connected to thinks he's being investigated and—"

"You're referring to Drummond?" She cocked one brow.

My butt cheeks clenched. "Yes. Did he call you?"

"No. I just keep my ears open." She picked a piece of tobacco off her lip and rubbed the fleck between her fingers. "But I don't foresee trouble."

My optimism diminished a degree, but I forced myself to appear upbeat. "I spoke with him. Rumors are circulating, and if he gets implicated, it could be damaging."

Bes leaned forward and rested her chin in her hand. "You mean it could be *inconvenient*." Still watching me, she tapped her cigarette ash into a tray.

I threw out one palm. "Aren't you concerned? He's got stuff on both of us."

"Drummond has no bone to pick with me." She scoffed. "I was the one who took him in when your bitch snubbed him. Me, not you." She took a drag and exhaled through her nostrils. "I understand that kind."

That kind was a monster. Had Bes forgotten the code? Every good madam protected their girls.

I gripped the armrests and leaned forward. "Can you blame me? He sent my best girl to the hospital. I can't believe you'd take his side."

Bes blew a smoke ring and laughed. "Your girls are pussies. You coddle and overprotect them. Have you forgotten what it was like? It hasn't been that long. A little roughness makes you strong."

I was strong. And I never condoned violence. I tried another tactic. "That's not what you told me when I met you. Remember?"

An icy wave passed over her face. "What I remember is, you abandoned me."

I closed my eyes, and the worst memory assaulted my brain.

That snowy night in January, I was heading home after a double shift with barely enough money to cover weak coffee and pancakes. While passing an alley not far from our apartment, I heard a whimper and followed the sound to a girl lying in a supine position with torn clothes and a bloody face. Her leg was at an awkward angle, and when I tried to move her, she screamed.

After running for help, I stayed with the girl until an ambulance came. Word of my efforts got back to her manager, and that's when Angela Kleinman called me in and offered me a job. Bes had warned me about hooking up with strangers, but Angela ran a high-class escort agency and assured me with her resources and the right representation, I could finally leave skid row.

It was everything Bes and I had dreamed of. And though I'd begged Bes to come along, pride and stubbornness sealed her fate.

"Why leave?" Bes refused to see the opportunity at hand. "We got a good thing going already."

"Barely." I tried to get her to understand. "That girl could've been one of us."

"Bad things happen in fancy places, too. I'd rather keep my money to myself."

"Money won't matter if you're dead."

"I'll take my chances."

Leaving Bes was one of the most difficult choices I'd ever made. Had things been different, had she found the girl instead of me....

A ringing phone in the lobby roused me back to present time.

After a deep breath, I said, "I begged you to come, Bes."

Her brows crimped in annoyance. "That's not how I remember it."

She wasn't letting go of her anger, but people were counting on me so I couldn't give up. I glanced at a framed bill behind her desk. Money was the way to get to her. "Have you ever considered merging companies? There's power in numbers and together we could build our businesses into—"

"You're kidding, right?"

The sharpness in her voice stunned me for an instant. I palmed my chest. "No, I—"

"You think I'd work with you after everything you've done? That's rich." She laughed and her stony expression intensified. "I'd rather risk jail than trust you again." She snubbed her cigarette into the ashtray and punched the intercom. "Regina."

"Yes," said a wispy voice.

"Please show my guest to the door."

"Don't bother." I grabbed my purse and pushed back my chair. "I'll see myself out."

Before I left, I searched her face for a trace of the kindness I once knew, but only read a blank page. On my way to the door, I turned for one last look. Bes was staring at her smoldering cigarette. The ashtray it rested on was the steely one with the filigree pattern I'd found outside our apartment in a box of throwaways. I'd cleaned it up and given it to Bes on our last Christmas together. She'd kept it all these years. She couldn't hate me.

I laid my hand over my heart. "I'm truly sorry, Bes."

She took a moment to respond. "Good luck, Faith."

This time, there was sincerity in her tone.

Chapter Four

During the elevator ride downstairs, thoughts of Bes and the apparent pain I'd inflicted replayed until the doors slid open to the lobby. Over by the building's legend, I took a moment to regroup. I'd bombed. Big time. Hurt was still a fresh wound in Bes's mind, and partnership was out of the question. Unless a miracle occurred, I had to accept Drummond's deal. But if I took it, how would I infiltrate Finn's circle?

The answer came to me at the sundries shop.

Soda was not the kind of drink I craved, but I needed something to neutralize the angry cauldron bubbling in my stomach. While waiting in line to purchase a ginger ale, I saw a magazine on a stand beneath the cash register. The cover featured a picture of Finn Billings, and everything about the guy looked off. His suit hung on his frame like it belonged on someone else, his hair was too fluffy, and a mole on his right cheek practically jumped off the page. I picked up the magazine and squinted. This was the Republican's new messiah? The guy desperately needed a makeover.

An imagined green light flashed before my eyes. Marshall knew my expertise and had been more than satisfied with the results, so it wouldn't be impossible to convince him to let me work with his son. I'd have to employ tact when I broached the topic, but the makeover was definitely my *in*.

I added the magazine to my purchase and headed outside.

Traffic was heavy on the avenue and dark clouds threatened more rain. While waiting for the light to change, I checked my messages. There were five missed calls from Jeanine, but I doubted any of them were emergencies. Jeanine called all the time, usually about things she swore needed my attention but didn't. Things like: *What color stationery should I choose for our thank you cards?* Or, *should we switch to biodegradable paper towels for the kitchen?* Who cared about biodegradable paper? The planet would be fine and there were too many inhabitants, anyway. Seven and a half billion too many.

The light changed, and a powder-blue taxi pulled to the curb. The driver was sitting on one of those beaded cushions that looked like a medieval torture device, and talk radio played in the background. As I finished giving the driver my address, my cell phone rang. The caller ID read: PIA, aka, pain in the ass, aka, Jeanine. It was tempting to let voice mail take over, but Jeanine was relentless when she got something in her head. She'd keep calling if I didn't answer.

"Relax," I said. "I'm on my way."

"Jesus, Faith. Didn't you get my messages?"

"No, I just—"

"Where are you, dammit?"

"Calm down." I slid the seatbelt from beneath my butt cheek, buckled myself in. "I told you I'm heading back."

"You'd better hurry." Her next words sent a vibration down my arm. "The police are here."

Chapter Five

Inside my suite, Jeanine bum-rushed me at the door. Her face was pale, and a ballpoint pen dangled precariously out of her beehive.

"I didn't know what to do." She paced. "They're in uniform and they're sniffing around. The girls will freak. This is bad. So bad. Dear God, it's bad."

I removed my raincoat and laid a hand on her shoulder. Police meant trouble, but I put up a chill façade because my assistant looked like she was about to spontaneously combust. "Breathe, J." I mimed a cleansing breath. "We've handled worse."

She shook her head. "One was asking personal questions. I didn't say anything, but—"

"Did you offer them coffee?"

"Twice, but they declined." She pointed to my door, and her words came out lightning fast. "The phones were ringing off the hook, and when I turned my back, they went into your office. Do you think they're here to arrest us? I can't believe I donated to the policemen's ball. Never again." Her cat-eye glasses slid down her nose. "I'm sorry I let you down."

I squeezed her shoulder. "You didn't let me down."

She pushed her glasses back in place. "What are you going to say?"

My gaze shifted to my door. "Not sure."

****

Two men dressed in light blue short-sleeved shirts and grayish-blue pants were inside my office. One was bent over my desk, glancing at a stack of papers, but I wasn't worried about that. Anything that could be construed as incriminating was inside my safety deposit box, and the names in my little black book were written in code and were always on my person. Years back, I'd contemplated writing a book on pandering, but another madam beat me to the punch.

I hugged my purse between my arm and armpit and glanced at the second man.

He stood by the window, arms akimbo, back facing me. Tufts of spiky brown hair jutted from beneath his uniform baseball cap. The heart-shaped birthmark on the back of his neck gave it away.

I hung my coat and purse on a hook behind the door and cleared my throat. "So, this is my taxpaying dollars hard at work?"

The man at the desk looked up. The man facing the window spoke without turning. "Quite a view up here. You must've put in some backbreaking work to get this. My office has a view of the waste bins. Tell me," he slowly turned, "where's the justice?"

I sniffed and shrugged. "Who said life is fair?"

The man at the window chuckled. "That's an understatement."

The man by the desk came toward me, but the man at the window halted him by raising a palm. "Could you give us a minute, Dave?"

Dave nodded and left the room. After the door shut, I walked over and wrapped my arm around the other man's waist, careful not to knock into the radio clipped to his belt. "It's been too long, Bobby."

"Phones work both ways, you know." He pulled me close, and the years melted away.

Familiar, dangerous feelings came back. I broke from his embrace and held him back at arm's length. "Let's see what they've done to you, Gordo."

"Gordo?" He patted his midriff. "It's a stereotype that cops just eat free donuts."

I chuckled. He was still in great shape. In fact, not much had changed. Same cleft chin, same nut-brown eyes, same mischievous smile. If not for the laugh lines bracketing the corners of his mouth, one would doubt he was legally able to drink. His grandfather's gold cross was in its usual place on his neck. No ring on his left hand.

I brushed imaginary dust off his shoulders and caught a whiff of something musky, body wash or cologne. "You always looked good in blue."

"And you look good in everything."

He still knew how to stroke my ego. I fingered his badge. "Officer Diaz."

He gave me a mock salute. "At your service."

"The job suits you."

"The pay sucks, but it's an honest living."

An honest living. One of many differences between us.

The sound of a ringing phone came from behind my door.

"Come see this." I steered him back to the window. "If you look all the way to the right, you can see the old apartment."

He followed my finger. "That place smelled like cat piss, and the roaches were bigger than the rats."

"What did you expect for four hundred a month?"

37

"It certainly wasn't the Ritz. And those stairs were killer." He rubbed his chin. "They ever fix the elevator?"

I fingered a window blind. "I doubt it."

"Remember the day we got stuck inside it? And the ice cream melted everywhere."

"We ended up drinking it from the carton." I covered my mouth to suppress a giggle. "That was the longest two hours of my life."

Bobby shrugged one shoulder. "I thought it was fun."

"Well, yeah. Sure it was."

Awkward silence.

Bobby removed his cap and raked a hand through his hair. "You should check out Hyattsville. I got a single-family, four-bedroom with a decent garage, pretty cheap. The yard is tight, but my neighbors are cool."

"You know I'd rather die than live in suburbia."

He sighed. "I'm aware."

I touched his elbow. "But I'm happy for you. You always wanted a big house, full of kids."

He looked down and ran his finger over his cap brim. "And you didn't."

The conversation was heading south.

I pointed to the credenza. "I'm gonna have a drink. What can I get you?"

"Nothing, thanks. I'm on duty."

"Suit yourself."

At the bar, I filled a shot glass with scotch, downed it, and winced as the burn struck my throat. After, I joined Bobby on the couch. He took the right side, I took the left, but the distance separating us, just enough to cross my legs without touching him, felt like miles. My brain was a little muddy from the booze and earlier events, and there was a mountain of work waiting for me, but Bobby came for a reason.

I smoothed the fabric on the seat cushion and accidentally grazed his knee. "You're obviously not here for a social call. What's going on?"

He set his cap on the couch's armrest and twisted to face me. "I came to give you a heads-up. As a friend."

"We didn't do friends well."

His cheek muscle twitched. "It was your decision to end it, not mine."

"We both know it wouldn't have worked." I glanced at his badge. "Not with your career."

He leaned forward and rubbed his palms together. "There are investigations going on. A cowboy at the F.B.I. is hell-bent on trimming fat. He's proposing cutbacks, consolidating departments, and there will be job losses nationwide. The guy is creaming to expose something. Thinks it'll transport him up the ladder if he does. There's a rumor circling that one of the candidates might have been misappropriating funds and hanging out with…someone in a questionable line of work." Bobby looked up. "You've been careful, right?"

"And here I thought you came to give me crap about unpaid jaywalking tickets." I laughed, but my attempt at humor didn't seem to go over well.

"This is serious, Faith."

"Relax." I patted his knee. "I'm always careful."

He glanced at my hand. "That L.A. girl was careful, too."

But that was different. The infamous west coast

madam had been at the top of her career when the Feds took her down. Against her better judgment, she'd taken on a client even when the warning bells rang. Not trusting your instincts was suicide in the biz. Fortunately, Jeanine did thorough background checks and vetted each prospect before she gave them information. I trusted Jeanine. I trusted Bobby, too. He'd risked a lot telling me this, but that was his way. He always put others before himself.

I squeezed his knee. "After all these years, you're still trying to take care of me."

A spasm of irritation crossed his face. "Why'd you do it?"

"Do what?"

"Give up?"

The question triggered a protective reflex. I leaned back and crossed my arms. "I told you from the beginning that loving me is a dead-end street."

"You could've tried harder."

What Bobby failed to understand was letting him go was the kindest thing I ever did for him.

"Forget it." He put his cap back on his head. "I'm not mad, I'm just disappointed. We were good once. And people shouldn't be alone."

I looked into his eyes. "There's a difference between being alone and being lonely."

His gaze bore into mine. "True, but you'll never be happy until you let someone in."

The intensity of his stare made my resolve weaken. A passing cloud darkened the room a degree. I faced the window and whispered, "I'm safer alone."

Bobby exhaled and stood. "Watch yourself, Faith. The sharks are circling."

At the door, he handed me a business card and tipped back his cap. "Call if you need anything. Day or night."

I tucked his card into my bra cup and stared at the credenza. Deep inside the third drawer was the antique jewelry box from the Eastern Market, the one I'd fancied on a day we'd spent hunting flea market treasures. Later that week, Bobby surprised me with the gift in my living room. Clear as day, I saw him on his knee, opening the box to reveal what was inside, the night of his proposal. The night I broke his heart with my answer.

Over the years, there were times I tried to give the box away but never could. Somehow, having it close by was enough. A reminder of what was, what might have been.

I hooked my index finger into my necklace and twisted the pearls around my finger. "How's your mother?"

Bobby dug his cell phone out of his pocket. "The same. She's still at the assisted living facility. On good days, she recognizes me. Unfortunately, there aren't a lot of good days."

"I'm sorry." I touched his forearm. "You'll send her my regards?"

He gave me a thoughtful look. "I know the flowers are from you."

"What flowers?" I blinked twice but kept my expression even.

He rubbed his cell screen with his thumb. "They arrive on Thursdays. White lilies. At first I was confused because there wasn't a card but then I remembered. Valentine's Day. I gave you red roses, and you told me you hated them. You said white lilies were your favorite. I mentioned that lilies were my mother's favorite, too."

I tugged my right earlobe. "I have no idea what you're talking about."

A chirp on his radio interrupted the silence. Bobby lifted his radio from his belt and keyed the response button. After replying to the call, he clipped his radio back on his belt. "Duty calls." He headed toward the entrance. As he approached Jeanine's desk, she swiveled her chair away from him and faced the wall.

"Send your mother my regards," I called.

Bobby paused and gave a small nod.

After he left, I walked over to the credenza and removed the jewelry box. The enameling was still vibrant, each flower petal still intact. When I lifted the lid, a flesh-toned ballerina pirouetted on one foot while *Fur Elise* played. Cradling the box, I headed to the window and leaned against the glass.

On the street below, a police car pulled away from the curb. With my gaze fixed on the empty parking space, I tried to imagine another life, one where Bobby and I stayed together.

He was a decent person, but I'd broken things off to protect him. He deserved someone honest, someone who'd give him a house full of kids and attend PTA meetings and bake sales. Someone who….

The door opened, and Jeanine leaned in. "Everything okay?"

I nodded.

"We're not going to jail?"

"Not today."

"That's a relief." She joined me at the window. "So

42

that was him?"

I shrugged but didn't answer.

She exhaled a long breath. "Okay then."

The ballerina made another rotation.

I touched a flower on the box. "When you have a moment, call Bethesda Florist. Have Tracy double Mrs. Diaz's order."

"One time?"

"Every time."

Jeanine removed the box from my hands and shut the lid. When the music quieted, I felt a sense of loss wash over me.

She put the jewelry box back in the credenza and headed to the door. Before leaving, she studied my face for a moment and said, "Holler if you need anything."

I stared at the empty space where the police car had been parked. For a long while.

Chapter Six

Time was almost up, Drummond needed an answer and I'd exhausted my options.

That morning, my biggest concerns had been financial dilemmas and coffee stains. Now I was dealing with the police, an over-zealous F.B.I. cowboy, and a senator who would stop at nothing to protect his own skin. In the span of one day, my life had attracted more drama than a Spanish *telenova*.

A siren wailed outside my office building. I dumped in the trash the remnants of a tasteless kale salad Jeanine had encouraged—correction, forced—me to eat, then swiveled my chair toward the window and looked out. Night was setting in, and the buildings across the street looked razor-sharp against the dark, gloomy sky. I flipped through a pile of unopened bills stacked in my inbox and checked the stock market. Not good news. Low numbers, apparent unease from newly imposed tariffs on steel. I rubbed my temple with my knuckle.

Since I'd failed to lure Bes into partnership, Drummond's offer was the only lucrative solution, but before I agreed to ruin Marshall's prodigy, I had to see if the Golden Boy was as squeaky clean as the press portrayed him.

Leaning on one elbow, I squeezed the yellow rubber ball Jeanine gave me to combat stress and speed-read every article I could find on Finn. His life was pretty much what I imagined: dreadfully dull and as clean as my countertops.

He'd been in the Cub and Boy scouts and even earned Eagle scout rank. He liked birds and had taken summer classes at the Chevy Chase Audubon society. There was a picture of Finn tagging a wren, and in the photo, he wore a wide-brimmed hat that covered half his face.

Hats were hard to pull off. Period. As bad as the picture was, he looked happier in that one than in the other photos I'd seen. I cracked my knuckles and continued reading.

He attended Gonzaga High School and later graduated from Georgetown. He didn't play sports— *quelle surprise*! but had been a member of the chess and computer clubs. Aside from attending Marshall's political events, Finn had kept a low profile.

I zoomed in on his college graduation photo. His posture belied weakness, and his graduation hat hung at a lopsided angle. He was attractive(ish) minus the mole and his nest of wiry hair, but he didn't look like a leader; he looked like a computer geek.

I stared at Finn's lopsided hat and shook my head. Poor guy. Growing in the shadow of a man like Marshall—someone loved by the masses—must have been challenging. Finn would always be compared to his father. I grabbed a sheet of paper and jotted down some notes.

Attributes—Good height - people associate that with power. Dark-blue eyes that conveyed trust. Normal-sized nose. Straight, white teeth, a plus, since politicians had to smile a lot. Pretty lips which curved up in a pleasant line. A smile that made a person feel safe.

Faults—posture, poufy hair, outdated clothes—I tapped my pen against my cheek—the mole. A makeover would improve things drastically. New clothes, trim his locks, foundation to even out his ruddy pallor. Yoga? I chuckled. Jeanine would love that.

My laugh died in my throat. He was Marshall's son, a seemingly innocent man. Could I sink that low to honor a deathbed promise?

I opened my desk drawer and reviewed the balance in my checkbook. Overdrawn. Savings dwindling. There was no other choice.

My cell phone felt like a weight in my hand as I scrolled through my contact list. I paused on D.B. aka douchebag, counted to five, and pressed his number.

"Is it presumptuous to assume good news?" Drummond said, instead of hello.

This was it. No turning back. My soul to the devil.

I gave my stress ball repetitive squeezes. "One thing, first."

"Yes?"

"I'll only agree if you make it an even two."

There was a pause. Then, "Fine."

I imagined Drummond's greedy smile and him washing his hands like a cartoon villain.

"We'll flesh out the details another time," he said. "I'm meeting someone for drinks. Talk soon."

The line went dead, and a piece of my dignity evaporated with the terminated call.

My hand shook as I filled a water glass with scotch. There wasn't enough alcohol in the bottle to prepare me for my next task, but at least I wouldn't be sober as I ended a decade of trust. I took a big swallow of the vodka—yuck, not scotch, my mistake—and carried the glass to my desk.

My phone seemed to mock me. I picked a piece of glitter off the case.

The sooner your obligation is fulfilled, the sooner you can tell Drummond to jump off a bridge.

That was the momentum I needed. I knocked down half my drink and dialed the number, one I knew by heart.

It had been ages since Marshall and I last talked, but when he came on the line, I recognized his distinctive southern drawl, and I imagined him wearing the seersucker suit I'd branded him with. "Good evening, governor. This is Faith. I hear congratulations are in order."

He let out a hearty laugh. "Not yet, darlin', but soon."

His laugh was infectious; I couldn't help but smile. "Well, if your son's anything like his father, he's sure to win."

"From your lips to God's ears."

I winced and swirled my vodka. "They'd be fools to vote for the other guy."

Marshall chuckled. "I trust you enjoyed that bottle I sent?"

I glanced at a crystal decanter on the credenza. "Aged cognac is my guilty pleasure. You certainly know how to spoil a girl."

"Nothing's too good for you," he teased. "And speaking of spoiling, how's that lady friend of ours?"

"Evangeline is doing well, but the doctors said she still needs to keep off her foot."

"Terrible news about her ankle. Please convey my regards to her. You'll send her the usual for me?"

I set down my glass and jotted a note onto a legal pad. "Chocolates and something sparkly. Consider it done."

"Thank you. When you speak with her, mention I know an excellent orthopedic surgeon, should the need arise."

"You're a peach, sir. I'll pass along the information."

"Much obliged."

I picked up the magazine I'd purchased in the sundries shop. "I'm sure you're busy, but I called for a reason. There's something I'd like to offer you. A premature congratulatory gift, so to speak."

"Your vote is all I ask for."

"That goes without saying." I gazed at Finn's picture. "In regards to your son—with all due respect—he has a good chance at winning, but…" I paused before presenting my next words. Men in power had big egos, and insulting Marshall's progeny would be detrimental to my effort. I glanced at my list of Finn's attributes. "Your son has a lot of potential but he needs a little *oomph*. Here's what I'd like to offer." I leaned back and propped my feet up on the desk. "Let me work with him, and come June, Finn will be the talk of the town." No lie there.

"Is that all?" Marshall blew out a heavy breath followed by a hearty laugh. "You nearly gave me a heart attack." He coughed. "So what I'm hearin' is, you're gonna do some of that fairy godmother stuff?"

I glanced at one of my framed awards on the wall. "That's exactly what I have in mind. You know how I work. Just give me the green light and I'll make it happen."

"Guess I'll hafta trust you on that. After all, it was you who helped me get the seat."

The first time I'd met Marshall, I knew we had to go with the southern gentleman look. We furnished his wardrobe with bow ties, suspenders, and seersucker suits. At first, Marshall worried the public wouldn't accept his unconventional look, but I assured him they would. And they did.

However, it took more than a fancy wardrobe to sway the public. It took confidence, the one thing Marshall had but his son seemed to be lacking.

Fortunately, I was good at building self-esteem. I'd helped people come out of the closet, taught shy ones how to assert themselves, taught frustrated spouses how to pleasure frigid wives. Clients had shared everything from baby announcements to their kids' graduation pictures. Some even told me I was better than their therapists.

"What're you planning?" Marshall asked. "Bow ties and suspenders like his dear ole' dad?"

"No, sir. The suspenders are yours and yours alone."

"I imagine you might have your work cut out for you."

I slid my feet off my desk. "Then I should get started right away."

"I appreciate this," Marshall said. "My boy means the world to me."

His words inspired a heavy feeling in my chest. I opened my desk drawer and popped an antacid into my mouth, chewed quietly.

"Send your bill directly to me," Marshall said. "No need to worry Finn with such matters."

"There won't be one." I coughed and forced out the words, "I'm doing this free of charge."

"Free?" Marshall belted out another hearty laugh. "Well, I'd be a crippled chicken in a fox's den to refuse that. That's mighty generous."

And painful to offer. I patted my chest where it felt like the antacid was stuck. "Consider it a gift to the campaign."

He cleared his throat. "But I gotta warn you, my son's a tad hesitant to change."

Finn was young, okay looking, and presumably heterosexual, and bedding men was my forte. How hard could it be?

"Don't worry, I'm a professional."

Marshall chuckled. "Indeed you are."

He gave me Finn's personal number, and I promised to keep in touch.

After we hung up, I dumped out the vodka and refilled my glass with Marshall's cognac. The liquid was the color of autumn leaves and had a sweet nutty, caramel smell.

Holding the glass high, I toasted my friend, and then I downed my drink and wiped my lips with the back of my hand.

No more Spanish soap operas. I was back in control. In two months, there'd be money in the bank, and Drummond would just be a memory.

Famous last words, right?

Chapter Seven

As I opened the front door to my apartment, the scent of furniture polish and vanilla-scented air freshener stung my sinuses, the smells apparently intensified due to the closed windows. The timers had turned on the lights in my living room and had started the heating system. I kicked off my shoes and frowned, remembering my barely-worn, coffee-splattered, red-soled heels. Rest in peace.

After sifting through a stack of bills and junk mail, I headed to the living room and surveyed the area.

Everything was in order, organized, impeccable. Never-read art books were stacked on my end table beside a kidney-shaped silver bowl. The fringe on my Arizona-white area rug was combed to perfection, and the polish on my built-in cabinets gleamed. There was dampness in the air despite the running heat, so I ignited the faux fireplace. One of the add-ons I'd chosen for the fireplace was cobalt glass chips. When lit, they glowed like lava and cast a fiery blue hue.

Javier had decorated my place, and though the furniture he chose was hip and trendy, the place was far from homey. There were no family photos, no mementoes, nothing that remotely proved I existed. My apartment could have been a model home in a suburban community in Anytown, USA. Someone could've moved in and never known I'd lived there.

Even my digital intelligent personal assistant had been evicted. At first, it was nice to have something to talk to, until the night it woke me, laughing on its own. I chucked that creepy thing right in the trash. So much for company.

I turned on the stereo and let the stink of the day wash away with the music.

At the bar, I popped the cork on a 2014 Lafite, a noble Bordeaux, and filled my glass to the rim. Mixing alcohol with wine was generally *verboten*, but I'd already survived a day filled with poor choices and ghosts from my past.

Flicking my nail against the glass, I savored the ping from the delicate crystal. Good wine was a worthy investment, and I always took great care when stocking my supply. The Bordeaux had a bold fruity smell and a pretty garnet color, like jewels. The first sip was to test, the second sip to savor. Yes, this was a damn fine wine.

I'd been saving the bottle for a special occasion, but saving my company seemed to be a pretty good reason to celebrate. The plan was set in motion. All I had to do was get Marshall's son to my apartment, take some pictures, and be done with the whole affair.

Bottle and glass in hand, I settled on the comfy spot on my couch. I'd chosen my apartment because it was the one that provided the best view, but I could probably count on one hand the nights I actually appreciated the cityscape. I sipped some wine and gazed out the window until I worked up the courage to dial the number Marshall had given me.

Here went everything.

One ring.

I chuckled at my own joke.

Two rings.

I hiccupped into my fist.

Three rings.

Maybe I should've sobered up a bit before I called.

I was about to disconnect when a surprisingly deep voice came on the line.

"Hello?"

I jumped in my seat. "Hi. This is Faith Crawley, I'm a friend of Marshall's."

"Ah, okay."

Finn apparently hadn't inherited his father's charm. I leaned forward and set my wineglass on a coaster. "Marshall and I go way back. He speaks highly of you, and he'd like me to help with your campaign."

"You're in politics?"

Obviously his dad hadn't mentioned me. "Not exactly, but I do work with people in positions of power." No lie there. "I guess you could say, my company helps people," I crossed my legs, "bring their best foot forward."

"So you're not in politics?"

"No." I exhaled. "But rest assured, I'm not new to the scene." Cradling the phone against my shoulder, I straightened a coffee table book that was out of place. "I've worked with plenty of movers and shakers. Unfortunately, I'm not at liberty to disclose names, but remember the mayor who got caught with a prostitute and a mound of cocaine?"

"Of course. You're referring to the late Marion—"

"That's right. Remember how he almost lost his council seat after those Asian American racial comments?"

"Certainly."

"Let's just say, I helped him keep his seat."

A pause. "That's impressive."

"Thank you." I searched the couch cushions for the remote and muted the stereo. "Mr. Billings—may I call you Finn?"

"Ah, sure."

"I've been around D.C. a long time, Finn, and I know what people want. My job is to help prepare you for the limelight. I've worked with major players and helped even the shyest people come out of their shells." I stifled a giggle provoked by the image of Finn wearing a tortoise shell. Definitely should've called before I drank. I cleared my throat. "The public will scrutinize your every move. Fortunately for you, my company is great at vamping people's image."

Another pause. "You said my father referred you?"

I rolled my eyes upward. Was the guy even listening? "Marshall and I go way back."

"And he thinks you can help with my campaign?"

"Your father has the utmost confidence in my abilities."

"What exactly would this entail?"

I curled my feet under my legs. "It'll be harmless. We'll get to know each other and discuss your goals. Once we do that, I'll have an idea on the best course of action."

He took a moment to respond. "That's awfully generous, but I'm quite busy these days."

Marshall had warned me Finn was hesitant to change, but big money was on the line. I smiled to sound friendlier. "I guarantee you'll be thrilled with the results."

"So, we're going shopping together?"

"Yes, well, more than that." My smile faded. "Why don't we meet for a drink and see what happens. My schedule is flexible so we can work around yours. How does that sound?"

Another pause. "Okay, I suppose."

Finally, some concession. "Excellent. I'll text you my bio. Look it over and call me back if you're satisfied."

"That won't be necessary. If Father endorses you—my apologies—Ms. Crawley, you said?"

"Call me Faith."

"Okay, Faith." There was the sound of paper shuffling. "My afternoons are swamped, but I might be able to meet you sometime after work." More paper shuffling. "Would Thursday work?"

I gave a thumbs-up. Success was on the horizon, but I didn't want to get too confident. "Thursday's perfect. You're in Crystal City?"

"Originally, but I've been working downtown these days since it's closer to the Hill."

Another plus. I gave my wine a longing look. "There's a Cuban restaurant and rum bar on the outskirts of Chinatown. It has great ambience." And killer mojitos. And hot waiters.

"That sounds nice."

Nice? I winced. People who liked rainbows and baby pandas used the word nice. Nice was not part of my vernacular.

"What time are you available?" I asked.

"My last meeting should be finished by eight. Could we say, nine, to be safe?"

Safe. Another word I abhorred. "Nine it is."

"I'm sorry," he said. "I didn't get the name of your

company."

"Perfectly Polished. I'll send you a link to the restaurant and to our website. You can read the testimonials."

"Okay."

He didn't sound overly enthusiastic, but at least he agreed to meet me. I flexed and wiggled my toes. "Before we hang up, there's something I should emphasize. My intent is not to change what's inside you, but to enhance what you already have. My goal is to help you win." And get my money.

"Father trusts you," Finn said. "That's saying a lot."

His praise inspired a tingle in my throat but I washed it away with a hard swallow. "See you Thursday at nine."

"Wait," Finn said. "How will I find you? I don't know what you look like."

I draped a hank of hair over my shoulder. "I'm five seven with hazel eyes and long brown hair with a blonde stripe on the right side."

"A stripe? Like a zebra?" He laughed then caught himself. "Oh, gosh. Forgive me. That probably sounded rude."

I laughed to put him at ease. "No need to apologize. I look forward to meeting you, Finn."

"And I you, Faith."

I thought he'd hung up, but I heard soft breathing.

"You still there?"

He gave a nervous laugh. "Sorry, guess I'm technologically challenged."

I chuckled. "We all are to some degree."

After we hung up, I steadied the bottle over my

wineglass, but hesitated before refilling it. Angela had chided me for my love of the grape, said wine lovers were pretentious pussies.

"Liquor makes your insides strong," she'd told me on numerous occasions.

Even while she was hospitalized, she'd begged me to smuggle in her booze. I'd refused until I was certain her departure from our world was inevitable. Memories of that day played in my head.

There were beeping machines. Her hospital room smelled like warm cheese. The bright sunshine outside warred with the glaring fluorescent lights overhead.

Despite her weakness, Angela held my wrist in a viselike grip. She was going on about the girls, insisting I protect them.

I shushed her and told her she'd be out of the hospital soon enough, that nothing held her down long. Her despondent expression made me soften, and I kissed her knuckles—a bold move since Angela wasn't the touchy-feely type. It must've satisfied her, because her grip relaxed and a peaceful expression spread over her face.

Her eyes looked like they were somewhere else, but I grasped her hand as though holding on would keep her with me. When her face changed to an empty shell, I knew she had finally passed. Angela's mojo, her essence, whatever one would call it, was gone. All that remained was the lifeless mass of the woman who once reigned over D.C. We buried her flask and her cigarette case with her body.

A crack of lightning outside my window washed away the memories. My body jolted from the sound, sending a small geyser splash of Bordeaux up and out of the bottle.

As I mopped up the spill, everything became crystal clear, as clear as my empty wineglass. Angela wasn't coming back, and feeling sorry for myself wouldn't save our empire; focusing on what I could change would. There was no question of what had to be done.

I had to destroy Marshall's son.

Chapter Eight

After a restless night of tossing and turning, I woke the next day in a pool of clammy sweat, leftovers of a nightmare still playing in my head. Drummond was in charge of my company, Marshall was Jeanine, and I was a destitute prostitute begging for a job. The evil duo laughed at me and had Security toss me out of their office.

The dark shadows in my room indicated it was early too early to be up, but too late to go back to sleep. After untangling myself from the bedsheets, I rewarded myself with a leisurely session with Big Red. Jeanine thinks it's strange to name a vibrator, but, as I explained to her, people name boats and cars and neither of those things are intimate.

****

Once the bed was made, pillows stacked, I trudged to the kitchen. My head felt like it was too heavy to be supported by my neck and my tongue felt as dry as the wine cork I found under the counter.

It even hurt to run the water. No big surprise since I'd drunk enough wine to fell a horse. I searched my cabinets for something to give me a kick-start, but only found immune boosters and B12 vitamins. I settled on the vitamins, put on the coffee, and grabbed my cleaning supplies.

While the coffee brewed, I worked a toothbrush

over some grout stains behind the sink. Obsessive-compulsive disorder was considered a weakness by some, but I found it empowering. It was my way of controlling things that were out of my hands. If I couldn't control my empire, I'd at least make my surroundings sparkle.

A gust of steam and a hiss signaled the end of the coffee cycle. Java in hand, I headed to the bathroom to get ready for the day.

By the time I exited my apartment, the burden I'd woken with had lifted from my shoulders. The stock market futures were up, my weight was down—well, it hadn't risen—and I found two crumpled Ben Franklins in a breath mint tin in my purse. The day seemed promising.

It was time to make money.

****

The sky was dingy gray, but the air held the fresh scent that followed a good rain's washing. The sidewalk was waxed with a thin layer of wet green leaves, and a gray curtain of fog enshrouded the tops of my building. A bus lumbered up the street and expelled a plume of exhaust that smelled like burnt beef.

Generally, I liked the walk to work. Jeanine said cardio was good for my heart, but, more importantly, it gave me an opportunity to go by the chichi boutique where the cute pink stilettoes I'd been ogling were still on hold for me.

Seven blocks into my trek, I was singing a different tune.

Jeanine was wrong. Exercise was stupid. Overrated, actually. People only did it to delay dying. Smoking was probably going to kill me before I got in shape, so why bother? I paused to catch my breath and headed into my local coffeehouse in search of caffeine.

The café was occupied with predictable inhabitants—writers plucking away on their laptops, glued to seats they weren't sacrificing, ponytailed moms in gym wear, and businessmen talking loudly into their cell phones.

The smell of burnt beans and the sounds of Indie music and frothing machines came at me from all sides. The line snaked out the door, and the cashier was complaining that the register had run out of printer tape, but neither of those things bothered me. Not even the woman talking on her cell who cut in front of me. She completely ignored my presence, but nothing was going to ruin my day.

Or so I thought.

The barista screwed up my name. One would think that after years of ordering the same drink in the same place, someone behind the counter would get my name right, I mean, Faith is not unusual, it's only one syllable, but apparently the cheeky pink-haired barista thought *Fith* was what I'd said.

It took a second to register when she called it out.

"Double shot low-fat macchiato for Fith." She cupped her eyes and scanned the area.

"Here." I shook my head and headed to the counter. It really wasn't rocket science, but I guess that explained why the gal cleaned latte machines and I ran a million-dollar business. Well, once upon a time, I did.

At the condiment bar, I dumped two packets of artificial sweetener into my drink. All was well. The coffee was good, and I'd made arrangements to save my company. Nothing *else* would ruin my day.

Until....

It was almost in slow motion. From out of nowhere, some little hellion escaped the clutches of his haggard-looking caregiver and came barreling full-force my way. As the little bugger made impact with my lower half, a tidal wave of scalding-hot macchiato splashed over the rim and onto my dress.

"Dammit." I jumped back and slammed into the counter causing a second macchiato tidal wave to hit my legs.

The child let out a sound that reminded me of cats fighting. There wasn't a drop of liquid on the kid, but the way he went on, one would've thought he'd been burned by fire. Eventually, his caregiver came over, not to offer an apology for ruining my ensemble, but to placate the brat with a hefty-sized chocolate bar.

[The incident confirmed my theory that:

1.The world was overpopulated

2.Kids were meant to be not seen and not heard

3.Contraception should be free]

Fortunately, my shoes were spared.

Unfortunately, things spiraled downward as the morning progressed.

The chichi boutique holding my stilettoes was closed for inventory, an e-mail alerted me my checking account was overdrawn—again, and two blocks from my office building, the skies opened up, and rain pelleted the sidewalk like rounds from a machine gun. By the time I entered the lobby, my two-hundred-dollar blowout was spent and my dress felt heavier than a bucket of wet sand.

In the grand scheme of things, these were only minor irritations. I still had some reserves in my savings, and my dress and hair would eventually dry. Before I rode the elevator upstairs, I took a mood-stabilizing pill to ensure a peaceful morning.

Nothing, from that moment forward, would ruin my day.

By the time I entered my office suite, my spirits were higher, but then I saw Jeanine.

She was humming to herself while tending a half-dead African violet plant. Her bright-pink jumper, wide hoop earrings, and shiny gold creepers neutralized the benefits of my mood-elevator. I glanced at the plant's wilted leaves. Was the thing ill from over-watering or from being exposed to Jeanine's attire?

The radio on Jeanine's desk was playing a twangy country music song. Wincing at the sound, I set my travel mug beside the music player and lowered the volume.

Jeanine turned and smiled. "Oh, hey there. You're wet. Didn't expect you in," she checked her watch, "so early."

Her perky demeanor was almost more offensive than her attire.

I sighed. "Yes, it's raining, and yes, I'm early." I pointed to her desk. "Any emergencies?"

"Nothing critical." She set down her watering can and dug a pink pad out of her pocket. "We have one potential—he checked out, so I set him up with Krystal." She flipped a page. "There was a call from a reporter named Alexander Clough at *The Post*. He's doing an article on something like lifestyles of the rich and famous—or maybe he said infamous—anyway, he wants a quote from you." She flipped another page. "A request for PR help from some diplomat family in

McLean. Seems their little princess made a scene at a restaurant in D.C., and the manager's threatening to sue."

I held up a palm. "Could you handle that one?"

"Already on it." She flipped another page. "A call from your bank—the third in two days." She looked up and squinted. "What's that about?"

"Transferring funds." I waved her on.

"Phillippe wants you to know the mink jacket you like is on sale. You have a meeting with Toastmasters Thursday—"

"Cancel that. I have plans."

She made a notation. "Lastly, Javier needs—" I interrupted her with a loud exhale. "Never mind." She tore off the messages and handed them to me.

I folded the papers in half and pocketed them. "I'll be in the cave. When you have a moment—"

Jeanine reached for my travel mug. "Dry clothes and coffee coming right up."

****

The rain continued to hammer the city for the majority of the morning.

During my lunch break, I called Alexander Clough and gave him a few quotes to use in his article. It was wise to stay on good terms with reporters, especially after watching other celebrities go up in journalistic flames. The more helpful you appeared, the more likely they were to paint you in a positive light. One never knew when one might need a favor from the press.

Later that night, while stuffing bites of tasteless tofu chunks, or as Jeanine calls them, a healthy alternative to white meat—yuck, not even close—into my mouth, I scoured the Internet for other articles relating to Finn. Information was ammunition, and I needed to prepare for our upcoming meeting.

It was a short read. Over the years, Finn hardly changed. His hair grew thicker, but he basically kept the same style, a wardrobe of tan chinos, button-down shirts, and forgettable ties. He maintained a consistent 4.0 GPA in college, and he volunteered at charitable events, like most candidates.

Yawning, I scrolled through more pictures. Brookside Gardens. Humane Society. Audubon society. More Audubon Society.

Finn certainly liked birds. All kinds of birds. Did plenty of bird stuff. Double yawn.

His life was as predictable as Beltway rush-hour traffic.

I dumped my tofu into the trash, headed to the window, and cranked the handle to let in fresh air.

The rain had stopped, and the sky was resplendent, ablaze with layers of pink and purple. The sounds of honking cars filtered into my office. The flower vendor across the street closed up shop, and streetlights came on one by one. A car's backfire jolted me, evoking the gunfire in my old neighborhood. Spooked by the memory, I shut the window and returned to my desk. There was no way I'd ever go back to a place like that.

The door opened, and Jeanine came in with the budget report. Not good news.

After a minute of calculations, I pushed the spreadsheet aside and rubbed my temple. "I don't understand." Math had been my worst subject, but even someone who never got past Algebra II could see something was awry.

Jeanine snapped a gum bubble. "My thoughts

exactly. I reviewed this three times, and the numbers don't add up."

I tapped my fountain pen against my cheek. "What does Tony say?"

"He wants to meet this week." Jeanine leaned back and crossed her legs.

I glanced at her horrible gold creepers. "Don't offer too much."

"I never do." She shrugged.

Jeanine usually handled these situations well, but Tony was sharp, and accountants didn't like missing links; they wanted all the puzzle pieces to fit together.

On paper, we were safe. We paid our taxes and we reported everything from the consulting business. The money earned from my side business went unreported, which required creativity. Although we'd been careful, I feared our good luck had run out. Tony was getting itchy and difficult, like a mosquito bite on the back of the knee.

I straightened a pile of papers on my desk, signaling Jeanine's dismissal. "You'll let me know what happens."

"Will do." She mimed brushing dirt off her hands. On her way to the door, she halted by the air filter and sniffed. "Please tell me you haven't been smoking."

Had I? Probably, but that would've been hours ago.

I held up a palm. "Not the time for a lecture, J."

She frowned. "I'm just saying, maybe if you believed in something you'd try to live longer."

I opened my mouth to defend myself, but she silenced me with a hand. "I know, I know. Crossed the line. Fine, I'm leaving." She flipped the switch on the air filter and exited the room.

Sometimes it was hard not to fire her.

I exhaled and stared at the air filter. Jeanine bitched about my bad habits because she cared, but she didn't understand my perspective. Just because I didn't believe in an omniscient being didn't mean I didn't value life. In fact, not believing in an afterlife made me live each day to its fullest. Sure, I smoked and drank a little, but so what? Life was about lassoing happiness, and booze and cigarettes made me happy.

My thoughts were interrupted by the vibration of my cell phone. Even before I checked the caller ID, I knew it was Tony. Sometimes you just know.

I reached for my yellow legal pad and crossed out his name. "You're on my list of return calls."

"Then I saved you a dime," Tony said.

"That's what we pay you for, right?"

He laughed. "Among other things."

"Tell me something good."

"My wife still loves me, I lost two pounds, and my son's finally graduating."

"Must be your lucky day."

"Think I should play the lottery? Jackpot's over a million."

"You always say the lottery is tax on the stupid."

"You got me there."

I rocked in my seat. "How's biz?"

He sighed. "Tax season always gives me indigestion, but it helps with weight loss. That being said, I'm hanging in. Knock on wood." He knocked something. "Honestly, it never slows down."

"You filed our extension?"

"Of course."

I picked up Jeanine's spreadsheet. "So, I reviewed

the latest report and I'm confused."

"You're confused? That's my line."

"You're the only accountant I know with a sense of humor. Seriously, Tony, I'm missing money."

He sniffed. "Let's be frank, Faith. I'm on your side, but I can't help you if you don't work with me. I've been asking for receipts for months yet you seem to disregard any requests I make. If you don't send me the information I need, my hands are tied."

An image of Tony handcuffed to a bedpost flashed before my eyes. I blinked hard to obliterate the image. "I'm not trying to impede your work." I was. "And it's not that I don't want to help." I didn't. "I'm just horrible at remembering things." I had excellent recall.

He cleared his throat. "I understand, but I'm canoeing upstream without a paddle. Even Jeanine dropped the ball on this. She said she's waiting for you, you tell me you're waiting for her, somebody has to be accountable."

Yes. That would be the accountant.

I gnawed a cuticle. "C'mon, Tony. Can't you bend a little?"

"Bending is frowned upon."

I opened my desk drawer and removed my yellow rubber stress ball. "There are gray areas in any business."

"Accounting is black and white, not shades of gray."

I squeezed the ball with repetitive pulses. "I'll try to get you those receipts. You just concentrate on finding out where my money's going. We shouldn't be in the red. Even with this crappy economy."

"I'll do my part. You just promise to send me what

I need."

What he needed, I couldn't provide—invoices linked to my side biz, names of clients I couldn't reveal. It was hard to dodge the I.R.S., and disclosing documents, even ones from the PR business, was tricky. If I gave Tony what he wanted, there'd be questions. Questions I couldn't answer.

My tendons in the fist gripping the ball looked like they were about to burst through my skin. "I promise I'll do what I can."

"That's all I ask."

After Tony hung up, I threw the squishy ball across the room. It hit the wall with a soft thud then rolled somewhere out of sight.

Dammit. I had to let Tony go.

That ruined my day.

Chapter Nine

The sound of a woodpecker hammering wood outside my window woke me the next morning.

Blinded by my eye mask and still groggy from the sleeping pill I took before bed, I buried my head under my pillow and tried to return to the dream I was having. A shirtless calendar boy, Mr. September from my kitchen calendar, had been rubbing suntan oil on my back—or was I rubbing oil on him—anyway, there was oil….

My alarm clock rang.

With a groan, I silenced the noise. By the time I found my robe, Mr. September was just a memory. I was almost at the door when I heard a vibrating sound in my nightstand drawer.

Big Red?

I backtracked and opened the drawer. My cell phone displayed D.B. Ugh. Not the way I wanted to start my day. I answered the call and put him on speakerphone.

"Just checking to see if there's been any movement," Drummond said.

I licked the fuzz off my front teeth. "I've got the ball rolling."

"Excellent. You'll have everything worked out before the fundraiser?"

The virtue of patience was lost on Bill Drummond.

"Long before."

"Good."

He continued talking, but my attention was elsewhere. The cable knit dress I'd planned on wearing that day was draped over my desk chair, but something was missing.

Years ago, the infamous west coast madam had been bugged, which led to her career's demise. Angela had warned me to take notice of my surroundings and keep everything in the same spot.

Cradling the phone against my shoulder, I picked up my dress and scanned the items on my desk. Scissors. Stamps. Stapler. What was missing?

It hit me.

My electronic tablet wasn't on the desk.

I dropped my dress.

"Faith?"

"Sorry. I have to run." I disconnected before he could respond.

My tablet wasn't in the drawers. It wasn't on my bureau or my nightstand. A nauseating wave of adrenaline washed over me. After a thorough sweep of my apartment, I started to call Bobby but decided to recheck the bedroom first.

On hands and knees, I reached under my bed and palmed the carpet. Eventually, I felt the leather case that held my tablet. It was sandwiched between the wall and the back wall of my bed.

How'd it get—oh, right. I'd watched a few *videos* before I went to sleep. Stupid porn site. Those producers have zero imagination. They should use female writers.

My heartbeat resumed its natural rhythm but my

paranoia didn't subside while I dressed. Cradling my electronic gadgets and work paraphernalia, I exited my apartment as quickly as possible.

Caffeine was probably the last thing I needed, but Drummond's urgency coupled with the fear of being bugged inspired me to do something proactive before I hit the office.

The coffeehouse was, as usual, filled to capacity. People chatted loudly in the line behind me, their conversations competing with the sound of a spritzing frothing machine. A barista poured steamed milk into cups on a low counter.

After retrieving my double shot macchiato with an illegible name scrawled on the spine, I headed outside to catch some rays.

Spring seemed to have arrived overnight. The sky was a cornflower-blue, free from haze, and the air was crisp and dry. The scent of bread and burnt coffee rode piggyback on the breeze. I grabbed a seat at a table in the shade but the sun peeked through the leaves above me and warmed the top of my head and shoulders.

The coffeehouse door jangled as it opened and closed with the constant flux of people entering and exiting.

Balancing my drink in one hand, cell in the other, I researched portable surveillance equipment on the web. There was plenty of spyware to choose from, priced at all ends of the spectrum. I wasn't sure which model or brand to buy, so I went with one that looked simple to operate.

My search led me to a link with a four-hundred dollar, law enforcement grade, motion-activated, HD camera/DVR built into a cell phone. The device came with a motion-detection mode and recorded to a memory card. It pained me to drop so much cash onto something as lame as surveillance equipment, but this investment would eventually lead to a sizeable payoff.

I hesitated before hitting the purchase button. Was it legal to record someone without their knowledge? Probably not, but bribery and prostitution wasn't exactly on the up and up.

A homeless man shuffled by and parked his shopping cart filled with cans, newspapers, his imagined treasures by my table. Then he extended his hand and gave me a pathetic look. "Spare some change?"

The poor guy looked like life had taken a dump on him, and I felt guilty digging into a wallet that probably cost more than the guy's monthly intake.

"Here." I handed him a twenty spot. "You take care now."

"Jesus saves." He fisted the money and returned to his shopping cart, ambled away.

I zipped up my wallet. Jesus wasn't going to save me, but I was going to save my company. I hit the purchase button on my cell, clicked for expedited shipping, and headed to work.

The recording device would arrive the following day.

****

Thursday afternoon, I was gathering my items to leave work early so I'd have ample time to prepare for my meeting with Finn, when Jeanine came in the room unannounced.

"You busy?" she asked.

I locked my file cabinet and pocketed the key.

"Actually, yes."

She marched to my desk and stood with her feet hip-width apart, like she was poised for battle. "Where are you going?"

I tossed my cell phone into my purse. "I've got a meeting."

She glanced at my open appointment book and arched one brow. "News to me."

"I'm sure I mentioned it."

"Regardless." She removed a pink pad from her pocket and popped a gum bubble. "You're not leaving until I get your *plus one* for the fundraiser."

"Can it wait?" I held up my wrist and pointed to my watch. "I'm running behind."

"Sorry, no. I need a name."

I exaggerated a heavy sigh. "What's the urgency?"

"Urgency?" She flopped onto a chair and set her pad on my desk. "You've been blowing me off for weeks. If you keep dragging this out, all the good bachelors will be snagged."

Ms. Annoying Pants had a point. Prospective bachelors in D.C. got snatched up faster than designer shoes at half-yearly sales. I stared at Jeanine's high hair dome while running through my options.

Mike, the guy in 3-B had a hot bod, but I'd heard he was relocating to California. The physical therapist I met on the subway had given me his card, but I tossed it because he had halitosis. The owner of my favorite boutique was gay. My dentist got married. Tracy the florist was married. Tanning salon owner, also married. Crap. Everyone was either gay or married.

I searched my desk drawer for my rubber stress ball but came up empty. Glancing around, I spotted the missing ball beneath the couch. Maybe I should stop throwing things. "I'm going stag." I pushed back my chair and stood up halfway, signaling the end of the discussion.

"Stag?" Jeanine laughed so hard one of the pens in her hair dome fell out. She picked it up and planted it back in place. "Hello, you're an image consultant and a madam. How would that look if you showed up alone?"

The image of me surrounded by a herd of balloon-size-lipped banshees flashed before my eyes. It would look bad, that's how it'd look.

I sat back down.

"Well?" Jeanine asked.

I sniffed. "I don't care how it looks. It's the millennium. It's perfectly acceptable for women to attend events alone."

Jeanine cocked her finger in my direction. "And this is why you'll never get married."

"Who said I want to?" I searched the table for something to grip, settled on my pen. "Half of all marriages end in divorce, the other half cheat."

"Well, stag's not an option." She drummed her nails on her armrest then raised her finger in an *aha* moment. "Let me help. I can find you Mr. Right, or, at least Mr. Right Now."

Having Jeanine select my date was not ideal, especially if her taste in men was as bad as her taste in clothes.

I squeezed my pen. "I don't think…"

Jeanine's smile drooped.

She reminded me of the wilted violet plant she kept trying to revive. Perhaps it wouldn't kill me to let her help. "Fine." I let out a resigned sigh. "But only if he meets my criteria."

"Which are?"

I ticked off items with my fingers. "Good hair, nice legs, and strong teeth."

She held up a hand. "Are we talking men or horses?"

"Hilarious." I resisted the urge to roll my eyes. "Make sure he's educated, handsome, wealthy—did I mention good teeth?"

"Twice."

I leaned on my elbow. "Why aren't you writing this down?"

She threw out her palms. "You think that after all these years I don't know what you want?"

"I'm not sure *I* know what I want."

"Well, I do."

"Okay." I leaned back and made a gesture with my pen like a conductor. "Tell me what I want."

She removed her cat-eye glasses and set them on my desk. "Your dream date is five-foot, eleven inches. He has dark, wavy hair and smoldering eyes. He votes in each election but isn't hyper-partisan. He's a critical thinker, and agnostic but not a Nihilist. He holds the door, but doesn't balk at women's empowerment. He doesn't want kids. He'd never be caught dead in a hybrid car and he couldn't care less if the grocer gave him paper or plastic bags. He can cook but prefers carryout. He stays fit, but hates fad diets. He appreciates music and listens to talk radio. He watches movies at Carter Barron Amphitheater, stays up late, likes to party, loves to sleep in. He's obsessed with the stock market but doesn't day trade. He likes the beach but despises the drive to Ocean City. Valentine's Day is sensationalized, but he'll surprise you with flowers for no particular reason. He's a lion the bedroom and a fox in the boardroom. Women confuse him but he worships the ground they walk on."

She picked up her glasses, huffed breath on the lenses and wiped them. "Well?" She put her glasses back in place. "How'd I do?"

I relaxed my raised brows. "You nailed it." Maybe it was a good idea to let her help. "Okay, genius, you have a month to find me Mr. Right."

She sucked her teeth. "Sorry. No can do."

"Why not? You just described the perfect man."

"That's the problem." She knocked the side of her head. "He doesn't exist. You have this laundry list of your dream guy, but you completely ignore the fact that love doesn't work that way. The right person usually comes when you're not looking, and the person you fall for rarely is what you imagined. You'll never find Mr. Right if you don't take risks. You have to be vulnerable. You can't just buy love."

"That's where you're wrong." I pointed to one of the awards on my wall. "We sell it every day."

"We sell sex and companionship, not love."

"Semantics."

A phone rang in the lobby.

In seconds, Jeanine was on her feet and at the door. "This isn't over," she called.

It never was.

During the elevator ride downstairs, I reviewed what Jeanine had said. Maybe I was too picky. Maybe the guy I envisioned didn't exist.

But why settle? Why not wait for someone who inspired that rush of butterflies? Was there a Mr. Right

out there?
        Or like Jeanine said, a Mr. Right Now?

Chapter Ten

The sky was illuminated in crimson colors of the setting sun, and the streets were bubbling with the sounds of honks, traffic light chirps, and pedestrians' conversation.

I was still a bit off-kilter when I arrived home, jostled by Jeanine's conspiracy theories about finding Mr. Right. Pressed for time, I quickly showered and shaved. Finn seemed to be enamored with flowers, so I dabbed a generous amount of gardenia-scented perfume behind my neck, wrists, and ankles.

It was time to dress, and clothing was the first ammunition, but nothing in my closet jumped out as a winner. I slid hangers across the rack. My zebra-patterned Lycra minidress was too suggestive for a first encounter. My velour jump suit was comfortable, but it was a bitch to unzip. My sweater dress shed angora hairs and they always ended up stuck in my lashes. My pleather cat suit was a Halloween costume. Beige skirt, too blah. Lace dress, too itchy. Sailor pants made my hips look wide.

I dropped a handful of hangers and slumped onto a chair. First impressions mattered, and I needed something that would convey sophistication yet still be sexy—sophisticated slut, if there were such a thing.

Upon further inspection, I finally found the winner: a striking knee-length knit sleeveless cocktail illusion dress with a banded waist, metallic sequins, contrast bands, and sheer tulle panels. I added onyx bangles and a pair of black heels then headed to the coat closet.

The forecast called for chilly temperatures, and it pained me to conceal my dress beneath something bulky, so I grabbed a light quilted jacket and hoped the restaurant would be warm.

Before leaving the apartment, I set up the portable spy camera on my bedroom desk and tossed a condom into my purse. It was presumptuous to assume I'd get lucky on the first meeting, but like a Boy Scout, a good madam was always prepared.

****

The driver dropped me off at the corner of H and 9th with time to spare. Outside the restaurant, I turned to face the Friendship Archway, the gate that marked the entrance to Chinatown, and inhaled the eclectic aroma of Chinese five-spice powder, succulent meat, and car exhaust. Melded together, they were an unusual, yet somehow pleasant, fragrance.

After a quick lipstick check and a lift-squeeze of *the girls*, I headed inside.

The happy hour crowd had dispersed, and the dining room was filled with *suits* and couples seated at intimate tables. Table candles flickered, and snippets of conversations and laughter came at me from all sides. Peppy Latin music flowed from overhead speakers.

The hostess sat me at a table by the window, and soon after, a waitress took my order for a coconut mojito, a house specialty, and a side order of plantains. While waiting for my drink, I mentally rehearsed my introduction.

Hey. Hi. Hello there. They all felt wrong.

I took a sip of mojito and jiggled my ice. Something was off. I was off. Strange, since I usually mastered this stuff. Perhaps, I was overthinking things.

I glanced at two *ballers* at the bar and returned one of their smiles.

Yes. I was overthinking things.

Normally, I took the lead with guys who were socially awkward, but allowing Finn to feel like he was in charge would loosen him up and help earn his trust.

The front door opened, and a long-limbed man with poufy hair and slumped shoulders came inside. He didn't have Marshall's tan, in fact, he was rather pasty-skinned, but he wasn't bad looking, aside from needing a haircut. His suit was two sizes too big for his frame, and the mole on his right cheek was visible even from a distance. A small American flag was pinned to his lapel.

Finn cupped a hand over his eyes and looked around. The hostess pointed in my direction.

Here we go. I straightened my shoulders and waved.

At the table, Finn tugged his tie. "Faith?"

"That's me." I stood to kiss his cheek but he thrust out a meaty hand.

"Sorry I'm late." He gave the area a quick glance. "I'm usually on time, but the meeting ran over."

I took his hand and smiled to put him at ease. "You're not late."

"That's a relief." He pumped my arm, releasing a whiff of fabric freshener from his clothes. I took mental notes. Moist palms, no eye contact, poor posture. Three strikes for a future politician, but I'd award him a sympathy point for the nice smile.

Finn draped his jacket over the back of his seat and took his chair. As he lowered, he knocked the table and disrupted a few items, including my mojito. Fortunately, nothing spilled.

"I almost didn't recognize you," he said. "The lights are so dim; I didn't see your blonde streak." He tilted his head and squinted. "Two colors, just like you said."

I wasn't sure if he meant that as a compliment but I continued grinning. It was going to be one of those exhausting fake smiles kind of meeting.

I gave him a quick study. He looked better up close, but candlelight had a way of making people look good—as did mojitos. I looked down then up. Long fingers. Bulky ring. Slate-colored eyes. Bright, white teeth—a dentist's dream. Don't look at the mole. Don't look at the mole. Do *not* look at the—

I stared at his mole.

"It's good to finally meet you." I shifted my gaze to his lapel pin. "Marshall has talked about you for ages. I'm glad we'll have the opportunity to work together."

"About that…" Finn slid his arm back, dragging the tablecloth with his sleeve. The candle nearly overturned, but he caught it in time. "Whoops. That was close." He rubbed his palms together. The room was cool, but the poor guy appeared to be sweating. "You said you've known my father a while?"

Yes. Why? What did he know?

I straightened the tablecloth. "I helped Marshall on his first campaign."

"Ah." Finn didn't expand his sentence.

"Let's get you a drink." I handed Finn a menu.

"You should try their mojitos. Coconut is the best."

He squinted as he perused the list. "I'm not a fan of coconut. Not really a big drinker, either. Just an occasional beer."

I speared a piece of mint from my mojito and sighed. This was going to be fun.

The waitress returned and set my order of plantains on the table. Finn ordered a Mexican amber lager and politely accepted the chip I offered.

"Interesting place." He twisted to look around. "Come here often?"

"When I can." I tapped my foot beneath the table in time with the salsa song playing in the background.

The waitress returned with Finn's beer. He sucked the foam from his glass and when he lowered it, there was a frothy mustache on his upper lip. I gave a nonchalant finger swipe to my own lip, but he missed my cue and slid his thumb up and down his glass then rubbed the condensation between his fingers.

"Um," I tapped my upper lip, "you have…"

This time he picked up my signal. He quickly licked his lips and gave a sheepish smile, bringing out two adorable dimples.

It was so cute, I almost laughed, but I stopped myself from embarrassing him further.

His cuteness wore off as the minutes ticked away. The conversation was tanking, and I was starting to lose the little patience I came with.

A waiter passed our table carrying a tray with sizzling meat. I swirled the ice in my glass. Finn was a bigger challenge than I'd estimated but big money was at stake. If I didn't help him relax we'd never move forward. Time to vamp things up.

I leaned back and pushed out my breasts. It wasn't an original move, but it seemed to work, because Finn immediately put down the plantain chip he'd been munching on and his gaze dove to my cleavage. When he looked up and met my eye, a blush tinted his cheeks. I smiled to encourage him, but he quickly looked away.

Strike one.

I slid the candle to the side to clear the space between us then stroked my clavicle and flashed a come-hither look. "Marshall told me you're quite handy. That you enjoy working with your hands."

Finn picked up his cocktail napkin and folded down a corner. "I love fixing things." He tore off a corner of the napkin. "When I was young, we had a workshop in our basement. I spent hours there, tinkering with electronics, reassembling alarm clocks. Once, I made a birdhouse, complete with electrical wiring. It was fun, until the fire."

My brows arched. "Fire?"

His neck reddened. "Never mind." He balled his napkin strip and rolled it around the table.

It was time to pull out heavier ammunition.

I lifted my sugarcane straw and sucked the end in a suggestive manner.

Finn picked through the plantains until he found one to his liking, ate it, and brushed off his hands.

Strike two.

I dumped my straw back into my drink. *Don't give up. Find something he can relate to.* I leaned on my elbows to provide him with an ample view of my bosom and twirled a piece of my hair. "Tell me what you like to do for fun."

Finn exhaled a wistful sigh. "Fun's limited these

days. With the campaign and the upcoming gala, I rarely have time for extracurricular activities."

"Well, you're here tonight." I stroked my clavicle.

"Yup." He tore off another napkin strip and added another ball to his collection.

The background noise was escalating. Laughter and Columbian music drowned out our stilted exchange. As I glanced around the restaurant, I wondered what the other diners saw. Probably a man who looked like he'd be more comfortable in a lab and an overdressed girl who'd rather be on a date with her vibrator.

Don't give up. Be empathetic. Flirt, for Pete's sake.

I rubbed my finger up the side of my glass, caught a water droplet. "You must be under an immense amount of pressure. I can't imagine what you go through. Anyone would feel overwhelmed." I licked the tip of my finger. "Only a strong person can do what you do."

Finn ripped off another napkin strip. "You get used to it. Oh, that reminds me." He twisted and removed something from his blazer pocket then set something wrapped in blue paper on the table. "This is for you."

"For me?" Too soon for jewelry, but one never knew. "How thoughtful." I unwrapped the item, a small pin, still warm from being in his pocket. *Vote for Billings.*

I flipped the pin over and studied the clasp. He wasn't expecting me to put it on, was he?

Finn's eager expression confirmed my answer.

My smile faded as I pinned on the ornament. The second I moved my hand, the pin flipped forward. I held it in place with my thumb.

Finn seemed pleased, but he was still preoccupied with his napkin. He gathered his collection of paper balls into a small pile and reached for another piece of napkin.

As I released the pin, the disc flopped forward.

Strike three.

I stirred my drink so hard, liquid splashed over the rim. In my entire adult life, I'd never experienced rejection, at least not from a heterosexual man. He was sitting next to one of D.C.'s most infamous madams and all he found interesting was…paper?

Paper!

I slugged down some mojito. My drink was as watery as our conversation, but I was damned if I was going to throw in the towel. Not yet, at least. "Tell me more about you. What are your hobbies or things of interest?"

That seemed to ignite something. Finn lifted his chin and scratched his jaw as though rummaging through his mental file cabinet. "I guess you could call me a rock hound. I used to collect specimens and polish them in a tumbler. A while back, I had quite a collection." He folded his hands together. "Do you like rocks?"

Sure, if they're over three carats and come from a jewelry store.

"Rocks are cool." I picked up a plantain chip and nibbled it. "Maybe you could show me your collection some time?"

"I'd like to." Finn sighed. "But Father gave it away."

"Why?"

He shrugged. "He thought it was a distraction. He said geologists are poor and that was no career for someone like me. Father has big plans for my future." He touched his flag pin. "I suppose he's right."

That wasn't cool. I set my unfinished chip on my bread plate. "If it's something you enjoy—"

"It's not a big deal."

His pained expression made me think otherwise but it seemed like a sensitive subject, so I decided to let it go.

Finn took a long swallow of his beer and glanced at the exit. I needed to make some kind of connection before the evening was over.

"Tell me about your history in politics."

Finn dragged the candle toward him and dipped his finger into the melted wax. "I was born into it, and it was all I knew. My paternal grandfather worked for the town council. His father was also a councilman. You know my father's story. Naturally, I followed in his footsteps. It wasn't a question." He looked up, and his expression was serious. "In our family, one does what one's told."

I got that. Marshall was a force of nature, and I knew all about domineering parents. I scooped up a piece of mint from my glass, chewed the pungent leaf, and scanned the bar. Stronger alcohol would loosen Finn up, but the waitress was nowhere in sight.

I tried to shift the conversation to something happier. "How's the campaign going?"

Finn removed the wax coating from his fingertip. "It's overwhelming. The fundraisers increase voter approval but they're demanding. Father insists I make appearances at practically everything these days." He rolled the candle wax into a sphere and added it to his pile of napkin balls. "Don't get me wrong, I like working with people but..."

I waited. "But?"

Finn's eyes had a faraway look. He pushed aside the candle. "I'm not sure I'm right for this."

The image of winged dollars flashed before my eyes. In my head, I grabbed them back and pocketed them.

I pointed at his flag pin. "I bet you're excited about the gala. Marshall is going over the top. They say it'll be the event of the season."

Finn twisted what was left of his napkin around his finger. "That's what they say."

He looked about as excited as a kid heading to the dentist. As he tore off another napkin strip and rolled it into a ball, I visualized a sinking ship. All that effort, all that worrying about my dress and the right shoes, perfume between my thighs....

I slid my mojito glass to the side and grabbed Finn's hand. His eyes widened, but I kept his hand in a firm lock. "I totally get it. Everybody wants to be famous, but people don't realize how hard it is growing up in the limelight. You're always the center of attention, judged for everything you do." Keeping eye contact, I rubbed my thumb over his knuckles. "I know you have your work cut out for you, but we need a good leader. And I can help you."

Finn swallowed, and his Adam's apple rose and fell.

I curled my fingertips over the top of his hand. My white nails shone like dinner plates, and I felt the bump of his college ring. "I'm sure it was hard being analyzed for everything you do. If you want to share, I'm an excellent listener. You can tell me anything."

Flickering candlelight danced on Finn's face. After a long moment, he spoke. "It wasn't easy, but I never complained. There were always reporters, people snooping into our business. Father handled it well, my mother, too. I guess when you're raised with it, you don't know anything different."

I nodded. "But you gave up so much."

He shrugged. "You get used to it."

"Do you?"

His cheek muscle twitched.

We both turned as the waitress passed our table. I pulled my hand away to hail her but she was too fast for me. I returned my attention to Finn. "If you could start over, go anywhere, or do anything you wanted, what would you do?"

"That's a tough one." He lifted his chin and tilted his head to the side. "I guess I'd be somewhere out west. California or Nevada—somewhere with lots of trees and wide-open spaces. Don't get me wrong, I like this area, Virginia has nice land, it's just…"

"Yes?"

He raked his hand through his hair. "Here, I'm too close to everything. I don't think I'm cut out for the political scene." He looked down at his paper balls. "I'll never be my father."

True. They broke the mold after Marshall. I looked down at my *Vote for Billings* pin. "Your father is an amazing person, but I'm sure you have special qualities of your own. You'll write your own story."

"Forget what I said. It's selfish to talk like that. People depend on me." He swallowed some beer and gazed intently at his glass.

An Argentinian ballad was playing, and Finn looked more melancholy than the song.

I dipped my index finger into the candle and touched the warm wax. "It's not selfish to have dreams. Without them, what's the point of living?"

"Living," he repeated.

A simple word, but he looked like he was having trouble digesting it. Clearly, politics wasn't his passion, but it was my job to make him think I was there to help in that department. My first task was to upturn his safety net. I dug my cigarettes out of my purse and lit a smoke with the candle.

Finn's head snapped up. "What are you doing?"

"Proving something."

His eyes grew wide. "You can't smoke in here. It's against the law."

I leaned back and crossed my legs. "Who says you always have to follow the rules?"

"Lawmakers." He fanned the air. "Please put it out. We'll get in trouble."

"What's going to happen?" I laughed.

Finn glanced at the hostess stand. "They can kick us out."

I took another drag. "You can't let fear be your guide. Sometimes you just act and worry about the consequences later. You should try that, you know, live a little."

He shook his head. "I couldn't."

"You don't know what you're capable of until you try."

The waitress came over and placed an ashtray on the table. "I'm sorry, the manager asked me to ask you to extinguish that." She smiled. "You understand."

"Of course." I smiled and stubbed my cigarette in the ashtray.

"I can move you guys outside. It's okay to smoke there."

"No need." I dabbed the corner of my mouth with my napkin. "We're perfectly fine here."

The waitress picked up my empty glass. "Can I get you anything else?"

Finn had his head lowered.

I handed her my menu. "All good for now, thanks."

After the waitress left, Finn looked up and whispered, "See. I told you."

"You're overreacting." I gestured indifference with a wave of my hand.

"But—"

"But nothing. You underestimate people. She wasn't mad. She offered to move us." I leaned my elbow on the table. "Don't let fear hinder you from having fun."

He rubbed his finger around the rim of his beer glass. "Easier said than done."

Perhaps, but he had to make an effort.

It was clear he needed help—more than a makeover—a complete overhaul, but a noisy restaurant was not an ideal teaching environment. I excused myself to use the restroom, and on my way back, I bumped into a man wearing woodsy-scented cologne. That's when inspiration hit.

"Finish your drink," I said when I was at the table again.

"Now?" Finn lowered the menu he was perusing. "We haven't eaten."

I flagged down the waitress. "Finish it or don't. We're leaving."

Finn glanced at the entrance then back at me. "Are we going far? I have an early meeting tomorrow and—"

"Finish. Your. Drink." I brushed Finn's paper balls off the table with a grand wave and challenged him with my stare.

He chugged his beer and wiped his mouth with the back of his wrist.

I let him pay the bill.

Chapter Eleven

On the way out the door, Finn surprised me by stepping around to open it for me.

"After you." He bowed slightly.

I chuckled. Guess he had inherited some of Marshall's charm.

The air hit my chest like a hard punch, and I immediately regretted the thin jacket I'd brought. A shot of cinnamon-flavored whiskey would have warmed my insides but Plan B required sobriety, and the buzz from my mojito was just wearing off.

To stay warm, I visualized warm beaches and tan cabana boys. I glanced at Finn, hoping he'd notice my discomfort and offer to wrap his arm around me, but he was preoccupied with something in his hand.

A family of four passed by. A balloon had broken free from a child's grasp and he chased after it until it was far from reach. Although the sky was dark, I saw the balloon tilt and teeter upward. Up, up, up it sailed, and disappeared into the clouds. *Sorry, kid. I know it sucks to lose something important.*

I checked the street for taxis but there were none to be found. When I looked back at Finn, I saw him opening the lid on what appeared to be a toy.

I stepped closer and pointed at the artifact. "What on earth is that?"

He dialed a number. "You mean my phone?"

"If you could call it that." I wrinkled my brow. "They still make ones like that?"

"I've had this for a while."

"Why don't you have a smartphone?"

He shrugged. "Never needed one."

"Everyone needs one. Even teenagers have smartphones. You're in politics, you have to stay connected. You need a new phone."

He gave me a sheepish grin. "What's that adage? Don't fix it if it ain't broke."

I rubbed my temple. How mad would he be if I broke the phone for him?

A cab turned the corner. I raised my hand and stepped toward the curb to hail the vehicle, but Finn caught my wrist.

He quickly released me. "We can take my car, if you like."

"Where'd you park?" My question dissolved as a black stretch sedan pulled in front of us.

Sweet. Finn had a limo.

"Father insists." His explanation sounded like an apology. He walked over and opened my door.

"Got your dumbphone?" I teased.

He chuckled. "Hilarious."

Inside the vehicle, I set my purse on the floor then unzipped my jacket. The limousine had a simple gray interior with a small bar area, empty glass decanters, and a sound system panel with too many buttons. The seats looked like they'd just been polished, and I caught a whiff of the scent of leather conditioner.

I'd ridden in plenty of luxury sedans, but I preferred public transportation. Taxis and car services had diverse drivers who loved to share stories.

Listening to people is what helped me become an empathetic companion. It helped my dates open up to me.

Finn climbed into the vehicle on the opposite side and sat close to the door.

Well, almost everyone.

I slid closer until our knees touched. I smelled beer and fried plantains on his breath.

Finn seemed uncomfortable with my close proximity. He bounced his knee. "Well, what should I tell the driver?"

I twisted to face him. "Tell him to take us to Canal Road."

"Could you be more specific?"

"Sorry." I patted his knee. "No."

He tugged his tie. "Are we going to one of the rest stops?"

"Negative."

"Fletcher's Boat House?"

"Wrong again." I giggled. This was fun.

Finn rubbed his jaw. "Will we be parking there? Are we staying long? I need a plan."

I squeezed his knee. "Sometimes you have to let go and be spontaneous. Let's call it 'consensual kidnapping.'"

He glanced at my hand. "You're serious?"

I cocked one brow. "Do I look like I'm joking?"

Finn exhaled a heavy breath and leaned forward to give the driver instructions.

As the car pulled away from the curb, Finn's foot started to shake. He was wound up head to toe, but a little adventure was the medicine he needed.

To alleviate some discomfort, I suggested some

music. "Got anything good to share?"

His expression brightened. "Sure. What do you like?"

"Everything." Father had forbidden music in our home but Mother had snuck albums in during his absence, cultivating my appreciation for jazz and blues. Later I opened my ears to other genres. Music was something to be embraced and appreciated, not banished.

I stroked my shoulder in a suggestive manner. "Surprise me."

Finn hit a few buttons on the sound system, and a song I recognized came on. While John Coltrane sang about favorite things, I tapped my fingers on the seat, keeping time with the music.

Things were looking up. Finn's posture had unwound and his expression had softened. All I had to do was keep the momentum rolling.

During the ride, we shared small talk. When Finn asked questions about my business, I gave evasive answers. It wasn't that I was lying, per se; I *had* worked with the personalities I named, just on a more *intimate* level with some.

Midway through a story, Finn interrupted me by raising his hand. "You're telling me your client is afraid of spoons?"

I palmed my chest. "I kid you not."

Finn laughed so hard he coughed.

I shook my head. "You have no idea what we had to deal with. Word spread after the guy made a scene in a downtown hair salon. The shampoo assistant had offered him a coffee, and unbeknownst to him she brought…"

"Cutlery?"

"Exactly." I chuckled. "The entire week everyone was on edge. The hotel, restaurants, the concierge. Celebrity or not, no one wanted him around. It was a PR disaster. Fortunately, I'm good at resolving these types of things."

Finn studied my face for a long moment. "I imagine you're quite the expert."

I blew imaginary dust off my nails. "You could say that."

A car in the lane beside us honked as a pedestrian stepped off a curb into traffic.

Georgetown was a hotbed of activity. The sidewalks were filled with shoppers and people perusing menus on restaurant windows. At the intersection of M Street and Wisconsin Avenue, we passed the bronze-domed building that was once Riggs Bank.

We passed the mall, various retail shops, restaurants, and a boarded-up building that had once housed the watering hole I used to frequent, where I'd catch live music and play backgammon with strangers.

The limo slowed as we hit a patch of traffic near the infamous "Exorcist Stairs." The narrow passageway was lit with a halogen light that made it look ominous. I'd hiked those bitches on plenty of occasions, once, in stilettoes. Not my smartest decision.

I pointed toward the landmark. "Ever climb those?"

Finn twisted toward the alley. "You mean the stairs?"

"Yes, those."

He shook his head. "Can't say I have."

My brows arched. "Surely, you've seen the movie?"

Another head shake.

I blinked in disbelief. Every Washingtonian had either forged the climb or seen the movie. It was a rite of passage, harrowing for those who feared heights, but the payoff came at the top. Standing there—cupping your hand over your eyes to get an unobstructed view of the city, nausea swirling in your gut, the fear of falling—it was a ritual everyone had to experience.

I gently knuckled his rib. "You're lying."

Finn looked me square in the eye. "I never lie."

Every politician claims their word is golden, but politicians had a tendency to massage the truth. Finn, however, was no ordinary guy.

I faced forward and folded my hands. It was starting to sink in, the loss we'd suffer losing an honest candidate.

The limo turned onto Canal Road, and the smell of deteriorating vegetation attacked my nostrils. Georgetown's canal had an odor one could only call *distinct*. Even on the driest of days the smell inspired one's gag reflex.

I held my finger beneath my nostrils. "We're close now. Another mile or so."

Finn glanced out the window. "Where are we going?"

"You'll see." I played with a piece of my hair. "Just tell your driver to drop us off at the light."

Finn rubbed his chin. "There's nothing there."

I glanced at the endless rows of trees. "Don't be so sure."

A minute later, we approached the intersection. It

was time for the next step, a part that relied on trust and compliance.

I tapped the window. "Okay, here."

Finn squinted and craned his neck. "There?"

"Yes. Tell your driver to pull over."

"But there's no—"

My hand was already on the door handle. "Do it, Finn."

"Wait. Stop. Hold on." He grabbed my elbow then quickly released it, exhaled. "I'll tell him."

Finn knocked on the partition and motioned with his index finger. The driver pulled to the side of the road. When the limo came to a full stop, I grabbed Finn's hand and practically dragged him out of the vehicle.

We stood on the embankment and waited for a stream of cars to pass. Somewhere nearby, spring peepers made loud chirping noises. Trees invaded by ivy loomed overhead, and the stench of rotting vegetation was stronger, probably from an earlier rain. I looked down at my dress and frowned. Plan B would ruin my outfit, but if I made a breakthrough with Finn, it'd be worth ruined clothes.

"Follow me." I zipped up my jacket and headed up the road.

"Where are you going?" Finn called.

"Just come."

He lingered behind. "There's nothing here."

I stopped short and glanced over my shoulder. "Sure there is."

"Faith…" Finn's voice trembled. "This is impractical. There's nothing around except trees and hills."

I huffed and turned to face him. "There is more. You're just not *looking*." I pointed toward the sky and waited for Finn to follow my finger. Eventually, he lifted his chin.

Overhead was an abandoned bridge. It was a heavy monolith, blackened from time, soot, and neglect. The bridge had missing planks, one dangling at a precarious angle. The tunnel beneath the bridge used to be a shelter for the downtrodden, but even the homeless had moved on. Left behind were graffiti, broken beer bottles, and the rancid smell of urine.

Finn's eyes were as big as marbles. "You're not serious?"

"As a heart attack." He didn't laugh. "Come on. It's fine." I grabbed his hand.

He studied something overhead. "Please, not there."

"Why not?"

"It looks dangerous."

I exhaled a slow breath. "Do you trust me?"

"I hardly know you."

I squeezed his hand. "Can you try?"

He hesitated then said, "I guess so."

I grabbed his arm before he could change his mind.

We crossed the street and scrambled up a craggy hill. Rust-red earth and dark leaves deadened the sound of our footsteps. Occasionally, I heard the snap of a twig, a distant car honk.

At the summit, we paused to catch our breath. The drop was significant, and it was foolish bringing him there, more importantly, to what lay ahead.

I flicked a hitchhiking burr off my dress and faced Finn. "Doing okay?"

He gave a thumbs-up then bent forward, his hands on his knees, and took slow breaths. A line of sweat ran down his cheek.

We must have shared a mutual antipathy for exercise.

Finn wiped his brow with his knuckle. "That was something." He walked toward the tracks, cupped a hand over his eyes, and took a small step back. "This really doesn't look safe."

That was the point.

I joined Finn by the tracks. "I didn't bring you here for safe. I brought you here to teach you something. Safe doesn't make impressions, and safe won't win elections." I flashed him my most reassuring smile. "You have to trust the process."

After a moment of apparent deliberation, he brushed off his pants and said, "Okay."

"That's the spirit."

I gave myself a mental pat on the back. Maybe this crazy idea would work, after all.

Finn waited for me to start along the tracks, then followed and eventually caught up. One by one, we crossed the planks. For the first minute, our steps were easy, carefree. A blanket of pebbles, dirt, and overgrown weeds carpeted our tracks, and our heels made clomping sounds as they made impact on the railroad tiles. We made idle chit chat about the increase in potholes and the weeks of rain, but I sensed Finn's hesitation as more and more ground disappeared.

Ahead was the challenge, the place where the tracks gave way to the bridge with a twenty-foot drop.

Over the years, people had died there. I'd read about the ones who'd voluntarily ended their lives for reasons unknown. I understood them. The bridge was the place I'd visited on my darkest of days—times when I felt like life wasn't worth living, times when childhood memories were too much to bear. After Mother passed, Father unleashed his anguish on me in the form of weekly belt lashings while citing his precious bible quotes. Time healed the bruises, but some wounds were so deep, they left permanent scars on your heart.

Salvation came as I helped my girls. Each person I took in eased my suffering. In time, the bridge became my happy place. It was my hidden gem. A place to journal and eat mozzarella sandwiches on Sunday afternoons. A place for reflection. After sharing so much of my body to the world, I'd needed something private. Perhaps the bridge would help Finn, too.

The clear night provided a grand showing of stars, and the yellowish moon glowed like a plastic jacks ball. The air smelled earthy, but it wasn't the moon or stars or crisp breeze that inspired the rush of adrenaline, it was being in a remote location with a powerful man, his fate held between my manicured fingers.

I moved closer so Finn could feel my hair brush his neck. As I took a carefree step, a wind gust blew dirt in my eyes, and my heel slipped. I moved to shield my face and lost my balance.

Finn grabbed my elbow and steadied me. "Careful." His firm grip on my arm tightened. "Almost lost you, there."

Guess I wasn't the only person holding someone's fate between his fingers.

My heart felt like it was going to burst through my ribcage, but showing weakness would make Finn second-guess what we were doing, so I smiled and linked my arm through his. "Don't worry. I've done this before."

Finn still had a concerned look on his face as we continued on. After a minute of slow, calculated steps, he came to a dead stop.

"I think we should go back."

"Not yet." I swatted an insect away from my ear. "This is where it gets interesting."

"But your shoes, the planks—"

"I'll be fine." At least, I hoped I would.

He unlinked his arm from mine. "I can't do this. People depend on me. What if something happens to us?"

"Nothing's going to happen." I smiled to mask the agitation creeping into my voice. "I've done this a thousand times." Well, a few. "I'm not worried so neither should you. Didn't you say you trust me?"

He looked to the side and shrugged.

I crossed my arms. "So, you're going back on your word?"

"No." He rubbed the back of his neck. "I'm a man of my word."

I stared at the spot where I'd almost jumped. I had almost given in to the darkness when a voice in my head intervened, reminding me of how much I'd overcome. I'd backed off the tracks that day and literally ran for my life. By the time I was on the ground, I'd vowed to never give up, never look back.

I touched Finn's shoulder. "Sometimes you have to take a leap of faith."

"I'm not that brave." Emotion crumbled his words.

"You are." I pointed ahead. "This is a turning

point. It's time to change your life. We'll do it together."

He stared for a long moment and finally said, "Okay, but please let me lead."

I intertwined my fingers through his. "I wouldn't want it any other way."

Slow, slow, his steps were painfully slow. As the dirt disappeared and gaps took its place, my resolve faltered and I questioned my motives. There was a good likelihood something awful could happen. I didn't want to die, and there was no way I was going out of the world on some rickety bridge. Like Finn, people depended on me. Who would protect the girls if I was gone?

Finn's chin was set in determination, his gaze set forward. He was fully invested. There was no backing down.

I took a deep breath and mentally recited my mantra. *Don't look down, never look back.*

Soon, we arrived at the point of no return. It was a place where time and the elements had weathered the wood. Here, there were more missing planks than whole ones. We paused for a moment to calculate our course. The wind whipped my hair, and a sharp breeze sliced through my clothes. In addition to being poorly attired, my shoes weren't made for hiking.

I shivered. Me and my crazy ideas.

Finn held his free hand to the side to steady himself. "Watch your step."

We crossed another board and again he paused. The plank in front of us hung by a nail.

After a minute of waiting patiently, I said, "What do you plan to do?"

"You're asking me?" He gaped at the plank with wide eyes. "This was your idea."

I shrugged one shoulder. "Life is unpredictable."

His brows crimped in apparent annoyance. "Not for me. I need plans. That's my life—schedules and routines."

I released his hand. "No matter how hard you try to control things, life has a way of changing course. You can wrap yourself in a protective bubble, but shit happens. The sooner you accept this, the happier you'll be."

He balled his fists. "I trusted you."

I touched his elbow. "And I trust you to get us across."

Lips pursed, he patted his leg with one hand, as though running through a big calculation. His expression was grave, and I understood his concern, but I couldn't let him retreat. The challenge would make him stronger.

"You've got this," I said.

He twisted to the side and looked down. I mimicked his actions. The drop was worse than I remembered, but I was willing to take the risk. Could Finn?

I took his hand and squeezed it. "Trust your instincts."

"All right," he finally said. "We leap across on the count of three."

"Leap?" My shoulders tightened. "Are you crazy? I'm in heels."

He jutted his chin. "It's not far. Three feet, max. You can do it."

There was a sound of cars in the distance. Images

of Finn and me splattered on the ground flashed before my eyes. A tremor came over me and shook my right leg.

Think. Think fast.

"I have horrible balance," I blurted out, followed by a strange laugh. "And I suck at yoga."

Finn stared into my eyes. "Do you trust me?"

He was throwing my words back at me. I looked down at our entwined fingers. His hands looked strong, probably from his years of woodworking, and his grip was firm and reassuring. I looked up and regarded his face with fascination. His gaze pinned me, his piercing blue eyes almost black in the moonlight. They were kind eyes. Solid. Trusting.

"Okay," I said. "I trust you."

He faced front. "On three. One…"

I inhaled the swampy air.

"Two…"

I exhaled a slow breath.

"Three!"

It was only one or two seconds, but the leap felt like it played in slow motion. Midair, I replayed the obstacles I'd overcome. My father. Living on the streets. Losing Angela. There were still hurdles to scale, but for a moment, that slow motion moment, I was free.

We landed hard, but upright. Finn's grip was a vise, and there was a wild look in his eyes, something raw and animalistic. His hair was ruffled, and his cheeks were ruddy, but his smile stretched ear to ear.

"Wow." He slapped the side of his face. "That was amazing."

For a moment I couldn't move. My feet were locked in place, but every muscle vibrated, and I was hyperaware of the earthy scents, the hum of traffic far away. I felt alive, indestructible.

When the shock wore off and my adrenaline cooled, I released Finn's hand and patted his back. "You did it."

He twisted and pushed a piece of hair out of my eyes. "*We* did it."

His touch instigated a warm vibration down my spine.

"How do you feel?" I asked.

He palmed his chest. "Good—no, great!"

"Don't get too cocky, we're not across yet."

He straightened his shoulders and made a grand wave. "Onward."

The stars twinkled, distant cars honked, and somewhere in the woods, animals called to one another.

It amazed me how one small change could make such a difference in someone's life. Truth be told, I doubted the events would change Finn's personality, but he was making progress. Small steps led to big climbs.

And the first leap was always the hardest.

Chapter Twelve

Safely across the bridge, Finn walked over to the side of the cliff and peered over. Leaning down, he grabbed a pebble and tossed it over the edge.

The ground vibrated as cars passed below us. Even though I stood at a safe distance from the edge, my knees wobbled at the jeopardy I'd put us in.

Finn scooped up two more pebbles and walked over to me. "One for you," he handed me one stone and pocketed the other, "one for me."

The rock was lumpy and was covered with a fine sheen of dirt. As I rubbed the pebble between my fingers, I remembered a video I once watched on the mating rituals of penguins that showed how male penguins would scour entire beaches until they found the perfect pebble to present to a female. Was Finn trying to impress me?

I squeezed the pebble. "Thank you."

"It's just quartz, which is pretty common. You can find it anywhere." He dug his stone out of his pocket and examined it. "But it'll be a nice memento."

The rocks I usually fancied came from jewelry stores, but I appreciated the gesture.

I curled my fingers around the stone. "I won't forget this."

An alarm chimed on Finn's watch. He pushed a button to silence the alert and motioned to the hill.

"Guess we should get moving."

With sluggish steps, I plowed on. Walking in heels made my ankles sore and my mouth was parched from earlier anxiety, but I didn't complain. The idea, crazy as it was, seemed to have brought us closer together. Hopefully, the momentum would continue.

We headed to the overgrown path that led downhill. Before descending, I scouted for the driest area, more worried about ruined shoes than broken bones. "Careful going down," I said. "It's probably slippery from all the rain."

Finn removed a small bottle from his jacket pocket and squirted hand sanitizer onto his palms. "This is child's play after leaping across that bridge."

I gave his arm a playful jab. "And you doubted you could do it."

Although the path was a relatively easy slope, Finn insisted on holding my hand on the way down. The warmth of his palm was comforting, and the bump of his college ring hardly bothered me.

Once we reached the street, I turned and looked up. From below, the drop looked perilous, confirming my theory that a fall would've landed us in the morgue. I'd come many times in the past, but this time, instead of focusing on my own drama, I'd come to help someone else. By the look on Finn's face, it meant something special to him, too.

Still holding hands, we waited at the light and crossed the road when traffic was clear. Once we stood on the embankment, Finn took out his cell and dialed the driver.

I leaned over his shoulder and pointed at the relic. "Dumbphone still working?"

He chuckled. "Like a charm."

The pungent odor of rotting vegetation made me queasy, and I nearly cried when I looked down and saw a snag on my dress where Finn's pin hung from a thread, but I accepted the loss. For progress, one made sacrifices.

Headlights appeared, and Finn pointed to the street. After the limo parked, Finn came around to open my door.

Inside the vehicle, I put the rock on my lap and waited for Finn to join me. He wasn't like other men and I'd met plenty over the years. Politics hadn't soiled him—not yet, at least—but even those with good intentions eventually crossed to the dark side.

Finn climbed inside and clipped on his seatbelt. "Everything okay?"

I twisted toward him and smiled. "Everything's great."

After I gave him the address to my building, he passed it along to the driver.

The limo headed down Canal Road and turned right onto the Whitehurst Freeway. Finn turned on the CD player, and Billie Holiday sang a song about strange fruit.

I hummed along.

"Do you sing?" Finn asked.

"Only in the shower. You?"

"If you mean well, then no. But I admire those who can carry a tune."

I chuckled.

He turned down the volume on the stereo. "My father introduced me to the greats when I was young. They don't make them like they used to."

Angela had played jazz records on a dilapidated turntable until I eventually replaced it with a modern player. "Sure they do. In fact, I know a great place to catch live acts. We could go sometime."

Finn took a moment to mull over his response.

I was starting to regret asking but then he smiled and said, "I'd like that."

The smile I returned quickly faded as I remembered my mission. Finn was a job and feelings would only muddle my judgment. I faced the window and focused on the sights.

The limo was passing Washington Harbor where boats and yachts docked in front of popular restaurants. A fleet of canoes was stacked outside the nearby rental house.

The famous and distinctive buildings we passed were some of the things I loved most in D.C.—along with the symphonic honks of traffic, smells of ethnic food and the chaotic bustle of people.

Finn tapped my shoulder. "You seem lost in thought."

I twisted back to face him. "Just enjoying the ride."

He pulled out his pebble and held it flat in his palm. "Remember I told you this is simple quartz?" When I nodded, he continued. "What's interesting is inside." He held the stone closer to me. "On the surface it's bland, but if you look closer, you can see the milky-white mottling that comes from minute fluid inclusions trapped inside while the crystal forms. The color and the inclusions dictate the value. You've probably heard of amethyst or rose quartz because they're stones people romanticize, but quartz has hundreds of varieties. Speaking of amethyst, in mythology it is believed that amethyst impedes getting drunk. As legend goes, Bacchus the god of wine drank from an amethyst cup so he wouldn't get drunk so…" Finn lowered his hand. "I'm sorry. Sometimes I don't know when to stop."

"Don't apologize, it's interesting."

He bobbed his leg. "I get too excited about rocks."

I patted his knee. "It's good to be passionate about things that interest you."

Finn looked down at my palm resting on his knee but I kept my hand in place.

"Tell me more about yourself. Something the general public doesn't know."

He shrugged. "I'm pretty much an open book."

"Come on. I told you I'm a good listener."

He opened his mouth then quickly shut it.

"What?"

"It's silly."

I slid my hand off his knee. "Like I'd laugh after we just defeated death?"

"Good point." He rubbed his pebble. "When I was young, I dreamed of being a famous geologist. My grandmother taught geology, and from the time I was small she shared everything she knew with me. Sometimes we'd take trips to Great Falls, and while we hiked she'd point out different rock and mineral species. We'd gather quartz, mica, sandstone, and other aggregates, but sometimes we'd find cooler things. Pyrite and the occasional fossil. I'd get excited when we came across trilobites and arrowheads, and she'd give me a look that made me feel special. Gran was important to me. She didn't expect me to be a leader, she was just happy to be around me.

"One summer she took me to visit a state park in Arkansas that was famous for diamond discoveries. We didn't come away with anything precious, but the memory left a lasting impression." He flipped his rock over. "After that trip, I knew exactly what I wanted to do with my life."

I tilted my head. "What happened?"

He tucked the pebble into his blazer pocket. "My father had other ideas."

The limo hit a bump and my pebble fell to the floor.

I steadied myself and twisted to face Finn. "It's your life, not his."

He touched his flag pin. "I have an obligation to my country."

Fear was a powerful weapon, and I understood loyalty all too well, but the day I took control of my life and got away from my father was the day I was finally free.

I grabbed Finn's hands. "You can't live other people's dreams."

He sniffed. "Sometimes we do things for the greater good."

I let that hang in the air, unchallenged.

For the rest of the ride we were silent. The sights blurred as we drove by, but the cityscape didn't distract me from noticing the way Finn's leg touched mine, the smell of the woods that came off his skin, and the way his chest rose and fell with his breath.

Outside my building, Finn came around and helped me out of the car. "May I walk you to the door?"

"Sure."

We took two steps and Finn halted. He rushed back

113

to the limo and returned to my side holding out his hand. "You forgot this." He placed the pebble in my palm.

Penguins.

The halogen streetlight above illuminated Finn's face in a soft amber color. As he smiled, dimples appeared at the corners of his mouth. The mole on his cheek was prominent, but it gave his face character.

I tucked a piece of hair behind my ear. "Thanks for a memorable evening."

He shrugged. "I should thank *you*. I can't remember the last time I let loose like that."

I took a step closer. "There's more to come during our next meeting."

He touched his lapel pin. "I almost forgot you're here to help with the campaign."

Otis, my doorman, stepped outside, tipped his cap, and retreated inside. The lobby door whooshed close.

Leaning to one side, I lifted my heel and twisted my foot, twirled a piece of hair. "Would you like to come up for a nightcap?"

Finn shoved his hands in his pocket. "Maybe another time."

"Of course." I lowered my heel and dismissed a small pang of rejection. "Anyway, our work is just beginning. I have plenty of ideas in mind to share when you're available."

"More death-defying adventures?"

"No." I held up one finger. "Well, maybe."

He laughed which I took as a green light. Feeling emboldened, I reached up and kissed his cheek, letting my lips linger on his cheek a few seconds longer than they should have.

"Call me," I whispered in my most seductive tone.

"I…will definitely do that." He walked backward a few feet, stumbled, and caught himself. Then he faced forward and headed to the limo.

I stayed outside until the vehicle turned the corner.

Small moments became turning points in my life—the night I left West Virginia; meeting Bes; saving Angela's employee; answering Drummond's call.

I wasn't sure what Finn and I had set in motion that night on the bridge, but one thing was true. We'd shared something. Something important. Something that made me question everything.

And that could possibly be the thing that would ruin me.

Chapter Thirteen

Detachment is one of the first things you learn when you enter the biz. To stay sane while selling your body, you bury your emotions. You put your mind elsewhere and treat it like any other job. I learned this concept while working as a dancer and later it was reinforced by my mentor.

"Kid," she told me, "in this biz, men either want to screw you or screw you over. Never do the former for free, and never let the latter happen."

It sounded vulgar, but her advice made sense. By the time I took over Angela's company, I'd hardened my heart. I dated, but never got emotionally attached to my suitors. Relationships weren't worth the trouble. However, every once in a while, someone interesting came along, and I found myself questioning my decision to remain a *bachelorette for life*. Usually after the second or third date, their flaws peeked out. I'd discover their dreamy eyes were the result of colored contacts or their pecs were attributed to implants. When I mentioned my favorite writers, they'd sport glazed looks. After that, I'd reconfirm my single status. No one surprised me. Until I met Finn Billings.

Despite my effort to ignore him, thoughts of Finn plagued my brain all morning.

While putting on my jewelry, I remembered holding his hand and feeling his college ring press against my palm. While applying blush to my cheeks, I pictured his mole. An article I read discussing personal politics and the ethical reach of talk radio reminded me of what Finn said about his duty to his country.

He was becoming a problem.

The local news was playing in the background and the broadcaster on the show had a sonorous voice like Finn's. I muted the volume and stared at the pebble Finn gave me as a memento.

What was going on? I wasn't easily taken in by strangers. Half my job was keeping a certain amount of distance so I could do my job and do it well. Part of the problem was that Finn didn't fit a specific category. Thus, my judgement was getting muddy.

I spun the pebble in a circle. Keep it in perspective. We had one fun night. So what? He was a job, nothing more. Getting attached meant I'd never fulfill my obligation.

I put the pebble back in my purse, turned off the TV, and headed to work.

****

The elevator chimed, the door slid open, and the odor of turpentine accosted my nostrils. Drop cloths blanketed the carpet and workers wearing white overalls were painting the hallway that led to my office. Inside my suite, I was accosted by the cacophony of ringing telephones.

Jeanine was beside her desk facing the wall, tending to her pathetic African violet plant. I never understood why people felt the desire to keep indoor plants. Too much work and little result. It made more sense to visit a public garden.

I cleared my throat to get Jeanine's attention, and

117

when she turned, I winced in horror.

She was decked head to toe in shamrock green, and even her nails were the color of leaves. There was so much green a leprechaun would be jealous.

"Well, look who finally decided to show up." Jeanine set down her watering can and tapped her watch. "It's almost eleven. You ignore my calls all morning and then stroll in here like the queen?"

I removed my scarf and trench coat and pushed back my oversized sunglasses. "Actually, I was going for the Jackie O look."

Jeanine batted her eyelashes. "Jackie who?"

"Onassis. A former First Lady."

"Right." Jeanine's cat-eye glasses slid down the bridge of her nose.

I pointed at her dress. "Should I mention St. Patrick's Day was last month?"

"Not funny." She gave me a look that made me wish I'd stayed home.

I took a step back. "Calm down, I'm only teasing."

She sank onto her chair and picked up a pink message pad. "You have no idea what it's been like here. The phones have been ringing nonstop, that singer we cleaned up last month—the one who started the afterschool program for underprivileged tweens—got arrested again, Tony's bugging me, and there's a new potential." She leaned on her elbows, folded her fingers into a bridge, and rested her chin on her hands. "Wait until you hear about this one. It's a doozy."

"Can't wait." The top-heavy stone on my ring slipped to the side of my finger. I twisted the gem back to its position, trying to forget Finn's ring. "If that's all for now, I'll be in my—"

"I know."

"Could you bring me a—"

"On it." Jeanine handed me the messages and grabbed my coffee mug.

****

Five minutes later, Jeanine entered my office, unannounced. I kept my gaze focused on the spreadsheet I was reviewing while she dumped a packet of artificial sweetener into my latte.

"Who's *F*?"

My head sprang up. "What are you taking about?"

She pointed to my spreadsheet.

At some point, I had drawn large and small letter Fs in the margins. *F* for Finn. My subconscious was betraying me again.

I quickly flipped the paper over. "It's nothing."

Her eyes held a suspicious glint but she shrugged and took the chair opposite mine, pulled a pen out of her beehive. "Wanna go over the potential first or should I just get to Tony?"

I sniffed the cinnamon-dusted foam atop my coffee, took a sip. "Tell me about the potential."

She pushed up her glasses. "He's a young Arab sheik, single, and filthy rich."

"Sounds good so far."

"Don't get excited." She fanned her face with the pad. "His name is Amir Hassan and he's an Arabian big shot. Lately, he's been jumping coast to coast, traveling among the party scene in L.A. and New York. He's been rubbing elbows with every first-name celeb—predictable, right?" She rolled her eyes. "Last year, he made the papers when he crashed after racing his luxury sports car on the 405. No one was hurt."

119

I licked foam off my spoon. "Doesn't sound like a potential. He sounds more like a P.R. case."

Jeanine held up a hand. "Let me finish. He's coming to town this summer and is hosting a party. He wants the…you know."

"The you know?"

She slid down her glasses, stared at me.

I lowered my coffee mug. "The ME Special?"

She scrunched her nose and nodded.

Goosebumps prickled my arms. The Middle East special was pretty sketchy. It was when rich, foreign men lured young girls to come to exotic locales. After the girls arrived, the men gave them *carte blanche* spending, and they were encouraged to shop and post pictures of the good life they were having. Once the lambs were caged, the men would bring these unfortunate girls back to their lair to gang rape and humiliate them. It wasn't common knowledge, but it happened on a regular basis. When the girls returned home, they were never the same.

"I was tempted to hang up right then," Jeanine grimaced, "but he's next in line to inherit his uncle's stake in the oil company and you said we needed new clients. But you've always told me to trust my gut, so there it is."

I stroked my lip. "How much did he offer?"

Jeanine furrowed her brows. "You're not considering—"

"How much?"

She glanced at her notepad. "Sixty. Or seventy if the girl will scream the guy's name when he climaxes."

I leaned back and stared at a framed award on the opposite wall. There was no way I'd ever send one of my girls, but if things didn't work out with Finn, I could go. The sheik's money wouldn't solve all my problems, but a small dent in my debt was better than nothing. And losing my company was worse than a little degradation.

I extended my hand. "Give me his number."

"No. No way—"

"Dammit, J." I slammed my fist on my desk, and coffee sloshed over the cup's rim. "I didn't say I'd do it, I'm just considering it."

She cradled the pad against her chest. "Business is slow but we can't be that desperate."

We were that desperate.

I grabbed a tissue out of my desk drawer and blotted the spill. "Just leave me his number."

She regarded me with an even look, not quite defeated but not willing to push further, and handed me the paper.

I dumped the damp tissue in the trash. "Now fill me in on Tony."

She flipped a page so fast it almost snapped off the pad. "He's coming tomorrow, and he's asking too many questions." She lifted her chin. "What should I do? He's going to catch on."

"Until we find a replacement, you'll have to keep distracting him."

"It's not that easy."

I glanced at her Kelly-green dress. "You're creative. I'm sure you'll think of something."

She laid her message pad on her lap and tucked her pen into her hair dome. "Last thing, and I know you don't want to hear it, but it has to be addressed." She reached over and pointed at my open agenda. "June fourteenth will be here before you know it..."

Here she goes. I sipped my coffee, buying time.

"...eligible bachelors get snagged quickly..."

While Jeanine droned on, my mind played a movie. In it, I was in an elegant setting surrounded by people wearing masks that covered their faces. I was standing in the middle of the crowd, my hair pinned in a ribbon style updo; I was dressed in a poufy gown with a cinched waist and capped sleeves a la' Cinderella. A tuxedoed man had accompanied me. He stood facing the opposite direction. He shook hands with a few guests. A waiter carrying a silver tray handed me a champagne flute. My date took a drink and turned to toast with me. I removed my mask with a gloved finger and indicated my date do the same. He fumbled with the string, but it eventually released and his mask dropped to the floor. It was then my date's identity was revealed...including the mole on his right cheek.

Jeanine waved a hand and whistled. "You in there?"

I nodded. "I was just running through options."

"Any luck?"

I fingered the stone on my ring. "Not yet."

"How 'bout this." She leaned her elbows on my desk, wafting a whiff of her syrupy-sweet perfume toward me. "You make a serious effort to find a date, and I'll help you find a dress."

As I opened my mouth to reject her offer, Jeanine's smile dropped, replaced by a pathetic hangdog expression. "Fine." I regretted my answer as soon as I said it.

"Really?" Her expression brightened. "You'll let me pick your gown?"

I glanced at her green nails. "Just promise to keep it tasteful."

She flipped out her palms. "Don't I always?"

A phone rang in the lobby, which saved me from answering her question.

After Jeanine left, I stared at the sheik's number. It was a last resort. Only if I couldn't make it work with Finn.

Since it was the age of information, unveiling things about someone's personal life was easy if one knew where to look. Social networks were a trove, especially if one paid attention to things like "check-ins," "likes," and tweets.

I scoured through every popular site I could think of but came up empty. In the social media world, Finn was practically invisible.

Another half hour of excavating finally revealed something interesting. A picture in a society page showed a charity event Finn had attended recently. He stood alongside a fair-skinned woman with jet-black hair and light eyes. She was pretty in a plastic way. Long hair, long neck, and legs like a gazelle. But, I noted with slight satisfaction, her smile looked rehearsed, not genuine. Finn looked stiff and uncomfortable beside her, and this also pleased me.

Squinting, I leaned closer to my computer screen. Who was this woman? Girlfriend? Distant cousin? A lover? Finn hadn't mentioned anything the prior evening. Did the shyest man in Washington have a significant other while I only had—I stared at the bottles lined on top of my credenza—booze?

I glanced at the bottom drawer. I had someone once. A dependable man with good hair and hard abs.

Someone who'd do anything to help me.

I grabbed my cell phone and called before I lost my nerve.

He answered on the third ring.

"First Division, Officer Diaz speaking."

"Hi. It's Faith." I took a deep breath. "I was wondering what you were doing the night of June fourteenth."

Chapter Fourteen

Fifteen seconds passed, and Bobby still hadn't responded. I watched the wall clock's hand tick and sank back into my seat wishing somehow the chair could swallow me whole. It had been a mistake to call him. I blamed Jeanine. If she hadn't strong-armed me into going to Finn's fundraiser in the first place, I wouldn't be acting like a stupid schoolgirl waiting for the hot quarterback to ask me to the dance.

I cleared my throat. "You still there?"

"Sorry," Bobby said. "You caught me off guard."

I bit my lower lip. "If you're busy, I understand."

"You haven't told me where we're going."

"Right." I knocked my head. "It's one of those stupid uptight affairs you'd probably hate, and I'm sure you have better things to do, and you'd have to rent a tuxedo, which I'd pay for, of course, but you probably have better things to—"

"I'll go."

I coughed. "You will?"

"I said I would."

"You told me once you'd rather die than be caught in a monkey suit."

"If you don't want me to go then why'd you ask?"

Good question. Habit, I supposed. Bobby had always been my go-to guy. He'd helped me out of a jam or two or ten. "I do want you to go. Thank you. I owe you one."

"You know I'd do anything for you."

His sentence stirred up a bag of mixed emotions. Bobby was always trying to make the world a better place. His mother had named him after the former president's brother with the hope her son would grow to be a great leader.

I pictured Bobby sitting behind a desk that was too small to hold his mountain of paperwork with an untouched cup of instant coffee growing cold by his phone. He was too good for the dregs of society he championed for.

I swiveled my chair away from the credenza. "I have someone waiting for me."

"Okay," he said. "Send me the information on the ball, Cinderella."

"Will do."

My cell rang just as I set it back on the desk, and I picked it up in a hurry, assuming it was Bobby calling back from the station.

"Hello, Faith."

Wrong. Not Bobby; it was Drummond.

"Just checking to see if that package arrived."

Package had to be code for Finn. "It arrived last night." I was hesitant to reveal too much.

"Excellent. I was concerned when I hadn't received an update. You're not having second thoughts?" Despite his chipper tone, there was the undercurrent of a threat.

I blinked to erase the image of Finn's shy smile. "Not at all."

"Good, because that would be unfortunate for everyone. Keep things moving along."

After the call ended, I pushed my cell across my desk as though it were contaminated. Drummond was impatient, so waiting for Finn to make the next move was no longer an option.

I disinfected my cell with a handy wipe and dialed Finn's number. When he came on the line, his voice sounded deep and husky, like he'd had little sleep.

"Hi. This is Faith. Faith Crawley."

"Of course. I recognized your voice. How are you?"

"Doing well, thanks." I relaxed back against my chair. "I was calling to see how your day was going." God, that sounds boring. Say something brilliant. "The moon was luminous last night."

"Yes, it was."

Less brilliance, more sexy. "I enjoyed your presence."

"Ah, me too."

Less sexy, less brilliance—argh, just get to the point. "Is this a bad time?" I opened my top drawer in search of my appointment book and stumbled on an unopened chocolate snack cake.

"I'm a little busy, but I have a moment."

I removed the snack cake and my appointment book, set both items on my desk. "The reason I'm calling," is to seduce you and get a boatload of cash, "was to see if we could get together. I'd like to start working on things as soon as possible."

"I was thinking about that and…"

Shoot. He was backpedaling. I couldn't let him off the hook. "Remember, Finn, we're working as a team. All you have to do is follow my lead."

"Like jumping on bridges?"

I smiled. "More like shopping."

"That sounds relatively harmless."

"Completely." I tapped my pen against my desk. "When are you free?"

Paper shuffled. "I could meet this Sunday if that works for you."

"Sunday's perfect." I made a notation in my appointment book. "Let's say one."

"So I won't need my hiking boots?"

I couldn't help but laugh. "Not this time. But wear comfortable shoes."

"You certainly like to keep me guessing."

"A little mystery is healthy."

There were three shopping centers in close proximity of each other in McLean, Virginia. One was the proverbial Rodeo Drive of the East Coast, one catered to boisterous teens. The one I had in mind was the perfect setting for a tip-to-toe makeover. I wasn't duped into thinking my job would be easy; Finn was headstrong, and there were barriers that would be hard to chisel, but spending a full day together would give us more time to bond.

"So we're all set. I'll text you the directions."

"Wait, Faith. Before you go. I wanted to say…"

Uh-oh. Had he changed his mind?

"I enjoyed getting to know you last night."

I exhaled a sigh of relief. "The feeling's mutual, Finn."

After the call, I picked up the snack cake to reward myself, but the second I drew back the wrapper, my stomach cramped. Apparently, hurting an innocent man didn't agree with my digestion.

Why did I feel guilty? I had reason to celebrate.

Before last night, everything was falling into place. Was I going to break a deathbed promise over a guy I barely knew?

Maybe he wasn't so innocent.

It was hard to imagine Finn as anything but genuine, but experience taught me people always had an Achilles' heel. Food. BDSM. Plaid Catholic school miniskirts—I sniffed my snack cake—chocolate! Everyone had vices. Why would Finn be the exception to the rule?

Not long ago, a conservative Christian politician had bashed a homosexual Olympian contestant for epitomizing the destruction of family values. Soon after, the same politician abandoned his wife to marry the woman he'd impregnated during his marriage.

I sank my teeth into my dessert and gazed at the picture of Finn on my laptop screen. Come Sunday, Golden Boy, I'll uncover whatever you're hiding.

Chapter Fifteen

The day slogged on, and aside from returning calls and ordering a pair of marked-down designer sandals online, I got little else accomplished.

Finn and Drummond were occupying too much space in my head.

To clear my thoughts, I headed to the window to smoke. As I leaned out, smells of bus exhaust and fried food hit my nostrils. Cars honked in the street below and a plane roared somewhere in the distance.

With the first drag, I was overcome by a coughing fit. My lungs felt tight, and logic told me it was time to quit, but the thought terrified me. Smoking, as awful as it was, connected me to Angela.

She had been a chain-smoker; her clove cigarettes were too strong for my taste, but I loved their smell and the silver-plated cigarette case she kept them in. It reminded me of all those nights in her living room, her ashtray overflowing with lipstick-stained butts, her scratchy records playing in the background, our talks on the meaning and meaningless of life, shared with glasses of Irish whiskey in our hands. She always had a butt dangling from the corner of her mouth, and her nails, when not painted, revealed yellowish stains.

I took a drag and tapped an ash onto the window ledge. Somewhere in the distance, a bell tolled, rekindling a memory.

Angela had taken me to a boxing match at the Convention Center in Atlantic City. We sat in the front row, Angela leaning forward, me with my arm shielding my eyes, traumatized by the violence. During intermission, she explained why she brought me.

"We live in a violent world." She told me a story about a boxing match between two heavyweight champions. One was favored to win the fight due to his superior punching power, but during the match his opponent provoked him to attack and force him back on the ropes. Everyone thought the underdog was outmatched, but all along he was feigning weakness. Eventually, the favorite tired, allowing his opponent to regroup. The underdog won.

"Rope-a-dope," Angela had called his tactic. "They thought he was defeated, but all along he was buying time."

"What does that have to do with us?" I couldn't understand why we were at the fight.

"People underestimate women, and that's their mistake. You and I are fighters, but the best way to outsmart people is by using this." She lightly knocked my head.

Use your brain.

That's it. I flicked my cigarette out the window.

On my way down the hall, I passed the pictures of my employees and paused at my hardest worker.

Monique aka The Brain, was the oldest in the lot, and though she wasn't as glamorous as the others, she had a good body, keen instincts, and intellect that earned her moniker. She'd wanted to be an English professor, but universities demanded a degree and teachers never got paid what they deserved. Bills and debt had motivated her to seek employment with our company.

Angela had groomed me to be her successor, and though I hadn't thought about retirement, the reality was, madams burned out early in the biz. Monique could handle the load when the time came to pass the proverbial torch.

Monique didn't answer when I knocked, but there was a light beneath her office door. I rapped again for good measure and peeked in.

The room was neat, impeccable, and empty. Rainforest sounds came from a portable speaker on a shelf by the window. There were papers stacked on her desk and a water glass sweating condensation. Monique was a neat freak, so I doubted she'd left a mess behind. I entered her office and closed the door behind me.

Framed motivational posters with cheesy *can-do* slogans dotted the wall, and a wireless speaker sat on an accent table beside a freeform soapstone sculpture.

I was about to take a seat, but I realized the sweating glass on her desk would leave a stain. As I lifted the glass, I saw something that piqued my interest. It was a brochure for a graduate school in Pennsylvania.

In the biz, privacy was golden, and I never meddled in my girls' personal affairs unless they sought my advice. I wanted them to be successful, because financially secure employees were happy employees.

But that didn't stop me from leaning over to read the brochure.

A voice from behind startled me.

"Hey."

I startled and spilled some water. When I turned, I

saw Monique in the doorway.

"There you are." I pointed to a pen by the brochure. "I was just leaving you a note."

Monique glanced at her desk then back at me. "I stepped out to get some supplies." She removed a few tissues from a box she carried and blotted the spill.

After I settled on one of her Scandinavian chairs, she offered me a drink, which I politely declined.

While she moved the tissue box to a corner on the desk, I glanced at her hand. Pretty pale pink nails, understated jewelry, nothing too sparkly, just a simple charm bracelet on her wrist and a cloisonné ring. Unlike my other employees, Monique followed the *less is more* doctrine. Her unruly curls were tamed in a French twist, and her dark hair shone as though it were wet. Her posture was ramrod straight, attributed, I assumed, to her years of practicing yoga. Her red lipstick played nicely against her creamy white skin, and the stud earrings on her lobes were modest-sized and appeared to be zirconias. What stood out was her scarf. It was the same paisley one all my employees wore, but somehow Monique's seemed different. It was something about the way she knotted it. Like she spent hours perfecting it before she put it on.

I crossed my legs and folded my hands together. "How've you been?"

She mirrored my actions. "Busy. Can't complain."

"Glad to hear that." I rubbed my finger along the chair's armrest.

She slid some papers to the side. "So, what can do for you?"

I brushed imaginary dust off my lap. "I've got a delicate situation and you're the only one I can trust.

You remember Bill Drummond?

"Unfortunately, yes."

I leaned closer to the desk. "Word on the street is, he's being investigated. I haven't seen anything in the papers yet, but I want you to shadow him. Nothing that would raise suspicion—just a drink, a little flirting. Keep him distracted, but be careful. He's probably got his radar up."

She reached for her phone. "Should I cancel tonight's appointment?"

"No." We needed all the business we could get. "Just report back when you have something."

"I'll get right on it."

I jut my chin toward her application. "You're applying to school?"

She nodded but she must have sensed my concern because she added, "It's a low-residency program. Ninety percent of the coursework is done online, and I'd only have to visit one week per semester."

"I'm sure we can cover for you, I just don't want you to burn out. You're my best employee."

"I promise I won't."

I reached over and patted her hand. "Let me know if you need help." I would've said a loan, but she had too much pride to accept charity.

"Thanks, Faith. That means a lot."

I pushed back my chair. "Let me know what happens with Drummond."

"It'll be top priority." She walked me to the door.

By the time I was back in my office, the weight that had been riding piggyback on my shoulders had lifted. Having Monique distract Drummond eased some of my burden. I had an ace in my pocket. The underdog would win.

I opened my laptop and flexed my fingers. Finally, I'd get something productive accomplished. Then the intercom buzzed.

"Tony's due soon," Jeanine said on the other end of the line.

Or not.

Chapter Sixteen

It wasn't that I didn't like Tony. Accountants were a necessary evil, and Tony was like a friend in some ways. Terminating his services was inevitable, but it took time to find good accountants, or at least, good ones who didn't ask too many questions.

I stuffed my financial report into a hidden compartment in my desk and locked the cabinet. There was nothing incriminating in the papers, but not long ago, some gung-ho lawyer tried to release names from a late madam's black book. Even post mortem, one wasn't safe.

I rubbed the cabinet key. Was I safe? Half my life I'd been running. Ever since... I glanced at the framed picture of my father on my desk, the one I kept to remind me.

At sixteen I left home with only a few babysitting dollars, some pictures, and a backpack stuffed with clothes. I used my only resources to shelter, clothe, and feed myself, and later I inherited a company which I built into two successful businesses. Yet there I was, almost at the big three-ugh, and still hustling. When would it end? When would I be back on top?

I stared at one of my framed awards. That this could be an inside job weighed heavily on my heart. My employees seemed happy, but I wasn't born yesterday. The employment expectancy rate of an escort—even a well-paid one—was slightly longer than the life expectancy of a Beta fish. Chyna, Monique, and Shivawn had been with me a while, but others came and went. Jeanine stuck to me like a week-old adhesive.

An alarm pinged on my cell.

Time to go.

I leaned out the door and scanned the lobby. No sign of Jeanine at her desk, no one in the reception area. The scent of fresh-brewed coffee wafted from the kitchen area, so I figured Jeanine was making a pot to share with Tony.

I darted past reception and turned the corner, almost colliding with the second person I was trying to avoid.

"Oh, good. You're still here." She held up two empty coffee mugs.

"Not really." I bowed my head, continued walking.

"Come back," she called. "I want to show you something."

"I'm late."

"Says you." She flagged me down. "Come on, it'll only take a minute."

As if.

"Fine." I exhaled. "You've got three."

At her desk, Jeanine set down the coffee mugs and cracked open a heavy binder. "So, I've been hunting dresses," she slid the binder toward me, "what do you think of this?"

It was a Flamenco-style gown, with flouncy layers that burst from the bottom of what looked like a sausage casing. The only thing missing from the picture was a mariachi band in the background.

Jeanine drummed her nails on her desk. "I know

what you're thinking."

That I was an idiot for letting her select my dress? "You do?"

She pointed at my waist. "You think it's too form-fitting. Don't worry, if you dropped three—four—six pounds, max—you could pull it off."

I clenched my teeth until urge to fire back a retort passed. "Well, I appreciate your effort, but it's not quite what I had in mind." I pointed to my watch. "Three minutes are up. Gotta go."

"Don't worry, I'll keep looking," she said.

The nursery rhyme about catching a tiger by the toe played in my head on my way to the door.

****

The corridor leading to the elevators smelled like fresh paint and the carpet had perfectly straight vacuum tracks.

When the elevator opened, I came face-to-face with a distinguished-looking gentleman with silvery-white hair. As I stepped inside the chamber, the man smiled and stepped to the right.

"Good evening." His voice was deep and there was something worldly in his robin's egg-blue eyes.

Staring forward, I replied, "Evening."

The doors closed, and a moment of silence fell. The elevator *pinged* our descent.

Pretending to be preoccupied with my phone, I snuck a sideways glance at the man. His bronzed skin indicated he lived someplace warm and sunny. He had long fingers, hands mapped with lines. Lace-up loafers. A pinstripe suit—Italian? A tie that matched his hair. A small pocket square peeked out of his blazer pocket, and a black umbrella was hooked over his arm. Fresh-smelling cologne. Gold band on middle finger. Interesting.

The man caught me staring.

I pointed to his umbrella. "Is it raining?"

"Not to my knowledge." He lifted the hook handle. "I carry this just in case."

"That's smart. Spring weather is unpredictable." I dismissed the memory of my ruined shoes in my office closet.

The man stroked his goatee with his free hand. "I rather like the rain. The way it makes the pavement shine like silver."

I touched my clavicle. "*Les Miz* fan?"

He chuckled. "Seen it many times." He jutted his chin in my direction. "You?"

"Only once."

"On Broadway?"

I shook my head. "The Kennedy Center."

"Lovely place. I saw *Phantom* there."

The elevator chimed, and the door slid open. The man reached inside his pocket and withdrew a business card holder. "I'm heading to a meeting, but I'll be in town all week." He selected a card and placed it in my hand. "It would be my pleasure to take you to dinner one evening, if your schedule allows." His eyes had a certain glint that belonged to someone with vast stories. Stories I wanted to hear.

The elevator door started to close, but the man used his umbrella to block the door. I looked down and read the name on his card. Theodore Kane.

A tingly feeling stirred between my legs. The guy was probably pushing sixty, but he had that old-school air of confidence like actors from black-and-white movies. I imagined a night in his company.

Theodore would take me out for a drink. One drink would turn to two, drinks would turn to dinner, dinner would lead to dessert, and dessert would lead to his hotel. We'd end up in his room, the penthouse, I'd imagine, and he'd order escargot and champagne. After eating, we'd make wild, passionate sex on six hundred count bed sheets, and later, dressed in hotel robes, we'd sip cappuccinos on the balcony and watch the sun rise.

The elevator door closed.

I reached for my business card then hesitated. Until my obligation to Drummond was fulfilled, my attention needed to be devoted to Finn.

Begrudgingly, I withdrew my hand. It took every ounce of strength to speak my next words. "I'm sorry. I'm busy the entire week."

"That's a shame, but of course, I understand." He folded my fingers over his card. "Another time, perhaps?"

Wine, dine, sixty-nine, some other time. I nearly cried.

"Yes." I smiled. "Another time."

Theodore hit the button and the elevator door reopened. He made a grand gesture for me to exit and followed me into the lobby.

I hurried to the entrance before I changed my mind.

Outside, while hailing a cab, I saw Theodore step into the backseat of a black stretch sedan.

The image of winged bills passed by my eyes as a rust-eaten taxi pulled up to the curb.

I exhaled a heavy sigh and climbed into the cab.

****

Bills and junk mail were the only things waiting for

me at home. Even more disappointing was the silence and sterility of my apartment. My closets were full of bewitching garments and my drawers were packed with lingerie, yet there I was, alone on a Friday night.

What kind of sexpert was I?

Something had to change or I'd end up fat and wearing sweatpants, with twenty cats for company. Those icky thoughts brought on a shudder. I dumped my junk mail into the trash, kicked off my stilettos, and poured myself a generous glass of wine.

Seated on the couch, I scrolled through a few social media sites on my laptop. *Single? Let's mingle* ads popped up in my feed. I sighed and sipped my drink, a velvety Margaux that would have aged well had I let it sit longer, but life was too short to delay gratification.

The heating system kicked on with a low rumble and ruffled the living room curtains. I sipped more wine and scrolled through pictures of female fitness fanatics who somehow managed to balance happy-looking lives with kids and pets, whilst keeping their tiny waistlines intact.

Bullshit. I downed the rest of my wine in one gulp and slid my laptop onto the couch cushion. People on social media were fake. All that smiling. No one's that happy. Besides, who wants that life? Pets ruined furniture and kids were money drains. Everything about parenting looked exhausting. PTA. Carpools. Minivans. Who wanted to raise a kid in a world where people were valued for their looks, not their brains? Take Monique. She had a degree, but she turned tricks because she made more money selling her body than she could working a reputable job.

My stomach let out a low growl. Maybe I was

confusing hunger for melancholy.

The kitchen was spotless and the sparseness of my refrigerator seemed to mock me. All it contained was a smattering of caviar, jars of gherkins and cocktail onions, and grapes that were borderline raisins. There was a tin of oysters in the pantry that I had no recollection of ever purchasing and packages of fancy dinner napkins, never used. While rummaging through my cabinets, I broke down.

Why was I spending a Friday night alone? Jeanine wasn't. Tony had a family. Even Finn had plans. Screw this. I stormed back to the living room, refilled my wine, and licked off the dribble of liquid that ran down my wrist.

It took a minute to locate Theodore's card, but I eventually found it in my purse's side compartment. The card was a simple stock with silver letters that reminded me of his comment about shiny pavement.

On the couch, I stacked two throw pillows behind my back and dialed Theodore's number.

His husky "Hello" triggered a flutter in my tummy.

I reintroduced myself and explained my plans had been terminated. Theodore told me he was indisposed until nine, but he was pleased that I called and anticipated a memorable evening. His exact words.

After hanging up, I showered to refresh and rejuvenate. Thoughts of spending a night in an expensive hotel with a rich man vastly improved my mood.

I'd only been with a few *silvers* before, but the ones I'd entertained had been attentive and tender. Older men appreciated lovemaking the way I savored good wine.

I removed a new pair of seamed stockings from my bureau and sat on the bed while I rolled the pantyhose up my thighs.

Maybe I wasn't destined to find a Mr. Right, but Theodore was going to be my Mr. Right Now.

Chapter Seventeen

At nine on the dot, I entered the historic hotel. The place was a destination for the world's power brokers and visitors drawn to the nation's capital. It was charming yet sophisticated and was situated in a coveted location not far from The Hill. I'd been a guest there a few times throughout my career but never had the luxury of staying a full night.

My heels clacked against the marble as I passed through the lobby then quieted as I padded across a Persian rug. I passed a bubbling fountain, a round table with a grand floral centerpiece, and large gilded mirrors. If memory served me right, the lounge was down the hall and to the left, the one with the fireplace and obsidian-colored walls.

I checked my reflection in one of the mirrors before making my entrance. In honor of the occasion, I wore a tried-and-true favorite: my sleeveless, backless dress with a deep V neckline and an A-line skirt with a front slit that exposed plenty of delicious thigh. The dress was an attention grabber, one glamorous enough to make Theodore feel like he'd be getting his money's worth.

After a quick lift of *the girls*, and a spritz of perfume, I entered the lounge.

Theodore was sitting at the end of the bar, his beautiful white hair illuminated by an overhead pendant lamp. An ebony walking stick listed by his chair, and a rectangular pocket square peeked from his blazer. I loved men who wore such things. Pocket squares weren't functional, but men who wore them typically paid attention to detail.

The lounge was exactly as I remembered. The dark walls and stained-oak flooring gave the room the cozy feel of a library in a contemporary estate. There were modern indigo-colored couches, brown leather chairs, brass tables, and a black-and-gray swirled marble fireplace.

As I meandered inside, I inhaled the scent of burning wood coming from the fireplace and heard low chatter of subdued conversations. A bartender shook a concoction in a silver martini shaker. Piano music drifted from hidden speakers.

Theodore was lifting a glass to his lips when I came up beside him and touched his shoulder. He smiled and set down his drink. "I'm delighted you came." He lifted my hand to his lips.

Goose bumps prickled my skin as the hair on his goatee brushed against my fingers. I glanced at his walking stick—was it for fashion or function? I refrained from asking. Things like canes were personal. If he wanted to explain its purpose, he'd tell me in time.

He spoke to the bartender then led me to an intimate table by the fireplace. I tucked my purse beside my high-backed chair and waited for my host to get comfortable.

When the server came by, Theodore ordered us rounds of eighteen-year-old single malt scotch. My eyebrows rose as I saw the price on the menu.

One drink turned to two, then three, then more.

Laughs were exchanged, mine too loud, as Theodore entertained me with stories of his past. He'd been in the Navy, but his leg injury was result of a motorcycle stunt long after he left the military. He'd earned his fortune by managing and inheriting his family's dry-cleaning business, where he met his wife Anita—a customer. They had four children, all grown, with families of their own. I glanced at his ring.

"I'd misplaced her favorite dress," Theodore explained, "so I took her to dinner as an apology. I spilled her chardonnay but she forgave me and married me two months later."

"She must be the forgiving type." I chuckled and sipped my scotch.

"She was," he corrected. "Anita passed away five years ago."

I put down my glass and touched his hand. "I'm so sorry."

"Thank you." He sniffed. "Undetected ovarian cancer. She was a living angel."

Angel. Angela.

I held my drink up to the light. "Cancer sucks."

"Yes, it does." Theodore twisted his ring and sipped his drink.

I took a hearty sip of scotch then leaned back and crossed my legs, exposing a hint of thigh. "Do you believe in an afterlife?"

He stroked his goatee. "I would love to believe such a place exists, but as much as I want to see my Anita again, there's nothing to suggest it is anything other than a dream. My wife lived a good life, and we had many happy years together. For that I'm grateful."

"You and me," I slugged down the last of my

scotch, "we're on the same page."

Time slipped away, and my bladder reminded me it was time to visit the restroom. As I stood to excuse myself, blood rushed to my head. I teetered and lost my balance.

Theodore quickly came to my side. "Are you all right?"

I grabbed my chair's backrest and rubbed the side of my head. "A little dizzy. Must've gotten up too fast."

He took my elbow. "You look pale. Have you eaten?"

"Not since lunch."

He glanced at his watch. "The restaurants have stopped serving, but we could retire to my room. There's a comfortable couch you could stretch out on while I order something from room service."

"That's kind of you, but I don't want to be any trouble."

"No trouble at all. In fact," he grabbed his cane, "I insist."

Theodore seemed like he could afford just about anything, but one never assumed. Before we headed upstairs, I had to lay out my terms, but it had to be dealt with in an artful way.

I stroked my clavicle. "There's something we should discuss."

He dipped into his breast pocket and removed an envelope, then handed it to me. "This should suffice."

It was hard to keep my expression even when I peeked inside the envelope. It contained a larger amount than I would have asked for, but I decided not to mention that.

He offered me his arm. "Now that we have that out

of the way…"

My dizziness had diminished by the time we made it to the elevators, but Theodore insisted on holding my arm. During the ride, I stole glances at him.

His eyes were shadowed by dark circles, but his cheeks were unlined, and his goatee was trim. Something about the way he carried himself attracted me to him like a dryer sheet clinging to a sock. Power was an aphrodisiac.

Inside the elevator, canned Muzak played from hidden speakers. Theodore's key card allowed us passage to the club level, and the same card unlocked the door to an airy one-bedroom suite.

What a sight. There was a small dining area to the right with French doors beyond that led to a bedroom decorated in somber hues, a flat screen TV above a bureau in the living area, a long, striped couch, and accent chairs with brocade fabric, plus glossy wood tables and a desk. It was all typical hotel furniture, but the area was almost as big as my apartment.

Theodore opened the French doors and we stepped onto the balcony to get some fresh air. I heard the sounds of cars honking and splashes and gurgles from a nearby fountain, saw glimpses of the monuments. He continued the tour.

The bathroom had a big soaking tub with a window overlooking the city, two vanities, a fancy-schmanzy table no one probably used, and peachy lighting.

Back in the living room, Theodore ordered for us. My stomach growled at the request for escargot, champagne, and chocolate-dipped strawberries.

Theodore disappeared into the bedroom and returned to the living room carrying a few items.

"This is for dehydration." He handed me a water bottle. "These to tide you over." He handed me a package of crackers. "And these are to make you comfortable." He placed a pair of slippers on the floor.

"You're very thoughtful." I opened the crackers and nibbled two then washed them down with some water.

"Are you feeling better?" he asked.

"Much." I set down the water bottle and patted the couch cushion. "Come join me."

Anticipation was gnawing at me, and my arousal increased when Theodore sat beside me and loosened his tie. He made a circle with his head and massaged the back of his neck.

"Want help?" I cracked my knuckles. "I give excellent massages."

He twisted toward me. "My dear, I want you to know, I am immensely enjoying our time together."

I sidled closer to him. "Me, too."

He held up one hand. "But."

"But?"

"When I offered you the envelope, it was to enjoy your company."

I ran my finger over his knuckles. "And I appreciate that."

He patted my knee. "But company is all I desire."

That's it? I retracted my hand. Was he gay? No, my radar would've picked that up. Impotent? Maybe.

"You're not attracted to me?" I crossed my arms and pushed out my lower lip.

He leaned over and stroked my jaw. "Of course I'm attracted to you. There's nothing I'd like more than to spend the entire evening with you—until the morning if time allows, but—"

"No sex?"

"No sex."

His warm smile did not appease my bruised ego. Theodore was someone I looked forward to sleeping with, not just for the money. He made me feel like a lady, and even whores wanted to feel like queens sometimes.

Still pouting, I tugged on a couch tassel.

Theodore lifted my chin with his finger. "There are plenty of opportunities to lie with a beautiful woman, but I can't remember the last time I enjoyed a rousing conversation such as this—not since Anita."

He had to pull out the dead wife card.

I sighed and leaned against his shoulder. "Okay. We'll keep it *G*. Well, G-ish."

His chest bounced with his laugh. When he lowered his hand, his blazer sleeve drew back, and I noticed a pair of gold filigree cufflinks with the initials TSK on his French cuffs.

I pointed to his wrist. "What's the 'S' for?"

He twisted his arm. "Seamus. After my father."

I repeated the name aloud. "Seamus. It has a nice ring to it, but I don't believe in shame."

He chuckled. "I'm Irish. Shame was ingrained in Catholic school."

I traced the letter S in his cufflink. "Anita would want you to be happy. She'd want you to move on."

He covered my hand with his. "I am happy. Truly. I appreciate the things that I have. Even the things I don't have." He held my gaze.

A knock on the door interrupted the moment. Theodore let the room service attendant in and the man set out our meal on the table. After the man left, Theodore poured us glasses of champagne and returned to the couch.

He placed a flute in my hand. "I took the liberty and ordered a lovely rosé. This one is elegant and powerful," he clinked his glass against mine, "like you."

The name on the bottle was one I'd heard of but never tried. Since I had a small idea about Theodore's taste, it was probably the best on the menu. I took a small sip. The champagne slid down like a bubbly waterfall. Yup. Delicious. Anita must have been pretty special to have captivated Theodore's interest. I wished I knew him better. I wished I was thirty years older. Heck, I wished he'd screw me.

After I'd taken a few more swallows, he lifted the champagne bottle. "More?"

"Sure, why not?"

While Theodore refilled my glass, I stroked my knuckle along his thigh. "You know, you're quite a catch."

He pushed a hank of hair away from my eyes, and I caught another whiff of pipe tobacco. I nuzzled his cheek, and the bristles of his beard tickled my skin. As he opened his mouth, I smelled the sweet scent of bubbly. My palm was on his thigh, inching its way toward his zipper, when he stopped me by covering my hand.

"Faith."

"Hmm?"

He drew slightly back. "If I were two decades younger…"

"Age doesn't matter." I laid my palm over my

heart. "It's what's here that counts."

He patted my hand that rested on his thigh. "You should find someone who appreciates your magic."

Something inside me grew small and soft. There was no magic in me. I was born with good looks and later learned makeup skills. Men liked me because I listened and screwed well but that was because I got paid to do so. Practice at anything long enough and one becomes an expert.

I leaned back and crossed my arms. "If I'm magic, why don't you want me?"

"Of course I want you. You're a beautiful, intelligent woman. But the reason I invited you upstairs is because you're more than a pretty face. I don't need sex to enjoy your company."

"Why can't we have both?"

He grinned. "It would cheapen what we have." He picked up the champagne, refilled my nearly full glass, and handed it to me.

"Thanks, I'm good."

"Come now." He placed the flute in my hand. "Let's not let this spoil the short time we have together."

I laid my head on his shoulder, and he combed my hair with his fingers.

The hours ticked away, and soon the first sign of dawn appeared. Theodore retrieved two plush terry hotel robes from the closet and we wrapped ourselves in the garments and retreated to the balcony to watch the sun rise.

The air smelled fresh and dewy, and amber hues streaked across the sky. There were the occasional outdoor sounds of insect hums and bird calls.

Somewhere below, a fountain gurgled and a sprinkler spluttered. I lifted my chin toward the sun and let out an audible sigh. Theodore lit his pipe and puffed his cheeks. He wrapped an arm over my shoulder and held me close to his side. Sunbeams warmed the top of my head, and Theodore's cherry-scented smoke billowed around my face.

The evening hadn't gone the way I'd envisioned, but thanks to a twist of fate, I'd met someone decent, one of the few men who wanted nothing more than to be my friend.

Still, I wish we'd screwed.

Chapter Eighteen

After coffee, I gathered my belongings, along with the peach bath beads and mini body lotion I'd pilfered from the bathroom, and headed to the hotel room door.

Theodore followed close behind with soft thuds as his walking stick struck the floor. He'd mentioned his joints were stiff in the mornings.

In the hallway, I kissed Theodore's cheek. "Call me whenever you're in town."

He set his cane against the wall. "You forgot something." He dug into his pocket then put the envelope with the money in my hand.

Earlier that morning, I'd placed the envelope on his nightstand. The *green* would've come in handy, but I didn't feel right keeping it.

"I can't accept this." I tried to hand him back the cash, but he closed his fingers over mine.

"We're business people, and our time is valuable. You understand that." He laid his hand on my shoulder. "Put it to good use. A charity if you like." He squeezed my shoulder. "Don't let pride muddle your judgment."

There was no room for pride in my line of work, but this wasn't business. I swallowed down a lump in my throat and muttered, "Okay."

He ran his hand over his goatee. "You'll remember what I said?"

"Which part?"

He lifted his cane and and gently tapped my shoulder. "Find someone who appreciates your magic."

Exiting the building in my evening clothes reminded me of a scene from an 80s movie I once watched where a hooker left an opulent hotel dressed in tawdry clothes. She received plenty of stares and felt shame. It wasn't too far off the mark.

I headed to the corner to hail a cab, trying to mentally erase the similarities between movie and real life. I'd arrived, yet I was still fighting off imagined stereotypes. Put lipstick on a pig, and it's still glorified bacon.

I sneered at a prissy pot who stared too long. *Bugger off, lady. You don't know the real deal.* How the man I'd stayed with had acted like a gentleman. How he lay by my side, fully dressed, talking about his wife and the love they once shared. No one at this stupid hotel knew how Theodore made me feel appreciated, not cheap or objectified. No one knew how I wished I had someone like Theodore as a father figure instead of the judgmental tyrant who'd sired me.

A taxi came into view. Shoulders hunched, I climbed into the vehicle and gave the driver my address. As he shifted into gear, he knocked an air freshener that hung beside the steering wheel. The cardboard twisted, and the sweet piney smell reminded me of the woods behind my childhood home. It was a place I took boys with forgettable faces. A place I'd perform sexual favors in hopes of receiving affection in return. It never worked; all I received was a bad reputation.

The driver tried to engage me in conversation, but all I uttered were a few "Mmm-hmms." I didn't want to talk. I didn't want the tears to fall. All I wanted was for my head to stop spinning and the world to go dark.

****

My apartment was too quiet, not even a hum of the ventilation system. My stomach was empty, as was the fridge, but I was too exhausted to shop or go out. There was no one to call anyway, no friends to meet for coffee. Jeanine perhaps, but she was busy with her own life. I thought she had a dog. Or a boyfriend. Dammit, why didn't I know this?

My celibate encounter with Theodore sent me into a carb-craving craze. At noon, I ordered a large pizza from a nearby Italian restaurant and while waiting for my meal, I changed into a yoga suit that still had the tags on it.

I placed my dress into the dry-cleaning hamper, removed my jewelry, and set Angela's pearls on the tray on the bureau. As I fingered the middle pearl, a pang of sadness struck an internal chord. Angela and Anita both died of cancer but they weren't alone when it happened. What if I had a heart attack? How long would it take before someone found me? Jeanine might not notice since I'd gone on benders in the past. It might be days until a neighbor noticed the smell. My hand trembled as the idea developed in my head. I shook off the panicked feeling and headed to my closet to medicate.

On tiptoes, I unlocked my safe and retrieved my marijuana stash. The plastic bag contained a hybrid strain, aka "the one-hit shit," that was more expensive than the weed I usually bought, but was worth the money, because one toke took you exactly where you needed to be.

Leaning against my column of shoe shelves, I filled my swirly glass pipe with a pinch of green then lit and sucked the end. The rush came hard and fast like an earthquake jostling you out of bed.

I teetered and grabbed a shelf to steady myself. The pot could have been laced with something, which wouldn't surprise me since I was using a new dealer. Scott, my regular connection, was serving twelve months. His replacement was Max, a shaggy-haired Asian-American kid with light eyes and an unintelligible accent. Initially I was worried, because it takes time to build trust with a new connection, but Scott assured me Max was good people, and Max was able to score quality X—the real stuff, not the "Molly" millennials used—on a moment's notice, which was something Scott could never do.

In the past, the biggest concern was getting busted, but now one had to be wary of the dealers. What was the world coming to? If you couldn't trust your *hookup*, whom could you trust?

I ran my finger along my swirly pipe stem and soon my nerves settled and memories of Theodore were just that—memories.

****

The pizza arrived and I wolfed down six slices. Had Jeanine witnessed the carnage, she'd have gone postal, but, Jeanine wasn't there, so screw her judgmental ass.

I licked buttery crust flakes off each finger, poured myself a shot of whiskey, and stared at my sterile surroundings. My apartment was a metaphor for my life. Empty. Quiet. Clean.

Scotch glass and bottle in hand, I traipsed across

the carpet and opened the dining room window. Down below, a dog walker paraded down the sidewalk with a cluster of mixed breeds. Car honks sounded from the other side of the glass.

Saturdays were normally my favorite day of the week, but nothing felt right that day, and nothing held my interest. Not more pizza, not porn, not even another toke of weed.

I walked over to the stereo and ran my finger across the top. My inspection for dust came back clean. I pressed my finger against the ebony wood to leave a mark and put on a CD and refilled my drink. While Nina Simone sang a song about not having a life, I swayed back and forth in a drunken slow-motion dance.

Would anyone miss me if I was gone?

I returned to the couch and curled up in the throw blanket. While Nina sang another melancholy song, I tried to imagine a world where women weren't judged for enjoying sex, age wasn't a factor in relationships, and I mattered to someone other than the delivery boy.

Chapter Nineteen

The *rat-a-tat-tat* sound of a jackhammer jolted me from my Sunday morning slumber. The clock read nine, but my brain read dead. After rubbing crust from my lids and kicking the throw blanket off my legs, I followed the sounds of construction to the open window.

In my drunken stupor, I'd left it open, and now I was paying the price. The jackhammer's thunder sent a shock wave to my brain. I leaned out the window and shouted a few expletives. Stupid overtime-driven city workers. Didn't they know that people liked to sleep in on weekends?

Two cups of strong coffee and a nibble of leftover pizza made the world seem right. I poured a third cup to ensure concentration since a lot was riding on the day and carried my drink outside, onto the balcony.

The day was sunny, and the scent of fresh flowers rode in on a light breeze. Sunday air was generally free from exhaust, early in the day, at least, and at some point it had rained because the sidewalks looked dark and wet. Two pigeons were attacking a crust of bread.

A family of three in colorful attire walked down the street opposite mine. Anyone dressed up that early was most likely headed to church. Father loved Sundays because they were the Lord's day. I loved Sundays because it was my day of rest.

Normally.

I checked the time on my cell. There were three hours until my meeting with Finn, and everything rode on my success.

Back on the bridge, we'd had a breakthrough, but the time for hand-holding was over. The idea was to break him down then build him back up. It was an old trick of the trade, a method that had worked well with others in the past.

I texted Finn and instructed him to meet me at the mall in Zone F, inside my favorite men's store.

Dressed and armed with ammunition—credit cards, breath mints, and B-12 vitamins for energy, I took a sip of whiskey then called a car service and rode to Virginia.

****

If I believed in hell, I'd imagine it was a mall in suburbia. Malls housed the walking dead: geriatrics in comfy shoes making indoor laps, bored *au pairs* hardly paying attention to their screaming charges, and identical-looking teens staring dead-fish-eyed at their cell phones.

With online shopping one could avoid encountering the Stepford-wife types who stood by kiosks and chased you down to sample their Dead Sea scrubs or hair-straightening rods that—yuck—had been used on two-hundred people before you.

My shoes made soft *thwop* sounds against the marble as I entered the mall. Honoring spring, I'd chosen my chic safari-style day dress with gold trim and a front zipper to wear, a pair of gold hoops, and double-tiered Roman sandals.

Passing a popular seafood chain restaurant, I

picked up the smell of Old Bay seasoning and fried fish. At the next storefront window, I checked my reflection. *The girls* looked good, my abdomen was flat despite the previous evening's carbohydrate carnage, and my hair had stayed in place. Off to a good start.

As I strolled past the windows of my favorite stores, the familiar pang of *want, need, must-have*! called my attention.

There were leather purses in springy shades—yes!

Slinky stilettoes and strappy sandals—yes, yes!

Cropped tops, miniskirts, maxi dresses—yes, yes, yes!

Maternity pants—no.

I retreated from that window and headed upstairs.

Inside the men's store, I was greeted with a blast of air conditioning, an overpowering scent of sporty cologne, and nerve-jittering electronic dance music. I wandered past a few tables and clothes racks and paused to ogle a slim-fit Italian virgin wool suit. Even with the markdown, it was priced at almost a grand, but Finn could afford it, and good clothes were an investment.

I grabbed the suit and walked over to a thin guy with spiky hair and a closely-cropped beard. He turned from the table where he was folding shirts.

"Excuse me," I said. "Could you put this aside? My friend will be here soon, and we'll need a fitting room when he gets here."

The man set down a polo-style shirt and spoke with gleeful exuberance. "Sure. I'm Ahrend. Let me know if you need any help."

"Will do."

Ahrend examined my choice. "Love this. Isn't it

fab? It came in last week." He glanced at the tag. "Is this your friend's size?"

Good question. Finn was tall, but the way he hunched his shoulders it was hard to know his exact height. If I were to guess, I'd peg him as six feet with average build. I'd touched his arm the night we'd met but didn't feel anything extraordinary, so I deduced he was average everything. "I think he's a 42 chest, maybe a 34 or 36 waist. We can go with a size 40 or 42 for the suit, for now."

"He'll probably need to have it altered, but we can measure after your friend arrives." Ahrend pushed through hangars and pulled out a lavender blazer. "Think he'd like this? It's part of our new spring collection."

I doubted Finn would like anything that colorful, but the jacket was gorgeous, and I was in charge. "This is great. We're doing a complete makeover."

Ahrend clasped his hands. "So fun."

I also doubted Finn would be as enthusiastic as Ahrend.

At one on the dot, Finn entered the store. He paused just over the threshold, looked down at the yellow sticky pad paper in his right hand, and looked around. The look on his face was similar to Dorothy exiting her shack, entering Oz.

He took a few steps and halted by a rack with turquoise sports coats. The navy blazer he wore sagged over his body like a sleeping bag and the tie around his neck had zero pizazz.

I shook my head. Tough love was in order. Finn was lucky I didn't carry scissors in my purse or that awful tie would be fabric scraps.

He meandered around a table, picked up a pair of citrine-colored shorts, examined them, and then dropped them as though he'd touched a hot poker. When he pivoted toward the exit, I took my cue and hurried over.

"Hey, you're here. Glad you made it."

He palmed his chest. "I was—"

"Right on time." I pecked his cheek. "I came early to do the preliminaries."

He furrowed his brow. "Preliminaries?"

"That's my shopping lingo for hunting sales and trends."

"Ah." He tugged his tie. "The clothes here, they're...different from what I'm used to."

"Exactly the point." I took his hand and led him back to the table with shorts. "Here's your first lesson. Most stores put their latest and most expensive stuff up front to hook you in as soon as you arrive." I twisted him around. "Belts, ties, and accessories are usually displayed midway." I moved him a foot to the right. "Impulse items like cologne, socks, and sunglasses are usually near the registers, like in a grocery store." I pointed over my shoulder. "End of season and sale items they want to move are usually kept in back." I tilted my head. "Why aren't you writing this down?"

He opened his mouth.

"Never mind, we have a lot to accomplish, so we'll have to power shop."

"Power shop?" His laugh died at my serious look. "Oh. You weren't kidding." He gave his tie another yank.

"Fashion is no joke." I pushed his hand away from his tie. "And no more of that. It makes you look

163

nervous."

"It's that obvious?"

"Yes, and it stops today. Now follow me." I steered him to the register where Ahrend was lining up cologne bottles. "Hi again. This is my friend, Finn. Finn, meet Ahrend. He's going to make you fabulous." I winked.

Ahrend touched his chin and squinted. "You look familiar. Have you been in here before?"

Finn reached for his tie but caught himself. "It's my first time."

"Well, welcome." Ahrend came around and stood beside us. "I started a room and put some things inside—whenever you're ready—no rush."

I stepped in. "We need everything. Suits, shirts, sweaters, both casual and formal—no vests." I faced Finn. "Do you have a swimsuit?" He shook his head. I ticked off more items with my fingers. "A swimsuit, some belts, T-shirts." I lifted Finn's tie. "And plenty of these."

Finn looked down. "You don't like my tie?"

"Do you want me to answer that honestly?"

He sighed. "I think you just did."

Ahrend cupped a hand over his eye. "I have some ideas. I'll grab them and bring them to you." He headed toward the front, gathering items along the way.

Finn's face pinched with worry as Ahrend picked up a pair of tropical print swim trunks.

I patted Finn's arm. "Deep breaths, and go with the flow."

The changing area was deserted, and as promised, Ahrend had hung the lavender blazer, along with a few other items, on a hook outside the fitting room. I gathered up the garments and headed inside the stall.

Finn hesitated. "You're coming in?"

I hung the clothes on a rod. "Why not? No one's here and it'll be faster if I'm with you."

Finn opened his mouth, but before he spoke, I pulled him inside the room. After setting my purse on the floor, I sat on a cushioned seat and crossed my legs. "Well? What are you waiting for?"

He shifted his weight from one foot to the other. "Ah."

I made a shooing motion with my hands. "Go on. Get undressed."

He made no attempt to move.

"Oh, I get it. You're modest." I looked to the side. "There. Now hurry up."

Still no movement.

I looked back. Finn hadn't budged. "Seriously?" I threw out my palms. "We're adults here. You think you have something I've never seen before?"

"Well, I—"

"Look," I stood and placed my hands on his shoulders, "I need to see what I'm working with. I'm your personal consultant, remember?"

"Was that what we agreed to?"

"More or less." I sighed. "Don't you want my help?" He nodded. "Then let me do my job. From here on out, everything you do, from the way you hold your spoon to how often you floss your teeth, goes through me." I smiled and tapped my teeth. "You floss, right?"

"Twice a day."

"See, that wasn't difficult." I returned to the seat but faced the wall to give him a sense of privacy. "Now strip."

Clothes rustled, a zipper slid, and hangars jostled.

My foot shook in time with the electronic music, and nicotine withdrawal set in. "Almost done?" I asked.

Zip.

"All done."

I twisted around and examined him from head to toe. He was wearing a sapphire-colored slim suit with notched lapels and front flap pockets, a diamond-patterned light-blue button-down shirt, and a navy checkered-pattern tie. The suit was slimming, and the color complemented his steely eyes. He looked good, not quite a stud, but definitely better.

"Well, now," I said.

Finn stretched out his arms. "You like?"

"Yes, but…" I rubbed my lip. "It needs something."

He looked down. "A different tie?"

"Not that." I squinted and snapped my finger. "Be right back." I hurried out of the room and searched through a table near the register.

Finn was sitting on the cushion when I returned.

"This is what it needs." I pulled him up by his shoulders, popped a small linen square into his pocket, and unbuttoned his sports coat. Then I stepped back and crossed my arms. "Perfect."

Finn approached the mirror. "A handkerchief made a difference?"

"Pocket square," I corrected. I came behind him and brushed off his shoulders. "It's all about details and attitude." I twisted him around and put his right hand in his pants pocket. "You're going to be a leader so you'll have to summon your inner badass."

He turned toward the mirror. "I'm not a badass." He withdrew his hand from his pocket. "I'm just…me."

I moved his hand back to his pocket. "It only works if you believe it. Fake it 'til you become it. Imagine you've already won. You're giving your acceptance speech to a crowd of your voters. What would you say to them?"

He stared into the mirror. "Thank you for voting for me?"

"No." I knuckled his arm. "They thank *you*. You're going to get stuff done. They were smart to choose you, because you're going to," I leaned around, "what are you going to do?"

"If I'm elected?"

"*When* you're elected."

He straightened his back and gave the collar of his sports coat a quick tug. "When I'm elected, I'll bring change. The strength of our nation lies in our freedom and personal responsibility. We need free enterprise and government fiscal responsibility to allow individuals to keep more of the money they earn. The best government is that which governs least, one that is closest to the people, yet far enough to allow them freedom. The more we adhere to family values, the principles that made us strong, the better we will be. The Republican Party is the best vehicle for translating these ideals into positive and successful principles of government." He threw out one hand. "How's that sound?"

I feigned a yawn. "Like a sound bite."

He frowned. "My father helped me write that."

"And that's who it sounds like—your dad." I flopped down on the seat cushion and crossed my arms. "Don't get me wrong, it's good, it just doesn't sound like you." I leaned against the wall. "Who is Finn

Billings? What matters to him?"

He stepped back and twisted toward the mirror. "I believe in freedom, morals, and family values."

"Go on."

He lifted his chin. "I believe we need to focus on jobs and education. We should help the teachers teach, not just prepare kids for tests. Education is one of my top priorities."

Many of my girls were high school dropouts. We helped them earn their G.E.D.'s, because knowledge was power.

"I like that, Finn."

He grabbed his lapels. "And I think I like this suit."

"Great." I hopped to my feet and brushed off my hands. "But don't get comfortable, we have a whole wardrobe to fill." I peeled the lavender sports coat off the hangar and held it up.

"Purple?" Finn groaned.

I thrust the jacket into his hand. "Purple."

Chapter Twenty

Ahrend hooked us up with everything from flip-flops to formalwear. He took Finn's measurements for the clothes that needed alterations, and swapped out items that didn't fit. I thought we were making progress until a moment between changes. I'd made the mistake of sneaking a peek while Finn was in the process of disrobing.

He was dressed only in his underwear and a pair of knee-high black socks. His thighs were so white, they almost matched his underwear. I pointed to his bleached-white briefs. "What the heck are those?"

"Geez." Finn palmed his chest. "You scared me."

"You think you're scared?" I pantomimed a fainting spell. "Quick, take those off."

He looked down and wiggled his toes. "My socks?"

"No. Your underwear. Or maybe they're your grandfather's underwear. Whatever they are, they're horrible." The image of Finn's pasty thighs and black socks would forever be burned in my brain. "Take them off now."

His brows shot up into high arches. "You want me to take off my—"

"Yes."

"But you're right—"

"Either you do it, or I will." I walked over and held

out my hand.

"Okay, okay." He backed up and hit the wall. "Could you give me some privacy?"

I remained in place.

"I'll take them off, just," he held up his palms, "please?"

"Fine." I exited the stall and headed to a section with socks and underwear. After rummaging around the table, I grabbed a bundle of boxer briefs in various colors and patterns and returned to the dressing area.

Outside Finn's door, I reached over the stall. "Put these on."

He grabbed the packages. "What's wrong with my old ones?"

I looked up at the ceiling. "How long ago did you buy them?"

"I can't remember."

"There you go."

"But they're comfortable," he whined.

"Give them to me."

"This seems a little extreme."

I banged on the door. "Give. Them. To me."

A pair of white briefs sailed over the top of the door.

I hooked the underwear over my thumb and dropped the briefs into a nearby trashcan. Back outside Finn's changing room, I rapped the door lightly with my knuckle. "Are you wearing the new ones?"

"Yes, but I'm not modeling them."

"Fair enough." I chuckled. "How do they feel?"

There was a snap of elastic.

"Nice, actually." His feet paced the floor. "They're quite comfortable." He twisted one foot. "Who knew?"

Me, that's who.

"Put on another outfit. Think casual Friday."

There was the sound of hangers sliding across a rack, followed by a zip, a shuffle, and a moan.

I leaned my ear against the door. "What's wrong?"

"Everything."

"It can't be that bad."

He kicked his foot against the carpet. "It is."

I took a step back. "Let me be the judge."

He opened the door, and I gazed at my *protégé*. Finn was wearing a charcoal-gray cotton Polo with contrast detail at the sleeves. He'd paired the shirt with a pair of black slim-fit stretch cargo pants with zippers on the legs. Black socks. No shoes.

Hmm. Not bad. But Finn was scowling.

"What's the problem?" I asked.

He tugged his collar. "It's too tight."

I stepped inside the dressing room, untucked his shirt, and undid the top two buttons. "Better?"

"Yes, but," he zipped and unzipped a leg zipper, "are these necessary?"

I pushed away his hand. "Stop fidgeting, they're just for show. And, yes, they're necessary."

He shrugged one shoulder. "It's not me."

I spun him to face the mirror. "Forget the old you." I pointed at his reflection. "New and improved Finn is a winner."

He touched the contrast detail on one sleeve. "It's kind of flashy."

"You'll get used to it."

"And everything's so tight."

It was hard to stifle my exasperation. "I told you to trust the process. I promise, this new look will make you relevant."

"You think people care about my clothes?"

"Absolutely." I brushed off the front of my dress. "Looks matter and style counts. It sets you apart from the others. You have the brains and your father's backing but you need to improve your image. This is just the first part."

"First part?" He groaned.

"We've only just begun."

He backed up and sat on the seat cushion. "I think I need a drink."

He wasn't the only one who needed alcohol.

"No time for that now." I pulled him back to his feet. "We've got things to do. But first..." I extended my hand. "Your credit card."

He sighed as he removed his wallet from his old blazer. "I have a feeling I won't want to see the bill."

"Trust me," I smiled and plucked the plastic card from his fingers, "you won't."

Before leaving the changing room, I gathered the clothes he'd agreed to purchase and pulled off the tags on the shirt and pants he wore. "I'll tell Ahrend you'll be wearing these out." I grabbed the underwear package and headed to the checkout counter.

While Ahrend sorted out Finn's items, I leaned on the counter and stared at a row of sunglasses. The music was so loud, a bottle of cologne by the register vibrated. It took a while to ring up Finn's order, and I'd prepared myself for a hefty tally, but I still gasped when I saw the total.

"Is that everything?" Ahrend asked.

Finn came up beside me. I blocked his view of the register, grabbed a pair of oversize tortoiseshell sunglasses, and slid them across the counter. "A reward for my hard work." I smiled at Finn.

He winced and gave the okay to ring up the glasses.

While Ahrend bagged Finn's clothes, I leaned over and sniffed Finn's shoulder.

"What are you doing?" he whispered.

I tapped the tip of my nose. "Now that you have good clothes, you need a good smell."

He lifted his shirt collar and sniffed. "I shower every day. Isn't that enough?"

"No." My olfactory senses had been sharpened by the biz. In my line of work, one learned to recognize smells to get information. People associated smells with power, thus, a strong scent equated to a strong candidate. "And don't argue with your mentor." I grabbed a bottle of cologne off the counter. Finn made an attempt to block me, but before his palms were at face level, I'd fired off three squirts.

I handed Ahrend the cologne along with my credit card. "My gift for *your* hard work."

Finn chuckled and coughed. "You're something else."

I tossed back my hair. "You got that right."

Ahrend finished our transactions and handed us two large shopping bags. "It was a pleasure working with you. The alterations should be ready in a few days."

"Thanks for the help. He'll be back soon." I grabbed the bags and linked my arm through Finn's. He was in the process of reading his receipt, but I slapped his hand. "Don't bother. It was worth it."

Finn's face paled. "I hope so."

Out in the mall, I handed him his bags. "Ready for our next stop?"

Finn peeked inside a bag. "If we keep going at this rate, I'll be broke before dinner."

"I doubt that."

We rode the escalators upstairs. Up on the landing, I studied the mall legend.

Finn leaned over my shoulder, looking apprehensive. "What's next?"

I pointed to a familiar sign and smiled. "Fuel."

Chapter Twenty-One

The café was playing pop music at loud decibels, and the smell of burnt coffee beans wafted in the air. After perusing the menu, Finn ordered an English breakfast tea with low-fat milk, two sugars. I ordered a venti-sized chai soy iced latte with light ice and two pumps of vanilla.

Finn excused himself to use the restroom, and I browsed through the kiosks. As I turned the corner, Finn was exiting the restroom, tucking his shirt into his pants.

When he was back at my side, I said, "Un-tuck your shirt."

He looked around, apparently embarrassed. "I look disheveled."

"Do as I say." My patience was wearing thin.

He frowned but complied.

"English Breakfast tea and a venti chai soy latte, light ice, two pumps of vanilla," the barista called.

We headed to the counter to retrieve our drinks.

Finn examined the name on my cup's spine and shook his head. "They got your name wrong."

"Every. Single. Time." I led him to the entrance.

Balancing our drinks and shopping bags, Finn and I strolled through the lower level. It physically pained me to pass the pretty displays and not stop inside to try anything on, but we'd made progress, and Finn was

175

slowly letting his barriers down.

At the end of the row, Finn paused to dump his empty tea cup in the trash. "Are we done now?"

"Not yet." I glanced from his cowlick to a window.

Finn touched the back of his head. "Wait, you're not suggesting—"

"It'll be painless."

Finn took a big step back. "You've said that before."

I tossed my empty cup into the trash and steered him to the right. "Trust the process."

****

The salon was abuzz with active blow dryers, synthpop music, and conversations between customers and their stylists.

At the front desk, a woman with caramel-colored highlights and a bronzed complexion greeted me and asked if I had an appointment.

"No, but it's an emergency." I jutted my chin in Finn's direction.

The woman looked his way.

Finn lifted a bottle of hair gel off a shelf and sniffed the contents. He scrunched his nose, recapped the bottle, and returned it to the shelf.

The receptionist opened an appointment book and scanned a page. "Good news. We had a cancellation." She looked up. "Shampoo, cut, and blow-dry?"

I nodded. "Everything." I cupped a hand over my mouth. "And could you add in waxing?"

The woman made a notation. "We can do that."

Finn looked my way, and I gave him a thumbs-up.

An hour and a half was all it took to make Finn go from drab to fab, but it was obvious he didn't share my enthusiasm. When the stylist un-caped Finn, he kept checking the mirror and repeatedly rubbed the back of hminis neck.

I walked over to his chair and whistled. "Well, look at you."

Finn ran his fingers through his closely cropped do and scratched his hairline. "I hardly recognize myself."

I placed both hands on his shoulders. "New and improved Finn."

Finn exited with plenty of at-home products he swore he didn't need, clean brows, and a smooth shave. The bill was hefty but he looked like a million bucks.

Outside the salon, Finn dug through the bag. "This seems like a lot of work."

I raked my nails through my scalp and shook out my hair. "Looking good takes effort. You're a public figure and that means press shots, appearances, and TV. Trust me, you need this."

"Trusting the process."

I patted his shoulder. "Now you're catching on."

Finn and I talked about his new look on our way to the exit. He seemed to be warming to the transformation. A ponytailed woman in black spandex tights checked him out by the escalator and Finn blushed and smiled in response.

I smiled, grateful for the positive reinforcement. Someone or something had crushed his ego at some point, and the poor guy needed a boost. We still had to work on things like his tie-tugging tic, but that would be addressed during our next date—correction—appointment.

****

Outside, the sound of traffic trailed from the nearby

177

beltway, and weary-looking shoppers headed to their cars as the sun dipped on the horizon.

While Finn called his driver, I made myself comfortable on a nearby bench and lit a cigarette.

Finn joined me on the bench and tucked his shopping bags under his seat. "Thanks for everything you did today."

I twisted toward him and shielded my eyes from the sun. "No need to thank me, it was fun."

"Still," he rubbed his neck, "you were really patient."

A couple walking arm and arm passed our bench. Finn nodded a silent hello.

I took a drag off my smoke. "I like helping people. And now that you trust me, it'll make my job easier."

"Job." Finn said the word with apparent disappointment.

Stop the press. Did Finn have feelings for me? What about that woman in the picture? It was difficult to read clues from his expression because Finn generally wore a permanent smile. I cupped a hand over my eyes to get a better look. In the fading daylight, he looked young and handsome. The haircut made his eyes stand out and his new ensemble complemented his physique.

I patted his hand. "I thoroughly enjoyed our day."

"Me, too."

From somewhere inside the parking lot, a car alarm sounded off three chirps then silenced. The limo pulled up.

Finn stood to retrieve his bags and offered me his hand. "Would you like a ride to the city?"

A car service would blow another fifty.

I flicked my cigarette toward the gutter. "That'd be great. It'll give us time to strategize."

He led me to the passenger door. "Strategize?"

"You didn't think our work was done, did you?"

He opened the door. "I never know what to think when I'm with you."

I took one of his bags and climbed inside the vehicle. "I like to keep you guessing."

During the ride back to the city, Finn regaled me with stories of his youth. He recounted things he built in his garage, bird species he'd charted, rocks he collected, and a tale of him and his father camping during a monsoon deep in the foothills of the Appalachian Mountains in the Virginia woods.

"The tent blew away," Finn paused to laugh, "and my father fell into a gorge while trying to retrieve it."

"Marshall?" My eyes widened at the thought of the former governor drenched to the bone. "Did he at least get the tent?"

"Unfortunately, it got caught in the rapids and sailed downstream. We ended up sleeping in the car and drove home the next morning. My mother asked why we came back a day early, but we never told her what happened. It's a male pride thing."

I held up a hand. "Say no more."

"It was one of my best childhood memories. Before the storm, he'd let me light the campfire and we'd spent most of the day hiking and gathering. There were no distractions, no electricity, just us. Even the ride home was good. We actually talked."

Finn's eyes were misty, so I didn't push further.

The limo turned a corner and parked in front of my apartment building.

Finn walked me to the front door.

"Thanks for the ride." I held up my purse. "And the sunglasses."

"My pleasure," he said.

"Don't forget what I told you."

He ticked items off with his fingers. "Burn my old underwear. Apply mousse to my hair while it's damp. Purchase the pants press you found online and," he squinted, "what was the last thing?"

"Make an appointment at the tanning salon on Connecticut Avenue. Tell the manager you're my friend. He'll get you in."

Finn pinched his brow. "You were serious about that?"

My smile faded. "As a heart attack."

He shook his head and laughed. "Okay. I'll call the tanning place."

Otis came outside, tipped his cap, and stepped to the side of the door.

"So," I twirled a lock of my hair. "Do you have plans tonight?"

"Actually," Finn looked down at his loafers, "I'm meeting someone later."

My brows lifted and fell. Was it the woman in the picture? Why did I care? Regardless, I had a job to do. I opened the calendar app on my cell phone. "What about tomorrow? Remember, you promised me two days."

He sighed. "Tomorrow I'm working on a project for Habitat for Humanity."

No surprise. Finn the do-gooder.

"However," he kicked at something on the sidewalk, "there's something I wanted to invite you to, but I was afraid you wouldn't want to go."

"Nothing ventured, nothing gained."

He tugged his collar. "There's a gem and mineral show coming to town. It's closed to the public, but a friend in the industry got me tickets." He bowed his head and looked up halfway. "I don't suppose you'd like to join me?"

The poor guy's confidence was lower than the canal during the dry season. I stepped closer and laid my palm on his chest. "I'd love to."

"Really?" Finn had the euphoric smile of a kid who just got a puppy for Christmas.

I walked my finger up his shirt and poked his chest. "You gonna tell me the day and time?"

"Of course." He knocked his head. "It runs next Saturday and Sunday. The show starts at noon, but we can get there anytime. Maybe we could catch a bite to eat before the show—if you like."

Saturday I was sending a few of my girls to a bachelor party that night and needed to be on call in case something went awry. We'd had problems with drunken college frat boys in the past. The story of a Supreme Court justice nominee scandal came to mind.

I shook off the memory. "Sunday's better. Pick me up at eleven and I'll think of someplace fun to eat."

"I'm glad you'll come." He nodded enthusiasm. "I promise you'll be blown away."

Doubtful. But seeing him in his element would boost his ego and help us bond.

"See you Sunday." I pecked his cheek and headed to the door.

It was silly to think the invitation was anything other than platonic, but when I stepped onto the entrance mat, something made me turn back for another

181

look. Finn hadn't budged. He was staring ahead, grinning, palming his cheek in the place where I'd kissed him.

It took a lot of effort to face forward and remind myself not to get soft.

Chapter Twenty-Two

When big money is on the line, every second counts. I tried my best not to obsess over the calendar all week, spent hours holed up in my office doing the usual: making cold calls, dousing fires, dodging Jeanine—avoiding her when I could. She still found things to complain about—the way I chewed my salads, my lack of enthusiasm over her horrific gown suggestions, my smoking.

When Sunday finally came, I practically leapt out of bed. It was time for my third appointment with Finn, and the only thing that posed a threat between me and the Golden Boy was the mysterious woman in the picture. I needed to see what I was up against.

On my laptop, I did a reverse image search. First, I uploaded their picture then I dragged and dropped it into the search box. One right-click, and there she was.

Sabrina Longstead. She was a socialite, a former debutante, and disturbingly pretty in a probably-never-eats, way. She had light-green eyes that held little warmth but stood out against her pale complexion and dark hair. Her thin limbs were like matchsticks and her skin was ghostly white. I smirked. Most men liked girls with a little meat and color.

I drummed my nails on the table. Now that I had the woman's bio, the two hundred thousand dollar question was—did Finn have feelings for her?

Time would tell.

After breakfast and a hot shower, I prepared for my appointment.

What did one wear to a gem and mineral show? Everything I had was workday chic or working girl night. Neither sufficed. After exhausting my options, I remembered a garment I'd kept on a shelf. The bag holding the dress had a broken zipper, and when I unsheathed the garment, a retro mint-green lawn dress with a crinoline skirt and a ruched bust line, I caught a whiff of dusty rose-scented perfume. The scent brought me back to the day I found the dress.

I'd stumbled into an upscale consignment store that day to escape the rain with zero intent of making a purchase. Back then, Bes and I could barely afford groceries, and the clothes I wore were mostly miniskirts and scanty tees. The woman who owned the store saw me ogling the dress and insisted I try it on. When I saw the price tag, my hand fell to my side.

"It's perfect for you," she'd said.

"It's nice, but…" I had searched my brain for excuses but she must have read my mind.

"Pay me what you can today, and pay the rest later."

I'd tried to resist, but the woman mentioned something about me reminding her of her daughter. I gave the woman the crumpled five dollar bill I had, thinking I could skip a meal or two.

When I returned to the shop three months later, the store was dark and a FOR SALE sign hung in the window. I never had a chance to repay the woman's generosity, so I paid her kindness forward by sharing my hand-me-downs with my girls.

The intercom buzzed while I was strapping on my patent leather kitten heels. "Bring me luck today," I whispered to the dress. I grabbed my purse and headed to the door.

Chapter Twenty-Three

Down in the lobby, Finn stood by the window looking away from me. His shoulders were hunched, and his hands rested on the small of his back like one of our charismatic former presidents.

The clack of my heels hitting the marble must have broken his concentration, because his head sprang up before I made it halfway across the lobby. Finn was wearing one of his new slim-fit blazers, a white fitted shirt, a skinny tie, and his American flag pin. I tried not to frown at him pairing everything torso up with an old pair of chinos. Rome wasn't built in a day, but there was only a month and change until the gala.

I came over and pecked his cheek. His pungent cologne pleased my nostrils.

"Wow." Finn took a small step back. "That's quite a dress."

I pulled out the ends to flare my skirt. "This old thing?" No exaggeration there. I threaded my arm through Finn's and said, "I hope you're hungry, 'cause I'm famished."

He patted his stomach. "I'm always hungry."

"Me, too." Just ask Jeanine. I grabbed his elbow and threaded my arm through his. "I've got a great place in mind."

Outside, I pulled out my new sunglasses and looked up at the sky.

The day was sunny and clear, and a crisp breeze came from the north. Birds squawked from tree branches, and somewhere in the distance, a church bell tolled.

"So, where are we going?" Finn asked.

I opened a popular food app on my cell phone. "Since the show is near Chinatown, I thought we could get dim sum."

"Dim sum?" Finn's lips puckered like he'd sucked on a lemon. "That sounds too exotic."

Too exotic? I lifted my sunglasses and squinted.

Caviar facials were too exotic. Fish sperm sashimi was too exotic. Rhinoceros viper snakes were too exotic. White truffles were too exotic. Dim sum was not too exotic.

I lowered my glasses and patted Finn's chest. "Go with the flow, remember?"

He scrunched his brow. "The last time I did that, I almost fell off a bridge."

"Yet here you are, still in one piece."

Otis walked over from a shady corner under the awning. "Top of the morning, Ms. Crawley." He tipped his hat toward Finn.

"Morning, Otis. This is Mr. Billings. He's my…" What was Finn? A client? A friend? I pointed to his American flag pin. "Finn is running for the senate."

Otis held out a gloved hand. "My apologies. When you mentioned your name before Miss Faith came down, I didn't put it together. Your father was a great leader. Best of luck to you, sir."

Finn pumped Otis's hand. "I appreciate that."

Inside the limousine, I scanned restaurant listings on the food app. "There's a place not too far that has excellent reviews. It's called Ding Dong Dim Sum."

Finn laugh/snorted. "That's a real name?"

"Apparently." I put my phone in my purse.

Finn pumped his leg up and down like a piston. "Trusting the process."

****

Almost every major city has a Chinatown, and D.C. is no exception. Once, it was a quieter, eclectic place but over time it got bombarded with trendy stores that catered to tourists. It still held some charm, like the gilded ornate Friendship Archway decorated with over three hundred dragons and an insane amount of splash. Unfortunately, the good food scents compete with the stench of urine, feet, and sewage, but that was part of Chinatown's ambience.

It's also a place where one can find bargains. For less than five dollars, a colorful paper parasol, an embroidered silk pillowcase, or a kitschy waving cat statue can be had. Haggling is expected, and if one is good, all three items can be acquired for the price of a case of soda.

There's constant entertainment in Chinatown. There are people wearing clothes that look like pajamas, little women burdened with shopping bags that are twice their size, and the homeless who take refuge in dilapidated cardboard boxes. Bare-chested boys blare music from their portable players, and girls with oversized gold hoops and painted-on jeans walk by, pretending to ignore them. There are the occasional Doomsday preppers waving JESUS SAVES! pamphlets and men with megaphones camped out by the Metro station, ranting at passersby.

As the limo passed beneath the Friendship

Archway, Finn's hand tightened around the door's armrest. His tense non-verbal gestures made it easy to read his thoughts—*Look at those weirdoes. Are we safe? Jeepers, we're going to get mugged.*

I almost laughed out loud at that last thought.

"What's so funny?" Finn asked.

Guess I did laugh out loud.

"Nothing important." I grinned.

The limo slowed to allow a pedestrian to pass, and I glanced at a popular coffeehouse sign with Chinese characters. Even there, they'd probably screw up my name.

"Well," I faced Finn, "what do you think so far?"

He pumped his leg. "It's certainly colorful."

I remembered Sabrina's snowy skin. "Color is good. Don't you like the general public?" My question came out just as the limo passed a bearded man who was yelling at a trashcan.

Finn slid a few inches away from the window. "Yes. Of course." He tugged his tie. "But I'm better behind the scenes." There was a thin line of sweat on his upper lip.

The poor guy needed to relax. I gently moved his hand off his tie. "Everyone's going to love you once they get to know you. You're smart, honest, and kind. Those are rare characteristics these days."

My syrupy praise must have helped because the exclamation mark line that had formed between his brows disappeared.

I pointed toward a mass of people on a corner. "Sometimes, when I'm overwhelmed, I put on a hat and glasses and blend into the sea of people. It feels good to disappear sometimes."

Finn rubbed his palms together. "That sounds nice, but I couldn't do that. Too many people need me now."

"You could if you wanted to. You have to take care of yourself first. You know, like on an airplane when they tell you in case of an emergency, you put your oxygen mask on first before you help others."

He nodded. "I see what you mean, but it's easier for you. You're a free spirit and I'm, well, I was raised with schedules and rules. My school dictated everything from the times we ate to the time we slept to the times we were allowed to use the bathroom. Not you. Nothing gets in your way. You must have had great parents."

If he only knew how wrong he was.

The limousine pulled to the curb and parked in front of a row of restaurants.

Finn came around to open my door, and as I exited the vehicle, I closed my eyes and took a deep breath.

"Is something wrong?" Finn asked.

"Not at all." I opened my eyes. "Now it's your turn."

"For what?"

"A game. Close your eyes."

"Here?" He looked left and right. "On the street?"

"Yes, right here."

He wore a blank look.

I sighed. "Could you just play along?"

He seemed reluctant, but he did as told.

"There you go. Now breathe."

He furrowed his brows. "Of course I'm breathing."

"Yes, but, like this." I placed his hands over his middle and gave him instructions. "Inhale through your nose, feel your abdomen expand, then exhale through your mouth, slowly let your belly fall."

He cracked his lids. "This is embarrassing."

I blindfolded him with my hand. "It won't work if you cheat."

"What if someone recognizes me?"

The streets were full of passersby, people preoccupied with their cell phones.

"Stop worrying," I said.

"I can't help it."

"You can. Let me teach you." I guided his hands back to his abdomen. "Deep breath in, hold one, two, three." His belly expanded. "Now exhale slowly, four, five, six." His belly contracted. "This time, when you inhale, tell me what you smell."

"And then we can eat?"

I chuckled. "And then we'll eat."

He followed my lead.

"To fully appreciate things," I said, "you have to summon all your senses—not just your eyes and ears—there's touch, smells, tastes. To be an effective leader, you need to absorb details. Train your brain to do this. Be aware, take notes, act and think like a detective. It'll help you read people and it enhances your experiences."

"I'll try."

"Now, tell me what you smell."

He lifted his chin and flared his nostrils. "Tar. Some kind of spice. Something sweet, like caramel. And, oh, not good."

"What?"

"I'd best not say."

A homeless man ambled past us carrying a jar of yellow liquid, and I pinpointed the source of the offensive odor.

"Now tell me what you hear."

Finn tilted his head. "Cars. Music. A whirring sound, like an air conditioner. A baby's howl."

To my right, a toddler was struggling to get out of its stroller. "Excellent. Anything else?"

He twisted his head to the other side. "A siren. A pigeon's coo. Wait." He cupped his ear. "A mockingbird. I can tell because their songs are quick and they rapidly change."

I'd almost forgotten his fascination with birds. I laid my hand on his shoulder. "Open your eyes."

He squinted in the sunlight. "How'd I do?"

"You get an A plus." I grabbed his hand. "Let's eat."

Twangy, tinny Asian music was playing, and voices babbled inside the restaurant. The place was packed, and we didn't have a reservation, but as soon as I dropped Marshall Billings' name, a table became available. The hostess led us to a prime spot.

"Always use your connections," I told Finn as he pulled out my chair.

"Duly noted." He sat and picked up his menu.

Over lunch, Finn told me a story about the first time he'd tried to cook. It was during his first semester in college and after months of eating out, he decided to make a simple chicken recipe.

"It was a disaster." He speared a dumpling and talked while chewing. "The pan caught on fire, and then the smoke detector went off. I threw the pan in the sink and turned on the water, but that made things worse. The kitchen was full of smoke, I couldn't find the fire extinguisher, and then somebody knocked at my door."

I threw out one palm. "And?"

Finn chewed his dumpling. "It was my neighbor. I let her in and she found the fire extinguisher. That stuff makes a mess, by the way." He twirled some noodles around his chopsticks, but they slipped off.

I twirled noodles around my chopsticks, scooped them into my mouth like a pro. "Go on."

He covered his mouth with a fist and laughed. "Did I mention I was only wearing my underwear?"

I exploded in laughter. "Not the tighty whities?"

He nodded. "I couldn't look her in the eye after that. Fortunately, she moved out of the building the following semester. Think she has a law firm in Arlington." He made a second attempt to scoop up his noodles. All but one fell off his chopsticks.

"Anyway," he slurped up the noodle and wiped grease off his chin, "that's why I don't cook."

I lifted my water glass. "Here's to delivery service."

Finn clinked my glass. "Hear, hear."

I set down my drink and smiled. He was kind of growing on me.

****

An hour later, we emerged from the restaurant cradling our plump bellies. During the ride to the convention center, neither of us spoke, but we sat shoulder to shoulder, legs touching. Finn stared forward, his gaze glued to the driver's plastic partition, back ramrod straight. It was hard to read his thoughts, but when the limo hit a pothole and I grabbed Finn's arm to steady myself, I caught him smiling.

Finally, some progress.

"Well," he twisted to face me, "you were right."

"I'm always right. But, about what?"

"Everything. The food, the clothes, that sensory game. I wish I'd met you sooner."

His words practically melted me, but it was hard to return a smile. The more time I spent getting to know Finn, the more I liked him. It would be harder to destroy him when the time came. I glanced at his American flag pin. If only there was another way.

The limo pulled in front of the convention center.

"Ready?" Finn asked.

I returned the smile he deserved. "Ready."

Chapter Twenty-Four

The lines inside the convention center snaked around the lobby. The carpet was soft and springy, a welcome relief after the hard marble stairs we'd climbed to enter the building.

We crossed the threshold and Finn pocketed his dumbphone and grabbed my hand. "Stay close, it gets crazy in here." His grip was firm, which surprised me, because his gestures were usually soft. He checked a sign then pointed to the first line. "I think it goes by alphabetical order."

"You lead, I'll follow."

At the registration desk, a heavyset woman with a neck that resembled rolled socks signed us in. She handed us two bags that contained pamphlets, key chains, magnets, and a foldout paper mapping the hundreds of vendor booths and displays.

As Finn perused a map, I looked around. "This place is mind-boggling."

He flipped the map over. "This is small potatoes. The Tucson show in Arizona is much bigger; the entire town becomes the exposition. Vendors set up stands everywhere, gas stations, convenience stores, even in parking lots." He folded and pocketed the map. "Let's get moving. We have a lot to see."

We headed into the main room, and I stopped in my tracks. An electric charge rushed through me.

So.

Many.

Shiny.

Things.

My fingers flew to my lips. "Holy—"

Finn retrieved my hand. "Keep moving, or we'll get trampled."

It was hard to budge. My knees had turned to pudding and I was still feeling tingly.

People around us were rushing by, and the air was thick with the scents of cologne and perspiration. I clung to Finn's wrist like a burr on a knit sweater and stayed that way as we headed down the first aisle. Chatter from the thousands of attendees sounded like a passing freight train, and eager faces at the booths we passed threw out hopeful hellos from each side. Their smiles disappeared as we kept moving, and they'd share the next smile with the person behind us. The room was warm from the tightly packed bodies, and after five minutes of absorbing the heat, lights, and noise, my head was spinning.

Finn took charge and led me down the next aisle. As I stared at a tray of champagne-colored diamonds, a popular song about diamonds being a gal's best friend played in my head.

Finn pointed to the tray. "They're basically compressed carbon, you see. Diamond has the same chemical property as graphite and coal, but the molecular structure is different. When the right temperature and pressure is combined, nature forms the carbon into diamond, and it becomes something beautiful instead of an expensive pencil." He chuckled at his own joke.

I smiled at his attempt at humor, but this was no laughing matter; there was some serious bling in front of me. It took a lot of restraint not to dive inside the showcase.

Finn prodded me on.

There were endless booths crammed tight, each composed of fingerprint-free glass cases displaying their valuables. Diamonds, rubies, sapphires, and emeralds. Ropes of freshwater pearls, long gold chain necklaces, and watches from Switzerland and China. Row after row, stall after stall, more of the same. After a while, everything blended into a sparkling sea of color.

I paused to drool over a six carat princess-cut canary diamond, and when I looked up at Finn, he waved a hand in front of my face. "You're not blinking."

Mouth agape, I shook my head. "It's like Oz after it switches to Technicolor."

Finn shut my jaw with his knuckle and whispered, "Don't look too eager, or they'll swoop in like vultures."

"Sorry. I can't help myself."

"I see that." He pulled me to the side. "Follow my lead. If they ask, we're just looking. Repeat, just looking."

"Just looking." A lustrous strand of golden Burmese pearls caught my eye. I gritted my teeth so my jaw wouldn't drop again.

We maneuvered down the aisle, zigzagging around those who had been snagged by hungry sellers. Finn took me into an area dedicated to rough crystals, fossils, and aggregates.

It pained me to leave the jewelry zone, but the rough stuff proved to be equally impressive. There were amethyst cathedrals taller than baseball bats, quartz spheres aglow on rotating motors, rocks and minerals I'd never heard of with names I couldn't pronounce. There were gemology and geology books, polishing wheels, and a tumbler, a machine Finn had once owned. Red cylindrical jars of cleaning liquid were stacked like soup cans in a grocery store. I double-checked a price tag on a hand-held testing device that cost more than my red-soled stilettoes.

There were ammolite fossils that I mistook for opals, and specimens with long names: hematite, chrysoberyl, and demantoid, in plastic trays. I rubbed my temple, hyper-aware of the hot lights and repetitive smiles. My head was trying to detach and lift off my shoulders.

Finn came to a sudden stop. "Are you okay?"

"I think I need some water."

He pulled me out of the way of passersby. "Let's take a break."

After consulting his map, he led me to the food court. While Finn went to buy us drinks, I made a pit stop. When I exited the restroom, I saw Finn standing by a window, his gaze fixed on a pamphlet. Sunlight streaking in shadowed his head in a luminescent glow. A flutter tickled my insides.

"Feeling better?" Finn asked.

I shook off the weird feeling. "Much better, thanks."

We sat at a table with someone's forgotten leftovers. After Finn cleared away the waste, he handed me a water bottle. "Well, are you impressed?"

I drank some water. "Am I ever. We'll need a week to see the whole thing."

He laughed. "Maybe half a week."

To the right of our table, a group of men dressed in black suits were huddled deep in conversation. They were chomping down fast food, one was writing up an invoice. Behind them, two Hasidic Jews were exchanging rectangular vellum papers. They talked, pocketed the papers, and shook hands. When I inquired about the transaction, Finn explained how million dollar jewelry deals were sometimes sealed with a handshake.

I was surprised, but only for a moment. After all, I'd sealed a 200K deal with Drummond with only a verbal okay.

People milled about and soon most of the tables were filled with visitors. Conversations and fried food smells came at me from all sides.

I poured some water onto my napkin and pressed the damp paper against my cheek. "How many shows have you been to?"

Finn rubbed his finger along the spine of his water bottle, making a wet trail in the slick condensation. "Seven—no, eight. But this one's my favorite."

"The gems are better here?"

"No." He gave a bashful grin. "The company's better."

There went another strange belly flutter. I peeled my gaze away from Finn's steely blues and chugged some water.

He mopped up my bottle's water ring with his napkin. "I used to attend these shows with my grandmother. She took me to the Tucson show, the Javitz show in New York, and the JCK show in Las

Vegas." He rolled his damp napkin into a ball. "I always dreamed of going with her to Minas Gerais in Brazil after I graduated, but…"

I waited a polite moment. "But?"

He squeezed his napkin and frowned. "She passed away."

I covered his hand with mine. "I'm sorry for your loss." I hated that sentiment, but my empathy was genuine. Besides, there was no good way to say, life sucks and good people die.

"Thank you." He stared at his water bottle.

A long period of silence passed. I was losing him to his grief.

I touched the top of his hand. "Whenever you're ready, I'd love to see more rocks."

His head snapped up. "You liked them?"

"Immensely." I capped my water bottle and pushed back my chair. "Just stay close, in case I feel faint again."

He gathered our bags and led me to the showroom.

We kept a steady pace, but the spring in Finn's step seemed diminished. Maybe we'd lost something back at the table. I tried to steer his attention to a happier place. "Know what I find absolutely fascinating?"

"Tell me."

I threaded my arm through his. "Fluorescence."

He stopped in place. "Fluorescence fascinates you?"

"Oh, yes. Those atoms, how they get all excited and charged up when they're exposed to ultraviolet light. And all they can do to release their tension is," I stroked my collarbone, "glow."

Finn's brows lifted into high arches. "How do you

know about fluorescence?"

"Oh, I've done a little reading." The Internet had a plethora of gemology factoids I didn't understand but knew would impress him. I straightened his American flag pin and let my hand rest on his chest. "I'd love for you to teach me more."

He squared his shoulders. "Well, I'm no expert, but I do know a little."

I batted my lashes. "Tell me about absorption."

He answered my question while we walked.

The biz teaches one to be good at faking things. Orgasms. Compassion. Laughter at bad jokes. Wear false lashes, synthetic wigs, padded bras. Sometimes false identities are used. Thus, it wasn't too hard to feign interest in the complicated crystal system Finn was trying to explain. I nodded at appropriate times, and touched my heart for added oomph when he showed me dendritic fibers in a crystal that he thought was special but to me looked like dried weeds.

I managed to stay awake while we watched a polishing wheel demo, and assured Finn it was no trouble to hold both five-pound bags while he went to a booth to receive a free magnifying loupe—correction, a third free magnifying loupe.

We continued walking and Finn explained, *ad nauseam*, about refraction, dispersion, and the intricacies of crystallography. By the end of a row, he stopped short. "Am I boring you?"

"What? No." I stifled a yawn. "I'm hanging on to every word." The lie was worth it because his expression immediately brightened and he pulled me closer. As we entered the next aisle, I glanced at my watch and frowned.

Two more hours until the show closed.

****

My imagined parole was granted around dinnertime. The vendors were pulling trays, cleaning glass countertops, and packing up shop. All day we'd hopped from booth to booth, collecting business cards, photos, magnets, and, at last count, six free magnifying loupes. We'd received fuzzy polishing cloths and plastic doohickeys I'd never need nor use—Finn could barely contain his excitement when I offered him my stash.

We observed strange specimens—who knew smelly sulfur was a gem? And we'd viewed some of the finest suites of jewelry I'd ever seen, up close.

On our way back to the entrance, Finn stopped in front of a booth. "Would you mind waiting here for a moment? I want to get another pamphlet before we leave."

Another pamphlet? I looked down at his gratuity bag. The thing was one advertisement shy of bursting at the seams.

"Go. I'll find a seat." I needed a break. My feet were on fire and my jaw hurt from smiling.

Finn headed to the Gemological Institute of America's stand and struck up a conversation with someone at the counter.

I found a chair and removed my shoe. It had been a long day, but the show had brought us closer. I glanced at the booth.

Finn was shaking hands with a man with thick glasses. Finn's expression was animated, lively. He was definitely in his element.

As I leaned over to rub my ankle, a pair of loafers

came into my vision. Then a hand with a familiar ring reached down and picked up my shoe. "Your glass slipper, milady?"

I looked up and smiled. "I didn't think Prince Charmings existed in this day and age."

"I belong to a secret society." He angled the tip toward my toe, slipped on my shoe, and helped me to my feet.

His quirkiness was definitely growing on me.

****

Dusk had set in, and the sky was a majestic canvas of rust, red, and amber. The shadows of evening were falling and the air was nippy, but I welcomed the breeze, having spent so many hours indoors.

At the bottom of the steps, while waiting for our ride, Finn and I discussed the show's highlights and what each of us had liked most. Finn appreciated the *phenomenal* gems, and I fancied the rare green diamonds.

"They're green because they were exposed to radioactive rocks when they formed," Finn explained.

"So they're beautiful and dangerous."

He chuckled. "I guess you could say that."

The crowd had thinned and the wind kicked up. As a sharp gust hit my back, I crossed my arms and shivered.

"You're cold?" Finn asked.

"A little."

He set our gratuity bags on the sidewalk then removed his jacket and draped it over my shoulders. "It's a shame to cover such a pretty dress but I don't want you to be uncomfortable."

Thank goodness he'd noticed. For a while I'd

feared the only thing that captivated his attention was rocks. As I drew the ends of his jacket together, I inhaled the odors of the day mixed with the citrusy scent of the cologne I'd given him.

"I'm really glad you came," he said. "It's been ages since I've been to a show."

"Why haven't you taken a friend?"

Finn shifted his weight from one foot to the other. "I don't have many. Most people like what I represent or suck up to me to get in good with my father. I don't have a lot of free time, so when I get a day off, I try to spend it with people that matter."

I mattered to him? It would've been a good time to ask about Sabrina, but I didn't want to spoil the moment.

Fragments of the setting sun cast red hues on Finn's face. In that light his eyes were as dark as the Australian sapphires we'd seen at the show, although earlier in the sun I'd seen flecks of green and gold.

The reds hues of the sky morphed to purple and blue. Finn's expression was tender and his posture was relaxed. The day was a success, but there was still work to be done, and my mind was jumbled with conflicting thoughts.

When I'd accepted Drummond's offer, I hadn't known what kind of person Finn was. But now I knew that Finn was the guy who opened doors, and said milady, and held a woman's shoe like it was a glass slipper. He was genuine and he trusted me.

I shuddered and rubbed my palms together.

Finn touched my arm. "Still cold?"

I sniffed and rubbed my nose. "Just when the wind blows."

He pulled me in, and I leaned against his chest. At the *thump* of his heartbeat, something stirred inside me. The movement started below my waist then crept upward. It was a butterfly rush. Excitement. Newness. The feeling that crazy actor had—the one who jumped on a talk show host's couch. Finn and I were close to something, a connection or change, something that couldn't be undone later on. Should I warn him about Drummond? Or at least, drop a hint? Maybe I'd tell him later. I was about to kiss him when a black sedan pulled to the curb.

"Looks like our ride's here." Finn stepped back and picked up our bags.

I smiled to disguise my disappointment.

On the way to my apartment, Finn returned a call, and I mentally prepared my next course of action.

First, I had to get him upstairs. He'd resisted last time, but since then, we'd bonded. I'd offer him a drink, but no weed. Did I have beer? Maybe a massage would loosen his tight springs.

Finn had ended his phone call but I was still running ideas through my head.

"…don't you think?" Finn asked.

I'd missed what he'd said but responded with a, "Mmm-hmm."

The car hit a pothole, and I braced Finn's leg to catch my balance. I straightened but let my hand linger on his thigh.

Finn covered my hand with his, rubbed his thumb over my knuckles.

It was happening.

****

Otis had to be the hardest worker in Washington.

When was the last time the poor guy took a day off? Those were my thoughts as my doorman stepped toward the limo and opened my door. "Evening, Ms. Crawley."

"Evening to you." I drew the ends of Finn's jacket together and climbed out of the vehicle. Finn was busy talking to the driver. "I hope you're keeping warm."

"Don't you worry." Otis tipped his cap. "I may be from the south, but my blood is thicker than catsup." He motioned me to the side. "Someone came by earlier. Of course I didn't let him in, but he said to give you something." He opened his blazer and retrieved a letter. "Said it was important."

I studied the envelope. "Old guy, slick black hair?"

"No, ma'am. Young punk, dark sweats, baseball cap."

"Thank you." I patted Otis's hand.

Long ago, I'd asked Otis to keep his eye out for anyone out of the ordinary. He originally declined the cash I'd offered, but when I reminded him the money would help pay for his mother's medical bills, he'd agreed.

I walked to a private corner near the door and read the paper.

YOU DON'T SEEM TO APPRECIATE THE GRAVITY OF THE SITUATION. MAKE IT HAPPEN.

My hand trembled with rage. Drummond had sent someone to my building? Unforgivable. My brain kicked into overdrive. Otis hadn't let him in, but Drummond had ways of working around obstacles. They could've ransacked my place. I had to get upstairs.

A hand tapped my shoulder.

"Everything okay?" Finn asked.

I turned and refreshed my smile. "Everything's great."

"You look whiter than that paper."

I shoved Drummond's note into my purse. "It's nothing—just a work emergency."

"On a Sunday?"

"Twenty-four, seven." My laugh sounded funny when it came out.

Finn rubbed his hands together. "I should probably get going."

"No, wait."

Dammit. We were so close. Drummond's antic had hindered my success. It was the feeling one gets while walking up a descending escalator.

I pointed to the lobby. "Why don't you wait in there while I run up and get the place in order."

"Look…" Finn took a deep breath.

The streetlamp's glow illuminated his face in a warm yellow light, and his shy expression reminded me of the differences between us, specifically, how he was innocent and I stole innocence.

My hard work seemed to be lost, but then Finn surprised me by saying, "We don't know each other well, but you've left quite an impression on me. I see people every day, but you're not like anyone I've ever met. You're different. Impulsive—in a good way. And you care more than others."

Okay. Maybe we were getting somewhere.

"So you'll come?" I asked.

"I'd love to, but," he shifted his weight from one foot to the other, "I've got an early meeting and you have that work emergency. I probably wouldn't have stayed long, anyway."

"Sure. I understand." I didn't. Not at all. "Guess I should give this back." I unbuttoned Finn's jacket and handed it to him.

"I'd let you keep it," he draped his jacket over his forearm, "but it cost a small fortune."

"Worth every penny, right?"

"Absolutely."

He gave me an awkward sideways hug, and I caught another whiff of his cologne.

"Promise me a rain check?"

"Promise."

He walked back to the limo and climbed inside.

I stayed outside until the vehicle was far from sight then removed Drummond's letter and tore it to pieces.

So. Freaking. Close.

Chapter Twenty-Five

No one had entered my apartment but I scanned the place twice to be sure. Once I was convinced things were in order, I swapped out my retro lawn dress for a satin negligée then sat at the kitchen table and fired up my laptop. The near-empty refrigerator hummed in the background.

The Bordeaux I chose to calm my nerves was a bottle I'd hoped to share with Finn, but Drummond had killed that opportunity by meddling.

I sifted through articles on Drummond's past investigations while I drank.

A little digging led me to an interesting story. After Drummond was elected, he voted for the president's economic stimulus package. It was no shocking coincidence to learn that Drummond's nephew owned a wind farm in west Texas that carried incentives for farmers to give parcels of land for building turbines. Drummond's nephew got beaucoup bucks in stimulus grants and tax credits, and apparently, that didn't sit well with the departments of energy and natural resources. They were trying to audit the son-of-a-bitch.

Good. He deserved that.

I finished my wine and crawled into bed.

****

Mondays were the busiest day of the week, but before I got to the office, I needed to throw a punch

Dana Ross

back at Drummond. A knockout punch.

Adrenaline was making me antsy, so I decided to walk to work. Entranced by the smells and sounds, I slowed by the entrance of a local park and took in the sights and scents of forsythia, rhododendrons, and sweet star magnolias. Insects thrummed, and bees flitted from flower to flower. A steel-colored fountain near the entrance was leaking water.

Inside the fenced perimeter were two men seated on beach chairs, playing a game of chess. Their spines were hunched forward, gazes glued to their game, their fists on their chins. I coiled my fingers over the diamonds of the chain-link fence and craned my neck to see the board.

Learning to play chess was the only good thing I took away from my childhood. Father never taught me how to play because he believed women were best suited learning skills like cooking and sewing, but he often played with men from our church, and the nights they sat on the porch drinking sweet tea, I'd eavesdropped on their conversations and learned their strategies.

Chess was like life. You had to plan your moves three steps ahead, take calculated risks, and sacrifice pawns because they were collateral damage.

The man on the left had his king in check. It could be argued that losing your king meant the game was over, but in my opinion, the queen was the most powerful piece.

I studied the board and whispered, "Castle."

Neither man looked up.

Castling was the only time in chess that a player could move two pieces at once. If the king and rook have never been moved and had no other pieces between them, they could swap places. It would save the man's game.

The man on the left made his move. A bad one.

"Checkmate," his partner said. Game over.

That was it.

I reached inside my purse for the dog-eared black notebook I always kept close at hand. The book was my lifeline. It contained coded information, names of people who would never want to be publicly linked to me. Jeanine knew the book existed, but had never seen it up close. My lawyer had been instructed to incinerate the book if something happened to me.

Calling a client's private home would be breaking an unspoken rule, but Drummond had sent someone to my home with a threat, so all bets were off. I flipped through pages until I found the name I needed.

A gentle voice answered my call. "Hello?"

I cleared my throat and smiled. "Hi, is this Rose?"

"Yes. Who's calling?"

I looked both ways, spoke softly. "This is Faith Crawley. Perhaps you remember me. We met at the Association of Women Business Owners meeting a few years back. We were talking about your sciatica, and I referred you to my chiropractor, Dr. Mark."

"Dr. Mark, of course. I remember now, you're the young lady with the consulting firm. Something about polish?"

"Perfectly Polished. I'm flattered you remembered. How's your sciatica?"

"Hasn't bothered me in years. Dr. Mark was a godsend. Within two months I was back on the golf course. I never got to thank you. I'm sorry, here I am going on. You're calling for a reason."

"Yes, a reason." I flicked the edge of my notebook. "I'm calling because I have information for your husband but I haven't been able to reach him."

"William is away on business. Is this regarding the campaign?"

"It is. And it's imperative I speak with him."

"He's been so busy these days. The campaign seems to occupy all his time."

Yet he still finds time to screw with my life.

An ambulance passed, lights flashing, siren piercing my ears. I cupped my hand over the phone's mouthpiece and waited for the noise to quiet. "Could you give *William* a message?"

"Of course."

"Tell him that I'm working to help his campaign, but my efforts have been hindered. Mention that I'd be happy to share the information with you."

"I'll pass along your message, and it would please me very much to see you again. Perhaps we could do lunch."

Rose Drummond was one of those ladies who lunched. A lady who spent her afternoons at functions that were basically excuses to wear nice hats, eat dainty, crustless sandwiches, and sip mint juleps. Rose wasn't a power-hungry bitch like most of that kind, but I'm sure she enjoyed the social status that came with being the wife of a senator. She was too good for him, and it would crush her to learn of his appetite for young girls. I didn't want to hurt Rose, but I wasn't going to let Drummond get off scot-free, either.

"I'd love that," I said. "Let's keep in touch."

I gave Rose my number, checked an item off my

cell's to-do list, and headed to work.

Checkmate, *Bill*.

Chapter Twenty-Six

Sending Drummond a warning had lifted my spirits, but my euphoria diminished as I arrived at my building. First, while rushing to the elevator, I skidded on the slippery floor and twisted my ankle. Second, the glass door to my suite had a greasy palm print on it and third, the entrance smelled like sour milk. But the cherry on my crappy morning cake was the dangling overhead light fixture in the lobby.

I stormed over to Jeanine's desk and shot her a terrible squinting look until she looked up. "Is it too much to ask to keep this place from falling apart?"

"Morning to you, too." She snapped a gum bubble. The hot pink dress and bow in her hair matched the candy she chewed. "What or whom, got your panties twisted?"

I removed my sunglasses and threw out my hand, ready to vent my frustration about the deteriorating conditions then realized my error. I wasn't upset about light bulbs and palm prints, I was pissed because I'd failed to launch with Finn.

"Sorry." I set my empty travel mug on Jeanine's desk. "I had a bad night."

"I figured." She leaned her elbows on her desk, folded her fingers, and rested her chin on top of her hands. "But I know something that'll turn that frown upside down."

I slid my sunglasses into their pouch. "Aside from winning the lottery, nothing will make me feel better."

"You're wrong about that." Jeanine blew a bubble so large it covered her face. After it popped, she sucked it back in her mouth and cracked her gum.

"I'm not in the mood for guessing games, so spill it."

"Wait 'til you see." In seconds, she was up and practically pushing me toward my door.

I wiggled free of her clutch. "I'm not in the mood for surprises either. Tell me what's going on."

"Seek, and ye shall find." She opened the door and made a grand gesture with her hand.

Things that excited Jeanine usually weren't good, so I braced myself for the worst—an unplanned renovation, a newfangled air purifier, another horrible gown choice. Those were things I'd expected to see, but when I walked inside my office, I was pleasantly surprised.

First, I caught a heavenly scent, and when Jeanine flipped the light switch, I witnessed the splendor.

On top of the credenza was a carnival of color, a tangle of flowers that practically exploded from their vase. There were pastel-colored roses, yellow tulips, pink peonies, white stephanotis, peach alstromeria, and greens. Some flowers had fallen back like silent fainting film stars, the others seemed to be wrestling for elbow room.

I palmed my chest. "Who sent those?"

"That's what I'd like to know." Jeanine placed her palms on top of my shoulders and steered me toward the credenza.

I drew in the sweet perfume of the peonies and

roses, the earthy scent of the tulips then dug an envelope out of the green fronds and turned my back away from Jeanine to read the card.

Thank you for accompanying me yesterday. I had a wonderful time. Sorry about leaving early. I'll make it up to you. - Finn

My cheeks felt like someone was holding a warm compress against them.

Jeanine leaned over my shoulder. "Who's the mystery sender?"

I pocketed the card. "Just a friend."

She lifted her cat-eye glasses and squinted. "That's a serious bouquet from *just a friend.*"

"Stop being nosy." I removed a lavender rose from the vase and stroked it along my jaw. The florist had smoothed down the thorns.

"Pooh. You're no fun." Jeanine grabbed a glass off the credenza and filled it with water. Then she put the rose in the glass, carried it to my desk, and took her favorite chair.

I fired up my computer while she filled me in on the morning events.

"It's been relatively uneventful. Just two potentials and one PR." She removed a notepad from her pocket and tore off a few sheets of paper and handed them to me. "Don't forget our staff meeting this afternoon. I'll make your latte while you look over your messages. Then we can talk about Tony."

"Do we have to?" I removed a bottle of painkillers from my drawer and swallowed a pill dry.

"Yes." She pushed back her chair. On her way to the door, she turned on the air filter. The machine gave a low hum that seemed to please her.

"Like it or not," she called as she passed over the threshold, "eventually I'll find out who sent the flowers."

"Just make the coffee," I yelled back.

****

I spent the next hour returning clients' calls and pairing matches. The PR case Jeanine had mentioned was a former child star, a darling of a popular sitcom, who had been out of work since she'd turned sixteen. Her new hobbies included pills, underage drinking, and causing general havoc at nightclubs. I scheduled her appointment at a month-long rehab center then made a note to pass her back to Jeanine for charity work once the kid was *sprung and clean.*

The fresh smell of tea roses wafted in the air. I glanced at my flowers and decided to take a break and check in with Finn.

Voicemail. I left a message thanking him for the generous bouquet and asked him to call when he had time.

I steepled my fingers and rocked in my chair. The flowers proved he cared, but not enough to take it to the next level. Something was holding him back.

I returned my attention back to the spreadsheet in front of me. The figures were puzzling since the girls seemed to be producing, and the question of why the funds were shrinking remained unresolved.

Jeanine opened my door, and a loud mechanical sound drifted from the reception area.

I covered my ears. "What's all that racket?"

"Carpet cleaners." Jeanine pushed aside my spreadsheet, set my coffee on my desk, and dumped a packet of sweetener into my mug. "They'll be done soon."

"Thank goodness." The bad smell had been overpowering when I arrived. I picked up my mug and sipped my brew. "What happened with Tony?"

Jeanine took a seat. "He seems placated for now."

"That's a relief."

"Are we going to fire him?"

"Eventually." I stirred my drink until the foam disappeared.

"Too bad. He always brings me gum." Jeanine popped a bubble and twisted her eyeglass chain around her finger. "So, I didn't want to tell you this, but the sheik called. He wants to know if we accepted his offer."

I set down my spoon. "What did you tell him?"

"I told him you were away on business." She crossed her arms. "You're still considering this?"

"Maybe."

"I knew I shouldn't have told you. Don't do it, Faith. The money situation can't be that bad."

I twisted the pearls at my throat. "You have to stop worrying about me."

"It's my job to worry. The day you hired me, I promised I'd have your back." She tapped the pin on her pink frock. "Later, you told me this meant something."

She was right, she was my pit bull. But if I confided with her about Drummond and things went south, she could be implicated. An image of Jeanine with her dilapidated beehive wearing an orange prison jumpsuit flashed before my eyes. I blinked away the visual and sipped my drink. "The coffee tastes different. Did you switch brands?"

She slapped her palms on her lap. "Don't ignore me. Think of the consequences."

The consequences sucked, but the idea of losing my companies was worse.

"Let me handle this. You worry about Tony."

She regarded me with a frosty stare. "I don't know what's gotten into you lately but you're awfully secretive."

I stared at her pin. "You're my rock, J." The image of her in prison resurfaced. "And you look horrible in orange."

She flipped out her palms. "That doesn't make sense."

I stared at her hands. Did prisons allow inmates to wear nail polish?

"You say I'm your rock, but we rarely talk anymore."

A guilt punch hit me in the gut, but I kept my lips zipped. Keeping her in the dark meant keeping her out of jail.

"We'll get a drink soon." I dragged the spreadsheet toward me and picked up my pen.

She stared at me for a minute then exited the room.

****

At three it was time for our monthly staff meeting. Generally I tuned out and let Jeanine run the show, but that day, I decided to pay attention. It was hard to imagine a traitor within my company, but there was no other explanation for the missing funds.

The girls were already seated in their chairs when I entered the boardroom, and the scent of flowery perfume hung thick in the air. I took a seat at the head of the table and looked around. While scanning the troops, I pictured Monique's wall poster with the slogan, *There's no* I *in the word team.*

Jeanine set a coffee cup in front of me and took her seat. She called the meeting to order by striking a rubber mallet against the table. I didn't remember agreeing to her having a mallet, but it seemed to make her happy.

While Jeanine read the minutes of our last meeting, I began my assessment. To my left was Chyna, formally Charles. Chyna had lush lips, ombred hair, and mammoth biceps. In heels, she topped six feet, but men didn't seem to be put off by her height, because she was soft and feminine and spoke with a whisper-soft voice.

Charles realized he was born in the wrong body at a young age. When he showed up at his homecoming dance wearing a dress, some schoolmates beat him up. Instead of his parents demanding reparation from the school, they tossed Charles out of their house. He hitchhiked to D.C. and ended up working the streets.

I met him outside the gentleman's club I once worked at, and saw him a few times on a popular corner. It was hard to forget him, tall and dark, always wearing a rabbit fur jacket.

One night, I saw him near Dupont Circle being pushed out of a car. His jacket was torn, and he had a bleeding cut over his eye. The car left before I could make the tag.

I took him to my place and called Jeanine. We cleaned his cut and sobered him up, offered him a job. The new name symbolized her new life, and I promised Chyna it would be the last time anyone put a hand on her. While working for my company, she'd undergone breast augmentation and hormone therapy to aid her transformation; I knew she was saving for a sex reassignment surgery, which was costly, but I doubted she'd steal our money to get it.

It couldn't be her.

Sitting beside Chyna was Yalena, a raven-haired beauty and former mail-order bride. Yalena had sought refuge with my company after the man she married decided to beat her with the frying pan she used to cook his dinner.

After we took her in, we set her up in an apartment in Adams Morgan and helped her earn her G.E.D.

The year she completed her requirements, we threw her a graduation party complete with a diploma-shaped cake. She was good at chess, and the games we played together sometimes dragged on for weeks. Once a month, she volunteered at a shelter for battered women.

It couldn't be her.

Jeanine was talking about health insurance. I continued my assessment.

Beside Yalena was Shohreh, a former Baha'i that had escaped from Iran after her family had been imprisoned and tortured for their religious beliefs. Shohreh showed love through cooking, and on special occasions, she brought in homemade halva, a Persian delicacy made with saffron, rosewater, and loads of butter. Clients loved Shohreh's zaftig figure and I loved her rebellious side. I glanced at her pierced nostril and smiled. America gave her the freedom to live as she pleased. She'd never betray us.

It couldn't be her.

Tiana was relatively new, which normally would have been a red flag, but the money started disappearing before she came to the company, so it wasn't her.

Krystal's looks were the kind that inspired people to write poetry or bad country songs. We nicknamed her Tiny because even in stilettos she barely graced five three, but her pixie features and baby-blue eyes made her one of our most popular girls. Krystal liked to tuck her bleached-white hair beneath colorful wigs, and each week she donned a new color. She was fun and flirty. And unpredictable. Could it be her?

I scribbled her name on a pad.

Last, there was Shivawn. Shivawn was an exotic beauty with long lashes, pendulous breasts, and jet-black braids that grazed her bottom. I'd once overheard the UPS man call her a "Brick House" which was, apparently, a reference to some seventies' song. There was truth in that. Shivawn's ass was so tight; a drill sergeant could bounce a quarter off it. Her rump pictures were wildly popular on social media and she'd received modeling offers that she turned down to continue working for us. Was it her?

No.

Yes?

I tapped my pen against my cheek then begrudgingly wrote Shivawn's name beneath Krystal's.

Monique was out with a client, but I knew it wasn't her. In fact, I was ninety-percent positive it wasn't any of them. The girls were the closest thing I had to a family, sisters I never had.

Most people viewed our profession as degrading, but in my opinion, it wasn't dirty, it was honest. We empowered women. We helped them pay off debt, start new lives, master their destiny. Some came to us broken, some stayed, some left, but they all became warriors.

While Jeanine ran through the details of our new dental plan, I remembered one of my father's sermons. It was one of his fire-and-brimstone diatribes he'd reserved for the sheep that paid penance after weekends of sin and debauchery.

My hand shook as the memory of Father's voice boomed in my head: "But among you there must not be even a hint of sexual immorality, or any kind of impurity, or of greed, because these are improper for God's holy people. For of this you can be sure, no immoral, impure, or greedy person has any inheritance in the kingdom of Christ and of God."

Clink.

"Faith." Jeanine snapped her fingers in front of my face.

I frowned. "Hmm?"

"Watch out." She pointed down.

My coffee cup had toppled, and liquid was snaking toward my lap. In seconds I was up, just in time to dodge the spill. Chyna ran for paper towels, and Jeanine struck her mallet against the table. "Meeting adjourned." She gathered her notes and helped Chyna mop liquid off the table. After the girls had cleared out of the room, Jeanine grabbed my elbow and pulled me close.

"Go to your cave. I'll hold your calls."

****

Even with the lights dimmed and the blinds drawn, I found it impossible to nap. The names I'd written down during the staff meeting played on repeat in my head. After the fourth failed attempt to clear my mind, I gave up and returned to work.

At my desk, I stared at the names on my yellow legal pad and drew question marks in the margins. Were the girls I'd selected capable of stealing funds?

My cell phone rang, and it took a moment to locate the device. By the time I got it out of the drawer, five rings had sounded. The number displayed was one I didn't recognize, but I answered anyway, hoping it was a client.

"Hello? Hi. This is Finn Billings."

My face flushed with warmth. How cute that he still used formal introductions. "Well, hello."

"Am I interrupting anything?" he asked.

"Not at all." I shut my desk drawer, leaned back, and crossed my legs. The sound of a car honk came from his end of the line. "Are you outside?"

"I'm heading to a meeting, but I wanted to catch you before I went in."

I glanced at his bouquet. "Thank you for the flowers. They're spectacular."

"I'm glad you liked them." He paused until the sound of a driver laying on their horn paused. "I didn't know your favorite, so I ordered everything."

"You're not exaggerating. I'd send you a picture but you don't have a smartphone." I walked over to the credenza and leaned over to sniff the bouquet. "There are petals in every color and the fern fronds are soft as tissues. Everything is so fragrant. They remind me of a place I used to visit." That place was the rose garden in Georgetown's Dumbarton Oaks. It had rained most of the week so the park wouldn't be an ideal setting, but I had another idea.

Earlier that week, I'd read an article in the style

section about a jazz-fusion band playing at The Alley, the latest hotspot that hosted local acts. Since Finn and I both liked jazz, it would be a good way to bond.

I fingered a fern frond. "Are you available tomorrow night?"

A pause and the sound of another car honk. "I could meet you after nine if that's not too late?"

Too late? I stifled a laugh. If only he knew the nature of my business.

"Nine is perfect. I'll text you the directions."

"That's all you're going to tell me?" he asked.

"I like to keep you guessing."

After we disconnected, I typed the information into my cell. Tuesday. Nine. Alley. Finn.

I had just put my phone in my purse when I heard it vibrate. I assumed it was Finn calling back. "Forget something—?"

"Hello, Faith."

The pleasant feeling I'd cultivated talking to Finn evaporated.

"Hello, senator. I see you received my message."

"Tsk, tsk, my dear." Drummond added a cold-hearted laugh. "You should know better than to trouble my wife."

And you should know better than to mess with me. "Well, now we have each other's attention." My tone was composed despite the fact I wanted to wring the guy's neck.

Drummond cleared his throat. "It would be *unfavorable* if you were to call my wife again. Poor thing. Her health is quite delicate." He sniffed. "Let's move on since we both have a common interest at stake here, yes?"

I flared my nostrils but played along. "As I said before, everything's moving along. There's no need for concern."

"That pleases me."

No, beating innocent girls pleases you. My smug smile disappeared. Hurting Finn put me on the same level as Drummond.

"You'll have this wrapped up soon?" His question sounded more like a command.

My foot shook beneath my chair. "Doing my best."

"It's good that we understand one another."

After the line went dead, I whisked everything off my desk with a grand sweep of my arm. Pencils, pens, spreadsheets, the legal pad with my girls' names—everything except Finn's rose—all lay on the carpet.

The mess reminded me I needed to regain control.

One by one, I picked up the items and placed them back on the desk. Once my workspace was in order, I moved the glass with the lavender rose to the credenza. Finn was collateral damage, a pawn in Drummond's chess game.

Despite my feelings for Finn, I had to finish what I'd started.

Chapter Twenty-Seven

Tuesday morning, I woke bright and early, energized for my appointment with Finn. Part of me was excited to see him, the other part dreaded hurting him, but Drummond was relentless, so I had no choice but to stick to the deal we'd made.

Before leaving for work, I put fresh satin sheets on the bed, decorated the room with scented candles, checked my condom stash, and assessed the area. Everything was in place. The only thing missing was the innocent lamb.

****

Jeanine was at her desk working the phones when I entered the office. She was wearing a bat-sleeved swirly print muumuu with every color one would find in a crayon box. Although her wardrobe was garish, there was something to be admired about my assistant. Maybe it was her spunk, or the fact that she was brave enough to wear polyester in my presence—whatever it was, there was no debating the fact Jeanine had guts.

I removed my sunglasses and waved.

"Yes...no...absolutely," Jeanine said to someone on the other end of the line. She covered her phone's mouthpiece and mouthed hello to me.

I pointed to my empty travel mug and set it on her desk. Jeanine pantomimed an open/close hand gesture to signal a heavy talker.

After she disconnected the call, she exhaled. "Man, that went on and on."

I popped my sunglasses into their pouch. "Potential or PR?"

She swooped up my cup. "Potential."

"Excellent." I clasped my hands together.

Jeanine lifted her glasses and squinted. "You're awfully chipper today."

"Am I?" I shrugged and leaned over Jeanine's desk. "Any emergencies?"

"Not really. Krystal called in sick—second time in two weeks, and there was a call from your bank." She tore two sheets off a notepad and handed them to me. "A package arrived—no, not your shoes," she handed me a piece of beige paper, "and our new stationery came in."

Krystal called in sick again? I was about to ask for more details but Jeanine motioned to the paper. "What do you think?"

I scrutinized the header. "It's different, how?"

She pointed at the lettering. "Embossed."

There was no point in complaining since the money had already been spent.

"Looks great." I unbuttoned my trench coat and hooked it over my arm. "You know where to find me."

She held up a hand. "Before you hibernate…" She opened a drawer and pulled out a small box wrapped in purple paper. "I know it's early, and I know you hate birthdays, but our conversation the other day got me thinking." She pushed the box across her desk with her pen. "Surprise."

I took a step back. "Thanks. But this isn't necessary."

"Don't thank me until you've opened it. But you will thank me."

I studied the box with as much enthusiasm one would have staring at a tray of dental cleaning instruments.

Jeanine made another hurrying motion. "Well, what are you waiting for?"

An excuse to be anywhere else in the world.

I picked up the box and gingerly tore off the wrapping paper. Inside was a gold-plated figurine pendant with a black cord, resting on a cottony square.

Jeanine came around and peered over my shoulder. "It's Athena, the goddess of wisdom and strategic warfare. I thought it would inspire you."

My lip quivered. "I—"

"I know, right?"

"It's so—"

"Perfect."

My whole life I'd built fortresses no one could penetrate. To survive, I'd kept people at an arm's distance. It was rare for me to lose my composure, but damn that Jeanine. She'd broken through my Berlin Wall.

"Put it on," Jeanine said.

I slipped the necklace over my head and adjusted the cord until the pendant lay over my heart. The metal felt cool against my bare skin. "You know I suck at—"

"Yeah, yeah. You love it, and I'm awesome." She shooed me away.

The fortune of a good morning was followed by an equally good afternoon. The bank creditor and I worked out a payment schedule, the shoes I'd ordered online arrived, and the prospect Jeanine had talked to when I'd arrived wanted to book a Full Girlfriend Experience: an entire weekend of companionship.

While trying to decide whom to pair the client with, I thought about Finn. Essentially, the Full Girlfriend Experience was the role I was playing with him. We were going on pseudo dates, we shared private conversations, and we were getting to know each other on an intimate level.

We hadn't *done the deed* yet, but that would be ancient history before the night was over.

At five, I left the office and headed to my therapy session.

****

Spa Eleven was the perfect therapy. Chen Huang, aka Tammy, my esthetician, was a master therapist, of sorts. I doubted she understood half the things I told her each week, but the system worked for us. She smiled as she pumiced my feet. She patted my knee just before she ripped off my bikini waxing pad. She brought me glasses of cucumber-infused water to rehydrate after my massage. She smiled broadly when I left the tip envelope at her station. It reminded me of prostitution—find someone you like, tell them your needs, they comply and get tipped well.

After two hours of plucking, tweezing, exfoliating, and being immersed in a solution that made me feel like beached seaweed, I emerged from the salon feeling soft and energized and vaguely smelling like the ocean.

Although I tried to keep things in perspective, I couldn't help but feel giddy. Even after years of entertaining, preparing for a night with someone new was exciting. The mystery was the best part. Not knowing what kind of kisser they'll be, or if they'll fumble with your bra hook or pop it open like a pro, whether their cheeks will be smooth or stubbly. Finn was an enigma, but I was pretty good at piecing together puzzles.

During the cab ride home, I texted him directions to The Alley.

Can't wait, he texted back.

After showering, I checked the hidden recording device, fluffed the bed pillows for the second time that day, emptied the wastebaskets, and rechecked my condom stash. Satisfied everything was in order, I headed to my closet to find an outfit that would ensure sexual success.

The black knee-length sleeveless dress with plunging neckline I chose from the rack seemed to be a winner. A few spritzes of gardenia-scented perfume, my coveted red-soled patent-leather pumps, and my Athena pendant for luck, and I was ready for action.

The Alley allowed patrons to bring their own alcohol, for a small corkage fee, so I grabbed a bottle of Bordeaux from my mini bar. The fee was worth every penny and then some, because bad wine was almost worse than bad sex.

Outside, Otis hailed me a cab, and I was on my way to change my destiny.

Chapter Twenty-Eight

The Alley was in the heart of the Shaw Neighborhood, specifically, the U Street corridor, a playground for revelers and music lovers. I'd suggested the area because it was closer to my apartment than Georgetown or Adams Morgan. The Alley had intimate seating, and it was easy to get a table without a reservation.

The bar was dimly lit, and the air smelled of peanuts and fried food. The sounds of laughter and loud conversations hit me as I wandered inside. Tables were occupied by people wearing suits and ties, as though they'd recently left their office, and the bar area had been taken over by bearded hipsters sipping on long-necked bottles and girls wearing band Ts and low-rise jeans.

Zigzagging through the crowd, I headed to the back and chose a table that would allow me to see the front door and watch for Finn. A brick wall behind the stage had posters with legendary greats such as Louie Armstrong, Billie Holiday, and Dizzy Gillespie.

The place was infamous for its sub-par service, but I managed to snag a waitress after I settled in. After uncorking my wine, she filled my glass, lit the table's votive candle, and promised to return when my companion arrived.

A group of men at the table beside me nursed their

beers while talking about sports. They clinked their glasses as they toasted one of their mates.

Onstage, a jazz quartet was setting up. People headed up and down the hall that led to the restrooms. I sipped my wine and reviewed Plan E.

Keep it simple. We would have a few drinks, take a stroll down the block, and when the mood felt right, take Finn back to my place, *click, click*, snap a few pics and get Drummond what he needed. The end.

The bassist struck a chord, and a twang resonated in the room. A pianist with dark sunglasses cracked his knuckles, a rotund saxophone player headed to the left, and the singer tapped the mic.

The front door swung open, and a tall figure entered the bar. I recognized Finn by the svelte lavender blazer I'd picked out for him during our shopping excursion. After a moment of watching him move left and right, seemingly lost in the crowd, I stood and waved until he caught my eye.

At the table, he slid an umbrella under his chair. "Am I late?"

"Not at all." I leaned over to kiss his cheek, but instead received an awkward arm-over-shoulder hug.

Finn removed his blazer, revealing a slim gray poplin shirt, another acquisition from our shopping trip. He draped his jacket over the back of his seat and settled down.

I craned my neck to check his pants. Slim-fit, no baggy chinos. He was making progress. I smiled and offered him some wine.

He squinted one eye. "Would you mind if I ordered a beer?"

"Suit yourself." Kudos for the ensemble, negative

points for snubbing a fine Bordeaux.

The waitress passed our table for the second time without bothering to check back.

Finn took in the sights. "Interesting place."

I motioned to the stage. "The band got good reviews."

He folded his hands. "You always impress me."

"Just wait." I rubbed my ankle against my opposite calf to check for any missed shaved spots. "The night is young."

While Finn perused the beer list, I sipped my wine.

"How go things at headquarters?"

He closed his menu and rubbed the back of his neck. "Crazy." His expression shifted from relaxed to strained. "We're weeks away and I imagine it's going to get a lot worse."

"You can count on that," I muttered into my glass.

An announcer came onstage to welcome the crowd and introduce the band. After a round of applause, the pianist, a thin man with a short goatee and dark shades, gave a signal, the house lights dimmed, and the band began to play.

Finn was making a pathetic attempt to hail our waitress who was halfway across the room. After his third attempt I leaned over and grabbed his wrist. "Watch and learn." I pushed back my chair, walked over to the waitress, and pointed in Finn's direction. The server followed me back to our table.

"What can I get ya?" she asked.

Finn ordered a microbrew and a side of French fries, with extra ketchup.

After the server left, I refilled my glass and swirled the deep red liquid. "You have to know when to take

Full Girlfriend Experience

the reins," I told Finn. "A leader knows how to assess a situation and take control."

He sighed.

I took another sip of wine. "I'm only trying to help."

"No, you're right." He still had a labored, strained appearance.

I felt bad for coming down hard so soon. "You're doing great, Finn. Change doesn't happen overnight."

He seemed pleased with that.

The band was playing a vampy rendition of "Take Five," an iconic melody. Finn bobbed his head and drummed his fingers on the table, keeping time with the music. "They're pretty tight."

"They are. But almost every band plays this song." I glanced around the vicinity. Some people carried on conversations, some were watching the band, bobbing their chins like Finn.

The song ended and patrons around us applauded.

Finn leaned forward and clasped his hands together. "How was work this week?"

"Relatively quiet." I curled my toes inside my shoes. "But I'm working on a big job."

"Hope it works out for you." Finn smiled.

Guilt stabbed my gut.

The waitress returned with fries and Finn's microbrew.

He took a few swallows, set his glass down on the table, and wiped his lip with his cocktail napkin.

As he tore a strip off, I grabbed his hand. "You have to stop those nervous tics."

"Sorry." He coiled into himself like a turtle retreating into its shell and looked down into his beer.

"Old habits die hard."

It was true, old habits did die hard—if at all—but I couldn't let him off that easy. I pulled his hand toward me. "Everything I say is for your own good. The more I get to know you, the more I can help. *Capisce*?"

He nodded. "I understand."

"Excellent." I released his hand and leaned on my elbow. Perhaps a game would lighten the mood. "Ever play twenty questions?"

He dipped a fry into the ketchup dish. "Can't say I have."

"It's easy. Just follow my lead and answer honestly. First question, what's your favorite food?"

He chewed his fry and swallowed it. "I guess I love a good steak."

"Me, too. What's your favorite color?"

"That would be blue."

"See, you're doing great." I scooted my chair closer to the table. "Okay, rapid fire time. You have to answer questions quickly in politics. What's your favorite season?"

"Spring."

"Chocolate or vanilla?"

"Vanilla."

I figured. "Favorite holiday?"

"Halloween."

"Technically, not a holiday, but I'll accept that." I extended my arm, hoping he'd return the fist bump, but it took him a moment to catch on. "Next questions will be harder. Ready?" He nodded. "What's your biggest fear?"

His chest heaved with a sigh. "Public speaking."

Everyone hated that. "Okay, digging deeper. Ever

stolen anything?"

"Never."

Of course he hadn't. "Ever get arrested?"

"Are you kidding?"

"Just checking." I shrugged. "What about suspended from school?"

"No way."

Time to get to the meat. I stared him square in the eye. "Have you ever been in love?"

"No." He didn't blink.

Interesting. "Any serious girlfriends?"

He hesitated, then said, "No."

I wasn't convinced. "Have you ever told a white lie?"

The waitress interrupted us before he could answer. I sipped my wine while our server swapped out Finn's wet cocktail napkin for a dry one.

"Get ya anything else from the kitchen?" she asked.

Finn motioned to me. "Did you want an entrée?"

"Nothing for me, thanks." The food I'd seen passing on trays didn't look like they were worth the calories.

The waitress took away our menus.

Finn took a long quaff of his beer then dipped another fry in the ketchup. "Did you learn anything interesting from my answers?"

I leaned my elbow on the table and rested my chin in my hand. "Not much more than I already knew. Basically, you're an honorable man."

He noisily chewed his fry. "Why, thank—"

"The problem is," I sat back and crossed my arms, "you lack self-esteem."

He pointed to his chest. "But I changed my clothes."

"It's more than a wardrobe, Finn, it's about confidence." I squinted and gave him the once-over. "You have strengths but you don't use them to your advantage." I paused to sip my wine. "What's your forte?"

He sipped his beer. "I'm financially secure so I won't be obliged to—"

"Not that." I swirled my wine. "I meant, what can you offer that," I angled my thumb toward a *suit* behind me, "someone like that guy can't."

The man I'd indicated was tall and handsome, almost a carbon copy of Finn except he sat with his shoulders squared, chest forward. The man laughed and his whole body shook.

Finn glanced behind me then looked away. "I couldn't compete with him. He seems so self-assured."

I slapped the table. "Exactly my point. You probably have more to offer, but you don't see it."

Finn hunched forward and cradled his beer glass with both hands. He looked so crestfallen I wished I could redact my statement.

"Tell me how to fix it."

"For starters," I clucked my tongue, "quit slouching."

He quickly straightened his shoulders.

"And no more tie tugging."

"Nixing the tug." He said it theatrically, so I obliged him with a laugh. Humor wasn't Finn's strongest suit, but his idiosyncrasies gave him a certain charm.

The band moved to a new song, their version of

"Moondance," and an idea came to me. My chair screeched as I pulled it back. Standing, I extended my hand. "Come with me."

Finn looked up. "We're leaving?"

"Not yet."

He squinted. "Then what are we doing?"

I wiggled my fingers. "We're going to trip the light fantastic."

He gave me a blank look.

I exhaled. "Dance."

"Oh." He glanced at the stage. "No one's out there."

"Good. We'll be first." He tried to coil into himself, but there was no way I was letting him off the hook. "Come on." I rocked my shoulders side to side and crooked my finger. "It's rude to keep a lady waiting."

He bowed his head and muttered something into his beer.

"What's that?"

He looked up. "I said I can't dance."

"Says every guy I've met." I tugged his elbow. "Just follow my lead."

He took his time unwinding from his seat. "You're going to regret this."

"Maybe, maybe not." I led him toward the stage.

It wasn't that I had a lot of experience in cheek-to-cheek dancing. I'd worked the pole and done lap dances at a show bar, and clients had occasionally asked for a striptease, but Finn looked like he hadn't had body-on-body time with a woman in ages, so a slow dance seemed like a good idea at the time.

But, while weaving through the crowd, Finn

knocked the back of someone's chair and toppled someone's glass. Fortunately, it was empty.

Finn's expression paled. "I told you this was a mistake."

"You'll be fine." I mouthed *sorry* to the man and nudged Finn toward the dance floor.

We paused on the laminate squares, and Finn stuffed his hands in his pockets. "Now what?"

I grabbed his hands and placed them on my hips. "Just do what comes naturally."

His diaphragm rose and fell. "Right. Naturally."

Or not.

The singer addressed the audience, asking if he could have this marvelous dance.

Yes, if my partner would comply.

Finn's feet were firmly planted, so I gently kneed my leg between his. He spread his legs a few inches, and I pulled him closer. "Close your eyes and pretend no one's around."

"This is embarrassing," he whispered.

"It's just us." I laid my head on his chest. "Ignore everything else."

He followed my lead and rocked from side to side.

"There you go," I said.

Finn didn't respond, but his breathing slowed.

An overhead light beamed down on my bare arms, and bass rumbled in my belly. "Listen to the layers in the song," I said. "Let the music take you where you need to be."

The stiff grip of his hands on my hips relaxed. He bent down, and his breath came out warm on top of my head.

I smelled his cologne and something clean, like

laundry soap. Our movements jelled, our feet were working in unison. Following my own advice, I closed my eyes and let the music carry me away.

A little dream entered my mind. In my daydream, Finn and I were in another setting, a homecoming dance where he was my date, dashing in a navy tuxedo. There was a lavender rose boutonnière in his lapel that matched both my gown and the corsage spray secured by a band on my wrist.

In real time, the music crescendoed, and Finn whispered, "This isn't too awful."

I pressed my breasts against his chest.

The song ended and applause followed. I imagined they were clapping for Finn and me, the homecoming couple, but reality came when a chair to our right toppled over and a heavyset man fell to the floor.

Finn and I both laughed once we realized the man wasn't injured.

"Thanks for the dance." I reached up on my toes and pecked Finn's cheek.

"It was nice."

I aimed a fingernail against Finn's chest. "From now on, strike the word *nice* from your vocabulary. Fun, sensual, awesome, or thrilling are acceptable alternatives, but *nice* is a word I associate with," not me, "boring."

"You're something else." Finn laughed and scratched behind his ear. "Okay, that was…exhilarating."

I snap/pointed my finger. "Good one."

Back at the table, we finished our basket of fries while the musicians continued to play. After a while, the band took a break and conversations around us resumed.

Finn struggled to verbally compete with the crowd. "Between meetings, party planning, and the election, I barely have time to eat, let alone take a break." He sipped his microbrew. "Now I understand why my father was never home. I don't know how he managed it."

His flag pin caught my eye. "In my opinion, if your job is doing something you enjoy, it doesn't feel like work. My days are long, but I love what I do." I glanced at Finn's cocktail napkin. He wasn't making paper balls and he hadn't touched his tie in over an hour but his worried expression had returned. "Are you sure this is what you want?"

He picked up his beer and downed the remains. "Pretty sure."

That wasn't convincing, but I decided not to press further.

To lift the mood, I told him about Jeanine and her fashion nightmares. "The worst one was the muumuu." The memory made me chuckle. "It looked like a rainbow vomited on her."

Finn let out a hearty belly laugh. "I hope you're exaggerating."

"Not one bit." I shook my head. "But she's a great person. Maybe you'll meet her one day."

"I'd like that."

And I liked that idea.

The waitress came by and removed our fries basket and Finn's empty beer glass. We'd had a rocky start, but Plan E was running smoothly. It was time to move things to the next level.

I finished my wine. "Let's get out of here."

Finn paid the tab and followed me outside, then ran back to get his umbrella.

The skies were clear, but the air was thick and muggy. The strip was hopping—people everywhere, smells of fried food, cars with rolled-down windows passing by, some playing music at near-deafening volumes. I loved the city's chaos, the busyness, the smells, the bustling. Aside from crickets, animal sounds, and the occasional car backfire, the place I'd been raised in was practically a ghost town at night.

Finn didn't seem to share my enthusiasm. He winced each time a motorcycle revved its engine. "Where to?" He tucked his umbrella under his arm and reached for his phone.

I removed my cigarettes from my purse and lit a smoke. "Let's walk. I need some fresh air."

He pointed at my hand. "Fresh air?"

"Semantics."

The sidewalk was congested with people loitering outside restaurant and nightclub doorways. Due to the mild temperatures, the masses had populated the bar scene. In Washington, as soon as a thermometer rises to fifty-five Fahrenheit, people shed their coats and boots and replace them with shorts and sandals.

We meandered down the street. Near the end of the block, a group of college-aged kids were hanging out by the entrance to a black-brick establishment. Lively music drifted from inside the bar and a flyer on the window advertised a band named Flogging Molly. A man by the door wearing a Rastafarian cap was smoking a clove cigarette. The scent evoked memories of Angela.

I linked my arm through Finn's. "This place has

good energy."

"Bars can have good energy?"

"Why not?" I paused to relight my smoke that had extinguished from the wind. "People can have good energy. You certainly do." I flicked my lighter and drew a flame.

Finn stood a little straighter.

We continued walking. Across the street was a colorful mural filled with bright reds, neon blues and greens.

"Check that out." I indicated the painted wall.

Finn followed my finger. "That's cool."

"Let's see it up close." When there was a break in traffic, I took a step off the curb but Finn stood in place. I waved. "Hurry up, slowpoke."

He pointed to the corner light. "We should cross legally."

I looked up and down the street. "Come on, it's clear."

He shook his head. "This is how accidents happen."

"You're kidding, right?"

"I would never joke about safety. Do you realize that almost five thousand pedestrians die each year from vehicle-related accidents?"

As a public servant, this would matter to him, but stressing over other people's problems wasn't my style. Despite his protest, I grabbed his elbow and practically dragged him across the street. Up on the curb, I laughed, feeling playful, but when I turned and saw the look in Finn's eyes, my giddiness disappeared. "Are you mad at me?"

He shackled his arms across his chest. "I told you I

wasn't comfortable doing that, and you completely disregarded my feelings."

I walked around and got in his face. "You're seriously upset about crossing a street?"

"*Illegally* crossing."

If Finn was perturbed about jaywalking, how would he feel about prostitution, recreational drugs, and other laws I bent?

I flicked my cigarette into the street. "It's healthy to break rules once in a while."

He stared at my burning cigarette. "Rules are made to keep people safe."

I huffed. "Sorry you're mad, but you're making this into a bigger deal than it should be. You can't get strung out on little things."

A raindrop dripped off an awning and fell on his blazer. He wiped the water off and adjusted his collar. "Little things matter to me."

Like the puddles pooling into the gutter, the night and all my hard work were slipping down the drain. Arguing my point would be as smart as shooting myself in the foot. Finn was upset, over a crossing light, of all things, but Drummond was equally antsy. If I wanted a chance at getting Finn back to my apartment, I had to swallow my pride.

As I opened my mouth to apologize, one of those annoying flower guys carrying a basket of long-stemmed roses approached us. *Go away, go away, go away—*

"Flower for the lady?" the man addressed the question to Finn.

"Allow me." It pissed me off that the flower guy naturally assumed the guy would be the buyer, but I was already on shaky ground with my companion, so I held my tongue and dug a five spot out of my purse. "Keep the change."

The man picked through his basket and handed me what he must have thought was a winner. "As lovely as you."

Red rose. Yuck. I smiled to get him to leave.

After the man walked away, I snapped the rose in half and tucked it into Finn's buttonhole. I threaded my arms through his, looked up, and batted my lashes. "Forgive me?"

At first he hesitated, a little too long for my liking, but then he shook his head and laughed. "It's impossible to stay mad at you."

"Remember that." I really hoped he would.

We crossed—legally—at the next block.

A meaty aroma spiced the air. The tantalizing smell was coming from the entrance to one of Washington's famous chili bowl restaurants. Unsurprisingly, a line of people snaked around the corner. Year after year, the restaurant chain won the cheap eats awards, and everyone from musicians to past presidents had eaten there. A guy with neck-to-toe tattoos walked by, and I tried to imagine Finn standing in line among the drunks and after-hours clubbers.

I tapped Finn's shoulder. "You hungry?"

He flared his nostrils and sniffed the air. "I can always eat."

I pointed to the red-and-yellow overhang. "Ever gone there?"

Finn shook his head. "Never been."

"Well, you're in for a treat."

His brows lifted. "We're going there?"

I nudged him toward the back of the line, the spot behind the tattooed man. "You'll thank me later."

****

A man whose long dreads were held back with a red bandana took our order.

Finn was pointing toward the tuna salad on the menu when I interrupted him. "Two chili dogs with onions and mustard, please."

Finn leaned over and whispered, "Chili gives me indigestion."

"Extra onions." I winked at the dreadlocked man.

He nodded and turned away.

Finn shook his head. "You're a bit of a bully sometimes."

"I know what I want, and I go for it, that's all." I let him digest that while I headed to the fixings counter to grab a handful of napkins.

After we retrieved our meal, Finn looked around. "No tables?"

"All part of the ambience."

Outside, we settled on a spot in front of an abandoned building near the alley and divided our meals. As I sank my teeth into my chili dog, a warm, satisfying rush of salty-sweet taste hit my tongue.

Finn set down his umbrella and took a bite of his hot dog.

"Good, right?" I asked, between bites.

Still chewing, he gave a thumbs-up. A mustard glob dribbled out of the side of his mouth.

"Hey, you got some…" I tapped my mouth.

Finn wiped his lip, but missed the glob.

"Here." I wiped his mouth with my knuckle and licked the mustard off my finger.

Finn's cheeks reddened. "Thank you."

"So," I sucked bun out of my teeth, "on a scale of one to ten?"

"If ten is the best," he took another bite, chewed, and swallowed, "then it's an eleven."

I clucked my tongue. "Told ya."

A rowdy gang of late-nighters headed our way.

Finn craned his neck toward the restaurant. "How do you find these places?"

I shrugged. "You live here long enough, you discover some gems."

He balled up his mustard-stained napkin. "How long have you been in D.C.?"

"It feels like forever."

A cockroach scuttled by on the pavement.

Finn watched the bug until it turned the corner. "Where did you grow up?"

I took another bite of hot dog and slowly chewed. "West Virginia."

"Really?" He stuffed his napkin into a paper bag. "That's hard to imagine. I thought you were a native."

I exhaled a heavy sigh, shucking off bad memories. "I hated it there. It was backward and stifling. I swear I'll never go back."

Finn uncapped a bottle and took a swig of water. "It doesn't sound bad to me. All that fresh air and clean living. I'd take the simple life any day."

"Simple isn't my style."

"I can see that."

A car stopped in front of the alley. Two passengers exited the vehicle and headed toward the restaurant.

Finn set his items on the ground, by his umbrella. "Tell me something no one knows about you."

He was playing my game, but his question caught me off-guard. To stall, I uncapped my bottle and took slow sips of water. "Nothing to report. What you see is what you get."

"Come on, you made me do it."

"Fine. Let me think."

Out on the street, a scantily dressed woman approached a parked car. I shifted my gaze back to the sidewalk to a hypodermic needle on top of a flyer. The wind jostled the paper, and the needle rolled away. A shiver traveled down my back. Whores and drugs, my life in a nutshell. But I couldn't tell Finn that.

He was waiting for an answer, and I owed him something honest. I squeezed my water bottle, and it made a sharp crinkling sound. "I'm terrified of poverty."

"What do you mean?"

"I grew up poor, and it was awful. My father was a preacher and we didn't have a pot to piss in. All my clothes were hand-me-downs from our church's donation bin. My mother would bleach out stains in my dresses and sew on missing buttons, but everyone at school knew the truth. Kids would talk behind my back or laugh when I passed. Once I overheard a conversation between two popular girls. One of them had donated her coat to our church, and apparently I was the recipient. She pointed at my coat and said she smelled poor on me. I never forgot how the other girls laughed in response."

I paused to sip some water. "After school, I ran home and dumped my coat into a ditch. My parents asked me what happened to my jacket and I made up a story. Father found the coat later and beat me for lying.

He forced me to wear it the next day. It was cold as hell, but there was no way I was wearing that jacket. I stuffed it into my backpack and practically froze during my walk to school."

A siren wailed as an ambulance passed.

"Winter was bad that year, and my knuckles cracked and bled from the dry air, but I refused to wear hand-me-downs. Didn't matter, everyone knew we were penniless. Even the teachers threw me pitying looks. I vowed that when I grew up, I'd never be in that position again."

I took a much-needed breath and looked at Finn. His expression was one I recognized. "Don't."

He pinched his brow. "Don't what?"

"Pity me."

He stepped closer and held my hand. "Not to diminish your feelings," he exhaled a mustard-scented sigh, "but if you think I feel sorry for you, you're wrong. I don't know you well, but what I see is one of the strongest women I ever met. That night on the bridge you showed me what the word fearless means."

The kindness in his eyes erased the sting of the memories. Something shifted and stirred inside me. I wasn't accustomed to sharing personal stuff with strangers, but there I was, telling Finn something I'd never even shared with Jeanine.

I squeezed his hand. "Thanks, but take some credit. It was your idea to jump."

Finn rubbed his thumb over my knuckles. "I would never have done something like that before I met you."

Moments passed but neither of us spoke. Instinct told me to pull away because feelings would muddle my judgment, because Finn was a job and I needed a clear head, because…dammit. I sniffed and looked away. He wasn't just a job.

A motorcycle whizzed by, disrupting my thoughts.

Finn released my hand. "May I ask you a personal question?"

"Go on."

"How did you get into your business?"

My small step back was involuntary. Exactly how much did he know? Marshall wouldn't have told him the real deal, but Finn wasn't stupid. Street naïve, but not stupid.

I drained my water and patted the bottle against my hip. Father always said the truth shall set you free. Let's see if he was right.

I tucked the water bottle under my arm. "My P.R. company stemmed from a matchmaking company handed down to me. I helped someone once and she later became a friend. When she passed away, I inherited her employees."

"I'm sorry about your friend," he said. "Were you close?"

My lip trembled. "Very."

Finn took my bottle and put it in the trash bag. "I know how hard it is to lose someone special."

I looked down at a trampled cigarette butt on the sidewalk. There was heaviness in my chest as I relived the moment Angela took her final breath. That day, something inside me went dark, and from that point on, I didn't let people get close. Finn was messing that up.

I sniffed to loosen the pressure building in my sinuses. "I'd give anything to have her back—even for just one day."

Finn nodded. "I was the one who found my

grandmother. She was sitting in our library with a book on her lap. I thought she was sleeping, because she looked so peaceful. We were supposed to go to the museum that day."

I felt an unexpected sort of kinship form. "I'm so sorry."

His eyes were misty, and his shoulders were slumped.

Seeing him like that, open and vulnerable, made my heart swell. There was a tearing feeling, like I was stealing something important, something he needed to keep. Finn didn't deserve additional hurt. Like me, he'd known loss of a loved one and probably never healed.

"Anyway." Finn brushed a crumb off his shirt. "You seem to really like what you do."

The happier shift in his tone alleviated the burden in my chest, but there was a tickle in my throat when I said, "They say I'm the best in the biz."

His mouth quirked and his dimples appeared. "What makes you an expert?"

The question tied my brain in a knot. I took a moment to contemplate my answer then said, "There's an art to it. People will tell you exactly who they are but we ignore it. We're blinded by what we want them to be, not who they really are. So I play detective." I tapped my temple. "My brain is a catalogue. After two minutes of talking to a client, I know exactly what they need. It's a gut feeling. A second sense, so to speak."

"Second sense?" He wrinkled his nose. "Sounds like voodoo."

"Not voodoo, it's scientific."

"Really?" He laughed.

"I'm serious. Watch and learn." I grabbed the trash

and his umbrella and guided him back to the restaurant's entrance. The rowdy group that had passed us earlier had congregated outside the door.

"Pick someone." I pointed my chin at them. "Anyone."

Finn studied the group. After a moment, he indicated two people standing closest to us. "See that couple?"

I nodded.

"What's their story?"

I studied the pair for a full minute then, "They're together, but the guy is secretly infatuated with the blonde to his right."

Finn turned, but I grabbed his elbow and pulled him back. "Don't be obvious." I stretched up on my tiptoes and spoke in a low tone. "The guy's wearing a wedding band and so is the brunette, but he keeps eyeing the blonde. He touches the blonde's arm when she talks, and she plays with her hair when he talks. Notice how he doesn't smile when the brunette chimes in. Maybe he dated blonde girl in the past. I'm not positive, but it's obvious he's into her."

Finn glanced at the people then looked back at me. "You got all that in sixty seconds?"

I blew on my nails. "Thirty."

"Just looking at them?"

"Well, I read their body language and non-verbal gestures. That kind of stuff."

Finn whistled. "Father was right in picking you to help me."

"I told you. I'm the best in the biz."

He fingered his American flag pin. "We're not so different. We both like helping people."

I mulled that over. Finn's world consisted of kissing babies, delivering favors, and hobnobbing with the stiff and famous. Minus the baby kissing, we weren't that different.

There was the sound of a bottle smashing then laughter.

Finn glanced at his watch. "Sorry to be a wet blanket, but—"

I touched his wrist. "You're not a wet blanket."

He smiled and led me to the curb.

Outside The Alley, Finn phoned his driver, and I checked my messages. Nothing critical, no panicked messages from Jeanine. While Finn responded to a text, I smoked cigarette and gave him a quick appraisal. His new slim-fit jacket and shirt drew attention to muscles I'd apparently missed before. One day at the mall made a vast improvement. Overall, the night had gone well. Finn and I were closer, but we still weren't where we needed to be. An imagined clock ticked in my ears.

I came over to within a foot of where Finn stood. "I was thinking, since it's not too late, why don't we go to my place for a nightcap?"

He pocketed his phone. "I'd like to but…"

"Remember, you owe me a rain check?"

"Yes, but—"

"You must see my apartment." I fingered a petal on his rose boutonniere. "The view is amazing, and I've got wines from every region—or if you prefer beer, there's a place down my street…"

"Faith," he gently grasped my wrist, "I appreciate the invitation, but it's not a good idea."

"Are you still upset about the jaywalking?"

"Not at all."

"Then what?"

He blew out a heavy breath. "I'm just not ready."

"Not ready?" My laugh came out too loud. "What? Are you a virgin or something?"

Silence.

Finn's eyes seemed to be haunted by some inner anxiety, and his posture looked like it strained under a heavy load.

Wait. Wait a damned minute.

It took a few seconds until the truth hit me.

My mouth formed a small *O*. I felt the blood drain from my cheeks and realized that was something that could be felt, not just seen.

Holy freaking mackerel.

Finn Billings was a virgin.

Chapter Twenty-Nine

We were silent during the ride to my apartment, and my mind raced with should've and would'ves. I should've read the signs. Had I known Finn was a virgin, I would've been more sensitive. If there was any way to undo what had transpired on the sidewalk, I would've tried, but by the look on Finn's face, it was too late. The damage was done. Me and my stupid failure to filter.

It all made sense. The hesitation. The early departures. His boyish innocence. I'd only met a few virgins in my past, but they were younger and eager to shed their chastity, unlike Finn, who seemed to embrace purity.

I needed a new plan.

I needed a cigarette.

Gosh damn. I needed a drink.

****

Despite his obvious discomfort, Finn walked me to my building's entrance. His eyes seemed to have lost their usual sparkle, and his playful smile was nowhere to be found. The heaviness in my chest almost sent me to my knees. Yes, I'd blown my chance, but it wasn't just about losing money; it was knowing I'd probably lost a friend.

"Take care." Finn turned toward the limo. He was leaving without pecking my cheek or giving me an awkward over-the-shoulder-hug or telling me off or something.

Dammit. I couldn't let things end that way. "Wait." I grabbed his wrist and immediately released it. "When will I see you again? There's that place I'd like to take you—"

His eyelid twitched. "I'll check my schedule and let you know."

On his way to the limo, the boutonnière fell off his lapel and landed on the sidewalk.

"Hey, you drop—" I stepped forward to retrieve the flower then halted.

Maybe it hadn't fallen accidentally.

The vehicle pulled away from the curb. I stayed outside long after the car was out of sight.

For someone who was an expert at reading people, I'd missed the signs with Finn. Only one thing was certain—I'd lost what we had.

* * * *

Early the next day, I woke with a bad song playing in my head, country music, of all things. In the dark dawn, all I could make out was the flashing alarm clock, an indication that the power had gone out during the night. I tossed and turned, haunted with memories of the previous evening's fiasco.

"Argh." I threw a pillow at the door.

Dwelling on the disaster wasn't productive, saving my company was, so I showered and dressed, determined to somehow salvage what I'd broken with Finn.

The weather app on my phone showed precipitation during the morning followed by sunny skies that afternoon, but from the look of the sky, I predicted a full, bleak day. I skipped both the walk and the coffeehouse and took a taxi to work.

As I entered the suite, I was accosted by ringing phones, the odor of classic perfume, and a screaming headache.

After chatting with Shivawn for a few minutes in the lobby, I gingerly approached Jeanine's desk.

Her attention was focused on the pages of a magazine. A small desk fan ruffled the papers on her desk and blew wind in her face. Two ballpoint pens peeked out of her beehive. She must have used a case of hairspray on her do, because the fan didn't disrupt a hair in her dome.

Tap, tap, tap. She clicked her purple nails on the desk. The tips of her nails were embedded with tiny rhinestones, and the grape-colored frock she wore confirmed my theory that fruit was best for eating, not wearing.

I unbuttoned my trench coat and cleared my throat.

Jeanine muttered, "good morning," without looking up.

I leaned my umbrella against her desk. "What's eating you?" Aside from grapes.

Jeanine sighed and flipped a page. "Just frustrated."

Welcome to the club.

I glanced at her reading material. It was the fashion magazine I'd left out as a not-so-subtle hint. The underfed-looking waif on the magazine's cover was holding a flower and her head was cocked at an odd angle. Despite her beauty, the model looked unhappy. The poor thing was probably starving which was common in the fashion world. My girls were encouraged to satiate their appetites. Beauty comes in all shapes and sizes, and the best lovers were comfortable in their own skin. And well-fed.

"Trying to vamp up your wardrobe?" I asked Jeanine.

She closed the magazine and looked up. "I *need* to find your gown. It's two weeks until the gala and we still haven't made a selection."

After last night, I doubted Finn would still want me there. Nonetheless, I had to make an appearance and I needed a dress.

My assistant looked more miserable than the magazine model. What Jeanine needed was guidance. I picked up the magazine and flipped through pages until I eventually found what I was looking for.

"Here." I pointed to a picture of a satiny off-shoulder gown with a long train. "I like the retro look."

As she examined the photo, her expression brightened. "Now I have something to work with." She twisted around to grab a coffee mug off the shelf behind her. "I'm going to make you an extra yummy latte today."

"That's why I keep you." No exaggeration.

I hooked my trench coat over my arm, grabbed my umbrella, and headed into my office.

****

9:00 a.m.

My first call to Finn went directly to voicemail. I left a message expressing my sincerity, but an hour later he still hadn't returned my call. He was busy, probably in a meeting. He'd call.

10:05 a.m.

My second call to Finn was answered by a

259

secretary who told me Finn was away from his desk but was somewhere in the building. It was close to his announcement day, I rationalized. Everyone's vying for his time. He'd call.

10:30 a.m.

During my third call to Finn, doubt picked at my brain. I hung up before the call went to voicemail, before a harried secretary answered, before I made a bigger fool of myself, if that were even possible.

I glanced at the lavender rose that had come from Finn's original bouquet.

Jeanine had soaked it in some preservative and had it set in a Lucite box. A few petals hadn't survived the transplant, but for the most part, the flower remained intact, a reminder of Finn's generosity and the friendship we'd cultivated.

10:37 a.m.

I picked up my phone, ready to dial, then immediately set the phone back on my desk. He'd call.

11:00 a.m.

Fourth call. I was eating a snack and mentally rehearsing the message I would leave, so I was caught by surprise and cheeks full of apple mash when Finn answered the phone. I quickly swallowed the food in my mouth. "Hi. It's Faith. How are you?"

"Doing well." His deep voice sounded sleepy, and there was the sound of multiple ringing phones in the background.

I cleared my throat. "I was calling to apologize for my insensitivity last night."

"There's nothing to be sorry for." His cool tone said otherwise.

I licked apple juice off my lip. "Still. I'd like to

make it up to you."

"As I said, I'm pretty booked."

"Please, Finn." Coming off strong was not the way to handle the situation, but I had to get back in his good graces. I palmed my chest. "Give me another chance."

A pause. "I would, but I'm really busy."

That was plausible, but he also could've been putting on the brakes because he thought I was trying to lure him into to my bedroom. To ease his fears, I said, "I arranged something fun for us to do, but it's in Maryland, and we have to go tomorrow—if that's okay."

Earlier that morning, I'd called in a favor. The dance Finn and I shared at The Alley had brought us together so maybe a formal lesson would lighten the mood. If anything, it would prepare him for the upcoming gala. I was on good terms with the owner of Two Steps, a dance studio in Bethesda, and my friend arranged to set me and Finn up with a crash-course in ballroom dancing.

"You're not going to give me details?" Finn sounded wary.

I glanced under the table at my peacock-colored custom-made heels. The value of fabulous footwear was underrated. "All you need to do is wear comfortable shoes."

"I've heard that before." He chuckled.

Laughter was a good sign. "So we're on?"

Another pause.

"I'm free after five," he said.

I pumped my fist. He didn't hate me.

There was the shrill sound of a telephone ring. "I have to run. See you tomorrow, Faith."

Holding my apple core with my thumb and forefinger, I carried the fruit to the trash, dumped it in the can, and brushed off my hands.

Hallelujah. I was back in the game.

Chapter Thirty

I never thought I'd see the day when I stood in a room with a future senator and twelve gray-haired, half-cadavers learning the foxtrot, but on that cold evening in May, that's exactly what happened.

After two grueling hours, Barry, the dance instructor with a Hitler-style mustache and high-waisted pants, finally gave us a break. While everyone congregated by the water cooler, I slipped outside to catch a few puffs.

Ballroom dancing was some kind of medieval torture. Muscles I never knew existed ached, my ankles throbbed, and the room's humidity had made my hair frizz. Even worse, dancing had left me winded and sweaty, two things I only appreciated if I was getting laid and paid for.

On the bright side, the distance between Finn and I seemed to have closed, probably because we'd been sandwiched together for hours. There was still another hour left of our lesson, thus, more chance to mend wounds.

Outside, I found a quiet spot in the alley to smoke. The night was clear and crisp, and a starry lawn glowed overhead. Leaning on a wall, I flicked my lighter and looked around. There I was, in the freaking suburbs, at some freaking dance school, standing next to a freaking trash receptacle that reeked of bad fish. I laughed and took a drag. Oh, the things one does for friends.

Overall, the evening had gone well. Finn and I seemed to be back on track, even after my failure to filter almost ruined what we'd built. Thankfully, Finn was the forgiving type, happy and carefree, like that sixties starlet who sang "*Que sera, sera.*" I hummed a few bars of the song, imagining Finn decked out in a top hat and tails dancing beside me.

"There you are." A voice from behind startled me.

"Mother fuc-!" The expletive died as I turned and saw Finn. "You scared me out of my socks."

"You're not wearing any," he teased. "But I am." He lifted his pant high enough to reveal a tangerine-colored knee-high.

I aimed my cigarette toward his ankle. "Those are nifty."

"Thanks. You chose them."

I chuckled, and he came up beside me.

"I was waiting by the bathroom, and when you didn't come out I figured you snuck outside for," he pantomimed air quotes, "fresh air."

"Guilty as charged." I flipped open my cigarette pack. "Want one?"

"No, thanks. I've never smoked."

I closed the pack. "Never?" He shook his head. "Not one puff?" Another head shake. I arched one brow. "What about pot? Everyone's tried that."

He crossed his arms. "Not everyone."

I took another drag. "You do realize no one ever falls for that 'I never inhaled' mumbo jumbo. It didn't even work for our past president."

Finn laid a hand over his chest. "On my honor, no cigarettes, no drugs—wait, does nasal decongestant count?"

"Hardly." I laughed.

The wind spiraled a pile of leaves beside us, and over by the trash, a stack of cardboard boxes toppled.

My body shook from the sudden drop in temperature. I fisted my free hand and blew warm breath on it.

Finn offered me his jacket. I leaned forward as he slipped his charcoal-gray blazer over my shoulders. The jacket retained the smell of his cologne and the warmth from his body.

A plane passed overhead.

Finn rubbed his palms together and hopped up and down. It was obvious he was cold himself, but he was sacrificing his comfort for mine. Virgin or not, Finn was a cool guy, as kindhearted and spotless as the press portrayed him to be.

The wind died down, and wispy coils of my cigarette smoke billowed around our faces. I fanned the smoke away from Finn's head and pointed to my cigarette. "Is this bothering you?"

Finn lifted his chin. "Usually it does, but for some reason I like it when you smoke. It makes you appear mysterious. Or French."

Well, that was a different tune from what Bobby and Jeanine would've sung.

I blew an ash off my finger. "I always wanted to go to France. They have the best shopping. And the food is supposed to be incredible. Don't even get me started on the wine. We should go there someday." I covered my mouth but the words slipped out before I could retrieve them. "I mean, *you* should go."

Finn smiled and stared at something on the ground.

"My grandmother spent a summer in Paris. She stayed in Le Marais. She told me everyone had to visit Paris at least once in their lifetime." He stuffed his hands in his pockets and looked up. "Maybe one day we could go together."

Butterfly wings tickled my insides. He probably meant *as friends*, but it was more fun to think otherwise.

A door opened, and the sound of merengue music drifted outside.

Finn turned toward the building. "It sounds like they're back in session."

I flicked my cigarette down the alley. "I guess that's our cue."

He offered me his hand. "Ready for more torture?"

I threaded my fingers through his. "Lead on, partner."

The lesson ended an hour later. Not only had Finn and I survived our crash course with the Dance Nazi, but we'd also befriended a couple named Edward and Selma who were at the studio honing their skills for their upcoming fiftieth wedding anniversary.

"You two dance well together," Selma whispered to me during a break between songs.

"We're just friends," I said.

"That's how my Edward and I started." She shot me a knowing wink.

Before leaving the studio, Barry the Dance Nazi gave us a round of applause and pulled us into a group hug. "I'm so proud," he said.

I swear I saw a tear in his eye.

****

There was an accident on Wisconsin Avenue and a

holdup due to a passing motorcade on Pennsylvania Avenue, which provided Finn and me with ample time to discuss the evening's highlights in detail.

After the limousine parked in front of my apartment building, Finn came around to open my door. When I stepped outside the vehicle, Finn grabbed my hand and spun me in a circle. Then he dipped me back and gazed into my eyes.

"Smooth." I grinned at him.

"You approve?" He raised me back to my feet.

"Fred Astaire's got nothing on you." I mock fanned my face. "You're going to wow them at the gala."

"Right." Finn scoffed. "Like I'd wow anyone."

I punched his biceps.

"Ow." He massaged his arm. "What was that for?"

"No self-deprecating talk."

He held up his palms. "Duly noted."

"You should know better by now." I jabbed my finger against his chest. "And you should be thrilled. The gala will be one of the biggest nights of your life. You're going to be a star."

"A star." Finn said the words slowly as though he was trying to attach the label to himself.

"That's right." I grabbed his shoulders. "You are a star. Don't you see that?"

He shrugged. "I guess it hasn't sunk in a hundred percent. But I am excited—and pretty nervous."

I released his shoulders and scratched my leg. The petticoat beneath my floral-patterned tea dress was tickling my thigh. "My best advice is to confront your fears. What are you worried about?"

"Aside from everything?"

I crossed my arms and arched one brow.

"Sorry. Bad joke." Finn thrust his hands in his pockets. "Promise you won't laugh?"

"Promise."

"This probably sounds silly, but this makeover, our adventures, it's been fun." He shrugged one shoulder. "I guess I don't want it to end."

A couple walking arm-in-arm passed by, and the image of Finn and me as an older married couple, one like Selma and Edward, with kids, grandkids, and some kind of rescue dog, flashed before my eyes.

I took Finn's hand out of his pocket. "It's not over yet."

An alarm pinged on his watch.

I spoke too soon.

Finn silenced the alarm. "I probably should go."

"Yes."

"It's late."

"Uh-huh."

Neither of us moved. No words were uttered, and the sounds around us seemed to quiet. Finn gazed into my eyes, and I resisted the urge to look away. There was another soft tearing of my insides again. Part of me worried he saw through me, the lies, the scandal, but part of me wanted to let go and dive in deeper. I held his gaze, even as the wind made my eyes water. It wasn't hard, because Finn's warm expression made me feel safe. I'd never experienced that type of intimacy with other men because I'd kept up barriers to protect myself, but somehow it felt right to let down my guard with Finn.

He leaned in, and the smell of briny sweat and faded cologne came off him again. It seemed like he wanted to kiss me, but I'd miscalculated his intentions before. To signal an okay, I closed my eyes and waited. Finn's breath was close to my neck. I licked my lips, anticipating the moment but I didn't feel body contact.

Come on, come on. Just do it.

The limo's engine revved, and I opened my eyes.

Finn glanced at the street then back at me. "I should go."

"Are you sure?" I asked.

He nodded. "I wish I didn't have to."

Stall him.

"We still have work to finish."

"I know."

"But we—"

He palmed my cheek. "I promise I'll be in touch."

The commitment was a relief, but I wanted to keep him there, let the night play out and see what happened. But Finn had obligations and it was selfish for me to want him for myself. Good sense told me it was delusional to think we would ever be more than friends, but I decided then and there, the relationship was worth holding onto.

I covered his hand with mine. "I'll wait to hear from you."

As the limo drove away, I vowed I'd do everything in my power to avoid hurting him. The ME Special wasn't an ideal choice but hurting Finn was worse than a little humiliation.

Inside my apartment, I tossed my keys onto the foyer table and looked around at my sterile surroundings. *You could lose all this, everything you and Angela worked for.* I gazed at the couch, the fireplace, my large picture window. Was it worth breaking a deathbed promise for a guy I barely knew?

Was it?

I tried to imagine a life with Finn, in a house with colorful messy rooms, kids, and some kind of dog. I shuddered and headed to the bedroom.

Sleep on it, Faith.

Chapter Thirty-One

Just before dawn, I woke with a start, the nightmare I'd had was still fresh in my mind.

In the dream, I was somewhere in the Middle East, shackled to a four-poster bed, naked, and spread-eagled. A camera was on a tripod was to my right; my hooded captor held a whip in his hand. The man slowly peeled off his hood, revealing Drummond's face.

I jumped out of bed and paced the floor, trying to shuck off the icky feeling, but bad dreams had a way of haunting you a while.

A smart person reads the clues in their dreams, and it didn't take a genius to decode this one's meaning. I had to sever the deal.

My call to Drummond went directly to voice mail. I left a message explaining that I couldn't do what needed to be done, omitting the part about Finn being a virgin, since it was his business and he'd disclosed that fact in confidence. I wasn't sure our friendship would last after the election, but at least I wouldn't be the one firing the bullet that ended his career.

****

Later that morning, I was sitting at my office desk, copying receipt figures into a per diem worksheet, when Jeanine came into the room holding an envelope.

"This came by messenger." She placed the envelope on my desk.

"Thanks." Head down, I continued my work.

Jeanine didn't budge.

I looked up. "Yes?"

She threw out her palms. "Aren't you going to open it?"

I glanced at the envelope. There was only my name on top, nothing more, but I had a bad feeling it was from Drummond. "I'm in the middle of something." Jeanine wasn't the type who let things go easily, so I added, "I'll let you know if it's important."

"Fine." She stretched out the word like a petulant teen and exited the room.

Once the door was shut, I reached into my top drawer and removed my ivory letter opener. The handle was carved from mastodon ivory, a gift from a former client, a veterinarian who'd caught flak after posting hunting pictures on the Internet. It had taken months to repair the damage he'd created. Charity work and public apologies had helped, but he'd received hate mail for over a year.

I sniffed the letter but didn't catch a scent. With clenched teeth, I sliced open the envelope and dumped out the contents. My jaw relaxed. It wasn't from Drummond; it was an invitation. Simple silver elegant lettering, on hefty cream-colored stock. My presence was requested at the Billings Estate for lunch, 12:00 p.m., Sunday. There was a phone number for *Regrets Only*.

Finn hadn't mentioned anything about lunch or meeting his family the prior evening, so I figured he'd wanted it to be a surprise. Seeing him on his home turf was intriguing but I'd heard rumors that Finn's mother Clara was stiff. If Marshall was there, it could be awkward, but if I wanted to be a part of Finn's life, this was a foot in the door. I typed in the day and time in my cell's calendar.

It was what normal people did, right? Meet the parents, share conversation, eat a meal.

How hard could one brunch be?

Chapter Thirty-Two

The following Sunday, I woke before the birds, anxious yet excited about my upcoming meeting with Finn and his family. After three failed attempts at falling back to sleep, I decided to get a jump-start on the day.

While waiting for my coffee to brew, I lined up the mugs in my kitchen cabinet in symmetrical rows. People didn't appreciate the value of an organized cupboard. Soon the coffee machine spluttered and *whooshed* its final gust of steam.

After my first cup was consumed, I mopped the floors until they shone, polished the stainless appliances, and ran the dishwasher. Cleaning my apartment myself wasn't just to save money; I cleaned to keep control.

The machine chugged and burbled, and talk radio murmured in the background. There was no mention of Drummond, but there was unrest on The Hill. Another adviser had left the White House administration, the second departure that month. The announcer mentioned an accident on 95 north. Two lanes were shut down due to an overturned tractor trailer.

I wrung out my mop and refilled my coffee mug, then headed to the bedroom to dress.

My search for the perfect outfit proved to be a bigger challenge than I anticipated. Nothing jumped out at me. In all the years I'd known Marshall, I'd never met his wife in person, but I knew her type. Tact and civility were their mantra, and appearances meant everything. I needed to look professional, but not the profession I worked. There was a lot riding on the meeting. If I impressed Finn's mother, there was a chance at maintaining a friendship with Finn. If I flubbed it, well, that would have to be addressed at a later time.

Eventually, I chose a tasteful dove-gray blouse, high-waisted navy knit pants, low-heel pumps, and a burgundy scarf. It pained me to conceal so much flesh, especially on a day that promised mild temperatures, but I wanted to show Finn's mother I was capable of blending into their world.

At the mirror, I looped the burgundy scarf around my neck, and took care to tie the knot the way Monique would have done. I stepped back to admire my handiwork and frowned.

I looked like a suburban housewife.

I retreated to my closet and switched to a pair of higher heels.

****

During the cab ride to McLean, I mentally rehearsed topics of conversation. Small talk and the weather were safe choices, religion was out, and if questions regarding my career arose, I'd have to give vague answers.

I opened my cigarette pack, sniffed the foil, and shut the lid. Smelling like an ashtray was not an option.

The taxi crossed Chain Bridge and hit Route 123. The road the driver took was narrow, uneven, wooded, and picturesque. We passed rolling hills, lofty estates, and gated McMansions that looked like miniature castles.

Soon we came upon an impressive set of high iron gates. The cab inched up a curved driveway past manicured shrubs and cone-shaped trees that dotted an expansive lawn. Colorful flowers burst from beds, and the scent of fresh-cut grass wafted in through the lowered taxi window.

I paid my fare and added an extra fifty, instructing the driver to wait for my return.

A set of lion's head door knockers gleamed in the late-morning sunlight. The smell of brass polish hit my nose as I buzzed the intercom. I was checking my teeth in my compact mirror for lipstick smudges, when a low-toned voice answered the intercom.

"Yes?"

I popped my mirror in my purse and spoke into the intercom box. "Hi. I'm here to see Finn Billings."

"Master Billings is not in."

Maybe he was running late. "How about Mr. or Mrs. Billings?"

"The family doesn't receive unannounced visitors."

I wasn't sure if there were hidden cameras around, but I removed the invitation from my purse and held it up to the intercom box. "The Billingses are expecting me."

"One moment."

Waiting, I paced beneath the portico. Back in the driveway, the cab's engine hummed. I was preparing to text Finn when the front door opened, and a wiry man with bushy gray eyebrows leaned out. "The missus will be down shortly." He motioned with a white-gloved hand. "She asked that you wait in the parlor."

Great. Now I'd be stuck doing small talk with Clara. Not a good way to start.

The man led me to a formal room with dark velvet drapes, chintz couches, and marble-topped end tables with spindly legs. A Persian rug covered glossy hardwoods, and an empty gilded birdcage occupied the right corner. A crystal vase held long, trumpet-shaped white amaryllis blooms. To my left stood an impressive baby grand with a gleaming three-tiered silver candelabra.

The man looked me over as though calculating whether or not I'd steal anything. Seemingly satisfied I was okay, he left the room.

I chose a spot on the loveseat and sat ramrod-straight, careful not to disturb the throw pillows. The scent of fresh flowers and wood polish hung in the air.

Time passed, and curiosity set in. I peered into the gilded birdcage which didn't look like it had been occupied in decades, then walked over to the piano and gingerly touched a key. A *C* note sang back, and memories of my mother escaped from the vault. On Saturdays, she'd polish the church organ with orange-scented wood cleaner and old diapers, her gnarled hands working over the wood until it gleamed.

"If you learn the piano," she'd told me, "you can play any instrument."

I'd taken lessons, but quit after the first six months. Mother was disappointed, of course, so I told her that I never had time to practice, that school was too demanding. What I didn't tell her was that my teacher liked to put his dirty paws on my thigh while I played. He had coffee-stained teeth and breath that smelled like black licorice, and to that day, whenever I saw an upright piano, I broke out in a sweat.

I struck another key, an *E* note sang back, and a soft Southern voice startled me.

"Do you play?" someone asked.

I retracted my hand and turned.

The woman behind me was tall and lean like Finn, yet she seemed to own the confidence he lacked. Her salt-and-pepper hair was cut in a stylish bob, and she was elegantly dressed in a tweed pants suit with white leather inserts and a high-collared blouse. A strand of large cultured pearls hung around her neck, and her diamond bangle bracelets jangled as she walked closer. Her posture suggested I was in the presence of a powerful figure. Marshall had the title, but Clara, apparently, had things of her own.

"Forgive me." I stood and backed away from the piano bench. "I should have asked."

"No need to apologize." She extended a thin hand. "I'm Clara. You must be Ms. Crawley."

"Please, call me Faith." I shook her hand, and again, her bracelets jangled. Her grip was strong for someone with small bones. "Thank you for inviting me. You have a lovely home."

"Alas, it'll be too quiet when Finn moves out." She gave an exaggerated sigh and then pointed to the bench. "So, you play?"

I fingered the knot on my scarf. "I used to. But not for some time."

"You'll humor me then." She winked. "It's not often I get an audience." She leaned in to flip a page in the playbook. The song displayed was Mendelssohn's "Lieder Ohne Worte."

She lowered herself onto the bench and began to

play. It was a plucky tune, with sharp, determined notes.

Watching her *tickle the ivories* reignited more memories. Mother playing the organ during Christmas. Me struggling to learn chords beside the piano teacher with curious hands. I took deep breaths until the vision faded.

Clara lifted her hands from the keys and twisted to face me. "My husband berates my grand-nephews when they play. He complains they're banging, not making music, but I disagree." She pressed the damper pedal and struck the keys with intensity, *a forte*. "Pianos are instruments to be heard." She slid her finger across the row and powerful notes filled the air.

When the song ended, I clapped. "You play well."

"Thank you." She sniffed. "I can hold my own." She lowered the key cover and rubbed a smudge off the top with her thumb. "Marshall uncovered her on a trip to London. It took six months and numerous tunings to restore the original sound, but now it's perfect." She stood and seemed to size me up with her stare. "Marshall loves to collect beautiful things."

A trickle of sweat rolled down behind my ear. I didn't know how to respond, but I was spared the embarrassment as the bushy-browed man entered the room. He carried a silver tray piled high with a gold-rimmed teapot, dainty cups, and biscuits. Taking slow, calculated steps, he set the tray on the coffee table and quietly departed.

"Let's sit and talk a while." Clara motioned to the couch.

I glanced at the door. "Will Finn be joining us soon?"

"Later, perhaps. You understand his line of work is important."

"Of course." A one-on-one with Clara was about as fun as a trip to the gynecologist, but getting to know her might help me understand Finn. I lowered down, again careful not to disrupt the pillows, then unfolded a napkin and laid it across my lap.

Clara poured the tea and handed me a cup. "Finn tells me you're doing some work for his campaign." Clara lifted her filled cup to her lips but didn't drink.

"That's correct."

She regarded me with a curious glance then smiled. "What exactly is it that you do?"

I set my teacup on the table. "I own an image consulting company. We help bring out the best in people."

Clara sipped her tea and set the cup back on the saucer. "My son's image isn't to your liking?"

I tugged the knot on my scarf. "Oh, no, ma'am. It's nothing like that. I extract and build up the good qualities people already possess."

She lifted a teaspoon and stirred her drink. "I imagine you charge your clients a hefty fee."

"Well, I…"

During the taxi ride, I'd felt confident, but the way Clara stared made me feel unsettled. And that comment. Was she aware that Marshall was one of my customers? Perhaps she saw through my fancy clothes. The woman was sharp. Clearly, I'd underestimated her.

I coughed to stall. *Think, think.* The key to telling a good lie was to keep it as close to the truth as possible. I smiled and lifted my teacup. "As a token of gratitude, I offered Finn my services free of charge. I've met your son, and I must say, he's quite charming—like his parents—but in my opinion, he needed a confidence boost. My company specializes in that."

Clara squinted. "I'm sorry, the name of your organization escapes me."

"Perfectly Polished."

"I vaguely recollect hearing that." She looked as though she were digesting a piece of rotten meat. "And in your opinion, someone who runs an image consulting company should be entrusted with handling a future politician?"

Yes. No. Dammit, she was messing with my head.

I gulped down some tea. "With all due respect, ma'am, Finn is more than qualified, my intent was to enhance his interpersonal skills." I set down my teacup and picked up my napkin, twisted it around my finger. "I've worked with politicians and celebrities in the past. I can provide references if you like."

Clara stared at my scarf and then the ring on my finger as though taking mental inventory. "No need. Marshall had mentioned your company."

Okay, we were getting somewhere.

I untwisted my napkin and set it back on my lap. "Finn will be running against William Drummond, and Drummond is popular with the working class. Finn needs to appear more approachable. If the public sees him with, say," I dipped my chin and looked up, "a girlfriend, he'd connect better."

Clara stirred her tea. "This is exactly why I've been encouraging my son to settle into a relationship."

My heart fluttered. So she approved of Finn's friendship with me?

Clara lifted her teaspoon, returned it to the tray,

and smiled. "I'm not one to interfere, however…"

She had to be dropping hints. Perhaps my suburban housewife façade won her over. I straightened my spine and mimicked her actions. Tea stir, set spoon down, smile. How does she sit so straight?

"…absolutely perfect for my Finn." Clara took a dainty sip of tea.

I scrunched my brow. "Sorry, I missed that. Who was perfect for Finn?"

Clara set down her teacup and folded her hands neatly, one over the other. "Sabrina Longstead, of course."

My lower half sank into the couch cushion. The Ice Queen? Not her. Anyone but her.

Sunrays slipped in from the curtained window, making a yellow impression on the floor. Clara repositioned her spoon, and a sunbeam bounced off the four-carat door knocker on her middle finger, practically blinding me.

Of course Clara liked Sabrina. The Billingses were accustomed to splendor. Mansions, grand pianos, priceless jewels. Clara probably had a treasure chest upstairs, baubles for every outfit. I'd dealt with high-roller types before. To win them over, you had to stroke their egos.

I sat as straight and tall as I could. "Sabrina must be special if you like her. Could you tell me more about her?"

Clara sniffed. "I'm not one to divulge personal details of my son's private life."

"We both have Finn's best interest at heart. Anything you share would be kept in confidence and would benefit his campaign."

"Yes. For Finn's best interest." She brushed something off her lap. "The Longsteads are dear friends. We met Don and Jacqueline back in the seventies when Marshall was first campaigning. They're good people—the right people—and our children played together when they were small. We summered together in Martha's Vineyard and spent winter breaks in Aspen. To our dismay, Finn spent most of our vacations with his nose in a book. Everyone knew he had his eye on Sabrina, but he never spoke about it. The girl was bright and spirited, someone who would push Finn in the right direction, but I think her confidence intimidated him." She paused to cough.

I handed her teacup to her.

"Thank you." She blew on the liquid. "Finn and Sabrina both attended Georgetown—Sabrina was in the law division, my son in political science. When he came home for the holidays, I'd inquire about their relationship, but he gave evasive answers." She sipped her tea. "Marshall and I always hoped they'd end up together. Sabrina is perfect for my Finn. She's well-bred, speaks French, German, and Cantonese fluently, and will make an excellent wife."

Wife?

I looked for something to grab, settled for the seat cushion. "I wasn't aware that Finn wanted to get married."

Clara set down her cup. "Of course he wants to get married. He must marry. A politician needs a partner, and a good woman can do wonders for a man's image. Choose the wrong kind," she dabbed her lip with her napkin, "and you can lose everything."

A clock tolled the hour.

Clara continued. "Whom you associate with is paramount. The right partner can make or break you. Consider," she cupped her mouth, "I'll refrain from saying any names, but there was a U.S. Senator from North Carolina who became *entangled* with an actress and nearly lost everything. That horrid woman. It seems her father was tied to a horse insurance fraud, and now there's a child out of wedlock. The poor senator's wife was never the same." Clara picked up her tea and stirred it, but didn't drink. "Can you imagine the horror? Here's a woman who stuck by her husband's side, helped him write speeches, attended luncheons and dinners, forever smiling and shaking hands, and how does he repay her? By sleeping with a woman of ill repute while she battled cancer. The poor dear passed away with the cloak of shame looming overhead. And for what? For her husband's weakness."

Clara glanced at my shirt. It wasn't transparent, and the collar was buttoned high, but I suddenly felt out of place amongst my host and the grand items in her parlor. I crossed my arms and held them close.

She sniffed and lifted her chin. "I understand that men have certain needs, but betrayal is unforgivable."

The uncomfortably long pause made it clear she wanted to let that sink in. After a moment, her expression softened. "As I was saying, Sabrina has the right background and no questionable history. She's perfect for my son."

Clara had a point, but was that what Finn wanted? The times we were together he'd never brought her up. In fact, I was the one who'd broached the topic. If he was so smitten with Sabrina, why was I receiving romantic hints from him? Was he using me to make

Sabrina jealous? I thought back to our personal moments. They were genuine. It wasn't an act.

I leaned against the couch cushion which felt as inviting as concrete. "Sabrina sounds like a," I stole Clara's description, "lovely girl."

"Sabrina is the right kind. Once the engagement is announced, everything will fall into place."

I coughed out the word, "Engagement?"

Clara straightened a plate on the table. "Nothing's official, but I'm certain things will fall into place soon. Nothing would please me more than my son having everything he deserves." She held my gaze. "It's my duty to make sure that nothing deters that from happening."

A nasty chill passed through my bones. Clara thought that marrying off Finn to some socialite was what was best, but my instincts screamed otherwise. Everything was wrong. The house, the empty birdcage, the coolness of Clara's expression.

Finn had told me he couldn't imagine me growing up in the country. Well, I couldn't imagine him growing up here. He was a puzzle piece that didn't fit.

Clara reached for a plate of biscuits. As she lifted the plate, another sunbeam caught her diamond and refracted into a rainbow pattern on the floor.

I glanced at her hand, at that giant diamond.

She held out the plate. "You must try one. We have them shipped from a bakery in Nantucket."

"Thank you, but—"

"I insist."

I chose the smallest biscuit on the tray. The cookie smelled good, but eating it would be a betrayal. I set the biscuit on my plate.

Clara was an easy read. She had no regard for what her son wanted. It didn't take a genius to realize that that politics wasn't Finn's dream, and I doubted he wanted to marry Sabrina. Apparently, his feelings didn't matter.

And given the way she regarded my scarf, my blonde streak, my insufficient ensemble, I wasn't worthy. Not for her home. Not for her couch. Not for the biscuits she offered, and certainly not for Finn.

My fingers were tingling due to the fact that my napkin was knotted around my fingers, coloring my knuckles purple. I released the paper and rubbed my hands together.

Air. Need air.

I tugged my scarf knot until it loosened and set my crumpled napkin on the coffee table. "Would you excuse me? I need to use the restroom."

"Certainly." Clara pointed to the parlor's entrance. "It's the third door on the right, just before the kitchen."

I hurried down the hall, past a grand stairway, more fresh flowers, framed photographs, and fancy collectibles.

Inside the bathroom, I turned on the faucet, grabbed one of their gold and plum-colored fingertip towels, stuffed it in my mouth, and screamed.

Once my anxiety subsided, I shut off the water, placed the towel back in on the counter, and paced the floor. Finn was Clara and Marshall's golden ticket. He'd continue Marshall's dream. Power was something people liked to hold on to. Former first ladies had stuck with cheating spouses, one in particular had weathered her husband's philandering so she later had a chance at the presidential seat herself.

Although the bowl was empty, I flushed for good measure and gave myself a mental pep talk while I reapplied my lipstick. Why was I worried? Finn and Marshall were on my side. Clara was just an uppity prune who valued appearance over people. I might not have as much money as her, but at least I had compassion for people's feelings. Didn't I?

I stared into the mirror. I'd almost sold Finn off to my enemy. That made me no better than Clara.

My hand shook as I capped my lipstick. I had to leave; the place was distorting my judgment. The meeting with Clara had tanked, but at least I knew what I was up against. And I'd learned a little more about Sabrina.

Back in the parlor, Clara was nowhere in sight. Desmond was clearing the table. "Ms. Billings extends her apologizes, but she was called away to attend to an urgent matter."

Like hell she was.

Head high, I marched over to Desmond and snagged the largest biscuit off his tray. "I'll see myself to the door."

The moment I stepped outside, I broke the biscuit in half and tossed the pieces into the shrubs. Freaking bitch. I unknotted my scarf and stuffed it into my purse. One day, Clara would get hers.

The cab was still in the driveway, the driver behind the wheel, still buried behind his newspaper. I knocked on the window, and he unlocked the door.

"Heading back to 14th Street?" he asked.

I exhaled a breath I felt like I'd been holding for hours. "Anywhere but here."

Gravel crunched beneath the tires as we headed

down the driveway. Before we turned the corner, I looked back at the house. A shutter in the upstairs window was hanging at a crooked angle. I smiled and faced forward. It was a small consolation that even the rich weren't impervious to flaws.

My cab driver let me off downtown, and I walked the streets in a mental fog for hours.

The weather was mild but I felt cold, despite the warm sunrays. No matter how hard I tried to forget Clara, my brain kept replaying snippets from our earlier conversation.

As I walked the streets, my feet felt like they carried weights. There was heaviness in my chest, and sadness in my heart for Finn. He needed to break free from his shackles, but he was too dutiful to do that on his own. I had to help him. I *would* help him.

****

The sun was dipping by the time I made it to my apartment building. My feet were throbbing from the day's trek, and my bones were chilled from walking outside without a jacket. Even my twelve-hour antiperspirant had failed me about five hours prior.

The reflection in the elevator's mirror revealed a ghastly sight: my makeup looked like it had been applied by the hand of a death-metal singer. I rubbed my feathered lipstick off and leaned against the handrail, still processing Clara and the meeting from hell.

I attributed the fact that it took a full minute to find my apartment keys to mental exhaustion.

"Open, dammit," I muttered, struggling to turn my key in the lock.

I took a breath and tried again.

The key twisted, and I pushed open the door.
It was then I saw the horror.

Chapter Thirty-Three

A tornado would have done less damage.

My purse slipped from my fingers.

I considered calling the police until I realized who the mastermind of destruction was.

Drummond.

A wave of fury rose up from my belly. That craggy bastard was trying to scare me because I said I was out.

The foyer, and what I could see of the living room, looked bad, but I wasn't sure I was alone.

I tiptoed over to the coat closet and opened the door. A few years back, a client had given me an autographed baseball bat which I'd kept in storage for emergencies. I groped around until I located the bat and headed into the living room.

The area was a disaster. Couch cushions were overturned, the area rug was thrown up, my prized ghost chairs lay on their sides, and my vintage Heisey Alexandrite vase had met an untimely end.

As I squatted down to pick up a piece of purplish-pink colored glass, a syrupy-sweet odor hit my nostrils. The feeling of a bowling ball socking me in the gut knocked my breath away.

Dammit. My booze!

I rushed over to the bar. There were splashes of amber and red sprayed onto the backsplash. The bottles were intact but empty, some still dripping onto the floor. On hands and knees, I touched the sticky pool of alcohol. Aside from pissing me off, I wasn't sure what Drummond's henchmen thought they'd accomplish by trashing my liquor.

I took a quick inventory. The gin, scotch, and ouzo were wasted, but my wine collection was untouched. It was a small victory, but I didn't rejoice since I hadn't seen the rest of the apartment.

My inspection continued. The TV and stereo systems were still in place, and my alphabetically organized CDs hadn't been swept through. Despite minor damage, nothing seemed to be missing from the living and dining rooms.

Bat in hand, I headed to the kitchen. My cabinets were wide open, my spice collection dumped onto the counters, but most of the cabinets were relatively bare to begin with. A set of dinnerware was destroyed. I checked the refrigerator. The condiments were still on the shelves, and my salvia stash was still hidden in the vegetable crisper.

I held the bat at chin level and headed to the back of my apartment.

There was nothing in the hallway except for my thirty-dollar perfect-red lipstick and an elastic hair tie. My bedroom door had been kicked in and hung on a hinge. I flared my nostrils and tightened my grip on the bat. Idiots. The door wasn't locked.

I peeked inside the room then entered. The dresser drawers were open, and lingerie and T-shirts hung out like guts from an eviscerated animal. Perfume bottles and my antique hairbrush-and-mirror set had been swept off the bureau, but the carpet had cushioned their fall.

The mattress and end tables were overturned. A few books had fallen off, and the pages were open like fans. My eye mask, whip, Big Red, and a pair of fur-lined handcuffs had been thrown across the room. I rubbed my neck, relieved the damage there was only a matter of reorganization, but as I turned toward my walk-in closet, it dawned on me.

My files!

I dropped the bat and rushed over to my desk. My cabinet lock had been jimmied, and papers and manila folders had been rummaged through. There was a loud *whooshing* sound, and my pulse roared in my ears.

Don't panic. Think it through.

All incriminating information I kept was written in code, but someone smart like Drummond might be able to translate it. The black book was in my purse. Anything sketchy was hidden in my desk.

I reached inside my bottom desk drawer and unlocked the hidden compartment. It was unlikely the intruders unlocked it, snapped pictures, relocked it, and then left everything behind. My relief disappeared as I leaned on the desk and realized there was too much space.

Where was my laptop?

I opened the top drawer, and a sick feeling washed over me.

Inside was an envelope with the words: A LITTLE INCENTIVE

I tore open the envelope. There were photographs of my girls. I zipped through the stack. Chyna, Shohreh, Shivawn, Tiana, Krystal, Yalena…I paused on the last photo.

Jeanine.

An incoherent sound clung to my tongue like a swollen taste bud. Beneath Jeanine's picture was another message: *If you value the safety of those near and dear to you, you will honor our agreement.*

My right hand trembled then the left. Terror hummed inside me, but the jolt of adrenaline shocked me into action. In seconds, I was in the kitchen ripping everything Drummond had sent into shreds. I dumped the scraps into the trash and washed my hands for a full minute. Lemon-scented bubbles blew around the sink, but no matter how hard I scrubbed, my hands still felt contaminated.

I gathered the trash bag and carried it down the hall to the garbage chute. The door groaned as I pulled it open, and a foul odor of waste attacked my nose. Down went the photos of the women I cared about, the ones I'd promised to protect.

Watching the bag slide down the gutter didn't make me feel better.

Rewashing my hands didn't make me feel better.

Finding my laptop beneath my comforter didn't make me feel better.

The leftover cabernet I drank didn't make me feel better.

The only thing that made me feel slightly better was the message I left on Drummond's voice mail: "You have no idea who you're dealing with. Do something like this again and I'll make you wish you'd never met me."

I kicked a plastic spice jar across the room, bay leaves that had never been opened. Fists balled, I stormed out of the kitchen, knocking aside another spice jar—paprika this time—in the process.

In the living room, I dug my cigarettes out of my bag. In all the years I'd occupied my apartment, I'd never smoked inside it, but a break-in merited an exception to the rule.

I paced the living room while I smoked.

Drummond wouldn't give up until I'd finished what I'd started. He'd crossed a line and was willing to go farther. I couldn't tell the police or Jeanine or Finn. Retaliation was imminent, later, when things were over. Whom could I call?

I cupped my hand to catch cigarette soot and opened a window to dump the ash outside. Clouds and buildings obscured my view of the sky but I heard laughter coming from someone's open window. A passing police car's siren howled, and an idea came to mind.

He told me to reach out if I needed anything.

I flicked my cigarette toward the street, removed my cell from my pocket, and dialed the number. He answered on the fifth ring.

"Hi, it's Faith. Sorry to bother you on your day off."

"It's no problem," Bobby said. "I was working in the garage and couldn't find my phone." He laughed. "It was in my toolbox."

"Could you—I—is this a good time?"

"What's going on? Is something wrong?"

The sweet smell of spilled liquor made my stomach roll. I glanced at a piece of broken pink glass. "It's complicated."

"Tell me. I can hear you're upset."

Bobby always fixed my messes. That was the kind of guy he was. He just couldn't fix me.

"I'm sorry. I shouldn't have called. Someone broke in—"

"Your place?"

"Yeah." I walked over to my upturned acrylic armchair, righted it, and sat.

"Have you called the police?"

"You know I can't."

"I'll be there in a half hour."

Part of me wanted him there for comfort, part of me knew he didn't need my complications. Bobby was a simple man with a house, a garage, and a good life.

"Don't come," I said. "I'll be fine."

I heard the roar of an engine.

"Lock your door," he said. "I'm on my way."

Chapter Thirty-Four

After a half hour of running the fan, most of the alcohol and cigarette smoke stench had evaporated. I swept up broken glass, cursing Drummond with each piece I found, and mopped my hardwoods with loving care. After, I lit the faux fire to combat the chill brought on by stress and opened the window. Bobby would give me hell for tampering with evidence, but I knew who the offender was, and leaving a mess intact was worse than the violation.

The intercom buzzed, and Otis announced my visitor. I wondered how Drummond, or more likely, his lackeys, had gained entrance to the building with the attendant on duty.

While waiting for Bobby to arrive, I checked my reflection in the foyer's mirror and winced. Angela had once warned me to never let an ex see me looking less-than-ten on the hotness scale. At that moment, I was a high "three."

In my bedroom, I shucked off my suburban housewife ensemble and traded it for a black dress with a cinched waist and a front zipper that ran from cleavage to shin. The clothes helped but I was still a fright, so I quickly brushed my hair and pinched my cheeks to redden my pallor.

My grooming session was interrupted by knocking on the front door. Three raps, a pause, then another. It was Bobby's signal, the one he'd used when we'd lived together.

When I opened the door, I saw him leaning on the jamb. He was wearing faded jeans with holes in the knees, a gray police academy T-shirt, and a leather motorcycle jacket.

"Wow." I pulled him in and pecked his cheek. "You look like shit, Gordo."

"I was working on an engine when you called. You're welcome."

I licked my thumb and rubbed a grease smudge off his chin. "I appreciate you coming, but I told you I was fine."

"I wouldn't have slept knowing you were alone after a break-in."

"You know I can take care of myself."

"This is different."

"Worrywart." I gave him a playful shove. His pecs felt almost as hard as the geodes I'd fondled at the gem show, but I wasn't surprised—I glanced at Bobby's gold cross—exercise was his second religion. Another one of our many differences.

He removed his jacket and threw it over his arm, entered the foyer. "Nice dress, by the way."

"Thanks." I folded my arms around my waist.

He craned his neck. "Show me the damage."

I locked the door and slid the chain, motioned for him to follow. "It's not bad. I tidied up the worst."

He stopped in place. "Why'd you do that? There could've been evidence."

"I know who did it."

He walked into the living room and whistled. "Looks like you've done well for yourself."

297

I took his jacket and laid it on top of my acrylic armchair. "I try."

He took out his cell phone and snapped some pictures. When he finished surveying the area, I gave him a tour of the rest of the apartment. In my haste, I'd neglected to inspect the bathroom, which was in a bad state. Makeup pots had been brushed off the counter and what was left of my gardenia-scented body lotion was dripping into the sink. SLUT had been written on the mirror with mauve lipstick, and my coveted, discontinued eyelash curler had been pulled apart and stepped on.

I picked up the broken wand and held against my chest. "I'll wring his freaking neck."

"Wring whose neck?" Bobby asked.

"Can't say."

He snapped a picture of the lipsticked graffiti. "Let's see the rest."

We headed to my bedroom. I cleaned up a clump of dirt on my carpet while Bobby transcribed notes into his cell phone recorder. He took a few pictures and studied the contents inside my nightstand.

I quickly closed the drawer. "I shouldn't have bothered you. You don't need this in your life."

Bobby laid a hand on my shoulder. "This is a serious threat. You could be in danger."

My translated, dog-eared copy of Friedrich Nietzsche's "Beyond Good and Evil," the first book I'd purchased with my own money, was splayed on the floor. My eyelid twitched as I examined the broken spine. "He's the one who should be worried."

Back in the living room, Bobby settled on the couch, arm extended over the backrest, foot crossed over his knee.

I picked up a throw pillow and placed it on the couch. "I'm overdue for a drink. What can I get you?"

Bobby rubbed his chin. "Got any beer?"

I headed to the bar and opened a bottle of Château Gruaud Larose Bordeaux, filled two glasses.

Back at the couch, I handed Bobby a glass. "Drink this. It's better than that piss water you like."

"Snob." He chuckled and sipped the wine. "Mmm. It's nice."

"It's not *nice*, it's divine." I held up my glass and swirled the liquid. "Notice the fine claret." I waved my hand over the rim to waft the fragrance. "Drink up, the stuff cost a hundred dollars."

Bobby coughed into his fist. "You're kidding, right?"

I put my feet up on the coffee table. "I never joke about wine."

He gently prodded my rib. "I remember when you thought wine coolers were *divine*."

"Don't remind me." I slapped my forehead. "Those were awful."

He uncrossed his leg and held up his glass. "To better fortune."

"I'll drink to that." I tapped his glass.

Bobby sniffed then drank some wine. "You're right, it is divine."

The heating system kicked on with a rumble, stirring another sweet-smelling breeze around the room. I pressed my lips against the rim of my glass and glanced at a rip in Bobby's jeans. Neither of us sewed and he used to say holes made things look cool which I assumed explained the pea-sized tear on his shirt collar.

The gold cross he always wore needed polishing. His thick, Latin hair looked wet and shiny as though he'd used product but I knew he never did.

Maybe Angela had it wrong about exes. There was something comfortable about being with them. They already knew your bad habits, they knew the right spots to touch you, and they thought you looked beautiful with or without makeup.

Bobby was watching me. The way cops do. Like they're taking inventory. Like they're sizing up your thoughts, dissecting everything, analyzing the clothes you're wearing, the angle you're sitting, the way you swallow, how many blinks your eyes betray you with.

I faced forward, trying to dismiss the feeling of being scrutinized. Bottles on the bar shelf were missing, and the empty spaces stuck out like missing teeth.

Perhaps Bobby saw me as someone overcompensating by the things she'd acquired. Or did he still see me as the girl fighting to keep her head above water? Maybe he saw me as one of his renovations to fix and flip.

I wasn't the person he once loved. That girl no longer existed.

Bobby set his wine glass on the coffee table. "When are you going to tell me who the evil mastermind behind this is?"

"Can't." I shook my head. "It's top secret."

"Then why'd you call me?"

"I didn't ask you to come. I told you I could handle it."

He fixed me with a level stare. "Doing a great job so far."

I leaned over and picked up a broken glass shard,

set it on the coffee table. "I cleaned my mess, thanks."

"You're doing it again."

"What?"

"Every time I try to help you push me away. Christ, Faith. When will you give in?" He emphasized his point by slapping his thigh.

"I've always been this way."

"You were different then. You may have been poor, but at least you gave a damn." He picked up his glass and downed his wine in one gulp.

"Animal." I slammed my wineglass down on the coffee table. "I told you this stuff is expensive."

He wiped his mouth with the back of his hand. "You think just because you have nice furniture and drink two-hundred dollar fermented grapes, you're better than me? Well, you're wrong. Maybe my salary sucks, and yeah, I like beer and nachos, but at least I can live with myself at the end of the day."

His arrow hit the target, the place where visitors weren't welcome.

"Whatever." I grabbed the Bordeaux, refilled my glass halfway, and drank. One, two, three gulps down.

Bobby took the glass from my hand and put it on the table. "I'm sorry." He moved closer and wrapped an arm over my shoulder. "I can be a total ass sometimes."

I held back a sob. "It's a hundred dollars, you know, not two hundred."

"Almost as good as light beer." His chest shook as he chuckled.

I leaned against his side. We sat in silence, gazing at the fire. The cobalt glass chips glowed like lava and cast a fiery blue hue. But the chips reminded me of the crystals I'd seen at the gem show with Finn, and a pang of sadness resurfaced. Hurting Finn was what had ignited this catastrophe.

The room was toasty but my toes were cramping from the cold. I kicked off my shoes and rubbed the ball of one foot.

Bobby took that as an invitation. He grabbed my foot, and took over, dragged his knuckle up and down my arch.

I leaned back and closed my eyes. "I miss those hands."

He massaged my toes, applied pressure to the pads. "I miss this."

When I opened my eyes, I saw him staring again. Not cop surveillance this time, just the gaze of a former lover. The dim lights cast a warm glow on his olive skin, and I recognized the longing inside his nut-brown eyes.

I hoisted myself up. We were heading down a dangerous slope. After the debacle with Clara, a break-in to my apartment, and a little too much wine, I doubted I was in a position to make coherent choices.

Bobby flexed his fingers and resumed my massage.

Was it a bad idea? He was safe, decent in bed, and a pretty good cook—from what I remembered. We'd broken up because of our differences; Bobby wanted things I couldn't provide, but truth be told, the reason I pushed him away was, I always killed the things I loved.

The chain holding Bobby's gold cross was twisted. I leaned forward to untwist it and let my hand linger on his chest.

He covered my hand with his, and I felt warmth radiate from beneath his shirt. Bobby had a high metabolism. He often slept with the windows open, even in winter.

I stared at his holey jeans.

One night, no strings?

Bobby brushed aside a hank of my hair and lifted my chin with his finger. "You in there?"

"I'm here."

He leaned over, and I smelled engine oil, the outdoors, and a musky scent of sweat. His lips grazed my earlobe, my neck, my jaw, my mouth.

The little voice in my head said *stop,* but my lips slowly parted. I tasted wine on his tongue, smelled his aftershave, the scent I'd found for him, years back.

I placed my palms on his chest, intending to push him away, but he grabbed my hands and moved them to his lap and then his mouth was on my chest, soft lips, faint stubble, going lower, and his tongue was making small circles and I smelled his musky scent, his skin, his garage, his home, and his finger stroked my jaw and traced my collarbone then down to my breast, and I felt him growing hard against my hand, my thigh, my hip, and his breath held cherry wine undertones and my pelvis betrayed me by thrusting against him, and my fingers were in his hair, my nails raked his scalp, his ears, the back of his neck, and I heard my zipper going down, and his hand was inside my dress, my bra, cupping a breast, and I wanted him, I wanted to be touched, to be taken, to remember, to forget.

I looked up toward the ceiling, and my mind played a scene. I was driving a car and took a sharp curve. The automobile almost hit the barrier. I continued driving and saw a DEAD END sign. Instead of slowing, I accelerated.

"I want you," Bobby whispered. He unzipped his zipper then eased down my body and nibbled on each hipbone.

Danger. Dead end. Nowhere to go.

He crawled up on his elbows and put his mouth back on mine. His tongue darted in and out with quick, teasing strokes. I accepted his kisses, keeping my mouth soft and open. He lowered his head. There was warm breath on my neck, a strong heartbeat against my chest. Dampness on his skin rubbed off on me, his musky sweat scent mixing with my perfume.

My moans betrayed me as he pushed aside the lacy barrier covering my chest and nuzzled my breasts. I stared at the ceiling, my head spinning, light, woozy.

Danger. Dead end.

I gripped the couch cushion. It was the wine. No, it was Clara and Drummond. No, it was…an image of Finn flashed before my eyes. I gasped and pushed Bobby back so hard he almost tumbled off the couch.

"Hey?" His bewildered look begged for an explanation.

"Sorry." I folded my hands across my chest and muttered, "I can't do this."

"Why not?" Bobby had the wounded expression of a kicked dog.

I scooted back and hugged my knees. "There's too much going on right now."

He raked his fingers through his hair. "I'd never pressure you, but it might help take your mind off things."

I rested my chin on my knees. Bobby and I were sexually compatible, but my heart was somewhere else. I lifted my chin. "It wouldn't be fair to you."

He sniffed and zipped his zipper. "I understand."

Clearly he didn't.

I straightened my legs and clasped the front hook on my bra. Something needed to be said to salve his ego. My survival instincts had taught me to be self-resilient, and Bobby had always taken that personally, like he needed me to be weak to prove I cared about him. I gazed into his eyes, knowing fully well that nothing good would come from sleeping with him, but I didn't want to be alone.

I reached for my pearls and realized I wasn't wearing them. This brought up another surge of emotion. "I shouldn't have led you on."

"You don't have to apologize. I came to support you." Bobby sighed and opened his arms.

I climbed inside them and snuggled against his chest.

He kissed the top of my head and stroked my cheek. "Your skin is always so soft."

"Thanks." I sniffed and tugged a thread on his jeans. "I moisturize."

He chuckled.

"Could you stay a little longer?" I asked.

His chest rose and fell with his breath. "As long as you need."

Chapter Thirty-Five

Something was buzzing in my ear.

Fly?

Mosquito?

It took a moment for it to register.

Bobby was snoring.

He snorted and kicked his foot. My right arm was trapped beneath him, and his breath was heating my cheek. As I wiggled my hand to get feeling back, an unpleasant tingle shot up my arm. Then it came back to me in snapshots.

Finishing the Bordeaux. Opening a second bottle. Me singing off-key. Him carrying me to the bedroom. The two of us tumbling onto the mattress. Removing my bra. Shit.

A quick check under the comforter with my free hand confirmed our underwear was still on. Bobby inhaled deeply. The issue of his wheezing due to his deviated septum had caused problems in the past. Not even earplugs helped. As he *sawed another log*, I ran through the advantages of living alone. No one hogged the blankets. You controlled the remotes. No one peppered you with questions like—was I your best, why don't you wear that dress I gave you, who's that guy following you on Instagram? And then there was Big Red.

I glanced at the door, still hanging on its hinge, and

gave Bobby a gentle nudge.

He snorted but didn't move.

The tingling sensation in my trapped hand was increasing, and my brain was screaming for coffee. I rocked and wormed my arm until it was free. Pins and needles shot up my fingers. I slid off the bed, dragging some of the comforter with me in the process.

The movement didn't wake my guest. Bobby's leg was tangled inside a sheet, his face and chest silhouetted in sunlight, his morning erection tenting his boxer briefs. The glow of his olive skin and muscular legs tempted me to climb back to bed, but I forced myself to look away lest I add another item to my list of poor choices.

On my way to the door, I picked up a wine glass that had fallen onto the carpet. In the hallway, I found the second wine bottle—gah, a merlot—which explained why my throat felt like sand and my head was about to explode.

The sky outside my living room window was pale pink, and the sound of a woodpecker working a tree trunk came through the open window. Somewhere outside, a trash truck beeped in reverse.

After putting on a pot of coffee to brew, I headed to the bathroom to find something to quell the ache in my head.

The medicine bottles scattered across the counter and floor looked like fallen soldiers in a war zone. I picked them up one by one and squinted as I read their labels. Aspirin wasn't strong enough. Anti-anxiety pills made me lethargic. Over-the-counter stimulants gave me chest palpitations. Erectile dysfunction pills were for a different kind of *head*.

I dumped out an extra-strength acetaminophen and washed it down with a handful of tap water.

Back in the kitchen, I scanned the news headlines on my cell phone while waiting for the coffee to finish brewing. After the coffee pot gasped its final gust of steam, I filled a paper cup with the steaming brew and carried it out onto the balcony.

A blue jay squawked and flicked its tail on the balcony adjacent to mine. Down below, a man wearing a neon vest was sweeping trash into a long-handled dustbin.

Golden sunrays warmed my shoulders, chasing away the chill of the apartment. Leaning against the railing, I sipped some coffee and winced at the bitter taste. It needed cream. The thought reminded me of one of Angela's wisdom pearls—"Never go back to your exes, kid. Think of them as spoiled milk. You can put the carton back in the refrigerator, but six weeks later it ain't any better."

Inviting Bobby over had been a mistake. The reasons we'd parted were still relevant. He wanted a family, and he expected women to stay at home and settle down. I wasn't the marrying type, and I hated the way people became property once they attached.

I dug my cigarettes out of my bathrobe pocket and checked the kitchen before I lit my smoke. Bobby's father had died of lung cancer and my ex used to lecture me about this each time he'd seen me light a cigarette. Bobby thought he was helping, but it only made me more defiant.

I took a drag and exhaled into the wind. Sunrays squeezed through the spaces between buildings, and the air felt warm and dry. Spring was a time for rebirth, and a fresh start was what I needed, not falling back to my past. I extinguished my cigarette in the remains of my coffee and headed back inside.

The living room still held a candy-sweet scent, but the area was in order, minus a toppled table lamp. As I bent over to right the lamp, warm hands gripped my hips. Bobby pulled me toward his pelvis. "I always liked you from this angle."

I gasped and turned to face him. "Oh. Hey. You're up."

He nuzzled his nose against my shoulder. "Morning, beautiful."

A warm tingle traveled down my back. There was nothing sexier than a guy's sleepy voice, but encouraging him would give the wrong signal.

"Morning." I stepped back and gave him a quick look.

His jeans were unbuckled, revealing the top of his gray boxer briefs, and his hair stood up in different directions. No shirt, no socks. His five o'clock shadow looked about ten-thirty, but the scruff only made him look sexier, and once again, I was considering poor decisions.

I set the lamp on the table and crossed my arms. "How'd you sleep?"

Bobby fisted a yawn. "Well, but not enough."

I pointed to the kitchen. "Coffee's up but I don't have cream."

"Black is fine." He stepped forward and pulled me close.

As his lips grazed my neck, Angela's warning rang in my head. *Spoiled milk doesn't get better in the fridge.*

I wiggled free and tapped my wrist that held no watch. "Whoa, it's late. I forgot I have a meeting."

Bobby rubbed the back of his neck. "You're going in today? What about the break-in?"

I looked around. "Everything's fine. You swept for bugs and I can handle the offender."

He buckled his belt. "You really should file a report so there's something on record. I know you won't, but as your friend, I had to say that."

Friends didn't usually get half naked and sleep together.

I pointed to the mantel that held no clock. "I'd better hustle. Coffee's on the counter and paper cups are in the cabinet."

Bobby ran a finger up and down my forearm. "If you're hungry, I can go to the store and grab a few things. You always loved my pancakes."

The thought of homemade, buttery, powdered sugar-topped pancakes was almost as tempting as sex, but I utilized restraint.

"Thanks, but I'm watching my waist." I patted my belly. "Gotta fit into a ball gown."

"I know. I'm your date."

"Right." I winced. Was there no end to my poor decisions?

Bobby twisted the chain that held his gold cross. The look of concentration on his face made me wonder if he was worrying about my lost soul or trying to understand where we'd gone wrong.

I touched his shoulder. "Thank you for helping last night."

He unwound his chain and shrugged. "You already thanked me."

"It deserved repeating."

"You know I'd do anything for you." He kissed the top of my head and let his lips linger on my hair.

"You're a good person." I broke away and hurried to the bathroom before tears broke from the vault.

While the shower warmed, I peeled off my robe and undergarments. Soon, the bathroom fogged with soupy steam. As I cleared a circle on the mirror with my hand, I saw a purplish-red hickey on my neck, and a memory came at me fast and hard like a metro train barreling full-speed into an underground tunnel.

I had told Father I spent the evening at a friend's studying. I thought I'd done a decent job camouflaging the hickey Stu Anderson had given me, but the second I entered my kitchen, Father's eyes had grown wide.

"Whore," he'd shouted.

Before I could spin a lie to defend myself, he was across the room with a fistful of my hair in his clutch. I screamed as he dragged me to the sink and rubbed my neck with a scouring pad.

"Father, have mercy." My pleas fell on deaf ears. His fingers knifed at my arm. I tried to fight him off, but anger had apparently fueled him with strength.

"Wash you, make you clean," he'd said. The veins in his thin neck looked like they would burst through his skin. "Put away the evil of your doings from before mine eyes; cease to do evil. Isaiah 1:16."

Once it was over, my skin was raw and bleeding. In my bedroom, I'd flung my concealer against the wall and hidden in my closet until the sun rose the next day. That night I plotted my escape.

A knock on the bathroom door interrupted the memory.

"Faith?" Bobby called.

"Yeah?"

"I'm leaving."

I pressed my index finger against my hickey.

Those who did not learn from their mistakes...

Bobby's your past. You can't right old wrongs.

"Okay," I called.

A door slammed.

Inside the shower stall, I twisted the lever to the highest setting and let the scalding-hot water cascade over my bent shoulders.

When I exited the shower and stepped onto the mat, I heard a buzzing on the bathroom counter. My cell phone screen was alit. I glanced at my towel hanging on the rack far from reach then looked back at my phone.

By the time I retrieved my towel and tracked water over the floor, I'd missed the call. In fact, I'd missed a few calls. The last number wasn't one I recognized, and after a minute, the voicemail alert pinged.

After drying my body, I listened to my messages. One call from Jeanine. A reminder for an upcoming teeth cleaning. Two robocalls. No message from Drummond but it was only a matter of time until he reached out.

Now that Bobby was gone, the reality of Drummond's threat sank in. He'd threatened my girls. He'd come to my apartment. Who knew what he'd do next?

The pressure in my stomach was building like an unattended teakettle boiling on a stove. I chugged a few swallows of bicarbonate and licked pink paste off my lips. There was no question about it; I had to get the incriminating photos. It was no longer about saving jobs. It was about saving lives.

But getting the pictures wouldn't be easy. Finn was filled with delusions about saving himself for the right girl. No more time for hand-holding. What I needed was something to loosen him up, but Finn barely drank, and alcohol only lowered one's inhibitions.

I opened the medicine cabinet and stared at the row of plastic bottles. There was something that would work. Something extreme. Something I'd never resorted to in the past, but had worked for others. Using it would bring me to an all-time low, but desperate times called for desperate measures.

I placed the bicarbonate in the cabinet and exited the bathroom.

It was time to call in another favor.

Chapter Thirty-Six

The Kennedy Showbar wasn't Camelot by any stretch of the imagination, but the popular gentleman's club had remained afloat for decades, despite the up-and-down economy. The drinks were top shelf, the beer was icy cold, and on weekends, men and women endured long waits to get in. When a brawl broke out, barrel-chested bouncers with thick necks kept the crowd at bay.

In my opinion, Kennedy's success was attributed to one person, its manager, Sammy Smalls.

He was Mr. Smalls to everyone else, but he was Sammy to me and to his wife Gwen. They were my extended family. Although they never had kids, Sammy and Gwen coddled their two apricot-colored Chows like children. Gwen had diamond-studded pink collars and designer bedding made for the pair, and back when they were pups, she'd paraded them around town in a stroller.

Sammy had a sharp wit, a list of colorful jokes in his arsenal, and intelligent eyes that were good at sizing up people.

The dancers liked Sammy because he protected them. The vendors liked Sammy because he paid in advance. I liked Sammy because, like me, he followed the formula: treat employees with respect, offer an affordable service, and always use discretion.

Before entering Kennedy's, I reapplied my lipstick, spritzed my wrists with perfume, and did a quick lift/squeeze of the *girls*. Head high, I walked down the stretch of carpet protected by a black domed awning.

The front window vibrated from the deep tracks of the music coming from inside, and the sound brought back memories of the time I'd worked the pole. Dancing was safer than working the streets, but it still stripped away your dignity.

A thick-necked bouncer held the door as I entered. Scratchy electronic dance music came at me from all sides, and the smell of disinfectant and greasy food permeated the air. The décor was sleek with brass and black lacquer accents. Purple neon lit the walls, and a revolving mirrored ball showered square rainbow reflections onto a stage. Dust particles danced in remnants of sunlight.

Only a handful of patrons made up the crowd. A man with a bad comb-over, a group of collegiate types, and two *suits* nursing their beers. Each customer wore an expression I recognized—the yearning to taste a divine woman's flesh. Only the suits turned my way as I headed toward the back bar. The others seemed to be mesmerized by the dancer onstage. She was pretty, a youngling in a scant gold lame bikini with tattooed sleeves and a tramp stamp on her back. She hung upside down on the pole, with one leg and one arm extended. Her long red hair swept the floor like a broom cleaning a kitchen.

With slow, sensual moves, she peeled herself off the pole and strutted to the edge of the stage. One of the suits reached up and tucked a bill into her G-string. The girl gyrated her hips in a way that would convince the guy she enjoyed his attention, but I recognized the vacant look in her eyes—the emptiness that came with selling flesh for fantasy.

At the counter, I flagged down the bartender. An overhead light cast a shine on top of his bald head. Mammoth forearms bulged from his rolled back shirt cuffs.

He picked up a shot glass and wiped it with a rag. "What can I get ya?"

"Whiskey." I pointed to a familiar green bottle on a shelf. "Straight."

He poured my drink and set it on a cocktail napkin. "Let me know if you want something to eat. The kitchen closes in a half hour."

"Thanks, I'm good." My stomach was empty, but I doubted I could hold anything solid down. The bartender threw his rag over his shoulder and walked down to the end of the bar.

Taking slow sips to savor the scotch, I swirled the liquid around my mouth and swallowed the burn. When my drink was finished, I swiveled my stool to face the stage. The tantric rhythm of a song I recognized from my dancing days pulsed throughout the room. The deejay had his gaze fixed on his computer, and bulbous headphones hung around his neck.

Intermittent lights flashed as a new song came on, and the dancer returned to the pole. She was a ballerina of sorts, her movements fluid and graceful. If things had been better and Sammy wasn't my friend, I would've offered the girl a position with my company. But I wasn't sure there'd be a company if I failed my mission.

"Refill?" the bartender asked.

I nodded.

He refreshed my glass.

I removed my cigarettes from my purse, flicked my lighter.

The bartender thumbed to a sign behind the counter. "Sorry, can't smoke in here."

I dug out my business card and handed it to him. He scrutinized my card then reached under the counter and handed me an ashtray. After lighting my cigarette, I said, "Sam in yet?"

The bartender wiped the counter. "Officially, no."

The cool burn of menthol hit my lungs. "I need to talk to him."

"He doesn't clock in 'til two."

"I'm a friend."

He tucked my business card into his pocket. "Be right back. But no promises."

"I understand." I set my cigarette in a groove on the ashtray. Wispy smoke threads curled up toward an overhead light. A new song came on, and the thump of bass reverberated on the counter.

I was finishing my drink, when a finger tapped my shoulder. I turned and saw a mop of blond hair. The guy was young and preppy, and wore wrinkled chinos and an untucked white Oxford. Decent watch. Probably a grad student.

"Hey," he said.

"Hi." I returned my attention to my drink.

The guy leaned against the bar. "What's a hottie like you doing all alone?"

I took a drag off my smoke and exhaled through my nostrils. "I'm meeting someone."

The guy looked around then fingered my blonde

streak. "Don't see anyone."

I was in no mood for playground games, so I bummed my cigarette and pushed away his hand. "Let's stop right here. You're looking for some fun, no strings attached. Well, I've got news for you, I don't give freebies and my strings would cost you. Like, thousands." I arched one brow. "Still interested?"

He backed up. "No, I—"

"And tuck in your shirt. It makes you look sloppy." I swiveled back to the bar.

He raked his hand through his hair and walked away.

The bartender appeared. "Sam says he'll see you."

I slugged down the last sip of my drink and followed the bartender.

Sammy's office was dark, cramped, and packed with papers. An ebony desk filled the majority of the room, and framed photos of breasty girls with come-hither looks lined the back wall. Sammy was at his desk, a phone cradled between his ear and shoulder. Seeing me, he waved and held up one finger to signal patience. Musical beats trailed from the dance area.

I waited in the doorway until he finished his conversation.

"Faith." He stood and extended a hand. "As I live and breathe."

I approached the desk and clasped his hand. "It's been too long."

He kissed my knuckles.

"Always the charmer."

"Gwen might say otherwise."

There were two chairs in front of Sammy's desk; one with a hole on the armrest that had been patched with duct tape, one with a cigarette burn on the seat. I chose the latter.

Sammy's attire hadn't changed. Shiny jacket, skinny tie, snappy gold cufflinks. His clothes always read something straight out of a Mafioso movie, but somehow it looked right on him.

"You're looking well." I offered him a warm smile.

"It's the tanning salon. Too much rain these days." He leaned back and folded his fingers over his belly. "You look good, yourself. Do something different with your hair?"

I draped my blonde streak over my shoulder. "Experimenting."

"It suits you." He moved a stack of papers. "Hey, I ever tell you the one about the priest and the Chihuahua?"

"Like, seven times."

"Okay, then." He chuckled. "What do you call a Mexican man with a rubber toe?"

I shook my head. "Roberto."

"Guess I need new material." Another laugh. "To what do I owe the honor?"

I crossed my legs and glanced at the bartender. "Could we speak privately?"

Sammy jutted his chin, and the bartender backed out of the room and shut the door.

I removed a smoke. Sammy leaned over the desk, lit my cigarette, and grabbed an ashtray from a drawer.

"I'm in a bind. I need something, and I need it fast."

Sammy stroked his chin. "I hope we're not talking about a piece."

The thought of getting a weapon had crossed my

mind, but I decided against it in case my place got raided. I inhaled, tapped my ash into the tray, and spoke through my exhale. "I need rope."

"Roofies?" I nodded. He steepled his fingers and put them under his chin. "I'm not asking why, but are you sure?"

I picked a piece of tobacco off my tongue. "I wouldn't have asked if it wasn't an emergency."

Sammy rubbed his jaw. Then he exhaled and opened a file cabinet. He slid hanging folders forward and reached his arm deep in the drawer. "Here." He placed a small bottle on the desk and pushed it my way. "Cut them and only use half. Trust me, you don't and they'll be sleeping through summer."

I stubbed out my cigarette and put the bottle in my purse, zipped it up. "Thanks. I owe you big time."

"Nah." He rolled a pen across his desk. "You've done plenty for me over the years."

"You're good people." I squeezed his hand and pushed back my chair. "Give my regards to Gwen."

At the door, he threw an arm over my shoulder. "Do you need protection?"

"I always carry condoms."

He stepped around and lifted my chin with his knuckle. "I'm serious."

I sighed. "I'm not at that point, but I'll let you know if that changes."

He kissed and patted my cheek. "You should come over for dinner. You're too thin. Lemme call Gwen. She always makes enough to feed an army."

I squeezed his arm. "Can't come now, but I will soon."

"I'll hold you to that."

I had a foot out the door when he caught my arm. "You need anything, you call. You hear?"

I blew him a kiss. "Loud and clear."

Chapter Thirty-Seven

Having Sammy's pills in my purse did not make me feel better. They'd do the job, all right, but the idea of hurting Finn weighed heavily on my heart.

Even Jeanine must've picked up my vibe, because she kept her nagging in check when she came in with my lattes and lunch.

I made it through the afternoon working on autopilot. I was reviewing the specs on a PR client, a has-been entertainer who'd gotten touchy-feely with a sixteen-year-old—who, he argued, looked twenty-two, but that was still no excuse—when my cell phone rang. It was Bobby, who had apparently misinterpreted my hopes of keeping things casual.

I answered the call with a strained smile. "Hey, how's it going?"

"Good. Just checking in," Bobby said.

I pushed my paperwork aside. "All's well. Just busy." I opened my desk drawer and searched for my rubber stress ball. While rummaging through papers and bills, I cut my finger on something sharp.

"Dammit." I retracted my finger. The sharp object was the card from the bouquet Finn sent the previous month.

"You sound distracted," Bobby said. "Is this a bad time?"

Yes. I slammed the drawer shut. "Sorry. I was in

the middle of something."

"No worries. I'll catch you later."

It wasn't hard to read the disappointment in his tone. In the biz, you needed resources, and sometimes keeping those resources meant using people. Men used my girls to satiate their carnal needs, and I used the johns to feed my payroll. I never intentionally set out to hurt innocent people, but it happened. Bobby was collateral damage.

I licked the cut in my finger crease. "I'll call you back when things quiet down."

"Anytime. I'm around."

After he hung up, I stared at Finn's boxed lavender rose on the credenza. The memory of the day the bouquet arrived and the nights that followed replayed in my head. There was no use delaying the inevitable. I swiveled my chair toward the window and called Finn's number.

He answered on the second ring. "Hello, Faith."

"Hi. Wait. How'd you—"

"I finally bought a new phone—a smartphone, thank you very much. See, I'm paying attention."

My laugh died in my throat. There was Finn, working hard to improve himself, and there I was, about to sabotage his career. He didn't deserve what lay ahead, but, like Bobby, he was collateral damage.

I walked over to the window and looked down at the street. "I was calling to invite you somewhere. If the weather cooperates, there's a place I'd like to take you. It's right up your alley."

"But not The Alley?

I chuckled. "No. Not there."

"No hints?" he said.

"Nope."

Paper rustled.

"Good news. I had a cancellation. Looks like Friday evening's open, if that works for you."

I fingered a vertical blind. "It works for me."

Part of me wished he'd declined. Part of me wished I'd just suffered my losses and filed for bankruptcy or run off to Brazil or somewhere it didn't rain all the time. If only I hadn't answered Drummond's call...

"What time should I pick you up?" Finn asked.

Having him chauffer me meant he'd have to return to my place after the surprise. If my charm couldn't get him upstairs, I'd have to do something stupid like pretend to sprain my ankle.

We arranged for him to pick me up after nine and he said he was excited to see me again. I told myself I wasn't a horrible human, that I had to protect others, and that it was all for some greater good.

Over by the credenza, I gazed at the boxed lavender rose. After a minute of staring, I moved the box down to the bottom drawer, beside Bobby's music box. Then I poured myself a drink and listened to the air filter hum and cars outside honking in traffic.

The *greater good*?

What was so great about all this?

Chapter Thirty-Eight

Friday morning it rained, but by the afternoon the clouds had dispersed, and the sky was clear, albeit gray. The place I was taking Finn that night was sure to be buggy, but it would appeal to his love of nature.

Despite my efforts, I couldn't get Finn out of my head all day. I thought about him while I smoked my first cigarette.

I thought about him while slipping on my thong, remembering the way his face paled when I demanded he retire his tighty-whities.

My ears perked when the barista at the coffeehouse called out someone's tea—in my defense, Jim sounds a lot like Finn.

And I couldn't help but feel a sting of jealousy when I saw the pictures in the paper's Style section.

Some people stare at car wrecks. Some people challenge themselves to eat hot peppers. Some people eat live bugs. People can't help themselves from doing things they know will hurt them. That had to be the reason why I couldn't stop ogling the disgustingly cute *couple* pictures of Finn and Sabrina.

Ugh. I crumpled the newspaper and tossed it into the trash. The gala was eight days away, and I had to accept the fact that Clara was right. Sabrina was on his level. Financially, socially, and probably morally. Hopefully she'd be there to help build back his life when all was said and done.

****

Rush hour was heavy, but I'd left the office early, hoping retail therapy would brighten my spirits.

I entered my apartment, carrying shopping bags, new lingerie, and a plethora of mixed emotions. Part of me was excited to spend time with Finn in a place that had meaning for me, part of me dreaded the pain I'd later inflict on my friend.

The air conditioning was running full blast in my apartment, and the windows were dripping with condensation outside. After unpacking my new hose and lace underwear set, I turned on the television to fill the oppressive quiet with background noise. Every cable news channel was a repeat. Election spin, who would win? I muted the TV.

In the bedroom, I checked my supplies. Fresh linens on the bed, scented candles on the bureau, condoms, lubricant, and adult toys in the nightstand drawer. The spy camera was hidden and aimed at my mattress. Everything was in place.

After my shower, I squirted a generous amount of perfume behind my wrists and ankles and realized I'd just invited every mosquito inside the Beltway to have me as their main course.

The dress I chose, a two-toned white-and-black form-fitted dress, hugged my curves like a racecar curling around a track. But did it make me look irresistible enough to get Finn up to my apartment and shuck his ideas of waiting for the right time or the right girl?

If it didn't—I shook Sammy's pill bottle—I had other options.

Finn picked me up at nine, looking dapper in his single-breasted crepe jacket with a lapel collar and welt pockets, a matching striped stretch-poplin cotton shirt, slim pants, and loafers, no socks.

Sitting beside him in the limo, I pointed to his bare ankles. "You're really breaking out of your comfort zone."

"All thanks to you."

He touched my hand, and my skin tingled and my insides went soft.

****

The driver let us off in front of Dumbarton Oaks, and Finn came around to open my door. Shouts, honks, and raucous activity trailed over from nearby Wisconsin Avenue. Friday nightlife was in full force.

Before we climbed stairs at the entrance to the park, Finn paused to read a sign. He craned his neck up toward the top of the hill and cupped his hand over his eyes as though blocking the sun. "Is it safe in there? It looks pretty dark."

"It's night; it's dark everywhere." I lifted my chin and sniffed. There was no scent from the rose garden, but the air smelled fresh and earthy.

A crack of thunder rolled in the distance, drowning out Finn's response. He took a step toward the limo, and I snagged his hand. "Where are you going?"

"To grab an umbrella."

I *tsked*. "Leave it."

He pointed to some low-lying clouds. "But it might rain."

"It's only water." I squeezed his hand.

He faced the stairs and exhaled. "Nothing to worry about. Trusting the process."

"That's it." Good thing he hadn't realized the park had closed hours earlier.

I'd walked in heels my entire adult life, but Finn insisted on taking my arm as he led me up the steps. He didn't release my arm at the top, and I didn't complain, because his skin smelled good and his chivalry was endearing.

At the top of the hill, Finn consulted the park legend. He had no idea where I planned on taking him, but I kept quiet and let him think he was in control.

Visiting the gardens each spring was a ritual. I loved to go when the air was fresh and I needed a break from the insanity of work. The hidden gem was situated in the heart of the city, near the cemetery, a few blocks off Wisconsin Avenue, Georgetown's main artery. Deep inside the park, however, one felt as though they'd stepped back in time.

On weekends, the park was usually overrun with tourists and screaming children, but on weekdays usually only a handful of locals came.

Those days, I used to listen to music and get temporarily lost in the wooded trails. Chipmunks would peek from behind tree trunks and cross the trail as though they were trying to lure me into a game of hide-and-seek. Eventually, I'd find my way to my destination: the coveted rose garden, and there I'd lie on my jacket or a light blanket and inhale the floral perfume.

Dumbarton's garden had an abundance of colored roses to gaze at. Over time, I familiarized myself with the varieties of the Rosaceae family; some I was able to identify by their scent. The dreadful dark reds were most pungent, the English roses smelled fruity. Hybrids smelled musky, the whites and yellows reminded me of clover. Grouped together, the scent could be overwhelming, and sometimes I'd gather my things and walk away to give my sensitive nostrils a break. Then I'd return for another dose and continue the routine until the stars filled the sky and my skin turned cold.

Finn and I continued along a path. A squirrel scampered in front us and Finn paused and signaled me to be still. The woodland critter shook its bushy tail, and Finn leaned down and slowly outstretched his hand. Then he made a strange clucking sound. The animal and I both stared at Finn for a moment. I broke out in laughter, and the squirrel took off in the opposite direction and scampered up a tree.

"It's good that you chose political science over veterinary school," I teased.

Finn straightened and brushed off his pants. "Sometimes it works."

"Aren't you afraid they'll bite?" I scrunched my nose. "And don't squirrels carry rabies?"

"That's an urban legend. Squirrels aren't carriers of rabies, they can get rabies, but they don't carry it." He paused and waited as though looking to see if I was impressed with that factoid.

I stared him square in the eye. "Stick with politics."

We continued up the path. Our conversation fell into an easy rhythm, and soon I picked up the scents of myrrh, honey, wine, and tea.

As the path turned to cobblestones, I slowed my pace. Flat surfaces were easy to maneuver in heels, but lumpy bricks were proving to be more challenging than I'd imagined. Moments after this thought hit my brain, my heel dipped into a crack and I lost my balance and stumbled.

Finn tightened his grip on my elbow. "Careful."

I squeezed his hand, then immediately relaxed my grip. His kindness was softening my hard shell, and I needed to stay focused. "I've done this a hundred times," I said. Just not in stilettoes.

He knocked his fist against his forehead. "I'm totally pro-feminism, but old habits die hard."

I laughed but there was another crack in my shell.

****

The garden was deserted, sodden and buggy, but the floral scent was intoxicating, a syrupy perfume mingled with pine from the surrounding woods. We meandered around and headed to a park bench.

Finn checked the seat and frowned. "It's damp."

"Clothes dry." I was lowering myself on the bench but he quickly pulled me up.

"Hang on." He stepped around me and wiped the bench seat with his hand. Then he laid his jacket down. "I don't want you to ruin your dress."

"You're awfully," I caught myself from saying sweet, "chivalrous."

"Yet pro-feminism, don't forget." He sat beside me, folded his hands in his lap, and looked around. "Nice job finding this place."

"It sorta found me." I stared at the sky, remembering the first time I'd visited the park.

It was the night I'd gotten picked up by a guy outside the seedy strip joint in Glover Park, at the top of Wisconsin Avenue. The guy took me back to his car and a short drive later, we were parked on a side street, outside the entrance to Dumbarton Oaks. My senses tingled. Something was off and I was right. The creep demanded I give him a blow job then and there, and when I refused, things turned ugly. I tried to escape the car but the guy caught my arm. I slugged him with my purse and clambered out of the vehicle. Up the stairs I went and into the park, and soon the sounds of Wisconsin Avenue and the lazy ass drunk's cussing were far, far behind me. Eventually, I stumbled upon the rose garden, and it took my breath away. That night I realized that from ugliness, something beautiful could be discovered.

Finn sneezed and the memory faded.

I looked up at the sky and pointed at the twinkling lights. "You ever wish on a star?"

"When I was younger. And hoping to get a girlfriend."

"Like that girl you went to college with?"

"Yeah." He chuckled.

My eyelid twitched as I remembered Clara's comment. *She's the right kind.*

I sniffed. "You're taking her to the gala?"

He responded with a nod.

I leaned forward and swung out my feet. "She must be pretty special."

Finn was silent for a moment then twisted to face me. "Sabrina and I have known each other since childhood, but I don't think she noticed I was alive." He fiddled his thumbs. "Now she seems interested, but she doesn't love me."

I dug my heels in the dirt. "Are you sure?"

He shrugged. "Relatively."

I tugged my left earlobe. "But you have feelings for her?"

His knee bobbed up and down. "Sabrina's

very…driven."

I pressed my palm over his bobbing knee. "Is that bad? You're passionate about the things you like. Birds, flowers, gemstones. At the gem show your face lit up when you explained how a lapidary analyzes a crystal's angles then cuts and polishes until facts appear and light shines through."

He chuckled. "I think you mean facets."

"Right. Those things. Anyway, pardon the *cliché*, but you're like a diamond in the rough, and I was the lapidary that polished off the dull parts to help you shine."

Finn regarded me with a thoughtful look. The wind blew a fresh gust, shivering a pile of green leaves, and I caught an earthy smell. The mosquitoes were out and were hovering around our arms. Finn swatted one away from his hand, but it returned a second later.

He slapped and scratched his arm. "Hungry little buggers." He scratched another spot. "They really like me."

I coiled a piece of hair around my finger. "They have good taste."

A bashful grin spread over his face.

We were silent for a while. As I listened to the sounds of nature, I imagined an alternate life with Finn. Hiking in Great Falls, biking in Rock Creek Park, Finn bird-watching in Woodside Gardens, us, sitting on the balcony, trading sections of the Weekend section on our apartment's balcony….

He slid closer to me. I steadied myself for one of his awkward hugs, handholding, whatever he'd offer. When his head was inches from mine, I realized he was building up the nerve to kiss me.

Yes. Finally. Do it.

I closed my eyes and parted my lips. And waited. And waited.

The moment was interrupted when a fire engine's siren rang. Simultaneously, Finn and I turned our faces toward the direction of the path.

So much for a moment.

Finn swatted a bug away from his ear. "Mind if we get out of here?"

We were insect bait, under attack, so I understood his desire to leave, but I didn't want to lose the momentum we'd built.

"We could go back to my place." I waved an insect away. "I promise, no mosquitoes there."

I thought I'd earned at least a chuckle but seconds passed with no response from Finn. I looked away, feeling foolish and dejected, and then I felt his hand on my elbow.

"There's something I should say."

Finn looked to the side as though he was struggling with the right words to offer. I prepared myself for rejection or another excuse, but he surprised me by saying, "I don't want this to end—not your work with me or the other stuff. This—us—our friendship. Sorry." He chuckled. "I'm not good at this." He cleared his throat. "What I'm trying to say is, I'd love to come to your place for a drink."

He regarded me with open fondness, twisting around the feelings in my head.

"I was hoping that would make you happy," he said.

"It did—does." Dammit. Winning felt like losing. I'd accomplished what I'd wanted and suddenly I wanted nothing less. I took a breath to regroup. "Let's get out of here."

Hand in hand, we headed back to the entrance.

Chapter Thirty-Nine

After weeks of plotting and planning, Plan D or E or whatever the heck I was calling my *Ruin A Decent Guy Scheme* was running smoothly and I couldn't hate myself more.

As we climbed into the limousine, I promised myself I'd enjoy our last night together, or at least make our time memorable.

During the ride, Finn regaled me with stories from his youth. He told me about the treks he and his grandmother made to remote locations and how she'd given him a rare variety of tourmaline called Liddicoatite, named after its founder, Richard T. Liddicoat, the former president of her Alma Matter, the Gemological Institute of America.

I slapped my palm on the seat cushion. "I remember G.I.A. You visited their booth at the gem show."

"You really do pay attention to details." Finn reached inside his blazer and removed something from an inside pocket. It was dark inside the vehicle, but when he opened his hand, I saw the pebble he'd taken the night we'd crossed the bridge.

Not to be outmatched, I withdrew a small velvet pouch from my purse, untied the string, held up my matching pebble. "I kept mine, too."

Penguins.

Dana Ross

****

After a brief tour of the apartment, I led Finn to the living room. The area had a tropical breezy scent from my unlit candles.

I slid open the drapes. "Make yourself at home. I'll put on some music."

Finn headed to the dining room and stared out the window. While he was preoccupied, I lit the faux fireplace and turned on the stereo.

"The artist did an impressive job," he called out. "My grandmother used to dabble in *trompe l'oeil*."

I looked over my shoulder. Finn was standing in front of my wall mural.

"Oh, that. Sometimes I forget it's there. My decorator commissioned some local artist and the thing cost me a bloody fortune."

I dug out my Van Morrison CD, hoping Finn would recognize the song we danced to at The Alley.

"It could be Paris," Finn said.

After the music came on, I joined Finn in the dining room. Arms crossed, I scrutinized the scene. It depicted old buildings, a river, painters with easels on a sidewalk. "Huh." I rubbed my jaw. "How did I miss that?"

Finn pointed to a patch of gold leaf. "Trompe l'oeil means to deceive the eye. Forced perspective."

Forced perspective. I took a small step back. Exactly.

We hung out by the dining room picture window for a while, and there, I pointed out visible landmarks. In the living room, Finn inspected a few knick-knacks, including a frame that still had the picture of the model family it came with. I sat on the couch and invited him to join me.

He settled down and perused a few conversation books on the coffee table. While he leafed through an architectural design book, I bent over to set coasters on the coffee table and while my back was turned, I inched down my dress's front zipper, just enough to pique interest. When I turned back toward Finn, his gaze dipped to my cleavage then quickly back up.

"Ready for that drink?" I kept my voice casual, as if I wasn't about to destroy his world.

He tugged his collar. "Absolutely."

"Be right back." I sashayed my hips on my way to the bar.

At the counter, I popped the cork off a new Bordeaux and waved my hand over the bottle's mouth. Younger reds usually needed an hour to aerate, but I was working on a tight time schedule. From what I'd read on the Internet, roofies needed about a half hour to kick in. It was getting late and Finn wasn't a night owl, so I needed to get the drug inside him before he tried to leave.

After collecting two clean wine goblets, I filled both halfway and dug the pill bottle from my pocket.

Finn said something about the weather, and I threw back a few "mm-hmms" as I forced the cap off the bottle. The *pop* sounded too loud for my liking, and I tensed, but Finn was still talking, so I dropped half a pill into his drink and stirred it with a plastic twizzler. Once it looked like the pill had dissolved, I returned to the couch.

Finn moved a throw pillow to the side. "Your place is quite roomy."

"Thanks. It works." I set the goblets on the

coasters. The glass with the gold charm was his. Or was it mine? Shoot. A moment of panic erupted then quieted. His was the one with the charm.

Finn stretched his arm over the couch's backrest. "I recognize this song. It was our first dance."

I toyed with my blonde streak. "Really?" Like I didn't know that.

While Finn tapped his foot, keeping the beat of song, I leaned over and picked up his wine. Panic-scrambled thoughts plagued my brain. Was the drug fully dissolved? What if it tasted funny? What if I hadn't used enough?

I glanced at Finn. His eyes were closed but his foot was still tapping. He was enveloped in the song.

My pulse thumped in my ears. It wasn't too late to stop. I could accidentally spill his wine. I could call Drummond and strike another deal, try to reason with him. I could….

Who was I kidding? There was nothing that would satisfy Drummond except Finn's career on a plate. I stared at his glass. Ultimately, this might help Finn. From what I'd deduced, politics wasn't his passion, it was his parents' plan. Maybe this was the catalyst to Finn's freedom.

I handed Finn his goblet then lifted mine. "A toast. To your future."

He tapped my glass. "To all your hard work."

I held my breath as he took his first sip.

"Mmm. Very nice." He took another swallow.

I sipped my wine and waited.

And waited.

And waited.

Time rolled on, and the honks of traffic quieted. In

the background, Tori Amos, a local Maryland vocalist, sang a song about leather, and air from the vent rustled the curtains.

While the stereo ran through my favorite songs, I tried to engage Finn in small talk. He looked relaxed and a tad sleepy, but it was hard to tell if the drug was working.

I refilled Finn's wine. "Back in the park, when we were talking about Sabrina, you mentioned something about her being driven."

He yawned into his fist. "I did?"

"Yes." I handed him his glass. "And I asked if it was a bad thing."

"Right." He paused for another yawn, and his eyelids drooped. He scrubbed a hand over his face and set his glass on the table. "Sorry. What was I saying?"

I crossed my legs and ran my finger around the rim of my wine glass. "We were talking about Sabrina."

"Sabrina." He said her name slowly, over-enunciating the syllables. "She's nice, but she's obsessed with power."

"A lot of people are." I uncrossed my legs and sat straighter. "Society has double standards. Strong independent women are viewed as bitches, while strong men are admired for the same qualities."

He rubbed his temple. "You're right, but…" He didn't finish his sentence.

Had the drug kicked in? I wasn't convinced.

I set my glass down and scooted closer to Finn. "May I ask a personal question?"

He squinted and rubbed his eyes. "Aren't all your questions personal?"

"Only the good ones." I glanced at his left hand.

"Do you want to get married someday?"

"Married." The word came out, slow and thick, as though he was struggling to stay awake. His chin did a bob, but he caught himself by snapping up his head and shaking it. Then he reclined against the couch cushion and spoke while staring at the ceiling.

"My parents' greatest fear is that I'll be a bachelor for life. They think a good woman will help my career." He snorted. "Like I care about that." He made an attempt to lean forward but fell back. "I've told them I'm waiting for the right person, but in their eyes every minute I'm unattached, I've failed." He twisted to face me. "My father had affairs for as long as I can remember." He winced as though the confession brought great pain. "My mother knew about the other women, but she played along and remained by his side. It hurt to see her do that, how she looked away and pretended not to notice." He slowly shook his head. "I vowed I'd never be like them. If I'm going to share my life with someone, it has to be someone who loves me for who I am." He pushed himself forward with his elbow. "I know what people say about me—the jokes that I'm naïve or gay—but so be it. Love shouldn't be rushed, it just happens. You know when you have a connection with someone. Even if…." He paused.

I waited a polite moment. "Even if?"

He fell back and closed his eyes.

"Finn?" I touched his shoulder.

He opened his eyes and blinked. "Yes?"

"You were saying?"

He rubbed his forehead with his fist. "Sorry. Forgot."

I touched his knee. "May I speak freely?"

He motioned me on.

I raked my nails back and forth across my collarbone. "I'm sure your parents have your best interests at heart, but if it's not what you want, then it's wrong. This is your life. If politics or marriage isn't for you, you have to speak up." I leaned over and squeezed his hand for emphasis. "Before it's too late."

He ballooned his cheeks and exhaled. "It's not that simple."

I grabbed his other hand. "Just tell them the truth. Trust me, lies have a way of eventually coming out."

"I'm not as brave as you."

"You're one of the bravest people I know. The problem is you don't know what you're capable of."

He glanced at his watch. "I probably should be going."

I released his hand. "I didn't mean to upset you."

"You didn't, I just have to…" His words were slurred and when he tried to get to his feet, he lost his balance.

"Easy, cowboy." I helped him settle back onto the couch. "Sit still. You look a little pale." It was true. His face was whiter than my rug.

He rubbed the back of his neck. "I feel…I'm…is it warm in here?"

"It's probably the fireplace heat. Here." I removed his shoes and tie, unbuttoned the top buttons on his shirt. "I'll get you some water."

I was on my feet when he grabbed my wrist. "Don't."

"No water?"

"Don't leave." His eyes were half-open, and again I found myself wanting to scrap the plan and tell

341

Drummond to go jump off Key Bridge.

I sat and stroked his hand with my thumb. "I'm right here."

"You're so good to me." He relaxed against the cushion and closed his eyes. "That's why I love you."

My spine stiffened, and all the air seemed to escape my lungs.

He what?

Finn loves me?

I gently shook his shoulder. "Hey."

No response.

I laid my ear on his chest. He was breathing, but his breaths were shallow. His complexion was still pale, but he had a serene expression. Not knowing he was drugged, one would think he was experiencing a happy dream.

I stood to get him water from the kitchen, but before I moved away from the couch, Finn locked his grip on my wrist. "Stay with me."

I sat, and he reached over and cupped my cheek. I felt the outline of his college ring on my skin. I saw his mole, the faint stubble of a five o'clock shadow. I laid my hand on his knee and felt the stiffness of the fabric of his new pants.

Finn ran a finger along my jaw then pushed back my hair and parted his lips.

Maybe his inhibitions were lowered because of the drug, but maybe it was real. I wanted it to be real. I wanted him. More than anything, I wanted his kisses.

Finn ran his fingers through my hair. His fingers tangled in my ends, and I felt his breath on my cheek. There were smells of wine and cologne, perfume, and the outdoors. His smell, mine, ours.

I tilted my head to encourage him to come closer.

He gripped my shoulders, and his mouth mashed against mine.

It was a high-school style kiss, tentative and unsure, but I felt the flutter of butterfly wings in my chest. I pushed my tongue inside his mouth, felt his muscles stiffen, then relax.

He stroked my arm, up and down, apparently too afraid to go past my shoulder, or, heaven forbid, my breast. His fingers pressed firmly into my skin, then released.

I pulled him on top of me, felt his weight siphon my breath. I arched my back and lifted my hips. His hipbone dug into my upper thigh.

"I waited for you." His breathing quickened then slowed. Quiet breaths, then silence. He collapsed onto my chest. No movement, and the end of his sentence never came.

"Finn?" I nudged his shoulder.

His head lolled to the side.

"You awake?"

He sucked in a breath but didn't respond.

I rolled him over and snapped my fingers in front of his face. Out cold.

It was time to act, but my feet didn't comply.

In sleep, the worry lines that shadowed his expression were gone.

I glanced at the hallway.

Get the camera. Move. There wasn't a lot of time.

I looked back at Finn. The pretty lines of his lips were curled upward as though he was in on a good secret. He looked so comfortable, I wanted to lay my head on his chest and cuddle beside him, listen to the music, and just be, but time was of the essence, and I wasn't sure how long the drug would keep him knocked out.

I glanced at the hallway.

Get up, take the pictures, and be done with it. He doesn't care about politics. You're helping him do what he can't do himself.

I stroked Finn's cheek. His mole was kind of cute.

Stop that. Think of the girls. Drummond threatened them. Now move.

I carefully removed myself from the couch.

In the bedroom, I grabbed the spy camera, retrieved my whip and handcuffs from the nightstand drawer, and brought everything back to the living room. If Finn woke while I was removing his clothes, I'd tell him he felt feverish and I was trying to make him comfortable. He'd believe me, because I'd earned his trust.

False perspective.

Finn didn't wake when I removed his pants. He didn't stir when I unbuttoned his shirt. He didn't blink or twitch or move a muscle as I put his clothes on the floor. I looked to the side while I pulled down his boxer briefs, one from the set I'd chosen the day we shopped together.

I exhaled and chewed my thumbnail. *You're wicked, just like Father said.*

My lip trembled. *Keep moving. Don't stop now, time's running out.*

Still looking away, I covered Finn with the throw blanket. Then I undressed, slipped onto the couch, and nestled against the warmth of his body. Poor Finn still had a serene look on his face.

I stroked his neck and slid my finger through the soft curls on his chest. When I touched his nipple, his skin puckered, but he didn't stir. The faux flames danced and a new CD was playing, but I blocked out the distractions and focused on what had to be done.

I leaned closer and stared at his mouth. His lips were dark red, the color of summer cherries. My chest felt heavy as I watched him sleep.

"I'm sorry," I whispered. "So incredibly sorry."

His lips parted as he exhaled. I held my breath expecting him to wake, but his eyes remained closed.

Do it. Do it now.

I moved the blanket, grabbed the spy camera, and slid the whip into his right hand. I snapped a cuff onto my wrist and positioned myself on top of him. After taking a series of photos I hoped would be juicy enough to appease the paparazzi, I grabbed Finn's clothes and dressed him in silence. The photos I'd taken didn't show my face, so I was safe, but knowing Finn would suffer and I'd be okay only made me feel worse.

I looked away to give him privacy as I slid his underwear back on. Once the briefs were in place and his pants zipped, I looked down and sighed.

It would've been nice to have been his first.

Outside on the balcony, I chain-smoked two stale cigarettes. My throat tingled from the menthol burn, and the city sounds bothered my ears. Salty tears ran down the side of my face, and wind chafe stung my cheeks. I felt cold and dirty, like there was no proper place to be, but I remained on the deck, alone with my thoughts and the guilt I deserved.

That night I ran from the guy and found Dumbarton Oaks, I'd turned something ugly into

something beautiful.
This night, I'd done the opposite.

Chapter Forty

When Finn came around hours later, he was groggy and disoriented, but didn't seem to remember anything that had transpired on the couch. I kept our conversation light so I wouldn't jostle his memory and gave him crackers and sodium bicarbonate to quell his nausea.

At the door, I asked Finn to text me when he got home.

An hour passed, and I still hadn't heard from him. Slightly panicked, I texted to ask if he was okay.

He texted he was fine.

****

Saturday afternoon, I telephoned Drummond, but my call went directly to voice mail. The answering service at his office informed me that the senator had been called out of the country and he wasn't returning until the end of the week.

I texted two words to Drummond—*mission complete*.

Later, he texted back and told me to sit tight.

****

Sunday passed with no additional word from Finn. I tried not to ruminate over the fact that he might have recollected something—something I wouldn't be able to explain, and rationalized he was a busy man with deadlines. I ordered Chinese take-out, left it cold and untouched on the coffee table, watched black-and-white movies, and numbed myself with wine.

Alcohol wasn't enough to mask the pain.

In the kitchen, I retrieved my salvia stash from the vegetable crisper then sat on my living room floor and filled my swirly glass pipe with the weed. It was legal. Legalish. In certain states, anyway.

The effects hit me while I was combing the fringe on the carpet with my fingers. My legs felt heavy, like they were sinking into the floor, but my torso felt weightless, like it was detaching from my waist. Rainbow colors flashed before my eyes, and when I looked up at the TV, I saw a cartoon version of myself, dancing, spinning, frolicking in a field of red poppies.

Still seated on the carpet, I stretched out my hands to touch the cartoon version of me on TV. Black flames appeared on the screen. The cartoon version of my face melted, and my imagined utopia vanished as a voice in my head told me I deserved to burn.

A chime pinged on my cell.

The drug wore off and I snapped back to reality and stared at my sterile white furnishings. After brushing carpet fibers off my fingers, I read the displayed message reminder on my phone.

The gala was one week away.

****

Except for a hangover headache, by Monday, I was starting to feel like myself—until I read the paper. It was beneath me—beneath the old Faith, to read a gossip column, but the second I saw the picture I scanned every word. The article featured a picture of Finn and Sabrina hobnobbing at some charity gig, and the columnist seemingly took great pleasure in informing Washington's female population, that, *sorry, gals, The Beltway's most eligible bachelor might be off the market.*

The press sometimes manipulated people to think what they wanted you to think, not necessarily the truth, and I knew Finn wasn't in love with the Ice Queen, but seeing her twiglike arms wrapped around Finn's waist made my blood boil.

I gripped the paper tight, like a racecar driver gripping a wheel. Sabrina wouldn't care that Finn's virginity was sacred to him. I doubted she'd be sensitive. I would've. I'd been trained in those areas. I would've appreciated his gift.

You also drugged him, lied to him, and were about to ruin him.

I balled up the paper and tossed it in the trash.

****

My mood hadn't improved by Tuesday, probably because it was four days before the ball and, ugh, my thirtieth birthday. The fact that both events fell on the day I'd ruin someone special to me didn't help alleviate my foul mood.

Father never allowed us to celebrate birthdays. He believed the only one worth recognizing was the Lord's, but that didn't make sense to a child, or a tween, or a teen, especially when her classmates would talk about all the fun parties they attended. I wasn't allowed to attend parties or give gifts—not that we had money for them, anyway.

By the time I was in my twenties I was accustomed to forgoing celebrations. Another year, another rotation around the sun. So what?

But this year, I'd be attending an event with my ex-boyfriend, making kissy faces to bitches and bifocaled bores. Even worse, Finn would be accompanied by the Ice Queen.

The incriminating pictures I took were hidden in a password-protected folder on my computer, and I was debating when and how to send them to Drummond, but his absence gave me a few days to think it through. Unfortunately, time was running out and decisions had to be made.

****

Tuesday afternoon, I was perusing an article on rare color-change cat's-eye Alexandrite chrysoberyls—shoes had taken a backseat to my newest distraction: rocks and minerals—when Jeanine rang me on the intercom.

I ignored the flashing telephone light and continued reading. A new vein had been discovered in Brazil. I visualized Finn in the hot, humid climate, a construction hat with a light, a pick in his gloved hand, and a smile stretched ear-to-ear. I copied the article to save for him then immediately deleted it. What was I thinking? After the gala, Finn would never talk to me again.

The intercom buzzed for the second time. "Pick up, I know you're there."

Gaze glued to my computer, I reached over the desk and hit a button. "Can't talk. Busy."

"No, you're not," Jeanine said.

For the love of Pete.

I punched the intercom button with my pen. "What do you need?"

"Geez," she said. "I was going to show you some dress pictures for the gala, but never mind. Go naked for all I care."

I knocked my pen against my forehead. It wasn't fair for me to take my frustration out on Jeanine. She was only trying to help, after all.

I rang her back and apologized. "Bring in the dress pictures—and a latte, when you have time."

"I'll add extra sweetener. Clearly, you need it."

The intercom light went dark.

Ten minutes later, Jeanine came into my office, straining to balance coffee, papers, and a hefty binder.

I cleared some desk space and leaned back as she set down my coffee and a muffin with a granulated sugary crown. After stirring sweetener into my drink, Jeanine slid the mug toward me and took a seat.

The coffee was so sweet I thought I'd get a cavity drinking it, but I smiled wide and gave my assistant a thumbs-up.

She scratched her chin. "Something's off. You haven't complained about my nail polish once this week and you missed your massage appointment."

I glanced at her bright yellow nails. She was right. I *was* off. "Change those."

"Too late. Anyway, let's review the afternoon messages." She removed a pad from her pocket and cleared her throat. "In order of importance, Tony—that's twice today—one prospect—yes, he checked out—the sheik—twice—and, lastly, Alexander Clough from *The Post*, who said he was doing a follow-up article and wanted a few minutes of your time." She tore the messages off her pink pad and handed them to me. "Want me to blow off the sheik or the reporter?"

I scanned the pink papers and then folded them in half. "I'll handle them."

"Suit yourself." She plucked a pen out of her hair dome and used the pen to push the muffin closer to me. "Eat. All of it. No excuses this time."

I tore off a piece of the crown and crunched the sugary topping between my teeth. "Happy?"

She sucked her teeth. "It's a start."

The office filled with sounds of people talking in the reception area.

Jeanine glanced at the door and spoke when the voices silenced. "Now the dress." She tapped the binder with a bright yellow nail. "We're out of time. You need to pick something—anything." She pressed her palms together in supplication.

The idea of attending the event with my ex and seeing Finn with Sabrina was about as enticing as standing in line at the DMV on a Monday, but there was no backing out. I had to make an appearance, if only to make sure Finn would be okay.

I took a sip of sweet coffee, winced, and set it down. "I'll find something."

Jeanine regarded me with a suspicious eye. "Today?"

"Yes. Whatever. Now go." I waved her out.

A phone rang in the lobby, and Jeanine sprinted out the room. Bottles on my credenza rattled as Jeanine shut the door.

****

An hour passed, and my heart fluttered each time I heard my cell chirp, but Finn was still incommunicado. I shouldn't have expected to hear from him since our work was complete, but part of me worried he'd remember what had transpired on the couch. I still had the incriminating pictures, but I hadn't decided what to do with them. To distract myself, I focused on the latest expense report.

Most of our company's numbers were down due to the lull. Monique was in Pennsylvania, attending her first grad school residency, Chyna was on sick leave, and Shivawn had thrown out her back. Like the Roman Empire, mine was crumbling, too.

A text from Jeanine came through—*Pick a freaking dress!*

Before I fired back a snarky retort, I decided to check what she'd left first, thus arming myself with ammunition.

I cracked open the binder and flipped through the first pages. No. No. Dear Lord, was that polyester? I flipped a page, ready to heave the binder into the trash, when something intriguing caught my eye. Hold on. What was this? I unlocked the spring holder and removed a laminated page.

It was a scarlet gown in a lustrous material, something that looked like satin or dupioni silk. It had an off-the-shoulder swooped neckline, origami folded details, a formfitting silhouette with curve-contouring seams, and a mermaid skirt with a short train. It was vibrant and glamorous, something I, myself, would've chosen, had I taken the time to shop.

I grabbed the phone and hit the intercom. "Jeanine! Get your overpaid, annoying ass in here, stat."

The door flew open.

"What's wrong with you?" She lowered her headset and glared at me. "I had a prospect on the phone. A good one."

I ran over and threw my arm over her shoulder. "You did it."

She pushed me back and held me at arm's length. "Did what?" She lowered her cat-eye glasses and squinted to examine my eyes. "Are you high?"

"Not recently." I pointed to the binder. "You found the dress."

"Which one?" She followed me to my desk and looked at the laminated sheet. "I had a feeling you'd like that one."

"It's exactly what I wanted."

I love red. Red incites passion. Red was fire, flame, rubies, and sunsets. Even my satin sheets were red. In fact, the only time I hated the color was on roses.

I paced in front of my desk. "Is it still in stock? Can we get it in time? Do they have my size? I don't even know what my size is." I patted my stomach and heard it rumble. "I think I dropped a pound or two."

Jeanine pointed to my waist. "More like five." She reached into her pocket and pulled out a notepad along with a spooled tape measure. Unwinding the spool, she motioned for me to raise my arms.

"You just carry around a tape measure?" The woman had untold depths.

"Shh." She wagged a finger. "Let me work." After taking all my measurements—even the ones I doubted were necessary, like my ankle girth, she pocketed the tape measure. "I'll call the store and find out if it's in stock. Keep your fingers crossed."

My eyes brimmed with moisture. "Now I know why I keep you around."

She fanned her face with her hand. "Like anyone else would put up with you?"

****

Later that evening, I was packing up my

belongings, hoping to leave early, when my cell phone vibrated on the desk. I was about to send the call to voicemail, but when I realized the caller was Finn, I answered with a breathless, "Hello."

"Hi. It's—oops." He chuckled. "I forgot you have caller ID."

I leaned back in my chair, comforted by the familiar sound of his voice. "Hi. Wow. How are you?" *Are you getting laid by the Ice Queen* is what I really wanted to ask.

"Doing well. It's been insane here. Three-and-a-half days until the official announcement."

"That's right." I swiveled my chair and glanced at the credenza's drawer that held his boxed flower. "You must be over the moon."

"Excited, for sure. And nervous." He paused. "I'm sorry I haven't been in touch. The last time I saw you—did I...was I a gentleman?"

A bleak, wintery feeling washed over me. He didn't remember. I should've been relieved but all I felt was heavier guilt.

I palmed my chest. "You were a perfect gentleman." But I wasn't a perfect lady. "There's nothing for you to worry about." Another lie.

"That's a relief." He sniffed. "I wanted to thank you for everything you've done. People have noticed the changes. My secretary said she hardly recognizes me."

Did Sabrina notice? My foot shook beneath my desk. Part of me wanted to hang up and forget everything bad I'd done, and part of me wanted to talk to him for hours. Truth was, I missed him. His old-fashioned charm, the way he tried to impress me with obscure bird and gem facts, his effort to better himself. But Finn didn't belong to me. He belonged to Sabrina and soon, the general public.

I picked up a pen and rolled it between my fingers. "You worked hard for this. What does Sabrina think?"

"She's been receptive."

Did that mean she deflowered him? It wasn't my business but I had to know. "So, things are going well for you two?"

A brief pause. "I guess you could say that. She's been helping with the campaign."

I dug my nails into my palm. "So, she's interested in you?"

"I, ah—"

"I'm happy for you, Finn." I was. I still hated the Ice Queen, but I cared about him.

"Thank you, Faith. I hope I'll see you at the gala. I couldn't get through the night without you—you know, in case I use the wrong fork or step on Sabrina's foot on the dance floor or do something awkward."

My throat tightened as I imagined Finn and Sabrina together at the ball, him holding her waist like he held mine at the dance studio, her close beside him. Maybe he'd step on her feet.

I mentally reprimanded myself for the mean thought. "You'll be fine. I'm sure you know which forks to use, and don't worry about the dances—just remember what Barry said, 'make the square, one, two, three, pause,' and as far as the awkward stuff…" I swallowed hard, holding back tears as memories of our nights together and his cute idiosyncrasies hit me. "Just be yourself."

"You're a great mentor. I look forward to seeing

you."

"Wait." I pushed back my chair and stood. "There's something I need to tell you."

"Yes?"

If I warned him of what was to come, he could bow out or prepare his family. Either way, he'd hate me, but at least he'd salvage his dignity. Maybe Marshall could stop Drummond. Maybe—

"Are you there?" Finn asked.

If I intervened, Drummond would retaliate. He'd already threatened my girls and Jeanine, what would stop him from hurting Finn?

I exhaled and sat back down. "I just wanted to wish you luck."

"Thanks. I couldn't have done it without you."

After we hung up, I poured myself a glass of Marshall's cognac. The sweet liquor burned as it went down and stirred up feelings of melancholy. In a few days I'd lose both Marshall and Finn.

I glanced at my framed awards. My employees would be okay after the fallout. Most of them were young with good bodies and good resources. Jeanine would help them. She'd honor the code.

Glass in hand, I walked over to the window and stared out. Across the street, a bus pulled to the curb. Passengers came off, new ones boarded. A traffic light changed, and cars moved up the street at a sluggish pace.

People were rushing to and fro, probably heading home to loved ones. No one waited for me at home. There were no dinners to fret over, no children to attend to, no pets needing to be walked—nothing.

I sipped more cognac and gazed at the darkening

sky. In the grand scheme of the universe, none of us were relevant. We were stardust, time travelers, cosmic vacationers. Things that seemed urgent today wouldn't matter five, ten, or twenty years later. Things eventually worked out the way they needed to be. The only way you mattered was to the people who cared about you. We lived, we died, we were recycled back to earth, then to the stars. The world went on.

I craned my neck in the direction of my old apartment and pushed aside memories of Bobby and Bes. I'd moved on, moved up since then, but what did I have to show for my life? A failing business. A sterile apartment. Fantastic shoes.

What did I expect? I carried a black book with names and events written in code. I hid passwords, burned receipts, dyed my hair, and camouflaged aging with makeup. How could Finn or anyone else love me when my life was a cornucopia of secrets?

And no matter how hard one worked to keep something hidden, one way or another, the truth always came out.

Back at my desk, I stared at the two pink message slips, one from the reporter, one from the sheik. After a minute of careful deliberation, the decision was made. I made a call then printed out the pictures of my evening with Finn, stuffed the photos into a padded envelope, and twisted away from the credenza while I phoned a messenger service.

Twenty minutes later, the photos were out of my hands.

Chapter Forty-One

I've done some questionable things in my time—a sex tape, giving head to a groom at his own wedding reception, orgies—but all my transgressions had been done with consenting adults. No one had been coerced into doing something against their will. The moment I sent out the incriminating pictures of Finn, I'd hit an all-time low.

Every muscle in my body ached after I hung up from the messenger service. I rubbed the quartz pebble Finn gave me, somehow willing positive energy his way, and realized the futility of my actions. The damage was done. Nothing could erase what I'd set in motion. The only thing I could do was be there for him the night it went public.

I tucked the pebble back into its velvet carrying pouch and tied the drawstring.

Thud. Whirr. Thud.

Someone was running a vacuum outside my door. Everyone had left; only the cleaning crew remained. I took my cue to exit.

Before leaving, I poured another shot of Marshall's cognac. The caramel-colored liquid reminded me of a gem Finn had shown me at the gem and mineral show.

"See this?" He'd held up something that looked like plastic. "This is Baltic amber. Essentially it's fossilized resin—tree sap, if you will. But it's not just

any tree sap. It's forty-four million years old." He'd
squinted. "Let that sink in. Forty-four million years."

To me, the gem looked like a glorified button.

"Look inside." His eyes glinted as he waited for
me to comply.

"Whoa." My eyes widened. "Is that a bug?"

"Yes. That's what makes it valuable."

I glanced at the price tag. "You better put that
down. We breakey, we buy."

He handed the gem back to the vendor.

I set my unfinished cognac back on the credenza
and headed out the door.

****

A warm wind gust hit my face as I exited the
building. It was a balmy evening with a black sheet sky
lit by an eerie yellowish moon. The air held the sounds
of music and the scent of good foods, so I decided to
walk and clear the muck from my mind.

Far from my office building, the streets morphed
from polished, clean sidewalks to litter-strewn. Many of
the stores I huffed past had drawn metal awnings or
barred windows. I slowed outside a park, similar to the
one near my office where old men played chess, and
watched a beetle scuttle over a mound of broken glass.

A tantalizing smell of curry and grilled meat led
me to a convenience store with a blue-and-white
awning. An Argentinian flag hung in the window.

Inside the store, I bought a mini bottle of cabernet,
a package of menthols, a meat empanada with a shiny
egg glaze, and a package of *alfajores*, round dessert
sandwiches filled with *dulce de leche*, rolled in coconut
and powdered sugar.

Back on the street, I nibbled an *alfajor* and licked

shredded coconut off my lips. The dessert, though moist, was tasteless. I tried an empanada but it also held little enjoyment. I dumped the food into a trash receptacle outside a white-brick church.

The church's courtyard was deserted and the fence was unlocked. I meandered in, wondering why a place of worship required barriers. Father's church didn't have a fence, just a yellow lawn that always looked thirsty. A sign with matching brick announced upcoming events.

In front of the steps, I stared at a pair of wooden red doors and took a swallow of the convenience store wine and blanched as it slid down my throat.

Growing up, I'd never seen my father intoxicated. He drank from the chalice he shared with his worshipers on Sundays, which I assumed was filled with alcohol, but a kid in my bible study class told me it was grape juice.

I took another swig from the bottle. When I was young, I usually tuned out during Father's Sunday lectures. The sermons he preached bored me to tears and anything he shared with his sheep were things he'd already force-fed Mother and me at home. The only time he captured my attention was when he gripped the wood of his podium until his knuckles turned white and shook a clenched fist in the air. That was the signal something big was brewing.

The wind rustled the bag holding my wine. As I stared at the stained-glass windows, I remembered one of Father's sermons. It was a story based on a passage from Romans. Clear as day, I heard Father's voice in my head.

"Therefore, just as sin entered the world through

one man, and death through sin, and in this way death came to all people, because all sinned, consequently, just as one trespass resulted in condemnation for all people, so also one righteous act resulted in redemption."

His advice was directed to the heretics, the miscreants in his flock, whom I admired, for at least they were fallible.

Redemption played like a skipping record in my head.

My cell phone chirped, indicating a missed call, and an idea came to mind.

I checked the time. It wasn't too late. She was probably still at the office. Hags like us had nothing to hurry home to.

I scrolled through my cell's contact list and paused on B. She would do it. Not without giving me a hard time, of course, but eventually she'd come through. She'd take care of them, even Jeanine.

The hazy yellow moon loomed overhead, and the scent of lilacs drifted from a nearby shrub, reminding me of Finn's bouquet. I hit the number before I lost my nerve.

"Maryland Matchmakers," a familiar voice answered. "How may I help you?"

"Hi," I tried to say, but nothing came out. I swallowed and tried again. "It's Faith. We need to meet…" I glanced at the red wooden doors. "It's a matter of life and death."

Chapter Forty-Two

I arrived at the office early Wednesday morning, with the intent of getting in early to tie up loose ends and getting out, nothing more.

The lights were out, minus one at reception. No employees were in sight but I smelled brewed coffee, and I heard Jeanine singing. As I came to her desk, I stopped dead in my tracks.

She looked up, I looked down, and we gave each other questioning looks. Hers was probably due to the fact that I was in before the NYSE opened, but mine was a reaction to her outfit.

She was wearing a tan wrap dress with a gold link bracelet, small stud earrings, and a dark-brown scarf knotted at her neck. The pit bull pin was in its usual place. I was caught off-guard because her outfit was simple and subdued, but the thing that surprised me the most was her hair.

No beehive.

I pulled off my sunglasses and blinked twice. Jeanine's long locks were down, tied back in a ponytail. My eyes widened as I glanced at her hands.

Beige nails?

Beige!

"Are you okay?" we asked in unison.

I pointed at her hair, she pointed at my blouse.

"What happened?" she asked. "Did you dress in the

dark?"

I looked down. My buttons were misaligned and there was a white splotch below my collar that looked like baby puke, but had to be vanilla coffee creamer.

"I must've spilled some—never mind. Just fill 'er up when you can." I set my travel mug on her desk and turned toward my office.

"Hang on," Jeanine called. "Before you hibernate," she reached under her desk and came back up holding a large rectangular box, "look what arrived."

I took a step back and pointed at the box. "Is it—?"

She nodded.

"Can I—?"

"Of course you can. You must." She pushed the box toward me. "Let's go try it on." She followed me into my office.

The room smelled like cherry ashtray, and the air conditioner was rustling the venetian blinds like the act of ghost fingers.

Inside my bathroom, I stripped to my skivvies. By some miracle, the dress fit and felt good. Not itchy. Not too tight. Now to show Ms. Annoying Pants.

I exited the bathroom and made a grand gesture with one hand. "Ta-da."

Jeanine clasped her hands together. "Wow. That is—wow."

I lifted a heel and twisted my hips left then right. "It's better than I imagined."

"Thank goodness." She motioned for me to turn around. "We were cutting it close."

"You can say that again."

She opened her mouth but I silenced her with my hand.

After I disrobed, I handed her the dress which she carefully folded back into the box.

"It's perfect," she said. "You'll be the belle of the ball."

"Gala."

"You know what I mean."

My skirt zipped up with ease—it had been a tight squeeze in the past—then I checked my blouse buttons to be sure they were properly aligned. I stepped back into my shoes and sniffed the air. "No coffee?"

Jeanine straightened some papers on my desk. "You seem to be a tad wound up today. Maybe you should drink tea instead."

"Tea? I'd rather wear a chastity belt."

Jeanine laughed.

My joke died as I remembered Finn. I fired up my laptop while Jeanine turned on the air filter. "You haven't told me how much I owe you for the dress."

Instead of answering my question, Jeanine pointed at my waist. "I'm going to order you breakfast from the deli. You're skin and bones. Don't make excuses, I know you haven't been eating, not even your secret dessert stash."

My brows lifted. She knew about my secret stash?

As if reading my mind, she said, "Yes, I know all about that." She lifted her cat-eye glasses and squinted. "You look pale. Did you switch foundations?"

I palmed my cheek. "I'm not wearing makeup."

"That's it." She leaned over the desk and grabbed my phone. "I'm booking you an appointment at Spa Eleven."

I grabbed her wrist before she could dial. "Not today. There's too much to do."

She set the phone back in the cradle. "Why not? It's quiet. I can cover for you."

"I can't." She didn't understand. I didn't deserve pampering or a beautiful dress. The only thing I deserved was to be left alone with my guilty conscience. I opened my drawer to retrieve my checkbook. "Just tell me how much I owe you."

She pushed her glasses back in place. "I'm paying for it. It'll be your birthday present."

I lifted my Athena pendant. "You already gave me one."

"Yes, but this is your big three—"

"Don't you dare finish that sentence."

She touched her pit bull pin. "You've always done things for me. Let me do this for you."

I glanced at her pin. She wore it every day, but this time it stood out because it wasn't competing with swirls or polka dots or other garish patterns. Moisture welled behind my lids and a tickle wormed up my throat. "Thank you," I finally said. "The dress is incredible. You're a miracle worker."

"Yeah, yeah. I'm awesome." She threw down her hand and turned to leave, but I jumped to my feet and pulled her into a hug.

Her shoulders stiffened, probably from shock because I rarely did such things, but then she relaxed and squeezed me back.

My nostrils tingled as I inhaled her fruity perfume, and the outline of her pit-bull pin pressed against my shoulder. "It's true. I couldn't ask for a better friend."

"Oh, my God." Jeanine wiggled out of my arms. "Are you dying or something?"

"Not that I'm aware of." I rubbed my shoulder

where her pin had pressed into my skin. "Maybe the birthday's making me soft."

She studied my face for a long moment then pushed me back onto my chair. "Don't lift a finger until I get back. I'm making you a latte."

She shut the door and left the room, and I sat alone with my perfect gown, the running air filter, and a calendar with a circled date that reminded me I was three days away from losing everything good.

Chapter Forty-Three

Saturday, June fourteenth.
Finn's fundraiser.
Bobby.
My birthday.
The Big Three—ugh.

I stared at the red permanent marker circling the date on my refrigerator's calendar and squeezed my pen, the one I'd used to slash through the squares the past two months that led up to this day, this time, this…

The pen fell from my fingers and rolled across the kitchen floor.

My resolve to not get emotional had taken a serious hit. I grabbed the pen and rolled it between my palms. Birthdays were dumb, overinflated, exaggerated celebrations. You got gifts you'd never use, and frilly cards with pink hearts from people too busy to invite you over for a drink, and you were alone in the world with no family while turning…thirty. Three decades. Three-hundred-sixty months. Over fourteen-hundred weeks. How many minutes? I wasn't sure, but it was a lot.

I sat at the kitchen table and dumped a thimbleful of whiskey into my coffee. Late-morning sun streamed through the window, and outside, birds chirped and cawed to each other.

The sky was cloudless, but my mood was not as

bright as the sunshine. I'd awakened an hour earlier with hunger pains and a scorching headache.

The weight of a sleepless night made my brain feel like it dragged three paces behind my body. I nibbled the protein bar Jeanine forced me to take home and poured another shot of whiskey into my coffee. There was a saying that alcoholics drank before five, but it had to be five somewhere, and I sure as heck didn't want to go through my bir—the day—sober.

With my coffee in one hand, whiskey bottle in the other, I headed to the living room.

While clearing off the coffee table books to make room for the cup and bottle, I saw a pamphlet I'd taken from the gem show. The brochure pictured the Hope Diamond, a forty-five carat dark-blue, cushion-cut beast that had once belonged to the owner of the Washington Post. Rumor said the owner let her dog wear the diamond necklace during parties and some believed the stone was cursed. I'd kept the pamphlet, thinking it would be fun to take Finn to see the stone at the Smithsonian.

A tight feeling tickled my throat. After the gala, he wouldn't want to visit museum treasures with me; he'd want to have me stuffed and mounted.

I pushed aside my mug and chugged whiskey straight from the bottle.

****

A sparrow's chirp outside my living room window woke me sometime later. I'd fallen asleep with my arm cradling the whiskey bottle and the throw blanket tangled around my legs. My cell was on the carpet beneath the coffee table. I'd missed two calls from Bobby.

I rubbed my temple and groaned. The night would be bad enough, and on top of everything, I had to spend it with my ex. It had seemed like a good idea two months ago, but so had Drummond's offer.

I fingered my Athena pendant. Drummond had won the last round, but I wasn't going down without a fight. Angela had taught me the story of the boxer and underestimating the underdog for a reason. If I was going down, I'd go out fighting.

After a hot shower and two cups of coffee, doctored with cream and sugar, not booze, I called Bobby. When he answered, I heard an engine humming in the background. "Please tell me you're not working with something greasy."

"Okay." He laughed. "I won't tell you."

I rubbed my temple. "At least promise me you won't smell like a parking garage."

"Isn't the fact that I'm wearing a monkey suit good enough?"

"I suppose." I paced the kitchen. "How does the tux feel?"

"Like a bag of cement."

My turn to laugh. "Well, I owe you one."

"You don't owe me anything. As long as they have free alcohol, I'm good."

"I guarantee they will."

Bobby had apparently forgotten it was my birthday. It was interesting, though, that he could recall the play of every Redskins game in the past fifteen years, but anniversaries and birthdays slipped his mind.

I exited the kitchen and headed into the bathroom. "Just promise me clean nails."

"You got it."

I opened a drawer and searched my lipstick collection for the perfect shade of red. "The limo will be here at nine."

"Doesn't the event start at that time?"

I painted my lips and blotted them with a tissue. "A diva never arrives on time."

"*Dios mío*." He groaned. "What have I gotten myself into?"

"Free booze and a date with a hottie."

Bobby chuckled. "See you at nine, Cinderella."

I practiced blowing a kiss in the mirror. "Nineish."

Chapter Forty-Four

With Bobby's arm linked through mine, I gathered the side of my dress train and descended the steps that led to the main floor of the Grand Ballroom at the Marquis Hotel.

Down on the floor, we moved to the side of the stairs and watched people fill the room. The place oozed with opulence. There were ladies in elegant gowns with statement jewels bespeckling their ears and throats, and men in formal wear, a vast sea of black and white. The smell of a thousand perfumes besieged my nostrils, and my ears vibrated from the sound of music, laughter, and rambling tongues. After a search, I caught a few recognizable faces along with others I couldn't place, but I was sure their last names were attached to fat bankrolls.

Bobby adjusted his bow tie and turned to face me. "You ready?"

I glanced at a dark patch beneath his nail bed and sighed. "As I'll ever be."

He tilted his head to one side then the other. *Crick, crack.*

Oh, no. He was doing neck cracks, which indicated a sure sign of nerves. I smiled and spoke through clenched teeth. "You're doing *the thing*."

"I can't help it." He winced. "These kinds of places make me uncomfortable."

"Just try to relax." I patted his arm. "Remember, they eat, sleep, and pee just like us."

Bobby pointed up to the second level. "The men's room upstairs had a bidet, so they don't pee just like us."

I laughed and scanned the main floor, hoping to find Finn. My breath caught as I took in more of the surroundings.

There were gilded mirrors, windows flanked with heavy drapes, and milky wallpaper with an iridescent sheen. There were fishermen's netting gathered with grosgrain ribbon, flower garlands, and balloon arches placed throughout. The tables had centerpieces made from long-stemmed hydrangea, and candles floated in water glasses. Tiered chandeliers and twinkle lights lit the hall. Covered round tables were surrounded by high-backed chairs that looked like giant pretzel sticks.

The catering staff circulated with trays of *hors d'oeuvres* and flutes of bubbly in gold-stemmed glasses. I followed a waiter's path with my gaze and zeroed in on my first point of attack—the bar area. The long line that snaked from the makeshift counter confirmed my hypothesis that Republicans loved free booze.

Bobby was fiddling with his tie again.

I came around and straightened his bow. "You look great. It's a nice change from those oil-stained jeans."

"Denim's almost as old as and cooler than these stuffy birds." He indicated a geriatric wobbling by with a woman whose cheekbones were almost at the same level as her eyebrows.

By the look of the five carat diamond on her finger, I deduced she could've afforded a better plastic surgeon. It was a miracle she could lift her bony hand with that rock weighing it down.

Bobby mumbled something.

I detached my gaze from the woman. "Sorry, I missed what you said."

He pointed at a man in a white tux. "Flag down that guy with the tray when he comes back. He's passing out champagne."

I stepped forward to make eye contact with the waiter, but the man headed off in another direction.

A hand squeezed my backside.

"Hey." I reached back and grabbed a wrist.

"Sorry," Bobby whispered. "Couldn't resist. Your ass is hot in this dress."

Couth was never his strongest suit.

"Let's slip out before anyone notices," he said. "We have the limo all night."

Still facing forward, I pushed his hand away. "I can't leave."

"Why not? Just go congratulate your friend, grab some *Dom*, and we'll bounce. There are tons of people here. I doubt he'd notice you're gone."

I glanced at the podium on the stage where Finn would make his formal announcement. A thick, ballooned arch hung overhead, reminding me of the balloon that broke free from the child's hand outside the Cuban restaurant, the night I met Finn.

A lump welled in my throat. "I can't go." I choked out the words. "He's a good friend."

Bobby scratched his temple. "You're friends with a conservative? Hell must've frozen over."

I ignored his jab. Bobby was a bleeding heart liberal, defender of the low man, but Marshall, Finn, and others I knew on the right weren't bad people, they just saw the world differently. Regarding politics, I was never hyper-partisan. I voted for the person least likely to screw our already screwed-up nation. My inclination was to gravitate toward candidates who supported women's advocacy, but I'd slept with both sides, the donkeys and the elephants. Once naked, we were all equal.

"Be a dear and get me a scotch, will you?" I said. "Single malt, if they have it."

Bobby coiled one of my ringlets around his finger and released it. "Anything for you."

I grabbed his wrist. "Make it a double."

****

By eleven the place was packed, and the scent of flowery perfumes was making my eyes water. Over the hour, I'd slugged down three scotches, polished off three plates of *hors d'oeuvres*, and had suffered through small talk with the lady whose facelift brought her eyes almost to her ears. I'd also crossed paths with a few recognizable clients. Some acknowledged my presence, some avoided eye contact. I didn't take things personally.

The effect of too much standing and too much alcohol was taking its toll. The straps on my designer vamp sandals were digging into my heels but on the plus side, the booze obscured my vision, making everything look soft and hazy.

People are pretty. I hiccupped and giggled.

Bobby flagged my attention. He was off in a corner, swapping an empty champagne flute for a fresh, full glass. "Want one?" he mouthed.

I hiccupped and shook my head.

Marshall and Clara Billings were making the rounds, Clara waving her cupped palm like a homecoming contestant, and Marshall pausing to clasp hands with fellow constituents, his hearty laugh sailing over the music and conversations.

Earlier, I'd run into Marshall by the restrooms. In passing, he'd flashed me a wink, and I'd felt a pang of guilt knowing it would be the last friendly acknowledgement after the news broke.

Leaning against a chair for support, I searched the room for Finn. There were black-and-white tuxedoes everywhere and my scotch-addled brain made it hard to pick my friend out of the crowd. Bobby was reaching for another flute—yikes. I squinted and gave the room another visual sweep for Finn. Tuxedo, tuxedo, tuxedo—there!

Finn stood alone by a table near the stage. I headed his way and opened my mouth to call to him just as Sabrina appeared in my line of vision. I stepped back so fast I almost tripped on my train.

She was prettier in person, dammit. Tall and lithe, like a willow branch, or a Degas ballerina. Her pale-green eyes matched the shade of her gown.

She wore an elegant suite of aquamarine jewels, and the choker on her throat was tiered with intermittently placed diamonds. Her dark hair was coiled in an elegant updo, and though she was dressed to kill, it gave me a little comfort that her thin limbs reminded me of the matchstick chairs by the table she stood at. I giggled at the thought of Finn's deep-tissue hugs snapping Sabrina's twiggy arms in half.

My smile evaporated as Sabrina patted Finn's arm. No biggie. She was showing off for his supporters. Finn probably didn't notice. A waiter passed by, blocking my view. Once he moved, I resumed spying on the happy couple. Sabrina wrapped her arm around Finn's waist, and a small strangled sound escaped my lips. That gesture was intimate, something *just friends* didn't do. I knitted my brows. *Oh, I bet she's loving this.* The attention, the pictures, his nice cologne—my cologne, dammit. I gritted my teeth.

Angela once told me jealousy was a witch mask women didn't wear well, and watching them was self-inflicted torture, like jabbing a needle into my eye, but I couldn't turn away. I had to see if Finn was enjoying her affection. I ducked beside a potted ficus, lit with twinkle lights.

Finn's expression was hard to read. I shifted my gaze back to Bobby.

He'd finished his champagne and was standing in line at the bar, probably in search of something stronger. The way he seemed to teeter, he'd be better off with a soda.

With a slight turn, I glanced back at Finn.

Sabrina was a few feet away now, talking with another couple.

Finn was chatting with a white-haired man whose belly was so distended, it looked like it was about to explode from its vest. The man laughed at something and gave Finn's back a hard slap. Finn, poor thing, winced and rubbed his shoulder. The bloated-bellied man took his leave, and Finn looked my way. Our gazes locked, and a wide grin overpowered Finn's face.

The room was cool, but when I saw Finn's smile, my face flushed with warmth. Oh, how I missed him, even his awkward hugs. The smile on my face dissolved as reality sank in.

Soon, everything he'd worked for would crumble. I didn't deserve his friendship, let alone, his smiles or bone-crushing hugs.

I glanced at Sabrina. She was watching Finn watch me. Her severely plucked brows inched higher as she examined the expression on Finn's face. Her mouth opened then quickly shut. Her gaze shot back to me, nostrils flared, lips tight. It didn't take a genius to read the message behind her look—*back off, he's mine.*

It was impossible to look away, even as she walked back to Finn and kissed his cheek.

I inhaled a tremulous breath. My legs threatened to collapse, and there was nothing close by to hold onto. I raced over to a nearby set of double doors that led to a balcony and dashed outside.

Music followed me through the open door. The band was playing Glenn Miller's "In the Mood," a song Angela had played on a few occasions.

At the railing, I sucked in gulps of fresh air. After a few deep breaths, my legs felt stronger, but I felt the pang of nicotine withdrawal. There were no smokes in my evening clutch, but I smelled cigarette smoke in the vicinity.

With a twist to the right, I pinpointed the source. A man with dark hair was flicking a lighter. I walked over to the man and bummed a cigarette.

"You're a lifesaver," I said as he offered me the pack. "I left mine at home."

The man cupped his hand around my cigarette and lit it. He was tall, medium build, with broad shoulders and gorgeous black waves. His wrist sported an oversized chronograph watch. Spotless tux. No ring.

"Lucky for me," he said. "Otherwise I wouldn't have met you." The man gave me a look that suggested he wanted something more.

Normally, I would've jumped at the chance to have fun with a hot ringless guy, but that night the person I wanted approving looks from was preoccupied.

I politely excused myself and walked away before the man's face was worth remembering.

There was a cozy corner with a steel table and chairs that no one had taken which granted me a view of the entrance. Since the dress I wore wasn't comfortable enough for sitting, I leaned against the back of the chair. Voices on the terrace attacked me at all sides. I tried to camouflage myself under the cloak of darkness but my red dress seemed to stand out the way a siren broke silence.

People milled around the terrace, women in shiny, bedazzled gowns, and men with stiff drinks and stiff shirts. As I took a drag off my smoke, I wondered if Bobby had noticed my absence. The sad truth was I hardly cared what he thought. What I cared about was Finn and the way Sabrina clung to him like he was her property.

I imagined her inside, on his arm, striking conversation with people who didn't deserve his attention. Was she laughing at his jokes? Or were they dancing now, his arm above her waist because he was a gentleman, her head on his shoulder? Was he wearing his new underwear? The ones I chose during our meeting—correction, date.

I took another drag. *Forget him. He's not yours. He never was.*

A hand tapped my shoulder.

"Jesus." I gasped and turned.

"Sorry." Finn held up his palms. "I always seem to do that you."

"It's okay." I coughed and laughed. "Congratulations, by the way."

"Thank you. I've been trying to talk to you all night." He pointed at my cigarette. "Figured you'd come for one of these at some point."

"Guess you have me all figured out." I flicked my cigarette over the rail and brushed off my hands.

An all-too-familiar look of concern appeared on his face. "Is something wrong? I feel like you're avoiding me."

I wanted to push him away but his kind eyes were making me weak. I wanted to kiss his cheek and hug and hold him and be there for him when his world came crashing down in—I checked my watch—seventeen minutes.

Finn took my hand. "Talk to me, Faith."

"Sorry, I'm not myself. Too much champagne." I sniffed and smiled. "The party's a hit. You must be relieved."

"Am I ever. It seems like everyone's having fun. But Republicans always like these types of parties." Still holding my hand, he stepped back to take me in. "You look beautiful—I mean, you always look great, but, wow. You stand out tonight."

"Why, thank you." I flashed a demure smile. "You look sharp, yourself." And he did. He had the right clothes, the right haircut, the right smell—everything. But deep down, he was still the humble man I'd fallen for.

Finn released my hand and thumbed to the door.

"Where's the guy I saw you arrive with?"

So he *was* watching me.

I shrugged. "Somewhere inside. Probably still at the bar."

"Ah."

A moment passed. I wanted to stop time or at least slow it down. In sixteen minutes the bomb would drop, and the person beside me would never speak to me again. I still had things to say, apologies to make.

Finn tilted his head in the direction of the music coming from inside. "Moonlight Serenade" was playing, another slow, breezy tune I recognized from Angela's collection.

Finn held out his hand. "May I have the honor of this dance?"

"You're such a ham." My laugh died as I caught a few stares.

People were milling by. Finn's hand was still out, and I worried how it would look for him to be associated with someone like me. Even if they didn't know my profession, I stuck out like a sore thumb. The lady who fit with Finn was somewhere inside.

I stepped back. "How about a rain check?"

He crossed his arms, held an elbow, and stroked his chin. "Don't you want to make sure I remember our dance moves before I make a complete fool of myself?"

I coiled a ringlet around my finger and smelled a faint hint of smoke on my skin. "I'm sure you're fine. By the way," I motioned toward the door, "where's your date?"

Finn stuffed his hands in his pockets. "Sabrina's making the circuit. She's in her element at places like this. I doubt she ever worries about wrong forks or spilling drinks—"

"Or stepping on toes?"

He stepped closer. "Or how to break off your shrimp tails when you're balancing a plate and a drink."

I stepped closer. "Or how to excuse yourself to use the restroom."

"Or how to jump over a bridge."

"Or how to—"

He bent his head, and his mouth was on mine.

My spine stiffened, and every fiber in my body was electric, tingly.

He was kissing me, right there, in front of everyone. What would they think? I placed my palms on his chest, ready to push him away, but he held me tighter, and memories flooded back. The bridge, his napkin balls, the rose garden, our dance at The Alley. I balled my fists, preparing to move, but Finn's lips mashed harder against mine.

It was social suicide. Sabrina was inside. Bobby was around. Clara would faint if she saw us. Marshall, too. And the press. God, the press.

Finn stroked my arm, and I smelled his cologne as he grasped the side of my head. He ran his fingers through my hair and it was over.

I was lost to him.

I kissed him back and tasted sour-sweet champagne. His lips were soft, his kisses firm. His scalp was damp but his skin smelled good and there was no place I wanted to be than right there at that moment.

The air held the scent of flowers, food, and exhaust. Car honks and conversations surrounded us. The sky was dark, smoky gray, and starless.

For one magical minute, Finn was all that mattered. I imagined us somewhere far away, an ordinary couple weaving a life together, Finn tending a garden, collecting rocks, and me, what would I do? Bake bread? Raise a family? Change diapers?

Diapers!

I gently pushed him back. Finn deserved an honest woman by his side. A wife. The mother of his children. I wasn't that person.

"What's wrong?" His concerned expression returned.

"I can't." I covered my mouth and ran for the door.

Inside, the energy was high. Music was thumping at a steady pace, and trays of champagne, held by bored-looking attendants, were circling the area. The band had an active gathering on the dance floor, and even the old-timers had broken from their seats to let loose for a while.

I checked the time. Fourteen minutes until the shakedown. When the people in front of me walked away, I cupped my hand over my eyes and scanned the room for Bobby. He was still in the vicinity of the bar, a glass in his hand, his bow tie undone. He was deep in conversation with three tuxedoed gents.

Finn entered the ballroom and Sabrina quickly came to his side. Unable to resist the magnetic pull, I twisted around to stare at them. The Ice Queen was holding Finn's arm. Laughing, she turned my way.

There was nowhere to hide. My red siren dress stood out in the crowd.

Sabrina's gaze narrowed, and my throat got an itchy feeling. People came over to her, providing me the escape I needed. I snatched a flute off a passing tray and gulped the bubbly, then flagged another waiter down, set my empty glass on his tray, and took a fresh flute.

This time, I carried my drink to a table in a far corner. With a little effort, I lowered onto a chair and then stared at a flickering votive candle in the centerpiece. Memories of the Cuban restaurant and The Alley surfaced. Finn had changed so much since our first encounter. He was stronger now. But was he strong enough to endure the fallout after the news erupted?

I lifted my champagne glass and knocked the drink down in two swallows. Effervescence tickled my nostrils and my throat tingled from sadness. Someone had left behind a cocktail napkin with a phone number written in ink. I tore off a strip of the paper and balled it up. Then I balled another strip. A third. A fourth. A fifth.

There was plenty of napkin left to construct more balls but I wasn't making myself feel better. Screw it. I swiped the collection off the table with a grand sweep and got to my feet.

In twelve minutes, it would all be over.

Chapter Forty-Five

It was five minutes before midnight, and excitement was palpable in the air. A zippy swing song was playing, and the dance floor was full. The moment was coming—the time when those who had donated to Finn's campaign would receive their imagined payoff for the campaign they supported. Finn was their investment, a commodity of sorts. He was the golden boy. Their political messiah.

I glanced at my watch, now obsessed with the time. Bobby was still huddled with the group of tuxedoed gents. We had to leave. Soon. Really soon. Now.

I stood on my tiptoes and waved to get his attention, but he missed my signal. Worming through the crowd, I caught sweet and spicy scents, and bumped a few elbows. Soon I was at Bobby's side, tapping his shoulder.

He turned, and the liquid in his glass sloshed over the rim. "Hey there. Where were you?" Not surprisingly, his breath reeked of alcohol.

"Pardon my intrusion, gentlemen." I smiled and linked my arm through Bobby's. "But we have an emergency." I pulled him away from the group.

"Where were you?" he repeated. His voice was thick and sluggish, and there was a wet circle on his shirt. One shoelace was untied, and his shirttail was falling out of his pants. His cheeks were blotchy and his right cufflink was missing.

I buttoned his top buttons. "What happened to you?"

"Free drinks are what happened." He laughed, and spittle sprayed. He wiped his mouth with the back of his hand and looked down to tuck in his shirt.

I adjusted his tie and prayed we'd make it out with a hint of dignity. Once he was back to a presentable state, I pointed to the set of doors with an EXIT sign. "We need to get out of here."

Bobby blinked as though he were trying to shake off whatever clouded his vision then he stepped toward a passing waiter. "One more drink."

I pulled him back. "There's champagne in the limo."

He shook off my arm. "What's the fire?"

"It's 'where's the fire,' and we need to go." My lack of patience made my words come out sharp. I stared at his lopsided bow tie and felt a stab of guilt. "Please, Bobby."

"Okay."

We were feet from the exit when the music quieted.

A man in a white tuxedo tapped a mic, and a high-pitched whine bellowed from the P.A. system. "Good evening, friends and fellow supporters…"

Dear Lord. It was happening.

I turned and scanned the area. Marshall and Clara were standing on the stage, Finn to their right, Sabrina waiting in the wings.

The white tuxedoed man continued, "We've all been waiting for this moment, so I'll pass the microphone and let Finn's father say a few words."

Marshall stepped forward, clasped the back of the white tuxedoed man, and shook his hand. He tapped the mic and waited for feedback. "I'd like to thank everyone for coming tonight. My darling wife." Marshall blew a kiss to Clara. "Our close friends." He leaned out and aimed a finger at someone in the crowd. "Except you, Joe Hanley, you old goat."

Laughter erupted in the audience, but the joke was lost on me. There was a time bomb ticking, seconds from detonating.

I grabbed Bobby's hand. "Come on."

"Wait." Bobby pointed to the stage. "Your friend is doing his thing."

A sharp pain hit my lower half. I tugged Bobby's elbow. "You'll read about it later. *Vamanos*." Let's go.

Bobby squinted. "Why are we—?"

Marshall continued, "…and without further ado, I'd like to officially introduce my son as the next—"

Marshall's sentence was interrupted by the flash of cell phone lights. Chirps and buzzing sounds came from mobile phones, and people bent their heads to look at their screens.

A man with a walkie-talkie walked over to Finn and whispered something in his ear. Finn mouthed, "What?" and even from a distance, I could see his confused expression.

Heads in the crowd snapped up. The room filled with murmurs and whispers. People craned their necks toward Finn.

The man with the walkie-talkie handed Finn a cell phone. He studied the screen, and his hand dropped to his side.

Gloom settled on me like fog rolling over National

Harbor.

Finn looked up and scanned the room. His gaze caught mine, and I felt the sensation of a trap door opening in my stomach.

The noise of buzzing phones and hushed mumbles escalated. Almost every face wore shocked expressions. Their messiah had been slain.

I lay my hand over my heart and mouthed, "Sorry."

Finn continued to stare.

A camera flashed. Then another.

Bobby squinted as a camera snapped our picture. I was so surprised by the sudden flash, I jumped and almost lost my balance.

"What's going on?" Bobby whispered to me.

I shook my head, my gaze glued to the stage, to Finn.

His face was transfixed with grief, and his shoulders were slumped. The man with the walkie-talkie quickly escorted him offstage.

Bobby scratched the side of his head. "Did I miss something?"

I felt the weight of a thousand stares. A loud sound whooshed in my ears, and my neck felt like flames. I covered my mouth and ran for the door, leaving Bobby behind, leaving Finn behind, leaving everything behind except my guilty conscience.

Outside, I stumbled to the curb, my heels feeling spindly and unsupportive. I coiled my arm around the closest lamppost for support and took slow breaths. Bobby came up behind me and spun me around to face him.

"For Chrissake, Faith. Tell me what's going on."

I covered the sides of my face with spread fingers.

388

"I can't explain. You'll know soon. Take the limo home. I'll catch a cab."

"What?" He crossed his arms. "You're in no state to be alone."

I plugged my ears to silence the car honks coming from the opposite side of the street. I needed to be alone. I needed everything to stop and time to go back so I could undo what I did. But that wouldn't happen; the damage was done.

A heave of nausea swelled in my stomach. I ran to a spot in the shadows, hooked an arm around a pillar, and braced myself for my stomach to empty its contents.

Bobby ambled over.

"Go home, Bobby." I grabbed my hair and waved him off. I didn't want him to see me vulnerable, pathetic. "I'm okay."

"Like hell you are." He came to my side and draped an arm over my back. "You're whacked if you think I'm leaving you like this."

He was stubborn, and if he stayed with me he'd only get hurt, because that was what I did—hurt people. I'd used Bobby like I used everyone. The only way to protect him was to make sure he'd leave.

I pushed away his arm and straightened to my full height. "Are you dense? I don't want you, you're nobody. You and your dumb job and greasy motorcycle. Go back to suburbia and leave me the hell alone."

My mind wasn't right, but I swore it looked like the sparkle in Bobby's eyes dimmed. I thought he would just slump off, but instead he flared his nostrils and punched the lamppost base. He let out a horrible sound that rang in my ears then stumbled and cupped his injured hand.

I reached out to touch his elbow. "Are you okay?"

"Don't." He said the word with so much hurt I quickly pulled back my hand.

"That was low, Faith. Really low." He held my gaze for a moment and then broke away as if he could no longer stand my presence. Cradling his hand in the crook of his armpit, he headed toward the entrance.

As he rounded the corner, I collapsed to my knees. Cradling my arms around my waist, I rocked back and forth. Greed had turned me into a person I didn't recognize, a person who damaged the innocent. I grabbed my hair and pulled it until it hurt, and a howl of release escaped from my lips. Make it stop. Make me stop.

The hem of a beaded gown came into my vision.

"The gutter is an appropriate place for you," a woman said.

I looked up and squinted. Clara Billings stood before me, arms crossed. Her severe expression reminded me of Venetian masks I'd once seen in a travel guide.

There was no point in defending myself, but words needed to be said.

My mental army sprang into action and every self-defensive instinct woke up. I grabbed the train of my dress and got to my feet. "I won't make excuses for what I did, but you have to understand, Finn doesn't want to be in politics. He only did it for you."

"You have no right to inject yourself in our family's personal affairs." She palmed the sparkly necklace at her throat. "My son is not your concern."

She glanced at the entrance, waved and smiled to someone, then turned back to face me.

I threw out my palms. "I was trying to help." I really was. In some way, at least. "He was living a lie."

Clara narrowed her gaze to my cleavage. "You don't know anything about him."

I straightened my shoulders. "I know him better than you think."

She lifted her chin and scoffed. "I highly doubt that."

I stared at the giant rock on Clara's middle finger, her necklace, the beads on her gown. "Finn's too good a person to tell you the truth, but you should know, he sacrificed his happiness to please you. If you really love him, you'll let him decide his future."

"You fool." She muttered something else, but halted mid-sentence. People were milling outside. Clara glanced over her shoulder at the crowd forming then shot me a warning look. "One day you'll pay for this." She leveled a heated gaze at me then collected herself and hurried off into the shadows.

Her threat fell on deaf ears. I'd already lost everything that mattered.

A bubble of nausea came out with a burp. I took a few breaths to compose myself then gathered my train, walked to the curb, and ducked under a velvet rope corralling the entrance. The line of drivers waiting for event attendees to leave reminded me of vultures waiting for prey to die.

A taxi waited at the end of the block. I walked over to the vehicle and slowly climbed inside.

"Good evening," the driver said.

I didn't respond. I just listened to the car honks and

conversations trailing from the entrance.

The driver pulled his rear mirror down and glanced at me. "You okay, miss?"

Back at the entrance, more people were filtering outside. I checked the time on my cell. Twelve-fifteen. My birthday, the worst day of my life, was over.

I faced forward, staring at the windshield, as the events of the evening overcame me. I tried to hold back emotion, but a tear broke free and ran down my cheek. Another tear followed. Both rolled off my chin, and landed on my dress. My stupid red siren dress.

I touched the wet spot and wiped my cheeks. "I'm fine."

"Where to?" the driver asked.

I wanted to go where no one could find me, where nobody I loved could be hurt by me. Away from the news, away from beaded gowns and gossip and tuxedos. Home, scotch, salvia, numb.

I gave the driver my address. He put the car into gear and headed up the street.

As the taxi turned the corner, I closed my eyes and mouthed a silent goodbye to Finn.

Chapter Forty-Six

The fallout was bad, but not the apocalypse that I envisioned. After a vague text mentioning I was only to receive half payment since the photos didn't go directly to him, Drummond cut communication. That was understandable, since I knew he'd further implicate himself were he caught in my web of destruction, but I didn't feel a trace of regret for the bastard. Ultimately, he got what he wanted.

The Republicans scrambled to do damage control, but their efforts were in vain. Finn's squeaky-clean image was tarred, their messiah had been crucified. Thus, even a weasel like Drummond seemed the viable candidate to voters.

In some way, I was relieved, if only for the fact Finn was finally free.

Marshall left scathing messages proclaiming his disappointment and told me to never make contact with him or his family again. Clara left messages warning me to steer clear of their family and if anything incriminating came out against her husband she'd seek retribution. She never mentioned Finn. I understood Marshall's position and regretted losing his friendship, but there was nothing he or Clara could do to hurt me. I'd lost Finn and that was all that mattered.

The only saving grace had come from the call I'd made to Alexander Clough at *The Post* the night I sent him the photos. As per our agreement, I granted Alexander an exclusive interview, and he, in turn ran a story about Finn, one that showed the good side of him. Finn would have to rescind his position, but I wanted the world to know they lost a hero.

Alexander refrained from printing libel, but some of the pictures made their way to the Internet and went viral. Finn made every headline. Everyone wanted to learn about the golden boy's fall from fame.

According to my insider sources, Sabrina dropped Finn. It was another blow he didn't deserve, but the Ice Queen only admired what Finn represented. Had she truly loved him, she would've stayed by his side.

People would eventually forgive and forget; they'd done it for lesser men. The former governor of New York. The late mayor of D.C. Others. Finn was young, rich, and handsome. Everyone loved a comeback kid.

Eventually, Drummond sent some money. I filed for bankruptcy, paid off a few vendors, and gave what was left to Jeanine and the girls.

Bes came through, but she didn't make it easy. She was eager to inherit my business and gloat over my defeat, but her softer, caring side, the side I remembered, promised to protect Jeanine and the team. All my girls, with the exception of one.

****

Tony called me two days after the fallout.

"So now you know," I said.

"Jeanine told me everything after the gala, but I had my suspicions."

"Like they say, 'All good things must come to an end,'" I mused.

"I'm sorry. And I hate to throw this on you now,

but there's something you should know."

"Just give it to me straight." What could possibly be worse than what had already happened?

"I traced the missing money. It's someone in your company."

"*Quelle surprise*." I laughed, but that was probably due to the fact that I was drinking at the time. "Who was it?"

Tony sighed. "Monique."

"Huh." I'd been medicating myself with booze and pills for two days, so I was numb enough to not give a crap.

He continued. "Apparently, she was running a side business and was siphoning off some of your customers."

I licked the rim of my glass. "That's a shame. I liked her."

"She embezzled as well. Jeanine found a box of receipts hidden in Monique's desk."

"Gotta admire her, she's got," I slugged down the rest of my scotch, "the guy at my deli calls it *chutzpah*. What do you Italians say?"

"*Che palle*," Tony said.

"What balls," I repeated.

****

Two weeks after the fallout, Jeanine arrived at my apartment. The superintendent let her in after she told him I'd been off the radar and she feared something bad might have happened.

She found me in the living room surrounded by empty bottles and take-out delivery boxes. My clothes and hair were filthier than my littered floor, so she dragged me to the shower and pushed me in, fully dressed. I cursed and threw a shampoo bottle at her, which smacked the side of her head, but she held on until I eventually gave in. It was a sobering experience, one I hoped never to relive.

Once I was clean, Jeanine dressed me in dry clothes, made me coffee, and let me cry on her shoulder. After that, we never spoke of the incident.

****

Three weeks after the incident, I emerged from my building, donning my oversized sunglasses, and wearing a wide-brimmed hat and a lemon-colored sundress.

It had taken hours to work up the resolve to cross my threshold, but once I was outside my building, the sun beaming on my shoulders, I felt, for the first time in weeks, human.

Otis hailed me a cab and tipped his cap as I approached the vehicle. "You take care of yourself now, Ms. Crawley."

I backtracked from the curb and placed a hand on Otis's uniformed shoulder. "After all these years, don't you think it's time you start calling me by my first name?"

"Sorry, Miss Faith. I'm old school, you know. Some habits are hard to break."

I lowered my hand and thought about Finn, the way he held the doors, the way he wouldn't cross illegally, the way he slipped on my shoe.

"You're right," I said. "Old school habits aren't bad. Not at all."

****

An hour later, I was standing on the embankment beneath the tracks near Canal Road. For my mission,

I'd worn the earthy-looking flats I'd purchased from a store near my apartment, shoes I'd once vowed I'd never be caught dead in, but what I planned to do required sensible footwear, and regarding death, the future was uncertain.

The climb uphill was more challenging than the night I'd hiked with Finn. The dry spell had made the earth crumbly, and rocks and dirt gave way with each step I took. By the time I made it to the summit, my feet were covered with brown dust. I'd been sedentary for weeks and chain-smoking, so the hike left me winded, and my heart trembled like a struck cymbal. The last time I spoke to Jeanine, she'd warned me that if I didn't quit smoking, I'd die, and for a moment I thought her prediction had come true. Once my breathing slowed, I continued on.

A warm, honeysuckle breeze tickled my nostrils. I followed the sweet smell to a nearby honeysuckle vine and picked off a flower that was the shade of my dress. I pulled the stem, pressed my lips to the flower's base, and sucked out a trickle of nectar. The taste brought back long-lost memories of West Virginia and summer and my parents.

I laughed aloud, imagining the look on Father's face if he were alive and reading the past headlines. Mother would have forgiven me because she was kind and that was her way. Alas, the good ones always died too soon.

I was scouring through a patch of pebbles, searching for quartz, when my cell phone vibrated. The display read PIA.

"Where are you?" Jeanine asked. "I thought you were coming in?"

I glanced at the bridge. "I'm out, and no, I'm not coming in."

She sighed. "I have questions." Sound of paper rustling. "The Better Business Awards, keep or toss?"

I swatted a mosquito off my shin. "Toss."

"Your framed interviews and the magazine covers?"

"Toss."

My skin itched where the mosquito had landed. I rubbed the area with my knuckle.

"Your—"

"Toss everything, J."

She sighed. "Everything?"

"Yes." I licked my knuckle. "Bes won't want them."

"Okay," she said. "I won't press."

That was a first.

A squirrel scampered around the base of a tree trunk and shook its bushy tail.

"Did Bobby call back?" I asked.

"He did, and said, I quote, 'Tell her I need time to wrap my head around things.'"

"Okay," I suspected he'd come around eventually. After all, Bes had forgiven me, but I figured it would be too late. I wondered if Finn would ever forgive me.

"What about...you know?"

Jeanine exhaled an exaggerated breath. "Let it go, Faith. He hasn't called back and I don't expect him to. You're torturing yourself, so please, let him go."

A flock of birds were flying in V-formation overhead. The clouds shifted, and with the shade came a fresh wave of grief. It wasn't that I expected Finn to forgive me, I just hoped for, I don't know, something. I rubbed dirt off the pebble I selected. "Go home, J. You've been busting your butt nonstop since this happened."

"Later," she said. "There's too much to do."

I fingered the Athena pendant that hung around my neck. "You're not so awful, you know."

"Actually, I'm awesome."

"Bes agreed to give you a raise."

"I'll believe it when I see it. Hey, why don't I come by on my way home?"

"Ah, no good." I glanced at the abandoned train tracks. "I don't know when I'll be back."

"I'm not taking no for an answer. I'll bring pizza. We're doing Hawaiian this time. Love you."

****

It was almost like sleepwalking. My legs shifted to autopilot and before I knew it, I was at the edge of the cliff. As I stood leaning over, scrambled thoughts pummeled my brain. The world had been around for ages and always would be. Secondhand smoke, breastfeeding in public, climate change denial, republican versus democrat, ultimately, did it matter?

People spent too much time agonizing about trivial things. They worried about which song should be played at their funerals or what kind of casket to be buried in, or which outfit they wanted to spend eternity wearing. My theory was, when you were gone, you were gone. You were worm fodder or a shark dinner if you drowned at sea. End of story. Finn's story would eventually be forgotten in time, as would I.

I aimed toward the ground and threw the pebble over the edge. There was no sound of its impact. With a breath, I stepped forward and dirt crumbled beneath my foot. A plane soared overhead. I waited a few moments for the sound to quiet then leaned over and stared at the ground below.

Don't think, just jump.

An image of Jeanine popped in front of my eyes.

She'll be fine. Bes will take care of her.

I inched my foot farther.

Jeanine's last words played in my head. *Love you.*

I touched my pendant.

Save everyone the heartache. You hurt people. You ruin everything.

Somewhere in the distance, a bird sang. It quickly changed its tune and I remembered Finn telling me that was the telltale sign of mockingbirds.

Forget him. Just do it.

The clouds parted, and sunbeams burst down. A passage from Deuteronomy played in my head: "I call heaven and earth to witness against you today, that I have set before you life and death, blessing and curse. Therefore choose life, that you and your offspring may live."

I took a step back and an image flashed before my eyes. It was the injured look in Finn's eyes the night of the ball. I covered my face with my palms.

Forgive me, Finn.

I took a deep breath, lowered my hands, and stepped forward.

Chapter Forty-Seven

There are those who believe in an afterlife and there are those that don't. I never believed in heaven or hell or omniscient beings, but I did believe in the goodness of humans. People like Finn, Jeanine, and Angela confirmed my belief that there were living angels.

The world probably would have been better off without me, but I didn't jump that day on the bridge.

I was seconds from leaping when I saw my life flash before my eyes, saw the faces of those I'd harmed. The movie in my mind was blurry and running too fast. Then it slowed on one image. The person I saw was Finn. That was what saved me.

I told myself that suicide was the easy way out. Living with the backlash would be hard. I vowed to make things right, and if I couldn't right my wrongs, I'd at least try to pay kindness forward.

And then I stepped away from the ledge, brushed my feet off, and went home.

****

My apartment was organized chaos. For weeks, I'd been knee-deep in packing mode, and my living room was crowded with an avalanche of boxes, rolls of packing tape, sheets of plastic bubble wrap, and newspapers I'd salvaged from the basement recycle bin—my apartment recycled?

The movers were coming to bring the heavy stuff to a storage unit, but I'd taken responsibility for packing my collectibles. I wrapped each with a loving hand, even the ones to be donated, and pushed memories aside as they arose.

Theodore called the day after the bridge incident, suggesting I needed a change of pace.

"Come to California. The weather is perfect, and I have a small guesthouse on my property. You're welcome to stay and convalesce as long as you like."

"I can't leave D.C.," I said. "It's home."

"A change of venue will do you a world of good. Come for a short while. Until you figure out your next step."

I knew his generosity didn't have strings attached, and my gut told me it was solid advice. Still, it was a big change.

"We're survivors," he said. "We fall down, but we pick ourselves up and brush off the dirt."

I accepted Theodore's offer, but doubted I'd ever be able to shake off my dirt.

****

It was the first week in September, unseasonably warm, and the sky was hazy and gray. The outside air was so humid it felt like I was breathing through a wet washcloth. Gnats buzzed around my head during the walk from the grocery store to my building. I held tight to the plastic bags I carried and didn't bother to swat the insects away.

Otis was outside my building, sitting on a small, collapsible stool. Seeing me, he sprung to his feet. "Need help with those, Miss Faith?"

I glanced at a twisted tassel thread on his uniform.

"I'm good, thanks. But I appreciate the offer." I reached into one of my bags and retrieved a clementine.

Otis accepted the fruit and tipped his cap. "Always at your service." His smile assured me he was one of the few people that didn't hate me. Adding Jeanine, Sammy, Bes, and Theodore, the tally of those people would be five. Maybe Bobby.

****

My apartment was dark, the air conditioner was humming, and the sharp odor of bleach from my earlier cleaning hung in the air. Getting to kitchen was like wandering through a maze since practically every inch of space was occupied with boxes and packing paraphernalia, but I managed to enter the room without tripping or knocking anything over.

After unpacking my groceries, I changed into yoga pants that were missing the drawstring and a comfy tee. There was a gray hair at my temple, and my blonde streak was dull and brassy, but aside from showering and shaving, I didn't feel worthy of primping.

Back in the living room, I poured a drink and turned on the stereo. Duke Ellington sang about a little brown book, and I chuckled, remembering my black book and how I'd tossed it down the trash chute after the gala.

The whiskey went down with a burn. I swayed to the music, remembering how my mother danced on rainy nights by the window, a secretive smile on her face I couldn't understand.

Sometime around nine, I heard a knock on the door. Jeanine had mentioned she might drop by. I pushed aside a roll of bubble wrap, peeled myself up off the floor, and surveyed the area. Over the past few hours, I'd made progress. Most of the carpet was visible, the box towers were organized according to size and shape, and there was a clear path to the door.

Another knock.

"Keep your thong on," I yelled. "I'm coming."

Jeanine usually brought pizza when she came by, and I'd started keeping a bottle of the fruity zinfandel she liked on hand. Though I enjoyed her company, packing had drained me, so I decided to make it an early night.

"I hope you brought paper plates cause everything's pack—" my sentence dissolved as I opened the door.

Finn stood in the hallway.

He was wearing baggy khakis, an unknotted navy tie, and a plain-white Oxford. Patchy stubble that looked like a bad shadow covered half his face, and his eyes looked tired and watery.

I gasped and palmed my heart. Eventually, a soft, "Hi," came out.

He didn't respond. He just stood there, staring.

I crossed my arms, hyper-aware of my own disarray. Memories flooded back. The bridge. Him on my couch. Camera flashes at the gala. My brain was speeding with a thousand questions, but I couldn't find the right words to say. I studied the hallway carpet then looked up. "Do you want to come in?"

Finn stuffed his hands in his pockets. His cowlick stood up like a soldier saluting, and there was something brown and unidentifiable on his shirt sleeve. "I don't know why I came," he finally said. "I shouldn't be here." He kneaded his brows. "I can't believe—why'd you?" He sighed. "What you did was unforgivable."

I opened my mouth to apologize, but he silenced me by raising his hand. "You ruined everything." He blew out a heavy breath. "My career. My reputation. I can't believe you were paid to—"

"I didn't keep the money."

His angry expression silenced my explanation.

I hunched my shoulders. "I don't know what to say except, I'm sorry."

"You're sorry?" His laugh was too loud.

I looked sideways to see if anyone had emerged from their apartment. A woman in 12-B poked her head around the corner. She glanced our way then retreated back to her apartment like a hermit crab retracting into its shell.

"Apologies won't change what happened, Finn said. "There's no way I can go back to politics."

"You could go back. It'll take time, but you could," I paused to swallow, "if you really wanted to."

Finn's neck reddened.

"I know you hate me, but please understand, I did it for you. You didn't want that life. You wanted other things but you were too afraid to pursue them. You still could—"

"Don't tell me what I can or can't do." He pulled his hands out of his pockets and balled his fists. "You lost that right."

His sharp words hit me like a punch in the gut, and for an instant I lost my composure. I sniffed away a tear and willed myself not to break down. I deserved the jab. It hurt, but I certainly had it coming. I looked down at Finn's hand. The stone on his college ring was chipped, and the stain on his sleeve looked like tea. I couldn't imagine what had happened to him over the past weeks, what the newspapers and tabloids hadn't reported, but it was obvious he was in pain.

I took a tentative step forward. "I wish—"

His nose wrinkled as though he'd smelled something spoiled. "You wish what?"

I hesitated. Did I honestly wish I could undo what I'd done? Erase everything? The dates, our times together. Did I wish I'd never intervened—let him live the life he dreamed of, correction, his family dreamed of? No. Deep down, that wasn't what Finn wanted.

I crossed my arms and stepped back. "Never mind."

The elevator pinged but no one came into my line of sight.

Finn scrubbed a hand over his face. "There's this giant part of me that hates you, but there's a small part of me that remembers the good you did for me. Your messages said you were trying to do what you thought was best for me, but it wasn't your place to decide that." He braced himself by leaning a hand on the doorframe. "I don't know what to think anymore."

His voice shook as he spoke, like whatever had stirred up my emotions had rattled him, too. His eyes were rimmed with tears, and seeing the disappointment and desperation on his face made me want to hold and console him, but I feared he'd reject me. Still, I had to try.

I took a tentative step toward him. "I am so incredibly sorry I hurt you and I will never forget what I did. Could the part of you that doesn't hate me come inside for a minute? I promise I won't keep you long."

His brows scrunched. "Your promises mean

nothing." He was silent for a moment, and I almost couldn't breathe. After a moment of deliberation, he looked down and muttered, "Maybe."

Maybe wasn't no.

I nodded, unable to speak.

Someone once told me about holding sand in your palm, and how squeezing it meant losing it, and if you held your palm open, it would stay. Finn couldn't be pushed, he needed to be handled like sand, but I couldn't let him leave. Not without one last try.

I extended my hand. "Please, Finn. Come inside."

He stared at my wrist.

While waiting for Finn's answer, I remembered the wounded look he had when the news had broken. My hand trembled but I kept it extended.

Down the hall, the elevator pinged again, and happier memories surfaced. Drinks, crossing the tracks, the rose garden, our kiss.

I tried again. "Just for a minute?"

His lips, normally curved in a playful grin, were stretched in a taut line, and there were creases at the corners of his eyes and shadows under his lids that seemed to age him five years. His gaze broke from mine, and I felt him slip away.

Finn looked up at the ceiling and exhaled a heavy breath. When he looked back at me, there was something in his eyes that made me feel hopeful.

"Okay," he said.

There was no certainty he'd forgive me, and I doubted he'd ever forget my betrayal, but perhaps it wasn't the end. Perhaps it was a new beginning.

"Okay," I replied. I shut the door behind us, slid the chain, and flipped the latch.

Epilogue

Happily ever after?
I quit smoking.
Not because of Finn.
Not because of Jeanine's nagging.
Not because of what it had done to Angela.
But Angela was the reason I quit.
Not her, my former mentor.
I quit smoking because of my daughter Angela.
Let me back up a little.

Finn wasn't the type to easily forgive and forget. The night he came to my apartment, we talked for hours and I'd begged his forgiveness, but it took months to mend what I'd broken, and things never went back to what we originally had. Eventually, after weeks of me giving him his space, he agreed to try again, but like a broken china pot that had been glued, the cracks were still visible.

We decided to reset. I moved to California, and Finn eventually followed. The slate had been wiped clean. We had a fresh beginning, far from D.C. politics.

Finn enrolled in classes and completed his Graduate Gemologist degree and was immediately offered a teaching position at the Gemological Institute of America on their Carlsbad campus. I'd taken temporary residence in Theodore's guesthouse which was hours away, but thanks to video chats and the occasional road trips to see each other, we built our friendship into something deeper.

As our relationship intensified and old wounds healed, we decided long-distance dating was silly. I moved to Carlsbad the following winter and rented a bungalow near the shore. Carlsbad is a quaint, coastal town, just north of San Diego. The seasons are mild, except for the days when the Santa Anna winds kick in and the fog rolls off the hills. Those days, when the skies were overcast and the breeze was intense, I remembered D.C., the place of my past.

I worked at a local coffeehouse during the day, waited tables in a dive at night, and took online classes to earn my G.E.D.

Never say never had become my axiom.

If a psychic had predicted my future, I'd have told her she was high. In all my life, I'd never imagined dating a guy like Finn or leaving D.C. or not working in the biz, but the one thing I did know was: the only constants were rush-hour traffic, death, and taxes. And half-yearly sales at my favorite upscale department store.

****

Finn was a loving companion, predictable, but gentle and kind. I was his "first" and was patient the night he sacrificed his virginity.

And that's when everything changed.

****

A child was the last thing on our minds. It happened the evening when Finn and I were out celebrating one of G.I.A.'s recent graduating classes. Too many margaritas, some bad karaoke, one missed birth control pill, and presto! I was pregnant.

409

You'd think I'd have gotten an abortion. You'd think I'd have numbed myself with drugs or run away. *D.C. Faith* would have done those things, but *California Faith* was a more honorable human.

Finn immediately proposed. I hesitated because I wasn't sure I'd be a good wife—let alone mother—but I eventually accepted. Because I knew I loved him, so maybe I could love a baby, too.

Maybe.

My knees shook the day of our nuptials. It was a simple ceremony at the courthouse, and only three attended the ceremony: Jeanine, Theodore, and Larry, one of Finn's co-workers.

For the occasion, I wore a cream-colored pantsuit, a wide-brimmed hat, a hammered gold bangle, and Angela's pearls. White lilies bound with a satin ribbon were my bouquet.

Despite Finn's attempts to reach out to his family, they never responded. Marshall called Finn the day of the wedding, but judging by the scowl on Finn's face when he ended the call, things hadn't gone well. I didn't push further.

****

Pregnancy wasn't the apocalypse I'd envisioned. Aside from the fact that my feet swelled a full size larger and the strange addiction I had to lemon rinds, I passed through three trimesters with little discomfort. People were nice and opened doors for me. A few of my customers at the coffeehouse asked to rub my belly.

Weird.

One sunny July morning, while I was dragging the recycling bins to our curb, my water broke. Three hours and one glorious epidural later, Finn and I welcomed a healthy baby girl into the world.

Angela.

I had a small panic attack the day we came home from the hospital.

Taking care of others had never been my forte. I was certain I was going to drop, break, or mentally scar my baby, but Finn pitched in and eventually I learned I didn't have to be perfect. All our child needed was love.

The nights I rocked my daughter to sleep, I remembered the way my own mother used to sway me in her arms, how she sang sad songs, and how she left the world too soon.

Through Angela, I finally understood unconditional love.

On rainy days, I'd lay Angela in the bassinet and play jazz on the stereo. Watching the outside raindrops hit the pavement, I remembered how Theodore admired the rain. In the postscript of his last letter from Europe, Theodore told me he was happy I found someone who appreciated my magic.

****

On Angela's second birthday, Jeanine sent her a pair of striped rainbow overalls. Angela called them over-awfuls because she had trouble pronouncing the word, but looking at the garish material, I realize my daughter had it right.

One day, I'll teach Angela about fashion. I'll teach her to be a critical thinker and how to shun convention. I'll raise her to be a warrior and teach her about art and online shopping and all the varieties of roses. Finn will teach her about gems and crystallography. He's already given her a gold-plated jeweler's loupe.

For now, I only focus on the necessities.

My family.
Our friends.
And very good wine.

A word about the author...

After leaving her career teaching gemology, Caryn DeVincenti, who writes as Dana Ross, moved to the sunshine state to become a full-time writer. She earned her MFA in Creative Writing at Wilkes University and is the regional director of the Florida Writers Association, Palm Beach County.

When not writing, Caryn nurtures her social media addiction, dances (poorly) to loud '80s music, and plays chase with her insane Cairn terrier.

Thank you for purchasing
this publication of The Wild Rose Press, Inc.

For questions or more information
contact us at
info@thewildrosepress.com.

The Wild Rose Press, Inc.
www.thewildrosepress.com

To visit with authors of
The Wild Rose Press, Inc.
join our yahoo loop at
http://groups.yahoo.com/group/thewildrosepress/